FRANK RYAN

Frank Ryan came to widespread acclaim with thrillers such as *Goodbye Baby Blue* and *Tiger Tiger*, which gathered fine reviews and found a readership of more than 300,000 in the UK alone. His non-fiction book, *The Forgotten Plague,* which was also first published by Swift, was a Book of the Year for *The New York Times*, while *Virus X* was an Amazon com best-seller and *Darwin's Blind Spot* was the "Amazon Featured Book" recommended by Charlie Munger at the 2003 Berkshire Hathaway annual meeting.

His books have been translated into many languages and have been the subject of more than a dozen television features and documentaries.

Also by Frank P. Ryan

Fiction
Taking Care of Harry
Goodbye Baby Blue
Sweet Summer
Tiger Tiger

Non-Fiction
Tuberculosis: The Greatest Story Never Told
(In the US this was published as *The Forgotten Plague*)
Virus X
Darwin's Blind Spot

The Doomsday Genie

Frank P Ryan

SWIFT
PUBLISHERS

SWIFT PUBLISHERS

First published in e-format 2007

1 3 5 7 9 8 6 4 2
Copyright © Frank P. Ryan 2007

A catalogue record for this book is available from the British Library
ISBN 978-1-874082-42-2

Swift Publishers
PO Box 1436, Sheffield S17 3XP

e-mail: bookenquiries@swiftpublishers.com

Cover artwork by Mark Salwowski

Acknowledgements

I would like to thank the people who encouraged me to write this book, in particular Bill Hamilton and Jonny Pegg, who were indomitably supportive. I am also indebted to Jennifer Rohn, who did such a superb job with editing and to Jamie Crawford for advice on the sublime nature of jazz. Finally, how can I express my gratitude to my fellow creator, Mark Salwowski, who clothed my dragon in such dazzling visual metaphor.

May your names be inscribed on the black rocks that decorate the beach of bones.

For Barbara whose support was essential as always

Prologue
Index minus 2 months

Prologue

03: 20/05h45

The three AH-64 Apaches stole in from the dawn horizon, like squat gray sharks invading a sleeping coastline. Emerging from the sea mists over a large desalination complex, they adopted a ground-hugging V-formation, the engines masked until they crossed over the security fence. The agricultural station was three miles ahead. From the air, the ripening fields of crops were laid out in radial slices so it looked like a gigantic target had been painted onto the desert. Cruising at 145 mph, the Apaches followed a raised embankment between two of the slices along which a solitary figure, wearing flapping Bermuda shorts, was jogging back to base after his pre-dawn exercise.

His hearing distracted by the earphones of his iPod, the man was oblivious to the dark shapes that were overtaking him out of the rising sun. A brief clatter of fire from a 30MM automatic caused his body to crash to the ground. The right earphone, detached from the shattered bridge over his head, fed a tinny whisper of Borodin's second string quartet into the disturbed air as the gunships swept onwards in what seemed an unhurried pace.

Soon visible, the central compound was a cluster of a dozen or so cinder-block buildings surrounding a massive glass and aluminum dome. The dome was the dead center of the radial plan. It was the bull's-eye in the target.

The Apaches went through a coordinated parabolic turn to line up facing the living quarters, out of which figures were emerging in various stages of undress. The attack was directed by a clean-shaven civilian located in the front cockpit position of the lead aircraft. He clicked on a video camera to record the scene, capturing people wearing short-sleeved lab coats over otherwise naked bodies.

A single barefoot figure emerged from one of the buildings. He gazed about himself for a moment, as if in bewilderment, before running into the dubious shelter of the dome. Within moments an alarm screeched from the apex of the dome: a red beacon flashing inside the entrance. It merely heightened the panic. The air shrilled with desperate shouts and cries as the heavy M230 chain guns rattled into action, mowing the people down with implacable efficiency. The guns continued firing for about thirty seconds, after which the Apaches wheeled skyward, putting enough distance between themselves and the compound to allow the deployment of their Hydra 70 folding fin rockets. The oblong buildings disintegrated and a cascade of burning debris descended over the wrack of bloodied bodies.

In the lead Apache, the civilian spoke to the military pilot. 'I want to make a record of the anomaly.'

The lead peeled off from the others, rising a further two hundred feet before adopting a spiral route around the fields, the boundaries of which were highlighted with razor-cut sharpness in the low glare of the sun. From time to time the aircraft hovered, the civilian directing the camera to record specific features in the fields below. The variety of crops was staggering. There were several types of maize, irrigated paddy fields of ripening rice, cereals, root crops, endless rows of small fruit-bearing trees. The "anomaly" appeared to be everywhere. The examination and recording was conducted with the same implacable precision as the killing.

The helicopter continued on its spiral mission for five or six minutes and then it rejoined the other two that were still hovering over the now blazing compound. There was a pause lasting half a minute or so: information being exchanged.

All three Apaches rose to six hundred feet so the CPGs could position their Target Acquisition Designation Sights onto the dome. From what was effectively point blank range, they each fired two Hellfire missiles into the building. Designed for the destruction of tanks and heavy armor in the field of battle, the combined effect was a massive overkill. An inferno mushroomed into the sky, against which the helicopters were reduced to gnats, tossing and pitching against the maw of red flames and black smoke.

These are the voices from a conference on genetic engineering. The scientists' voices were recorded on audio tape but subsequently suppressed from public awareness:

'A new technique of molecular biology appears to have allowed us to outdo the standard events of evolution.'

'It is not known what sort of risks this is going to create because we have no tests.'

'There may still be sound reasons why the Pandora's Box should not be opened.'

'We are already – probably – on the path of no return.'

1

Strange Deaths

Top Secret
Operation Globalnet
Surveillance Mode: E-mail
Retrograde analysis: Index minus 20/12
DELICATE SOURCE: RESTRICTION CODE:
eyes alpha
L of E/ he→ee

Dear Lyse,

Such excitement!

I've enjoyed this week in London. We spent the evening in a small hotel by the Thames. My new employer has booked the whole place for the inaugural celebration - although relatively unknown in the international league, the company certainly knows how to spend money. There is a terrace leading from the restaurant, where we sat out and enjoyed the pyrotechnic display they laid on over the river. Of course El Supremo had a hand in planning this. I was secretly pleased that it didn't quite rise to his grandiose expectations. But all the same, as a climax to the week of planning, the fireworks were fabulous - a delight to cap a wonderful evening.

E.S. did his best to spoil it for all of us even before the midnight celebrations. He insisted on a toast, with champagne, that I considered inappropriate: "To rewriting history!" I had no option but to put a damper on his silly games. Then he had the arrogance to rebuke me, as we gathered at the balcony, for what he considered my lack of enterprise.

If I have a single worry, it is going to be his leadership. But the night was too stimulating to allow hubris to spoil it. I will admit that I didn't sleep too well, in part through genuine excitement at the challenges ahead, in part through worrying about his future antics.

If only you had been here!

Love,

H.

05: 17/ 08h45

Thirless, Arizona, is a small town an hour's drive west of Flagstaff. It has little in the way of distinguishing features, nothing that would set it out as different from the many such small Midwestern towns that bead the former Route 66. Drive along Main Street and you pass by fast food chains, shopping malls and wide glass fronts selling real estate, with the promise of the "affordable luxury lifestyle" provided by their individually designed haciendas-with-pools, all guaranteed close to golf courses. The I-40, Route 66's brash modern offspring, is two hundred yards away, with its never ending drone of traffic between Southern California and the Four Corners states: heavy trucks, RVs and campers, tourists off to the mountains for a week's hiking, others heading northwest for the gambling thrills of Vegas or the scenic wonders of the Grand Canyon.

It was here in the parking lot outside the West End Mall, that MayEllen Reickhardt waited in her pick-up for the arrival of her friend, Lucille. MayEllen had driven twenty-seven miles with air-conditioning that was temperamental and she was feeling somewhat temperamental herself. A blue and cloudless morning. The temperature high. She wound down the window so she could light up a Marlboro and the heat enveloped her like the exhaust from opening an oven door.

When Lucille pulled up alongside, with husband Paco Cordoba at the wheel of a battered blue Mazda, she looked surprised to find MayEllen alone. MayEllen's husband Bill usually did the driving. Now MayEllen eyed the petite, yet shapely, figure of her friend, as Lucille climbed out of the vehicle and opened up the trunk. With a groan of undisguised jealousy, MayEllen kicked open the pick-up, sliding her not-so-shapely five feet nine inches onto the hot asphalt. Both women were similarly dressed in short-sleeved white cotton shirts and blue jeans. MayEllen had a thick tangle of bronze-colored curls, bleached tawny by the sun. Her eyes were blue - Bill called them her Molly Malone's. Lucille's eyes were Hispanic brown and her hair was straight and a glossy black. Both women wore high-heeled cowgirl boots. The chatted amiably as they ferried cacti from the trunk of the Mazda to join those already loaded into the back of the pick-up. The job complete, the two women called out belated goodbyes to Paco, who was already heading off.

Lucille just stood there, like she was waiting for MayEllen to explain Bill's absence.

'Bill ain't feeling too good.'

'I know a pretty good hangover cure – like this herbal tonic I got the recipe for that was handed down from my grandmother.'

'I don't think it's a hangover. I don't rightly know what it is - except I think it might be the flu.'

Lucille focused on just one of the billboards, the one that advertised a cream that made your skin twenty years younger.

'Do folks get the flu when we're almost in summer?'

'Lucille – I don't know.'

MayEllen and Lucille talked with a pleasant Western drawl. They moved slowly, people used to not hurrying. Thirless, where Lucille lived and worked as a waitress, was a town of twenty-eight thousand people. Everybody knew everybody. It made MayEllen glad that the farm where she lived - the B&M Cactus Farm – was further west and off the highway, a dead end along its own dirt road. It meant those nosy townsfolk, such as Lucille Cordoba, couldn't get to know every last wrinkle of their business.

Lucille hopped nimbly into the passenger seat, while MayEllen hauled herself back into the driver's seat. She plucked at the armpits of the shirt. Then she fired up the engine and set the pickup rolling down Main Street for a short distance, against the scenic backdrop of the distant Black Mountains. She took a left onto a dirt track that was lined by desert sand and tufts of sage and rabbit weed, bumping over the irregular surface before joining the I-40 heading east, like a precise surgical scar through what city-born Bill called "the Nowhere Desert".

'You're smoking again.'

'I should give you A-plus for observation.'

'I thought you'd given that up.'

MayEllen took another drag and said nothing.

Lucille adopted a huffy look but she didn't engage in argument with MayEllen. Few people did that and won.

It was a long haul, from Thirless to Phoenix, where the two women planned to meet up with friends and rivals at the Saguaro Annual Convention, named for the giant cactus that gave Arizona its yellow state flower. It was Paco and not Lucille who had the interest in cacti. MayEllen liked and respected Paco for that. He was her kind of a no-nonsense guy, raising the plants as a dedicated amateur outside of his regular work as a telephone engineer. And thinking about cacti made her think about the desert so that, from time to time, as she drove along at a steady fifty, MayEllen glanced out there at the passing dunes and buttes, and the thinly spaced plants that people wrote off as scrub. She knew that it was a much more deceptive landscape than that, with a huge variety of wildlife that most people failed to see. There was nothing she and Bill liked better than to ride through it bright and early on a cool Sunday morning on their Harleys. Best of all was at the time of the spring rains when it became an Eden of glorious color with hundreds of different flowering plants all showing their faces at once.

She said, 'I'm worried about Bill.'

'He must be feeling bad, letting you come on your own.'

'I didn't want to go and leave him but you know how ornery Bill can be.' A flash of memory: Bill's face turned up to her from out of the chair: her kiss. 'Honey' – wisecracking – 'I just timed it nicely. I got the flu. You got the trip to Phoenix. Go have a real bad time without me.'

MayEllen stared at the highway running off ahead of them, straight as a ruler line into the flat distance. 'There's something I got to tell you - something I probably shouldn't be telling nobody. Could damage our business.'

'You know I'm not one for talking, MayEllen.'

'I wish! But I'm going to tell you anyway.' She sighed, blinking quickly, still staring fixedly ahead. 'You know about those things they talk about on those UFO shows you like so much? What they call those field circles?'

'You mean those crop circles.'

'Well that's what I'm talking about.'

'MayEllen, are you telling me you've seen a crop circle?'

'Well, you know I don't believe in that UFO business. But anyway, I'm telling you we have one of them circles in our cactus field.'

'Oh, my God! How'd it get there?'

'How would I know? All I'm saying is I have this bad feeling about it. So now you know why I'm smoking again.'

Lucille probably wouldn't have believed what she was hearing from anybody else other than MayEllen. She took several seconds even to digest it. It was so unlike MayEllen to volunteer such information – that and the way she kept staring into the distance, like she couldn't face Lucille while she was talking about it.

'Oh, my! I thought you were just frettin' about Bill.'

'Sure I'm frettin' about Bill. That's what I'm trying to tell you. It only happened yesterday. I was making breakfast when he came back in out of the field and told me about it. Oh, Lucille – he was looking real worried.'

'I never thought you got circles in cactus fields.'

'I never thought so, neither. But he took me out to look at it. I didn't want to get up close. There was a disgusting smell. You know – like something gone rotten.'

'Yukkk!' Lucille wrinkled her snub nose. 'I never actually heard that crop circles smell bad.'

'Will you stop winding me up and just listen? Bill decided that the only thing to do was to get rid of it. So he chopped down all the plants in the circle and he set fire to them and buried the whole goddam mess.'

'Oh, my!'

For the first time in minutes MayEllen swiveled her gaze from the distance to her friend's pretty-doll face, and not for the first time she wished that Lucille would get herself a brain transplant.

'Don't you see what I'm getting anxious about? That stinking circle - it was only yesterday. And now Bill's sick.'

'Aw, come on, MayEllen. That's just plant stuff. Plants can't harm people. He's just coming down with a summer cold, or maybe the flu. You're just frettin' because he always comes with us to Phoenix, is all.'

'Maybe I am at that.'

MayEllen wished she had a cell phone. She didn't believe in cell phones. She believed they surely fried your brains. But now she just couldn't stop fretting about Bill. When she got to a point about twenty miles south of Flagstaff, she pulled into the parking lot of a motel and went into the lobby to call home.

It took Bill a long time to pick up the phone.

'Bill – is that you, honey?'

'Hey – MayEllen!' It didn't sound like Bill's voice at all, more a low wheezy growling. In the pause, she could hear grunting noises.

'Bill – are you okay?'

'Oh, sweet Jesus!' That grunting sound again. She realized what it was. Bill was vomiting at the other end of the phone.

'What's happening, Bill? Have you gotten worse since I left?'

Bill started making coughing noises. They weren't the normal noises of somebody coughing. Every time he coughed, it sounded like his lungs were being torn up by their roots.

'Oh, Bill! You sound in really bad shape.' The words were inadequate, hopelessly out of kilter with the hollow feeling that was invading her breast.

She waited for him to answer, her hand cramping with tension around the receiver. No answer came, only more of the same unpleasant noises. MayEllen was not the sort to panic. But those noises at the end of the phone made her panic. She knew Bill wouldn't have called the doctor. Bill hated doctors.

'I'm coming home,' she said abruptly. 'But first I'm calling Dr. Manning to go see you. You just hold on `til I get there.'

*

About four years ago, when the hospital had moved to its present site at the edge of town, it was hailed as a long overdue replacement for the old municipal hospital that had grown up around the defunct desert-air sanatorium. The new hospital, formally renamed "Thirless Memorial Hospital", was an airy five-story building equipped to deal with the modern-day stress-and-affluence related ailments. MayEllen dropped Lucille off at her home before heading for the hospital parking lot. She wanted to see Bill on her own. Inside the lobby there were signs in English, Navajo and Spanish and a bewildering color-coded directory, which you were expected to follow through lines laid into the floor. Today, these reminded her of the panic lines in the aisles of aircraft. Dr. Manning was waiting for her at the reception desk.

'Where's Bill?'

'Now, you take it easy, MayEllen. Bill's been taken to the Intensive Care Unit.'

Dr. Manning did that thing with his mouth, a sucking in of his lips. He tried to lead her toward some armchairs on either side of a coffee table by the window. MayEllen refused to follow.

'I want to see him.'

'I need to explain things to you before I take you to him.'

'What's the matter with him?'

MayEllen looked suspiciously around her. She could see that the woman at the reception desk was ogling them, like she knew something MayEllen didn't.

'Bill's very sick. I have to prepare you for how he's going to look.'

MayEllen led the doctor towards the elevators. She punched the call button. 'Top floor, right?'

'That's where the ICU is, yes.'

While she waited, she continued her interrogation. 'He's very sick? What the hell's the matter with him?'

'Do you know about barrier nursing?'

'I don't know nothing, Dr. Manning. And it seems to me I'm not getting any wiser from this conversation.'

The doors opened and they stepped in. The Star Trek voice, disturbingly soft and female, told them to "Mind the Doors". The elevator suddenly felt overheated and claustrophobic and MayEllen wiped sweat from her brow with the back of her hand. She had never seen Dr. Manning look this worried.

'Bill's illness is unusual!'

'What do you mean, unusual?'

He lifted his face up, watching the floor levels floating slowly by. 'There are some people here who will explain about that.'

They stepped out onto the fifth floor. There were no plants in pots, or comfortable armchairs by the windows.

Dr. Manning followed those maddening guidelines of dotted red and yellow inlay, which divided right and left. They took the red line, which went through twin doors, with the sign, NO ADMITTANCE – AUTHORISED MEDICAL PERSONNEL ONLY.

'Bill has some kind of a serious infection?'

'So they think, yes.'

'This barrier nursing business –?'

'A precaution, Mrs. Reickhardt. For your benefit and the benefit of the staff taking care of him.'

Dr. Manning never called her Mrs. Reickhardt.

'You're saying he might be contagious?'

'We have to assume so.'

'I still want to see him.'

'You'll have to dress up.'

'Then I'll dress up, whatever. But I want to see him now!'

'The nurses will show you what to do.'

Dr. Manning ushered her through a second pair of glazed doors into a u-shaped corridor with a dozen or so further doors opening off it. He didn't follow her. Three figures, one man and two women, were standing in the corridor. They were all gowned up like in the movies. She had the impression they had been waiting for her to arrive.

MayEllen scowled as one of the females introduced herself as Nurse Ritter, the "Infection Control Nurse." The nurse took her into an annexe with racks of gowns on the wall and overshoes, masks and gloves laid out in cardboard boxes on a low glass-top table. MayEllen's hands were shaking as she put on the protective gear. When she was gowned up, the nurse took her into a room off the corridor where a man was lying in a bed. He was connected through a battery of wires to an eight-channel video monitor. There were two separate drips running into him, through the skin on either side of his neck. A crash cart stood by the bedside.

'That ain't my Bill.'

'I'm afraid it is, Mrs. Reickhardt. I'm sorry.'

MayEllen stared at the figure in the bed and she almost fainted from dizziness. She just stared at what they were telling her was Bill. The dizziness worsened and she began to shake.

'What's wrong with his face?'

'It's swollen. A complication of his toxic state.'

Only Bill's hands and face were exposed and even his face was half hidden by an oxygen mask. All the skin she could see was blistered and peeling. His eyelids were so puffed up, he looked like some wino who had cooked all day under the July sun.

'I only left him at home this morning. He looked fine. Just a bit of a cough – a touch of the flu. He didn't seem all that sick.'

'That's something we want to talk to you about, Mrs. Reickhardt.' It was a man's voice, deep throated, sounding tired. 'I'm Dr. Valero. Your husband has been admitted under my care.'

Valero was a tall slim Hispanic, with a bony look to what she could see of him. He was wearing more complicated protective clothing, with mask that covered his mouth, cheekbones and his almost-black eyes. MayEllen turned her face away from the bed, an involuntary movement she had no control over. She thought: *It's just a nightmare. I'm going to wake up any moment.*

Just then Bill moaned, a strangulated sound, and his head turned towards her, his eyes struggling to peer out through the grotesquely ballooned eyelids. His lips, bloated like the eyelids, parted, and another terrible moaning sound came from behind the mask.

'He... he knows I'm here?'

'He's conscious to some extent.'

MayEllen put out her gloved hand and took the hand of the bloated figure in the bed. The fingers closed on hers, tried to squeeze.

Tears threatened, but she realized that she was too frightened to cry. 'It is Bill – it really is him!'

His hand was so hot she felt it burning right through the glove. MayEllen couldn't bear to see Bill in that terrible state. Impulsively she grabbed hold of his hand again and held onto it as the nurse took her shoulders, encouraging her to leave. There was a soft tearing sound and the skin of Bill's thumb came away from his hand, like a finger tearing from a rotting glove. MayEllen looked down at the shriveled skin of Bill's right thumb, now resting in her open palm. The nail was still attached to the skin.

She felt a hot wave rise up out of her chest and travel all the way to the roof of her skull. There was a roaring sound in her ears and a smell in her nostrils, like burning rubber.

05: 17/ 18h20

At the Ivan Wallin Field Reserve, an ecology station at the southern end of the Mojave Desert, Professor Ake Johansson carried a roll of computer printout back to his office from the mainframe computer down in the lab. The printout - covering the last few days' ICDITD measurements in Sector 5-32 - was frankly baffling. Clearing the surface of his desk of papers and journals and running the roll from floor to floor over the entire desk surface, he passed it through his hands a few feet at a time, stopping at intervals to draw thick red circles with a text liner around sudden jumps and dives in the charts drawn by one or more of the five different colored pens.

To the field ecologist it was apparent that something very strange was going on. Two days earlier he had spotted significant fluctuations in insect density measurements. He should have gone out and inspected the area today. But a committee meeting had taken up all of the afternoon. Now he continued to run the readouts through his hands, comparing fluctuations with baseline controls, to convince himself there was no computer glitch to explain it.

The electronic baselines were all normal.

Scratching at the gray twelve-hour stubble on his cheeks and his chin, he couldn't imagine a reasonable explanation.

Insect populations didn't go crazy for no reason. Johansson ought to know since he had been monitoring them in their desert ecologies for almost three decades. But suddenly those insect populations were undergoing bizarre fluctuations.

Ake Johansson had invented the technique of ICITD, or "insect counts in three dimensions," which coupled nicely with standard techniques of plant foliage estimation. Put the two together and you had the baseline food web of the desert, mathematically predictable against the natural ecosystem variables, such as elevation, shade, temperature and rainfall. This inter-relationship of insects and plants was the key to survival of the local wildlife in an ecology where the temperature ranged from below freezing to close to boiling point and the rainfall was limited to a few inches per year. The balance was always precarious and any unexpected change was cause for concern. He stared at the readouts, with a restless anxiety.

It was an anxiety he would have to endure overnight since it was far too late in the day to investigate it. He would go take a look at first light after he had seen the latest Landsat data.

*

The telephone rang in the office of the Heimholz Professor of Evolutionary Botany in the Department of Integrative Biology at U.C. Berkeley. The recording machine prompted: 'This is the voicemail of Kay McCann. I'm either busy with another call or out of the office right now. If it's important, leave a message and I'll get back to you.'

The caller identified himself as Ake Johansson, and he sounded irritated at having to leave a message.

'There's something of a problem, Kay. I've left the same message on your cell phone, which is currently switched off – I presume because you've already set out for Boston. I'm leaving this message on your office phone in case you check in while you're away. We need to talk.'

*

At the time Johansson was attempting to get in touch with her, Professor Kay McCann was wrapping the hotel issue white bathrobe around her after stepping out of the shower at the Sheraton Boston. She had switched off her cell for the duration of the American Association for the Advancement of Science meeting. She was glad to be off duty. She needed to focus down hard on her plenary speech in two days, the Friday morning. Three of her grad students were presenting posters on the Saturday half-day and she was also determined to give them her prime attention. Anybody, other than her son, Sean – who already knew how to get in touch via the hotel switchboard – could reasonably wait until she got back to Berkeley on Monday. Kay was also looking forward to tonight's welcome dinner, an opportunity for the course organizers and committee chairpersons to indulge in a little gossip before the busy program started.

While showering, she left the bathroom door wide open so she could wind down from the flight listening to some music from the TV sound program. And now, out of the shower, and just as she got halfway to the closet, a new track cut through her musing as abruptly as if somebody on the airwaves had called out her name. The band was U2 and the track was *I Still Haven't Found What I'm Looking For*.

She smiled.

Jesus, how something melted inside with that sacred memory – Billy Forrester, and the smoky crepuscular light of the woods at Big Sur, Plasket Creek! They had made love on the leather-smelling back seat of his 80s Mustang.

For Kay, then aged seventeen, it had been the initiation ceremony, as well as the first and last time with Billy. Looking back with the wisdom of maturity, he had been a little on the wild side, five years older than she and more versed in the art of seduction. She had never regretted it, not even for a moment. Seventeen now seemed like an age when you still believed in magic.

At the time the magic of a handsome man adoring you had seemed infinitely more attractive than her forthcoming exams and the world they heralded, the world she now inhabited, of career and responsibility.

She didn't want to let the memory go. When the song ended she missed it. She wished it would play just one more time over, so she could lose herself for a few more minutes in the nostalgia of being seventeen again and still believing in magic.

05: 18/ 03h21

In Atlanta, Will Grant was attempting to rouse himself from sleep to answer an urgent telephone call. 'Well, I'm telling you, Doctor, this is a very strange case. We've already sent you specimens. I certainly hope you're going to be able to help me here.'

Will rolled over in bed, to slide out quietly. It was a habit he had acquired over the years to protect his wife during nights on call. Even now he was unable to suppress the instinct to look at the place in bed where Marje's figure would normally have been sleeping.

'Just give me a minute.'

A pathologist with a special interest in plague viruses, he was fielding emergency calls for his department, which was the Special Pathogens Branch at the Centers for Disease Control. He had experienced difficulty getting to sleep and had sat up in bed until 1:00 am, drinking two or three generous shots of whisky and listening to nighttime jazz on his iPod. The whisky was still in his system, slowing his thinking. Meanwhile the voice on his bedside phone sounded far too impatient to wait for him to wake up.

'Look, Doctor - I'm chief of intensive care at the Memorial Hospital in Thirless. We have a worrying situation.'

Will rubbed at his right eye with the heel of his hand. 'Remind me. Thirless – where's that?'

'Thirless, Arizona.' An edge of irritation had joined the impatience in that voice. Will had only the vaguest of recollections of Thirless, Arizona - one of those desert stops along the highway - but big enough, it seemed, to have a hospital with an intensive care unit.

'I'm sorry to do this to you. But could you possibly give me your name again?'

The voice was angry now: 'My name is Ric Valero. I'm calling you about one of my patients. You awake now?'

'How can I help you, Dr. Valero?'

'I'm dealing with a man with a spreading gangrene of his skin. This is one hell of a toxic guy.'

Will pulled a soiled white T-shirt over his shoulders. 'Can you hold on for a few seconds. I'll go pick up the extension in my office.'

Padding through to the top-of-stairs landing, he checked on Janie, to make sure she was sleeping. Her bedroom door was half open and she was lying on her left side, her slender knees drawn up to her chest, her hands tugging a fan of sheet to her mouth. She also had the nightlight on. Janie had reverted to the nightlight after Marje's death nine months before. And now, in passing her bedroom by, Will felt guilty about the fact he wasn't spending enough time with her. The low light also illuminated the team picture of the Atlanta Hawks that filled almost the entire long wall by the side of her bed. He closed her bedroom door to nearly shut, making his way downstairs and into the office, where he flicked the light switch and picked up the extension, blinking in the sudden brightness.

Valero said, 'I don't mind telling you, this is the most toxic patient I have ever had to deal with.'

Will had pen and paper ready: 'Give me the patient's name.'

'Bill – William Reickhardt. Aged forty-seven.'

'Reickhardt, William, forty-seven.' Will switched on the coffee percolator he kept by his desk. 'Okay - fire away.'

'The development has been lightning fast. This guy was fit and well twenty-four hours ago. Far as I can tell, he gets some kind of a flu-like prodrome. His wife takes off on a trip to Phoenix, calls home just to check. Next thing he's coming in on a gurney with all lights flashing. He has a temperature we can't control. We're cooling him right now with two fans, aspirin and ice packs, and it's 105 and rising. And this rash –!'

'Describe the rash.'

'We watched the thing evolve. When he came in – *nada!* Then he gets a spot about an inch above the umbilicus. It becomes a branching root. Hell, we took pictures every five or ten minutes to capture the damn thing evolving. You just have to put a skin marker at the edge – any edge – and you can see it go past your marker in minutes.'

Stupefied by lack of sleep, Will took the first slug of coffee. 'Can you describe the rash in more detail?'

'Color – kind of blue-black, like classic gas gangrene. It smells like a kind of sickening sweet smell, which would also fit. But I never heard of any case of gangrene behaving like this.'

'What about its distribution?'

'It's spreading very rapidly, in that same arborescent fashion. Out over the abdomen, then up onto the thorax. It moved from his chest to his neck, head, legs and arms – in that order - in just a matter of hours.'

'The rash has become confluent?'

'If that's an appropriate term for something like this. Looks like every square inch of skin has become swollen and black. Dr. Grant – let me tell you how it really looks to me. It looks like this guy's skin has, in the space of six hours or so, just died on him while he was still alive.'

'Now you're getting emotional.'

'You'd get pretty damned emotional if you were here looking after this patient. The skin isn't all.'

'Go on.'

'We've taken MRI scans. You wouldn't believe the hassle, trying to get those done in somebody who could be contagious. But you should see the films. There are spreading lesions there too. Brain, liver, spleen.'

'Spreading lesions?'

'Spots that grow into roots and then they take up pretty much the entire organ.'

'So it's blood-stream spread?'

'No doubt about it. The same thing happening in the internal organs as we've seen in the skin.'

Another stupefied swig of the coffee, burning his mouth again. 'Did you say that you've sent specimens?'

Valero's voice fell. 'In two batches, liver biopsy, skin biopsy, bone marrow, throat and skin swabs, feces, urine - even cerebrospinal fluid. The CSF seemed curious to me in that the brain was so abnormal and yet the CSF was clear. I'd have put money on it being turbid. We didn't just send tissue in formalin. We sent you fresh frozen too, so you can get cultures, including viruses. Especially viruses. If we've thought of it, you've got it, two batches, special air-freight.'

Will shook his head, puzzled he hadn't heard of their arrival.

'This first batch of samples - how long ago did you send them?'

'Seven or eight hours ago. You should have gotten them three or four hours ago at the very latest.'

'Okay. I'll look into it.'

'This is the first time I've had the chance to call about the clinical situation. The earlier contacts were through our microbiologist.' Valero's voice was rising again in pitch. 'Look! You've got the picture now. Just tell me – do you have any idea what we're dealing with here?'

'You've considered the obvious possibilities?'

'We've considered them all. Necrotizing fasciitis? We've been onto that from the time of admission. But our cultures are negative up to now and an antibiotic cocktail that would kill every flesh-eating bug in the state of Arizona has made no difference.'

'You've considered plague?'

'Of course we've considered plague.' The voice became muted, as if Valero had put his hand over the mouthpiece to talk to someone. 'Oh, for goodness sake – well, yeah! Just a minute! Okay – I'm coming!' Valero's voice returned to the telephone, more stressed than ever. 'Plague is endemic here in the Southwest. We've done swabs, cultures and the immunofluorescence tests are up and running. To be read first thing tomorrow – sorry, 1 mean later this morning.'

'You mentioned viruses?'

'You think it could be some virus?'

'It's possible. But your local microbiologists must have done a screen for viruses already?'

'I checked with both the path lab here and the public health lab in Phoenix just before I called you. Nothing so far, but it's too early to be certain of anything.'

Will was silent a moment, thinking furiously.

Valero interrupted: 'Listen, something else has cropped up. I've really got to go.' Will overheard the whisper of an urgent conversation at the other end of the telephone.

'Dr. Valero – don't hang up – not just yet. I don't even have your contact number.'

Another distant whispered conversation. Will could make out anxiety-laden voices. He heard Valero's exclamation, 'Oh, for Christ's sake!' Then he came back on the line, sounding distracted. 'Listen, I'll give you one more minute. We've admitted another patient with a temperature of one hundred and four. A local doctor, called Manning. The man is Reickhardt's family doctor.'

'Has he got a rash?'

'No rash – not yet.'

An obvious alarm had entered Valero's voice. There were more disquieting sounds in the background. A woman's voice was calling Valero's name.

'Okay, I'll let you go in just a few moments. This man, Reickhardt, what about his systemic condition? His immune response?'

'All systems failure. Kidneys, liver, bone marrow. There never was a bone marrow response. No leukocyte response, no lymphocyte or specific antibody response – not even IgM. All systems down in his boots, from the time we first admitted him. This guy is already dead. He just hasn't gotten around to admitting it yet.'

'Give me your contact details. I'll get back to you.'

*

One of the things you learned from long experience with plagues is that panic, however understandable, is unhelpful – even dangerous. Will dialed the switchboard at CDC and spoke calmly to the desk clerk: 'It's Dr. Grant here. I want you to put a call out to the home of Mrs. Kristina Earle. It's urgent.'

'I believe she's already in the lab.'

Her reply surprised him. What were the chances that Kristina's presence there in the early hours of the morning was connected with the same emergency? 'Well, you'd better put me through to her.'

'I'll page her, Doctor.'

What did Kristina think she was doing, not calling him? After a pause of a minute or so, he heard Kristina's Atlanta accent, 'Hi!'

He couldn't hide his irritation: 'What's going on?'

'I'm in BSL-3 right now.'

'Processing samples, from the Thirless case?'

'That's right.' There was a hesitation in her voice. 'I'm aliquotting the second batch. Liver biopsy, second bloods and CSF.'

Will exhaled. 'Why didn't you call me?'

'There was nothing to suggest anything out of the ordinary. I didn't think –'

'You should have thought to call me, Kristina. I've just taken a call from a Dr. Valero and I didn't know a damn thing about the situation.'

'I'm sorry, Dr. Grant. But you got to get some sleep yourself. Or do you want me to wake you with every sample, any time of the night?'

She had called him "Dr. Grant". He sighed, realizing that she merely thought she was protecting him. His voice softened. 'Okay, Kristina – I'm coming in.'

*

In the atrium of Special Pathogens Will felt dwarfed in spite of his six foot two inches. The roof soared sixty feet overhead, capped by a church-like dome of frosted glass. In spite of the dimensions there was a feeling on entering of being hermetically sealed in. A stainless-steel cylinder about four feet in diameter ran from floor to ceiling, carrying ducts and cables. Over in the corner lay a mound of containers, respirator masks, rodent traps, plastic gloves, flasks and tubes for serum or blood - anything needed to fly out on some new investigation. Most intrusive, and contributing to the claustrophobia, was the sound, a continuous low rumble of heavy machinery positioned that came up through your feet, like from some Morlock factories deep underground. His office was off the ground floor, down a corridor. Opposite the office building, and across the green-carpeted floor, was the BSL-4 facility where he did most of his work.

Kristina was sitting at one of the small square tubular steel tables laid out over the green carpet.

'You coming here to check up on me, Dr. Grant?'

'You're damned right.'

'In case I let excitement get the better of me?'

Will flopped down in the chair next to her. He explained what Valero had told him over the telephone.

'Confluent gangrene?' Kristina showed surprise. 'I never heard of anything like that before.'

28

'Me neither.' He tapped his index finger on the opened pages of the laboratory log she had slid to him across the table. 'Okay – so what do we have?'

'Two separate arrivals of Thirless specimens. Batch one, throat swab, skin swabs and biopsy, blood and serum. I Gammacelled the blood and serum, so we could get some serology aliquotted and under way.' The Gammacel contained intensively radioactive cobalt-50 sealed off from the laboratory environment by ten tons of lead. It was used to kill potentially dangerous microbes before immunological screening could be carried out on the serum. The lethal dose of irradiation for a human being was 600 or 800 rads, but plague viruses were a lot tougher and some needed five million. 'Ditto,' she added, 'for a piece of the skin biopsy. Swabs, blood, serum and biopsy through the BSL-4 and the usual tests also under way.'

'You injected animals?'

'Oh, no – I forgot the animals!' Her eyes lifted up to confront his, like she was reproaching him for even thinking such a thing. There was a greenish tint to her dark skin in the artificial light. And a look in her eyes beyond the tired challenge that suggested an appeal.

'I'm ready to begin on the second batch, which I'm still processing, mainly more blood and serum, CSF, liver and skin biopsies.'

'Do me a favor, Kristina. Go check the results right now? See if anything at all is showing up?'

'You know we're clutching at straws this early.'

'I still want you to look, okay!'

'You're the boss.'

'I'm thinking about what Valero said – about the rapidity of disease evolution.'

Kristina's eyes were still returning his gaze. She must have been working patiently through half the night. Irritation would have been a natural enough explanation of whatever feeling he saw in her eyes.

She intoned: 'Level-4?'

'Level-4 you can leave to me.'

*

The walls of the BSL-4 suite were massively thick, designed to withstand a neighboring nuclear blast. As he walked down the long and empty upper corridor leading to the entrance, an incongruous peace came over Will, as if he were stepping not into danger but into a cool and refreshing shower.

It was far from the normal reaction. Few virologists, even those with extensive experience of working with plague pathogens, could live with the ever-present dangers of working in BSL-4. He knew people talked about him. Some called him "the iceberg". He ignored the banter because he knew they were wrong. He felt the fear as soon as he entered the building, every time. The day he stopped being afraid was the day he grew dangerously careless. And that would never happen. The difference between him and most other people was not that he was without fear but that he could work with it. In recent years, while Marje was sick, working with danger had become a useful distraction. But as her illness progressed, his wife's need for him, the increasing burden of supporting her, made his twelve hour working day a tougher ordeal. Marje had been a strong and resourceful woman. But the illness had been relentless. It had ground her down until she became so mentally fragile you didn't know what to expect coming home. In the end it had worn him down too. He had felt increasingly guilty with the distraction of work because he knew she missed him every minute that he wasn't at home.

'I feel a little better today!'

'That's nice, sweetheart!'

In his mind here tonight, walking the echoing corridor to BSL-4, he imagined he was still holding her. He felt the jitters that had invaded her body and soul so it felt like he was holding a frail and terrified animal.

At the door Will inspected the gauge that measured the differential pressure between the corridor outside and the suite of rooms inside. There had to be a pressure drop from outside to inside, the first step in an increasing vacuum with every room. He had passed through here thousands of times. But still he checked. The pressure was satisfactory. He put his pass card into the slot. Nothing happened. The pin light on the lock stayed red. This too was a safety precaution. If he lost his card or somebody stole it and tried to get in here, it would do them no good. Strange as it might seem, there were fanatics desperate enough to want to enter here. He dialed an additional special code. The light turned green. He took the card out of the door and passed through into the locker room. Here he stripped off his clothes and put on clean surgical scrubs, then surgical gloves. He passed on to another room, where some large and clumsy suits of a cerulean blue hung along a rack on the wall. The suits were complete with whole face visors, originally space suits, designed for NASA. Will's name was stenciled on one of them.

He put on the heavy rubber suit, wriggling his gloved hands into the thicker outer gloves that were taped to the wrists and pushing his feet down into the bootees that formed an integral part of the suit. From now on all manual operations were necessarily clumsy. He attached to his suit a HEPA filter, which would act as an additional safety screen for the air he breathed in the hermetically sealed laboratory. He performed each step with a practiced care. Nothing could ever be downgraded to routine. The air regulator was a heavy metal coupling that would supply and filter his air supply when he was inside. He slung the heavy metal coupling over his shoulder and put on some ear protectors before he pulled up the Ziploc that, with an additional rubber seal, enclosed him within the suit and helmet. Finally he put on Wellington boots. His body weight had increased by 25 pounds.

Once through the airlock, he coupled his HEPA filter to the nearest airline, a red coiled hose that dangled from the ceiling. The air now came in at 60 pounds per square inch, inflating the suit and draining out through four one-way valves, so he didn't blow up like an over-inflated tire. The familiar roaring invaded his ears, drowning out all outside sounds even though it was muted by the hearing protection. Kristina had already fed the new samples through the entry hatch and Will spent a good ten minutes in the prep room, getting ready to inject a second batch of animals. Then he moved awkwardly across the floor, coupling and uncoupling from one ceiling hose to another in the thirty seconds it took the suit to deflate. It took him over a minute to cross the thirty yards of floor to reach the door to the animal room.

Most dangerous of all in the Level 4 lab was the animal room. Like every door in this facility, it carried warning signs in large capitals and the biohazard logo in blood red. There were animal rights people who decried the fact they used animals here. But it was exceedingly unlikely they would attempt to break in – not unless they had some kind of a death wish.

The operative caution here was "sharps".

Animals were unpredictable. They voided secretions that were likely to be contagious. The animals - mice, rats and guinea pigs - were kept in their own cages, with their filtered air supply kept at a negative pressure to the surrounding room. But you had to cross those barriers when you needed to inject them. And that brought you into contact with sharps. Sharps were broken glass, the needles you used and the animals' claws and teeth. Sharps could penetrate gloves. They could even penetrate the heavy rubber of a Centurion suit. More often than not it was through carelessness with animals that scientists working in BSL-4 laboratories died.

Armed with his new samples of blood, tissue and cerebrospinal fluid from Bill Reickhardt, Will opened the final door and went in.

*

Kristina finished her tour of the culture and serology results five minutes or so after Will had entered the animal room. She returned to the table in the atrium, mopping her face with a paper towel while waiting for him to return. The seconds passed with excruciating slowness. She got to her feet and walked to the giant dispensing machine against the wall. Usually she made do with water. Tonight she hankered after a refreshing fizzy drink. A flashback: Will's voice cajoling her about her lack of appreciation for jazz:

'You're way too cool.'

She chuckled. Bought a Sprite and returned to the table, holding the cold can against her brow. She thought: You got Miles Davis tootling *Tutu*; I got Marvin Gaye. Give me the funky magic of *Sexual Healing*.

Will had upset her more than she had let on, giving her grief over the telephone. But then there had been that moment when their eyes had met. A thrill went through her, recalling that moment. His eyes were that glacial blue that seemed to frighten people. But they didn't frighten her, not Kristina Earle. She appreciated what others just didn't notice, the immense courage demanded by his day-to-day job, the manly qualities that included courtesy, the struggle with loneliness after the death of his wife. Kristina was married to a husband who had lost what physical attraction she had felt during their courtship to become a boorish and predictable slob who took her for granted. A Masters degree, doing homework on her mother's kitchen table had led her to a doctorate in medical microbiology. She had sweated blood to gain this full-time job of twelve hour shifts working with BSL-4 viruses. Kristina was breathing hard now, almost hyperventilating. The fact was she was close to tears.

Sexual healing: she wished. She could die for it. But she wasn't going to get it – not in this life.

Blinking suddenly, she was startled into reality by a pain in her fingers.

She had automatically begun to open the can of Sprite and now there was a sharp, tingling pain in her fingers where she had pulled at the tab. Her fingertips felt like they were swollen and inflamed. She couldn't open the can. She tried again to yank the tab open but she was forced to abandon it because of the stabs of pain that were shooting up her hands and into her wrists from her fingers.

She walked over to the four-story office block behind her, a building that was free-standing, yet entirely enclosed under the same high-vaulted ceiling as the atrium, like a small island in the three-dimensional space of the massive laboratory complex. She sat in the secretary's chair in the ground floor squeeze, switched on the desk lamp and examined her hands. Her fingers and thumbs were throbbing. The throbbing pain was worsening fast. Already it was past her wrists and darting half way up her arms. She was beginning to hate that omnipresent roaring of the ventilation machines, which prevented her thinking clearly. The vibration was irritating her very bones. At that moment, her training kicked in and she began to investigate her actions.

Could I have made a mistake?

All of a sudden a wave of terror invaded her, viciously, hungrily. It tore right through her like a shark through water.

Blinking a little faster than usual, she went over the precautions she had taken. The samples had arrived here from Thirless, sealed with a thick brown tape in a plastic-covered padded envelope. She had picked them up from the loading bay and taken them directly into the BSL-2 facility. In her mind, she went back through the routine of entering the door. She read the familiar sign in capitals: CAUTION: GLOVES REQUIRED IN THIS AREA. BSL-2 – no big deal: the ordinary pathogens you met in any hospital bacteriology laboratory. She recalled taking all the right precautions, of putting on gloves, walking on through into BSL-3. Now, involuntarily, she touched both her hands to her face. Her fingertips felt hard as hazel nut shells, and red-hot. She tried sucking them and the pain only got worse. The telephone was ringing, right there beside her. She didn't want to be distracted. BSL-3 –! She struggled to recall her exact sequence of actions.

The sign on the door: the usual biohazard logo, in carmine red. GLOVES REQUIRED IN THIS AREA. DISPOSABLE GOWN REQUIRED IN THIS AREA. CAUTION: MASK REQUIRED IN THIS AREA. DANGER: EYE PROTECTION REQUIRED HERE. As if she needed reminding that this was a battle zone. She relived her movements, precisely, accurately. Opening the package in one of the hoods: normal glove port precautions. She had taken particular care with the blood. She had spun down the clots, removing the straw-colored serum that was left, dividing the serum into aliquots, with full precautions. She held there, on that memory. You had to be particularly careful with serum. Serum was where you found the viruses. She had taken some of the serum into the Gammacell before diluting and dividing it up for antibody testing. In her mind, she was scrupulous in going through her earlier actions, her care in putting aside the hot stuff to be ferried over to BSL-4 for animal testing. At every step...

I used every precaution!

Kristina let out the breath she didn't even realize she had been holding. With fingers that throbbed, she picked up the desk phone.

It was Will's voice.

She had difficulty telling what he was saying to her. He sounded like he was shouting down the noise of a wind tunnel. He was talking through the radio microphone fitted into his suit.

'Say it again!' she spoke into the telephone. 'I can't hear you.'

What he was really doing was shouting – it was an automatic compensation for his ear protection and the noise in his suit. She had to hold the telephone slightly away from her ear as she listened again.

'Can you hear me now?'

'Yes. I can hear you.'

'Some of the animals are dead.' He hesitated a moment: in that same moment her pulse began to race. Will – the Iceberg – was worried. 'All of those in cages A, B and D. Are those the ones you injected intravenously?'

'That's right.' She had injected mice, rats and guinea pigs.

'Those in C, E and F have marked induration in the skin over the abdomens. It could be the beginning of the rash. I presume these were intradermal injections?'

'Yes.' The terror had returned. She felt her eyelids spring wide open. It was completely automatic. Her voice was a croak:

'It seems awful fast.'

She imagined the frown of thought that must be creasing his face. She thought: *like goddamn lightning!*

A judder of panic was careening through her. Panic at the sudden realization of something she had overlooked. She mewed, like a cat, at the throb of agony that had invaded the bones of her hands. In her mind, she was back down there: the loading bay, signing for and then picking up the samples. She recalled her actions with a stupendous clarity. That was the only time she had handled anything without wearing gloves. She had picked up the padded envelope, sealed in plastic, with her bare hands.

'Oh, Jesus!'

'Kristina - I'm going to have to ask you to come up here and help me do some autopsies.'

Her voice had fallen to a whisper: 'Okay!'

She heard the telephone cut to dial tone before she dropped it. Her eyes turned to the opened door, lifting up to those small square windows, like goblin eyes in that sheer stretch of reinforced concrete across the atrium. She didn't even put her hands out to protect herself as the building became a vortex, crazily spinning, and the floor rose up to meet her.

05: 18/ 06h22

Ake Johansson unhitched the tailgate of his silver Mitsubishi Montero so he could load equipment into it from a four-wheeled cart. The most awkward item was the 1800-06 Microscope Receptor, which looked like a complicated telescope with a lengthy cable that attached it to a keyboard. This was an optical sensor device that would enable him to assess plant foliage densities through radiant energy reflected back from their canopies. He had included a specialized camera that would allow him to tell one type of vegetation from another, avoiding one of the most time-consuming problems in any field sampling exercise. Normally the grad students would have been here to help him but they had been given some days off to attend the tripleA-S meeting in Boston.

'Lucky old them!' Johansson grumbled to himself.

The truth was Johansson didn't really envy the students one bit, any more than he resented the absence of his colleague and co-director of the Field Reserve, Kay McCann. Botany, and evolutionary botany in particular, was Kay's field of expertise and it was her field ecology equipment Johansson was now borrowing to investigate the anomaly.

The anomaly: strange to think about it in such terms. But he couldn't deny those Landsat images he had seen first thing this morning.

Johansson slammed down the tailgate, walked round, opened the driver's door to switch on the engine, then closed it again so the heater would take the morning chill out of the interior while he rattled the cart back to the lab. He decided to leave a message for the departmental secretary, to let her know where he was going and how long he was likely to be out of his office. Michelle wouldn't arrive for almost two hours so he put a blank tape into her Dictaphone and had fun talking to her *in absentia,* an actor with his soliloquy perching inelegantly on the edge of her desk.

'Michelle – I'm leaving this message for Kay. In the unlikely event that she calls in from Boston, let her know that I am investigating an anomaly.' Of course, Michelle wouldn't understand what he meant by that. If she had been sitting in her chair right now, she would have frowned up at him with bespectacled owlishness.

He continued: 'Things appear to be going slightly crazy on the Landsats in Sector 5-32 so I'm going out there to do some counts.' Then, smiling impishly because he was unable to resist the urge to titillate Kay's imagination, he added: 'You can tell her that we could be witnessing a new paradigm.'

Johansson suppressed a sneeze by squeezing his nose between finger and thumb. But the sneeze just bided its time and came along a moment or two later, so he had to grab hold of the silver cigar-case that was poking out of the breast pocket of his shirt and was in danger of skidding right across the reception floor. Hah! If Michelle had been here, she would certainly have been tutting. Michelle was so goddamn evangelical about smoking. These days the only place where Johansson could smoke his beloved cigars was out in the desert. In a continuation of his theatrical mood, he drew a smoking cigar and placed it under the Dictaphone. Then he strolled out into the morning sun.

He hadn't traveled more than a quarter mile before he stopped the vehicle and flipped a Havana from the case, lighting it ceremoniously with the heavy-set silver lighter Agnietta had bought him when they were honeymooning all those years ago in Havana. He savored his first puff of the day. These days even Agnietta insisted he enjoyed his cigars outside of her company, so he had come to associate the pleasure of smoking with his passion for the desert. It was a long-term source of regret that Agnietta did not share his love of the desert. But she had suffered his passions for twenty-nine years. For that compromise, for the depth of support he had enjoyed from his otherwise easygoing wife, Ake had made a sacrifice in turn, which was to let Agnietta spend all of her time in their home in LA while he was prepared to spend half his life in quasi bachelorhood here, whenever it was his turn on the roster to direct the field reserve.

After about forty minutes' driving, he parked on a butte that overlooked Sector 5-32. Stepping down from the vehicle, he lit his second cigar of the morning before striding the thirty yards or so to the edge, scanning the bowl of the valley below him with appreciative eyes. Solitude! It was as if the cool breath of an Olympian god had blown away all of the pollution and bustle of southern California and replenished its true soul, at once harshly primeval and yet exquisitely harmonious. Cigar clamped between his teeth, he returned to the vehicle and spent a few trips ferrying the 1800 equipment to a reasonably level spot on the summit. Over ten minutes or so, he connected the telescope to the spectroradiometer and the latter to the laptop computer that would enable him to do some quick foliage readouts over a range of wavelengths. As the first readout appeared on the screen, he squatted close to the ground so he could cross-reference the results with the printouts he had taken from the Landsat earlier that morning.

He spat the cigar from his mouth and ground it under his heel:

'*Skit också!*'

It had been a long time since Johansson had sworn in Swedish. Standing erect, he thought about what he had just witnessed.

It just made no sense.

Pacing up and down, he started muttering to himself. *Calm down!* It was no good panicking. He had to consider his logical options. There was so much to be done and he would have to do it all alone. He reprogrammed the equipment to go through a new range of spectra before returning to the vehicle, then reversed in cloud of dust and drove down into the valley.

05: 18/ 07h41

MayEllen Reickhardt was staring up into the face of a bald man in a space suit who had come to give her the bad news. He was an infuriating reminder that she was still incarcerated in the ICU, at the Thirless Memorial Hospital. The bald man wore gold-rimmed eyeglasses inside his heavy plastic helmet. He was breathing from a pump hanging from his belt, attached to a line that put air into the helmet. Introducing himself as Dr. Burke, he informed her that he was the director of epidemiology in the state public health department, at Phoenix.

'How are you feeling, Mrs. Reickhardt?'

'Never mind me. How's Bill?'

'I'm sorry.'

No surprise there: not really. But the pain that was registering was even worse than she had anticipated. All her dreams, everything, had evaporated right there in those two words expressed by that man with the hooded, bespectacled face.

'You're sorry?' It felt like she was playing some foolish game.

'Your husband died, earlier this morning.'

Tears burst out of her, in an overwhelming flood. She didn't try to stop them or to mop them up with a tissue.

'I know it will be little consolation, but at least the poor man is no longer suffering.'

His words should have offended her but they didn't. MayEllen had seen the way Bill had looked. That rash on his skin. The smell.

'Can I get you something? A glass of water?'

She didn't bother to reply. She was squeezing her eyes tight shut through the tears in an attempt to clear her thoughts. They had given her a double dose of the sleeping capsule, so she felt muzzy. 'I want to go see him. I want to go see his body.'

'I'm afraid we can't let you do that. It's for your own protection.'

Her face was wrecked, both her nostrils freely running with snot onto her lip. 'Why not? Where's Dr. Valero? He's my doctor.'

'Dr. Valero is busy with another patient right now.'

A nurse, also suited, tried to wipe her face. When MayEllen stopped her, she compromised by pressing tissues into her hands. MayEllen ordered Burke: 'Then call him in here. I want to talk to him.'

'I can't do that, Mrs. Reickhardt.'

She wiped her face with the wad of tissues. 'You mean you won't do it.'

'Your husband died from a contagious illness. The nature of the infection is still unknown. The cause of death will be established by autopsy.'

'I haven't given you permission for any autopsy.'

'In these circumstances we don't need your permission.'

'Where's my family doctor. I want to talk to Dr. Manning?'

'Dr. Manning has been admitted.'

Dr. Manning admitted! All strength suddenly gone from her, MayEllen flopped onto her back again. Chills, violent tremblings, were creeping over her. She couldn't come to terms with what was happening. Suddenly there was a lot of noise in the corridor. It sounded like beds being wheeled by.

'Is the hospital being evacuated?'

'No – not at all.'

She thought: *My God – he's lying to me.*

*

Kay McCann was leaving the breakfast room for the first lecture of the TripleA-S meeting when she saw the message addressed to her on the conference notice board:

URGENT. CALL PROFESSOR JOHANNSON

It was unusual enough to cause a flicker of anxiety. She checked the time on her watch: 8:15 a.m. She went back to her room to get her cell phone, switched it on and heard two recorded messages, one dated yesterday evening and the other very early in the morning. Both messages asked her to call Ake back. He didn't say what was wrong: he just said, 'We need to talk', and 'There's something of a problem.' She clicked his name in the menu and dialed his number. The machine voice prompt told her his cell phone was switched off. It made no sense. Why would he call her twice, sounding so fired up, and then switch off his cell? Had the problem, whatever it might be, resolved itself? Kay thought about calling Michelle at the Ivan Wallin reception desk, but Michelle didn't start until 8:30 and she never arrived early. Kay decided she would try Ake's office phone, on the off chance he wasn't already out in the desert. Once again she got no answer.

She didn't have time to keep on trying. She had to get to the lecture hall well in advance of the 8:30 kickoff. So she, in turn, left a voicemail message for Ake on the office phone, asking him to call her back after 12:00 noon.

By lunchtime, Ake had failed to call her back. Kay called Michelle: 'I've had two urgent messages to call Ake. I've been trying to get hold of him all morning and he's not answering. Do you have any idea what he wants?'

Michelle sounded her usual insouciant self, breezily informing Kay, 'Ake isn't here. He went out into the reserve early this morning. I had a message on my Dictaphone to say he was looking into a problem. He hasn't got back yet.'

'What's the problem?'

'You know Ake – always clowning about. He did say something about checking out a glitch he'd picked up on the Landsat data. What it was, he didn't say.'

'Can you play back his message?'

'I'm sorry, but I went over it with some more dictation. But I recall he intended to take your 1800 gear with him.'

Kay thought about that. It was unusual, but not incredibly so. Ake must be doing some measurements of plant and insect densities and she had to presume there was nobody from botany to help him.

'What time did he set out?'

'Real early would be my guess.'

Kay took a moment to think about it. Clearly there was a problem serious enough for Ake to contact her. No doubt he'd get back in touch when he got back to his office sometime in the afternoon. If not, she'd call him when she got home late on Saturday.

Unlike Kay, who worked out of Berkeley, Ake was affiliated to UCLA. For close to thirty years, he had been the Roscoe Pound Professor of Ecology. It had been Ake who had founded the Ivan Wallin Field Reserve, bringing together biologists and ecologists from all of the California universities. Kay felt a certain flicker of anxiety in not having gotten hold of Ake. But whatever the problem was, it would keep. In the meantime, she had a meeting to chair at 2.00 p.m.

05: 18/ 14h21

Susan Anne Mackenzie studied her reflection in the smoked glass door of her office in the pathology laboratory at the Thirless Memorial Hospital. It was only the second time in her professional career that she had worn a biosafety suit and the first time had been a practice assignment, under the watchful eyes of the suit suppliers. Since the hospital had adopted the revised Major Disaster Plan, some eighteen months ago, Dr. Mackenzie had been a member of the Major Disaster Response Team.

Now she shuddered.

Chief of histopathology at the hospital, her position wasn't too onerous in the normal run of circumstances. Her research interest was cardiac deaths, a predictable specialization given that heart attacks killed one in five of the overfed local population. But a pathologist at a small town hospital had to be prepared to investigate any kind of illness, including serious infection. And the present case, the case that had precipitated the Major Disaster Response, was almost certainly a contagious infection. There were two questions that needed answering. What was the precise nature of the infection? And how was it communicated?

At six in the morning, Dr. Mackenzie had attended a meeting of the Major Disaster Response Team, where she had represented not only the hospital pathology division but also the State Medical Examiner's Office, to which she was affiliated.

She knew that the intensive care unit was no longer functioning in its normal capacity. It was in the process of being converted into a high-security isolation facility. She also knew that her colleague, Dr. Ricardo Valero, was under investigation on his own unit because three other staff had gone down with the same mysterious illness as the body she was about to examine. Ric was not being allowed to examine his patients, not until the State Health Department decided he was free of the infection himself. Outside the front façade of the building, the largest fleet of ambulances she had ever seen was shuttling past the main doors as a hundred and eight patients were being moved out of the hospital, post-ops and medical cases that were too sick to be discharged home. They were ferrying people north to Vegas, East to Flagstaff and south to Phoenix. This morning Mackenzie had helped to make that decision, in reluctant support of the decision of the State Public Health officers. She had sat on the committee and voted for it against the apoplectic opposition J.J. Maher, her colleague, and the hospital clinical director.

It had been her involvement in the Major Disaster Response that had delayed the autopsy until the afternoon. Now she waited until Pedro, the mortuary assistant, had wheeled the body out into the center of the floor, above the steel drain.

She started her dictation. 'The body is that of a large obese male, aged 47 years, height six two and a half, 229 pounds. Signs of antemortem hemorrhage about the mouth, nostrils, ears and eyes.' The hemorrhage, she knew, was non-specific, and did not necessarily mean a hemorrhagic fever virus. Any disease that destroyed the liver was complicated by hemorrhage. 'The skin ...' she clumped in her gum boots around the circumference of the body, 'the skin exhibits marked antemortem changes of the sort I would normally associate with a body that had been lying for several days in a warm moist environment.' She raised the pitch of her voice so she would be picked up clearly by the suit's inbuilt microphone. 'I would describe it as a confluent marbling, with obvious pockets of gas. Reminiscent of a Fourier's gangrene – or possibly infection with a gas gangrene organism, such as a Clostridium.' Thinking ahead, to her summary and differential diagnosis, she wondered about an overwhelming infection with a mixed zoo of organisms, the kind of exotic event that might accompany total immunological failure.

Mackenzie had read Valero's notes before entering the autopsy room. They were cryptic, like a ship's log in a gale: admission findings, times of change, calls made. She had read them on a sealed tray, which the control of infection people had autoclaved under two layers of polythene. Even then they had insisted that she wear a virus-proof facemask, eye protection, and two pairs of surgical gloves.

'Making my initial incision now!'

She placed the scalpel on the skin of the chest, high up to the right under the collarbone. She cut down, making the left upper arm of what would become a great Y-shaped incision, folding back the skin of the chest to enable her to cut out the shield of sternum and the entire front plate of ribs, before carrying the single incision down through the linea alba to the pubic bone. As the turgid flesh gaped, she was unable to stop herself reeling back, with her forearm automatically rising as if to occlude her nostrils.

'Ah, shit!'

A whiff of putrefaction got to her inside the suit. For a moment it caused her to panic. It shouldn't have been able to get through to her in the suit. But she dismissed this and wondered if there was some way of increasing the flow of air from the pump attached to her waist.

Pedro was standing back, watching her with owl's eyes behind his mask. He looked ridiculous with his potbelly protruding through the green plasticized material of the biosafety suit, over which he, like Mackenzie, also wore a black rubberized apron that reached from his neck to his Wellington-clad feet.

'Let's get on, shall we!'

With the chest thrown open, she felt her way deep down around the floppy bulk of the lungs to cut through their roots and she waved for Pedro to hoist their oozing bulk out of the body. The lungs looked heavy, more solid than their normal spongy texture and a blackish purple. When he put them on the scales, they weighed almost twice the normal, even for a large male. There was a liquid slap as he flopped them onto the dissection table. Mackenzie used a long-bladed steel knife to slice them, cutting through the flesh at intervals of an inch or so, like a butcher slicing up steaks. The slices oozed chocolate-colored pus over the bright cutting edge of her knife. The liver was the same. Hugely swollen, it bulged out of its capsule as Pedro struggled to get it onto the table. He dumped it heavily, like a ton-weight fleshy balloon, then sluiced its surface with a small plastic hose. When she inserted the point of a scalpel through the glistening capsule, the balloon exploded, drenching Mackenzie in putrescent slime.

'Shee—it!' Pedro, mimicking her own reaction from minutes earlier, was staring at her, his eyes startled, like a horse ready to bolt.

'Go get the big hose and sluice me down,' she barked. 'Start with my visor and then move down over the apron. Go on - for Christ's sake, do it!'

She stood rigidly in the shower, waiting for the slime to dissolve to pink and then clear away into the floor drain. Mackenzie considered changing her suit. But that was just allowing her anxiety to take control. The suit was designed to protect her against any such transmission through surface contact. But she had to swallow a spurt of saliva before she could speak once more, tersely, into the suit microphone.

'There appears to be no recognizable liver architecture as such. The entire organ has undergone liquefaction. All I can do is to aspirate some of this for stains and culture. At least we might get some evidence of the causative organism.' She paused, knowing that her personal assistant, Henrietta, was jotting this down in the comfortable sanity of her office. Under normal circumstances, Mackenzie would comb through the small and large intestines, looking for pathology. But she didn't feel inclined to follow normal procedures. She shook her head slowly, thinking it through. She said, 'I'm going to take representative samples from those tissues that are most likely to show the causative agent.'

Certain tissues played a key role when it came to fighting off the invasion of some foreign life form. The liver, the spleen, the bone marrow, the lymph glands. The first changes would be seen in these organs. She planned to take samples for culture and microscopy. Other major organs, such as the guts, the lungs and heart, would also have to be examined and samples taken. And that would have to suffice. She wanted to get out of this suit. She had to suppress the urge to run from the autopsy suite. She knew that biopsy samples had been taken from the skin and liver last night. She would add these to the samples she was now taking, and in this way calibrate the progression of Bill Reickhardt's disease.

But there was also the brain.

Pedro was clearly thinking the same. He was watching her, with the Stryker saw in his hands. Mackenzie walked around the head to decide where to begin the incision. The scalp, with its thick gray hair, was thrown into sharp contrast by the gangrene affecting the skin. She used a scalpel to cut a circle around the back two thirds of scalp and then peeled it forwards, so it hung down over the face. The hair edge protruded over the concealed chin like an obscene parody of a Puritan beard. She stepped back. Pedro was still standing there, looking at her, as if hoping she would tell him to hold back from cutting into the skull.

Mackenzie swallowed again, deep-breathing to hold down that rising bitter reflux of nausea. There would be an aerosol of bone and tissue before the head was opened up wide, like a capped egg.

'Go ahead!'

The saw screamed and its arc of blade cut into a skull that seemed to lack its normal bony hardness. The sound was low-pitched and hollow, like a wood saw cutting into a wormy log. Mackenzie tensed herself, anticipating the smell of burning bone.

Just then a sound made her jump. It was the amplified ring of a telephone. Henrietta was talking to her through the speaker in her helmet.

'I told you I wasn't to be disturbed.'

'I'm sorry, Dr. Mackenzie. But it's the public health people, up in ICU. They want to tell you something important.'

'Okay – you better put them through.' Mackenzie stood there staring at Pedro, who was standing as far back as he could from the head incision. The brain was swelling out of the opened skull, like a rancorous semi-liquid cheese in a microwave. She watched it in amazement, as a little of it began to slobber out over the incised bone and flayed scalp, oozing slowly onto the metal table.

'Susan? Can you hear me?'

'I hear you.'

'It's Jez Burke here. I thought I should inform you about the condition of your colleagues.'

'Uh-huh?'

For Christ's sake, don't say it has gotten to Ric Valero!

'Thought I should warn you that two of the interns from the Emergency Admission Room have definitely started with the rash. It started on their fingers and worked its way up into the hands and arms.'

The Emergency Room. Mackenzie's mind began to race. The interns would have been the first to examine Bill Reickhardt on his admission, long before anybody even thought about a contagious infection and sending him up to ICU.

'What about Valero?'

'Nothing to worry us as yet. We're hoping he might be clear. But we're still keeping him in isolation.'

Mackenzie exhaled.

'We've also located Nurse Ritter. She's on her way in. She was comatose when we found her.'

He paused for a beat or two, as if inviting her to speak. But Mackenzie couldn't think of anything to say.

'Those same changes on her fingers. The involvement of the fingers seems important – suggests penetration of the skin at the point of contact. So I thought you should know about that. Be exceedingly careful with the autopsy. There appears to be a very high risk of nosocomial spread.'

Mackenzie's heart kept missing beats.

Burke paused again. She could hear his breathing amplified by the speaker system. 'You realize the implications?'

'You're going to investigate me and Pedro when I've completed the autopsy.'

His voice softened: 'If Valero turns out to be okay, I think we'll find that from the very first examination he took proper safety precautions.'

Mackenzie thought back to that spurt of slime soaking her suit. She rushed over to the wash basin and dropped the scalpel into it with a clatter. She had to steady her hands through leaning on the edge. She tasted another spurt of bile come into her mouth but she forced herself to swallow it back down. There was no way she could possibly be sick inside her suit helmet.

'Oh, shit and piss!'

A good old pathological expletive!

Wouldn't Nurse Ritter also have taken safety precautions? And still she had gotten the infection. No!

Mackenzie focused down, mentally calming herself. Common sense suggested an alternative explanation. Ritter must have done something wrong. She had broken the rules in some way. Maybe touched Reickhardt's body before she realized the man was contagious.

Right now, still leaning with both hands against the wash basin, Mackenzie did not feel altogether comforted by her own logic, any more than she felt an altogether professional detachment about what she was doing.

Only yesterday she had made arrangements to have a Sunday brunch with her son, Jason, and seven of his nine-year-old friends at O'Grady's. She had been looking forward to it. The waiters would make a fuss, carrying the birthday cake in high on a platter with nine sparklers burning. Now she wondered if she would ever see Jason again.

05: 21/ 13h50

Los Angeles Police Officer Tad Brentford was humming contentedly to himself. 'You gotta fish where the fish is!'

His rookie partner, Officer Joanne E. Laing, hooted uproariously.

Brentford was driving the black-and-white through the streets of San Francisco heading east on Alosta out of Glendora. Joanne wasn't a bad looker. She sported a good full figure, at least that was the considered opinion of this red-blooded male. She also had cuddly brown eyes, inquisitive as a squirrel's, under neat cropped curly brown hair. Tad was enjoying the mentor role on what would otherwise have promised to be a boring Sunday afternoon. They were following their second call, after visiting the Church of the Little Flower where the priest, Father Brown, had been the victim of a physical assault. His crack-head assailant had ripped the collection box from its plinth and smashed the priest's skull with it before making off with the one foot square wooden box rattling with small change. Tad and Joanne had shared a few jokes about that as they spent an hour and a half hunting the streets around the church. They had found no sign of crack-head or box. Tad had come away, bemused by the forgiving nature of Father Brown, a bald-headed black man with blood streaming down his face, who had already forgiven his attacker before the ambulance had arrived to take him to the hospital.

When Tad has asked him why he didn't find a church in a classier neighborhood, Father Brown had uttered those memorable words: 'You gotta fish where the fish is!'

They took a left onto Foothill, heading towards the National Forest, where a university professor called Johansson lived. Johansson had failed to show up for work at UCLA. People had gotten worried when he and his wife, Agnietta, didn't answer the telephone. Another professor, name of McCann, would join them at the house.

'Absent minded professors!' Tad shook his head, grinning.

'A few days' research in the company of his secretary.'

'Too absent-minded to let people know?'

Chuckling: 'You got it.'

Here in the leafy suburbs the Sunday streets were quiet, the houses spread out, with large gardens backing onto the pleasant vista. Overhead, the sun had dissipated the smog to reveal a washed blue that would have looked magical if they'd been down to swimsuits and looking up at it from the vantage of a pool and a crate of beers. They were still enjoying each other's jokes when Tad pulled into a wide, cobbled driveway, shaded by eucalyptus. A yellow Wrangler was already parked in the drive and a red-haired woman, wearing a chartreuse silk shirt and knee-length black skirt, was calling to a dog through the wrought-iron bars of two six-foot gates.

*

Kay McCann turned to watch the patrol car park by the side of her Wrangler. Two navy-shirted officers alighted: a middle-aged man, white T-shirt inside open necked short-sleeved shirt, introduced himself as Officer Brentford and his younger companion as Officer Laing.

'You the one who asked us to investigate?'

'Yes, I am. Now that I'm here, I'm even more worried.'

Kay suffered his macho inspection. From his expression, she assumed she passed his "Helen-of-Troy" scale as a face that would launch at least a hundred, if not the mythic thousand, ships.

He asked her, 'You know this Professor Johansson?'

'Ake and I are friends as well as colleagues.' She pronounced the first name in the Swedish way for no reason other than to annoy him, since it must have sounded like somebody attempting clear their throat. 'We cover for each other on the field reserve out on the Mojave. We keep an eye on each other's patch, home and work.'

There was a brass bell on the left-hand gatepost: Officer Brentford was pressing it as he was talking to her. Kay could have told him, if he had troubled to ask her, that there would be no response. She had been pressing it on and off for five minutes before their arrival. Agnietta's pet dog, Scratch, was barking inside the gates. The small dog – a mongrel Agnietta had rescued from a dog pound, with a patchwork coat of grays and browns – cut a lonely figure in the bone-dry midday heat. Kay watched Brentford inspect the mailbox, where he saw exactly what she had already seen: several newspapers and more than a dozen letters, journals and circulars uncollected from the other side of the wall. The gates were substantial and she waited for macho man to figure out that they were electrically operated.

'You know where we can get hold of the remote?'

Kay dangled it from her right hand. 'I decided I'd better wait until you arrived.' She pressed the button and the gates swung open. Scratch scampered out to greet her, barking excitedly around her legs.

Kay bent down to tickle him under one of his ears. 'Agnietta and her dog, they're real close. I can't imagine her letting him run around wild.' She set out to walk briskly on through the open gates but Brentford held her back. Laing had been looking from side to side at the neighbors' houses and now she shared a glance with her colleague. These were properties with large walled-off gardens that came with the same sort of detachment of mind as the physical separation of the real estate: people who rarely met. She asked Kay, 'This guy, Johansson, should definitely be at home? Not out of town on vacation or at some scientific meeting?'

'He's still supposed to be running things at the field reserve. But I called earlier and was told he left for home late Thursday afternoon.'

Brentford narrowed his eyes at the dog. 'Okay, let's go check it out. But I want you back there behind me – Ma'am.'

Kay grimaced but supposed he was only doing his job. She followed behind the two police officers as they made their winding way through a capacious and very unusual garden. There were no bottlebrush bushes or Bermuda grass, or lemon trees or the bitter orange hedges that people planted as decoratives in the hot dry climate. Bare rocks poked up through the sandy gravel between explosions of cacti. In the clearer areas it was scattered with milkweeds and brittlebush, penstemons and a variety of succulents, including saguaros and aloes, but the dominating – astonishing – feature was a huge variety of spiny shapes, flowering and non-flowering, that must have appeared unfamiliar ornaments to any visitor. It made her love her friend Ake all the more. Scratch hung back, trotting contentedly by Kay's feet. Her nerves couldn't help but jump as the gates clanged together behind them.

Laing appeared to slow her pace of walking so her partner could scope ahead. They were about halfway down the forty yards of approach when Laing remarked to Kay: 'Those trees - they're desert trees, aren't they?'

'They're ironwoods, yes.' She added, 'Ake brought a piece of the Mojave back into his yard.'

Kay decided she would stay back behind the two officers as they approached the front of the house. The carport, which was off to the left, was capacious, sheltering two vehicles with ample room to spare. Kay saw Ake's dust-grimed silver Mitsubishi Montero parked next to Agnietta's Honda Accord. The cars confirmed that both Ake and Agnietta were home. Scratch was whining in front of the door as they stepped up onto the deck that ran all the way along the front elevation. Officer Brentford rang the bell.

There was no response from inside the house.

Kay stepped back to look along the facing windows. Suddenly she noticed the silence. It was eerie. It wasn't just the house that was silent but the garden too. There should have been bees buzzing, cicadas chirruping – things out there grousing about the heat.

Brentford headed across to a long window opening out of the living room. The curtains had not been drawn back. His nostrils twitched. 'Hey, Joanne – you smell it?'

'What is it?' Laing's voice sounded high-pitched as she came across.

Kay also caught the smell: something rank, the smell of decay. The policewoman bent down to inspect a raised-level flowerbed that ran below the windowsill.

'I think these are geraniums.'

'They weren't here when I last called,' Kay remarked. 'My guess, they were planted by Agnietta.' She joined them in looking down at what should have been an exuberant display of flowers, but this was a coffin of dead and withered stalks.

'Very recently planted too!' Laing pointed to a cluster of black plastic gardening pots, piled up on the deck, next to the raised bed. She touched a trailing black stem with the tip of her index finger. 'Oh, phfeew!' she squealed.

Kay couldn't imagine why the policewoman had touched something that looked so putrid. Laing insisted on holding up the tip of her finger to Kay's nostrils. Kay averted her face. The dead flowers were the cause of the rank smell. To Kay it was eerily disturbing, this box of rotting flowers in the otherwise pristine and well-kept yard. The two women followed Brentford around the house into the back, with the dog barking and scampering around their feet.

Brentford hammered on the back door. No response. He turned the door handle, pushed. The door clicked open.

'Hey – that's odd!' he muttered. 'You live in LA, you don't go out leaving the back door unlocked.'

Pushing the door wide, he slipped his Smith and Wesson from its holster, stuck his head into the room, then followed it with his body. A medley of antique Scandinavian furniture decorated the gloom. But there was no sign of life. He sniffed in unison with Kay, who was now only two feet behind him. There was another bad smell, a sickly sweet, disgusting aroma. It added to Kay's growing unease, that and Scratch's lonely barking, and the unlocked door. Increasingly nervous, she followed Brentford and her nose to the big square kitchen.

A woman's body was lying on the floor. Her right arm was stretched out stiffly above her head, as if in parody of hailing a bus.

'Dear God – Agnietta!'

Kay's stomach contracted with the stink, which was coming from the decomposing body.

Brentford kept muttering, 'Jesus H. Christ!'

Kay watched him holster his gun, then inch his way closer. He had to press his kerchief hard against his nose to get within feet of Agnietta's body. Kay couldn't stop herself from retching. The body she could see past the probing policeman was black, or at least it was mostly black. Agnietta had been a Scandinavian blonde, with skin the color of milk. Whatever had killed her, her body had become covered with something horrible and black, like a fungus.

'You know what I'm thinking?' Brentford looked like a man struggling to control his own panic. 'This morning I read a bulletin about that mystery illness broke out in Arizona.'

Kay watched in horror as he poked at the blue-black scalp under the disarrayed blonde hair with the tip of a ballpoint pen.

'My wife's sister, Bernice – she lives in Flagstaff. So Milli calls Bernice. They're talking about what's goin' on. Bernice, she's a nurse, is convinced it's the plague. Got to be, she says, because plague turns folks' skin black. Did you know that, Professor? You know the old name for bubonic plague was the "black death"?'

Kay felt disinclined to answer. Her stomach was cramping up in waves, bringing spurts of vomit into her throat. Suddenly Brentford reared back, almost toppling the two women pressed up behind him. 'Oh, Jesus – fuck!' The blue-black scalp had detached with a tearing sound. They could see smooth white bone, the top of Agnietta's skull, oozing a straw-colored oily plasma. Brentford pushed them back into the living-room, retching himself. All three of them were close to hysteria.

Brentford was talking to himself: 'Arizona isn't very far from Southern California. And now it looks like we got that same bubonic plague.'

Abruptly, as if realizing what he was saying, he wheeled round and put an arm around Kay's shoulders, manhandling her towards the open back door. Officer Laing had beaten them to it. She was down on one knee in the yard with a bundle of tissues held to her mouth. She said,

'Damnation, Tad, my fingers are burning. I wish I hadn't touched the rotten plants.'

Kay's thighs were jerking and trembling.

Brentford looked from Kay to Laing and then back again, shaking his head. 'Look – hey, Joanne – I want you to leave this to me. Why don't you stay with the professor out here in the yard.'

Laing shook her head, determined to accompany him.

'Then you better keep your mouth closed and press the tissues against your nose.' He walked through the broad expanse of living room and into the corridor leading to the stairs. At the foot of the stairs, he swallowed hard, took several breaths, and then started to ascend. Laing just stood there in the hallway. Kay skirted the policewoman and she followed Brentford, pressing her handkerchief up tight against her nose.

On the queen-size bed in one of the two spacious bedrooms they found Ake's body, also bloated and black.

'Aw, shi—it!'

'What is it?' Kay gasped, unable to take a step closer.

'Flies, Ma'am! I've been called to a good many dead bodies in my time. But good God Almighty – I've never seen so many dead flies!'

2

The Field Reserve

Top Secret
Operation Globalnet
Surveillance Mode: E-mail
Retrograde analysis: Index minus 15/12
DELICATE SOURCE: RESTRICTION CODE:
eyes alpha
L of E/ he→ee

Dear Lyse,

I'm sorry we couldn't get together for Thanksgiving. And now it's the New Year and I haven't seen my little granddaughter in ages. Tell Penny and Martin that I've been asking about Simone. Her photograph takes pride of place on my desk, among the mosquitoes and the ants.

I should be able to get home soon. A few more months of concentrated effort and we'll all be ready for a two-week vacation - I promise.

Things are looking so much better, after all those initial misgivings. Ahmed's work on maize is very promising – also Chan's work on rice. I'm optimistic in both cases. The blessing of a hot climate is the fact that you can grow things quickly. You can alternate two separate crop cycles in one year. This has speeded everything up no end. The compound is so big now we could feed a small town. And progress - you wouldn't believe the progress we have made! We're expanding so fast we've had to double the number of dormitories and even these are becoming overcrowded. We've had to recruit tech labor locally, though the nearest city is almost two hundred miles away with nothing but sand in between. Even E.S., after that spiteful episode with Nancy Chong, when she refused to hop into bed with him, is showing signs of knuckling down. I only wish that his tact with his scientific team would match his hands-on ability with molecular technology. The fellow is undoubtedly a wayward genius.

I'm not one to get overly excited, but we have made a breakthrough - I don't think it's an exaggeration to call it a new biological paradigm. I'd love to say more but I'm not supposed to talk about it. E.S. has pioneered new organic vectors in the eight months we have been here. We have abandoned microprojectiles. Spectacular nano linkups with bioinformatics. There are radically new structure-class charts sprouting along the entire lengths of the corridor walls!

Of course it's a double-edged sword. The more exciting it becomes, the harder we work – and the more poignant the separation from you.

Lyse – there's a possibility – I hardly dare to mention it – but I have begun to hope we might be able to help people like Simone.

Love
H.

05: 22/ 06h55

'Goooood morning, all you good folks out there! This is your favorite radio host, TeeJay Nieman, on K-V-A-L. The station that gives it to you straight, no pre-recording, no editing, the Voice of America Live.

'So what have we got for you on this bright and cheerful Monday morning? Well, let me tell you – do I have something for you. A tale for those of you now traveling to work on those congested turnpikes and highways. With me here, in the studio, is MayEllen Reickhardt. Say hello to America, MayEllen!'

There was a muffled grunt.

Thirty yards from the shoreline of Lake Mead, Nevada, a man listened to radio with interest, tilting back the hand-stitched leather seats of a flame-red Ferrari 575M Maranello. Outside of the tinted windows, the morning was cold so he kept the engine idling and the heater running.

The strident male voice over the radio continued: 'Now don't be bashful. Say it again, loud and clear, so all those listeners out there can hear you!'

'Hello!' the woman's voice said, a little louder. It was a deep voice for a woman, audibly nervous.

The driver's fingers tapped on the matte-black carbon fiber that surrounded the dash and his eyes relaxed on the mist-shrouded lake at the bottom of a gentle slope that was planted with decorative shrubs. He had arrived early and now he had to wait. He wasn't gifted with a natural patience. The radio was a welcome distraction.

'We're going to hear MayEllen's story right after the jingle, so don't go away, folks. You know this mystery epidemic that's going around and frightening us all to death? Well, she has something to tell you that will make your hair curl. So hold tight there and we'll be right back.'

*

Kay McCann, heading south with her son, Sean, from their home in Beverley, was tuned to the same wacky desert radio station. While glued to the program, it made her feel decidedly jumpy. And now they had cut to the advertising, the volume had been hiked up a couple of notches. She turned it right down.

'Aw, Mom!' Sean, who was wearing his Lakers 2002 Champions T-shirt, curled up his right leg onto the seat and groaned.

'Just for the interval. It's interfering with my concentration. Deal?'

'Oooo-kaaay!'

She reached over and rumpled the upstanding mop of golden hair on her twelve-year-old son's head. Sean grimaced and shook her off.

Kay flicked the blinker to warn the madman close on her tail that she was turning right. The Wrangler had been a big mistake. She had allowed herself to be persuaded by the incipient puberty of a 12-year-old boy. Driven by a flame-haired woman, the bright yellow automobile was a pheromone come-on for aggressive males, and the roads seemed to be chock full of them this morning. She was relieved to get off the congested 580 and heading onto Interstate 5.

Sean lost interest in the radio station for the two or three minutes they devoted to advertising. He turned to look at his mother across the wide cabin with a mixture of curiosity and fear in his blue-green eyes. He had helped her pack the food and the changes of clothes. She had just pulled everything out of the kitchen cupboards, the freezer, cleared the drawers and hanging racks in the closet.

'Are they really going to close down UCLA, Mom?'

'I hope not.'

'They closing down Berkeley too?'

'You hoping I won't have to go back and we can live wild on the field reserve for good? There'd be no money to buy new computer games.' She laughed at his chagrined expression. 'Nah! Only kidding. It's not such a big deal as some folks are making out. There've been one or two incidents –'

'The man on the radio called it a plague.'

'He's exaggerating. One or two people died and people are getting jumpy – that's all it is.'

'Was that what the police called you about?'

'Something happened to a policewoman I met.'

'Did she die?'

'Yes - yes, she did.' Joanne: she recalled her name. Kay hadn't known that she'd died until she'd taken the call from the public health nurse in LA, who had frightened her by asking her questions of how she felt.

Sean looked over at her again. 'Like Ake?'

The man's voice on the radio cut through her need to reply. She restored the volume and heard him prompt his guest.

'MayEllen, let's talk some more about your late husband.'

'My husband, Bill,' she said. The woman sounded badly shaken. But then she added, in a rising voice: 'Some of you folks listening to this will have known my husband, Bill Reickhardt. We ran the M&B Cactus Farm outside Thirless for twenty years. My husband was the first person to get this mystery plague that's in all of the papers right now. I just come out of the ICU in Thirless Memorial Hospital, where I spent four godawful days.'

'Did you catch this bug?'

'No. I've been fine all along. But the doctors insisted on keeping me in hospital, kind of like a precaution.'

'They didn't want to let you go?'

'No, they didn't'

'You took your discharge? Against the advice of the doctors?'

'I took my discharge because there was nothing wrong with me. But my husband, Bill, died in that same ICU. I want to tell you folks how he died, and I'll have to warn you it wasn't pleasant. His skin turned black. He made awful moaning noises. The doctors didn't know what was wrong with him. I don't think it's right in this day and age that a man should have to die like that.'

Sean's eyes were round as a bug's. 'What's a plague, Mom?'

'A plague is an infection that kills a lot of people. But that's not what's happening here at all. We just have some people who died.'

'Spooky!'

Kay wasn't surprised that Sean felt scared. Ake wasn't he only academic to die. Eleven students and one assistant professor had also died at UCLA. From what she could gather from the television and newspapers, the deaths had been accumulating before anyone had connected what was happening in LA with what was happening in Arizona. Nobody had come up with any kind of explanation. 'And besides,' she said brightly, 'I can carry on working at the field station even while they're checking out all the Californian universities. Then we can go back to normal as soon as they have it all sorted out.'

'Yeah?' He almost sounded disappointed.

'You better believe it.'

But did *she* believe it?

A constriction tightened around her chest whenever she thought about Ake. He had sent her urgent messages and she had been more concerned with the tripleA-S meeting. How had she been so stupid? Ake never got in touch like that unless it was something urgent. *We have something of a problem!* His Swedish ancestry showing: no need for panic here, folks, only a plague! No - she didn't want to think along those lines. Something serious, no doubt about that. But it wasn't a plague, by any stretch of the imagination. Not with just thirteen or so people affected in the whole of LA. But were the authorities telling people the truth? Why, according to the media, were teams of public health doctors invading the university?

The man on the radio asked, 'Had Bill been sick for a while, MayEllen?'

'My Bill never had a day's illness in his life, except for the usual colds and things.'

'Did you say his skin turned black?'

'I had just set out to take some cacti down to Phoenix and I called him. I thought it was just flu. Then he made these terrible retching noises. I knew right then that something serious was wrong. I knew it had to be something real bad the matter with him.'

'Did you say he was making moaning noises?'

'That was later on, when he was in the hospital.'

'He was making these real strange noises?'

'Didn't sound like Bill at all. Didn't hardly sound human, those awful noises.'

'And then his skin turned black?'

'That's right.'

'Now let me get this straight. Bill was a white man before he turned into a black man – right?'

Kay turned the radio off before Sean got nightmares.

'Aw, Mom!'

'Okay – so let's talk about it rationally. This isn't a real plague. Not like the plagues they used to have long ago. There was a very famous plague back in 1666. The year of the great fire of London. Over there in England they had the big fire and the plague in the very same year.'

'They did?'

'Sure did. And they had to close down Cambridge University. You know who was an undergrad student then, at the university? Only the most famous scientist who ever lived - good old Isaac Newton.'

'I thought the most famous scientist was Albert Einstein.'

'Well, maybe there's room for two most famous scientists. Until Einstein came along, Newton was the guy. And Newton had to run away from Cambridge because of the bubonic plague.'

'Just like we're running away from Berkeley?'

'We're not running away. It's just that things are a little mixed up right now. Ake should be running things down there. I have to take over his duties for a little while.'

'Cool!'

*

An approaching plume of dust heralded the arrival of a second vehicle. The man in the Ferrari watched it drive up, a charcoal gray Lincoln Navigator. He guessed it had been clean when they had set out from LA, but now it was caked in dust, most of it, he guessed, from when they had left the road and followed the trail of his tires leading down to the lake. It swept round him in a wide arc, showering the desert with petals from the bushes decorating the slops. Flocks of dun-colored birds, smaller than sparrows, scattered, then wheeled in indignant circles out over the lake as the Lincoln came to a halt alongside the Ferrari.

He cut the engine, waited and watched.

Two men stepped out of the Lincoln. The smaller of the two was dark-complexioned, like an Italian. He wore a black Marine Corps baseball cap with a gold-embroidered logo, the bill pulled down low over deep-set brown eyes. Military tattoos encircled his upper arms. His partner, the car driver, was massively tall and broad across the shoulders. His hair was sun-bleached tawny, with a ponytail held back by a clasp of Navajo silver. It was the big man who opened the passenger door to a woman, who was rail-thin and cat-lithe in her movements.

The waiting man studied the woman with particular interest. He hadn't met her before, although they had talked on several occasions over the telephone.

In the flesh, she looked younger than he had expected, maybe early thirties, which put her five or six years younger than himself. It delighted him to find her magnetically attractive, with platinum blonde hair to the level of her chin. She wore a tailored suit light tan in color, the skirt riding high over magnificent tanned thighs that left him gasping in awe. The men were gorillas. Their legs stretched the fabric of their jeans and their denim shirts had their sleeves torn off to show their muscles. Donning an ivory-colored Panama and wraparound shades, the waiting man stepped out of the Ferrari, all of his senses attuned to their body language and expressions.

The gorillas didn't like the fact they couldn't make out his face.

Closer up, the woman's eyes were coolly assessing. Her handshake was probing. When she spoke, it was with a twangy accent.

She said, 'For communication purposes, you can call me Sam.'

'For those same purposes you can call me Ray!'

He knew her real name: Nora Seiffert. In fact he knew all he needed to know about the entire murderous band. Small-time gangsters desperate for a chance at the big money. Ponytail was Jamie Lee Weiss and his wiry tattooed sidekick was Tony Moldano. Both were ex-marines, discharged through dishonorable conduct. This was knowledge he kept under his Panama hat.

She nodded: 'Okay - Ray!'

The gorillas smirked.

He hauled a bulky aluminum case out of the trunk of his Ferrari and headed down the gradient of shale in the direction of the lake. They walked the thirty yards in silence until they were standing at the edge of the water.

Ray said, 'Okay – so let's talk business.'

'You got all of my attention.'

'I want a few things understood before we discuss the details. I don't want anybody else to know that we *have* had any kind of deal. Agreed?'

She shrugged, taking a black Sobranie from a packet she lifted from her jacket pocket, plugging it into her mouth, getting ready to light it.

He frowned. 'Do you mind? I don't want you blowing smoke in my face.'

A confrontation of gazes: he enjoyed that. It was just as well she couldn't see the exhilaration in his eyes. With labored slowness, she took the cigarette out of her mouth, keeping face-to-face contact all the time. 'You're paying.'

*

On Interstate 5, Kay McCann sighed, reassured by the sign to Bakersfield. From here she took the 58 towards Barstow. The traffic was only marginally better and the journey was becoming increasingly stressful. The radio was back on. Glancing over at Sean, she saw that he was enthralled. The man on the radio was making much of the fact that the plague had turned a white man into a black man. Those wackos sure knew how to pitch it so they got you hooked on the wildest notions!

But still, she recognized similarities with what she had seen at Ake's house. Ake's skin had turned black, and so had Agnietta's.

She turned down the volume again, so she could think.

There was an unreal feeling to this morning, had been ever since first rising. It was as if all nine and a half million people who lived in LA had suddenly grown neurotic about their own safety and survival. This man they were talking about on the radio, Bill Reickhardt, had clearly died from the same illness that had killed Ake and Agnietta - and the policewoman, Joanne. It was clearly some contagious illness. Joanne had fingered the dead geraniums under the back window of Ake's house. Then she had complained about her fingers being painful. She had been wiping her hand on her tunic just before she put her arm around Kay's shoulders, to reassure her, when all three of them had finally come back out into the garden.

She wiped her fingers then put them on me! Kay could not suppress a shiver of suppressed panic.

Sean reached out to turn up the dial. Kay slapped his hand away, a little harder than she intended.

'Aw – Moommm!'

Let him sulk. It was important she thought this out clearly.

Of course the impression was that the medical authorities would soon have it under control. Nearly all the cases had been linked to UCLA. That was why they had descended on the university like that. A preventive measure, sensible under the circumstances, even if it was also a little frightening. The city districts had all gotten their acts together. There was a committee of experts meeting once a day, issuing bulletins. And all this for just thirteen or so deaths!

Kay rubbed at her brow once again, distractedly. It was easy to let yourself get eaten up by suspicion.

'You hit me!'

'I did not hit you.'

'You hit me, Mom!'

Kay shook her head, feeling increasingly wound up.

At least a third of the vehicles traveling with her were trucks and RVs loaded up with cans and preserves, like they were expecting to be away from home for a while. Paranoia! She rubbed harder at her brow. To date Berkeley was unaffected. Nevertheless, no matter how she dressed it up as continuing to work outside of the department, in actuality she was running too. Her 4x4 was loaded up, pretty much to full capacity.

'You did hit me, mom!'

'I didn't mean to hit you. I apologize – honestly?'

He shrugged, then looked at her. 'I can't hear what they're saying!'

'Go ahead – turn it up.'

*

Ray opened up the aluminum case, took a folder out of the lid and then passed the case and its remaining contents to the pony-tailed gorilla. Handing the folder to the woman, he studied her reaction. She took her time, examining a list of names, details of occupations and addresses. She looked at the photographs. She whistled at some of the personalities.

'There's one more hit than I was expecting.'

He said, 'Is it a problem?'

'There's no need for it to be a problem. Problems always come down to a question of cost.'

'There's $250,000 in the case. That's $50,000 more than we agreed up-front. I'm willing to equal that if and when you get the job done quickly and efficiently.'

Her eyes widened – Jesus, he got off on the neediness there – as she returned to inspecting the hit instructions in more detail. 'There's a body you don't want found?'

He shrugged. 'I have my reasons. He just needs to disappear.'

'Like he just walked?'

'Exactly.'

She turned to Ponytail who had finished counting the money. He nodded. 'Two-fifty, like he said.' He closed the case and snapped it shut.

Ray said, 'Well?'

'You're expecting us to be kinda trusting.'

Ray hesitated. Her reaction was unexpected. He didn't like it. All of a sudden his instincts prickled.

He said, 'What's the problem?'

'We'd like to know who we're working for.'

'That was never part of the deal.'

The gorillas stood absolutely still, their eyes on the woman.

She looked at Ray for several seconds, her eyes narrowed as if trying to penetrate the shades. 'Okay,' she exhaled in a throaty purr. 'So how do we get in touch when the rest is due?'

'You'll get it when the job's complete. And I'll know. Don't worry!'

'Problem is I am a worrier.'

That overwhelming instinct again. Had he miscalculated the dominating nature of their greed?

'That's the deal. Take it or leave it.'

'I got a better idea.' She nodded to Ponytail, who removed a slim black cell phone from his hip pocket and handed it to Ray. 'It's brand new, unregistered. All you gotta do is keep it switched on. *We'll* call *you* when the job's complete.'

He caught the fleeting look of triumph in Ponytail's eyes as he passed the cell phone. 'So now I'm expected to trust you?'

'There's risks here that cut both ways – right? How do we know for certain that you'll pay us the rest?'

The tattooed gorilla was staring up the slope. The focus of his gaze was the Ferrari. Ray was taken by surprise again at the developing situation. It occurred to him that they could kill him, take the money and run.

'You and me both, we have to figure the odds. You've got $250,000 dollars worth of trust on my part. You'll get the rest. A grand total of half a million dollars when the job is done. We're going to have to trust each other.'

She slipped the cigarette from the packet, lighting it, taking her time about the action. She smiled at him, a predatory smile, as unrelenting as the cut of her skirt. She stared at him, still smiling, and then she blew out smoke in his face.

'You're the boss – *Ray!*'

*

'Heeeeyyyy! You folks out there! Stay tuned right now! You should be listening to this.' Kay McCann couldn't help but listen to the raucous voice coming over the radio. 'We got a woman, MayEllen Reickhardt, here in our studio and she has gone through hell and worse. This is no set-up. This is for real and it is live, on K-V-A-L. MayEllen, tell me – and all those folks who are listening to your story – what you and your friend, Lucille, just told me during the interval. The doctors told you they didn't know what was wrong with your husband.'

'They never told me nothing.'

'They never even gave you a proper death certificate, so you could bury Bill's body with proper dignity?'

'No, sir.'

'Well, there you have it folks. K-V-A-L has exposed it. There is a plague threatening America. And now we know how it first showed up. A living death in the first man to get it. And his illness happened after he dug up a UFO circle in his cactus field. I guess that now we're really getting somewhere. Hell, maybe now we can begin to put two and two together. And do you know the question that comes to my mind, and I guess it comes to your minds too? Secret meetings involving the medical authorities, those same people who wouldn't tell MayEllen the truth about her own husband's death. Those same people who kept her locked up in that hospital for four days against her will. Are those guys still keeping the truth from us the way they always do?'

An eerie closing jingle began to sound in the background and Tee-Jay Nieman dropped the pitch of his voice to a suggestive whisper. 'As we say goodbye to you on this bright and sunny May morning, ask yourself this question over your cup of decaf:

'Is America in the grip of a deadly Zombie Plague?'

05: 22/ 09h17

It was a relief for Kay to abandon the road, rattling and bumping over a dirt track that wound through a juniper-clad arroyo. Her vehicle was soon out of sight of the highway. She passed by a cluster of 1950s-style wood-framed offices, a rangers' station long defunct. After another eight miles of winding travel, the track dead-ended at a security gate in a seven-foot steel and mesh fence that stretched to the horizon on either side. There was a buzzer for visitors and a sign, IVAN WALLIN FLD RES. As she stood ready to open it, she thought again about Ake – the fact that he had been so desperate to get hold of her. Her hand shook as she swiped the lock and the gate swung back. She drove on through, watching in the rear-view mirror as the gate clicked shut behind her.

After a further half-mile drive through desert scrub, she arrived at a three-sided enclosure of single-story cinderblock buildings. She pulled into the large central parking lot, where there were about twenty vehicles, mostly 4x4s and pick-ups, randomly spread over the asphalt. Close to the glazed entry into the main reception, she tooted the horn. Two young men, grad students dressed in cargo shorts and T-shirts, came out to help her. They unloaded the food and beers onto a cart, leaving Kay and Sean to deal with personal items. Andy Yang, the Malaysian EM tech, came out to pester her. He was pleading with her to let him bring his latest girlfriend to join him here at the reserve.

'Not now.'

'She's a sweetheart. Wouldn't be any trouble. She could help out with things. Hey - she's a wonderful cook.'

'Forget it, Andy!'

Kay had no intention of encouraging his sexual adventures. Let him do what he had done with other girlfriends in the past. He would put her up at one of the cheap motels off the nearby highway.

As Yang headed off in a stew, Kay entered the building, looking for Michelle at her desk in the lobby. She found her at the center of a throng of people, all recent arrivals judging by the bags and boxes lying around the floor. Normally the field reserve was an oasis of tranquility, with no more than twenty or so scientists and students working quietly. Today there seemed to be far too many people milling around. Michelle, wearing bright blue framed eyeglasses, was blowing her nose into a bunch of tissues while answering the queries of several at once. Kay pushed her way through.

'Oh, Kay! Things are going crazy. You got messages - voicemail, fax and e-mail.'

'Anything important?'

'Mike – wanting to know that Sean's okay.'

Kay exhaled. The last thing she needed now was an emotionally draining conversation with her ex-husband.

'It's natural he's worried.' Michelle had always had a soft spot for Mike.

'Anything else?'

'We got a crisis in entomology. You heard the awful news about Ake?'

'I know, Michelle. I was with the police when they found him.'

Michelle had taken off her eyeglasses and was wiping them clean with a steri swab. Her nose was red and her eyes were pink-rimmed. Now her lips trembled as, in the background, a man began shouting. Kay recognized the voice of Jimi Pocock. He was a flaky assistant professor in zoology at Davis whose main interest was rodents. Somebody had taken some of his traps. Pocock was waving a Browning semi-automatic in the air, declaring that he knew how to deal with people stealing his traps. Kay stormed over to Pocock and snatched the gun out of his hand. Raising her voice above the excited babble, she warned them all: 'If anybody else has brought anything similar into this field reserve they can either head straight on home or hand it to me to be put in the safe.' She glared at Pocock. 'Have I made myself clear?'

Back in her office-cum-living quarters, Kay took advantage of the fact Sean was rummaging around in the bedroom to stare at the ugly squat shape of the gun. Unbelievable! She had no option but to talk to Pocock's boss and have him grounded. But now, with the sounds of Sean ready to emerge from the bedroom, she shoved the pistol and clip into the safe, spun the lock. When she turned around, Sean was watching her from the open bedroom doorway.

She said, 'You know what we need?'

He read what was coming: a bear hug.

'Knock it off, Mom!'

He dodged around her, heading for the glass jar with the quarters that would enable him to wallow in drinks at the dispensing machine in the R&R room. She laughed after him as he scuttled out through the door and down the long corridor, decorated with project posters.

Normality was what she needed. But she very much doubted that she was going to find it. *Ake – trying to get hold of her!* She called Michelle, asking her to join her for a more private talk.

'What's happening in entomology?' She recalled that Ake had said something about a problem, some kind of anomaly.

'I know that Ake was in his office, looking at the latest Landsat pictures before he left for home on Thursday. He was only back here half an hour before he took off again. He looked to me like he had a touch of the flu.' Michelle looked up at her, her chestnut hair cut boyishly short. 'Now people are talking about wildly fluctuating bug counts, I don't rightly know what, from some of his ICDITDs.'

'Who's talking?'

'I've had two grad students, Sara Goldsmith and Sameeha Prakesh, anxious to discuss their project with you.'

Kay knew the students and their project. She had helped Ake to plan their co-evolutionary population dynamics methodology. 'Okay. Let them know that I'll take over whatever Ake was going to do with them.

'When?'

'Not right now. Maybe tomorrow.'

Kay shook other worries out of her head so she could think straight about Ake Johansson.

'What time did Ake come back here on Thursday?'

'Mid-afternoon.'

'He talk to you?'

'Only to say he wasn't feeling so good.'

For a moment, the awful thought went through Kay's mind: Ake was already harboring the disease that had killed him. 'What else did he talk about? Try to remember. Did he say anything specific?'

'He mumbled something, but I didn't get it.'

Kay waited a moment or two, but Michelle was unforthcoming.

'What were his words, exactly?'

Michelle blew her nose. 'He was kind of excited. You know Ake - he didn't let you see he was excited but I could tell. Impression I had, he'd seen something unusual out there. Something he called a para something.'

'A para what?'

'He used a word I'm not familiar with. A para ... para... whatever.'

'Come on, Michelle. It might be important.'

'I wish I could recall. But I think it was something to do with evolution. An evolutionary para something-or-other. That I do recall - he was only here about half an hour and then he went home.' Michelle blew her nose again.

Kay couldn't help being puzzled. Ake had spotted something. Now he was dead, before he could explain to her what was so important.

She thought back to the horror of finding the two bodies. The dead geraniums – the flies! Should she call up the medical authorities? See if it was significant? *The Zombie Plague!* That wacky name was going to catch on.

Michelle wailed, 'Oh, Kay! We're all terrified. We don't know what to do.'

'What we need to do is carry on as normal. Why don't you e-mail Mike for me.' God knows, she had to force herself to calm down from her own emotional state. 'Let him know that Sean's okay. Tell him I'll get Sean to ring him once he's settled in.'

*

Susan Ann Mackenzie found Ric Valero in his office on the ICU. He was sitting in the half gloom, his face reflecting the milky white light of the x-ray viewing boxes on which he had mounted a series of chest films, all showing whiteouts. On a sudden impulse, Ric stretched out his hands and asked her to place a sheet of paper on top of them. She did so and they watched as the paper jerked and trembled.

'I don't know how much is caffeine - I've been drinking coffee all day to keep me awake - and how much is paranoia.'

She slumped down in an adjacent chair. 'If I put out my hands, I wouldn't need the sheet of paper!'

He said, 'I've seen almost nothing of home in the past five days.'

'You're going to have to delegate. If you don't demand help, those guys in admin won't give it to you.'

'Do you think I don't know?' He lifted his hands, as in apology, before wiping his face down with them.

Susan thought there was something different about him, something in his manner, the excited look in his eyes.

'What's going on,' he said, with a note of amazement in his voice, 'it's really incredible. In the cases of Manning, the intern staff, Nurse Ritter - and from what I've gathered about the tech who died in Special Pathogens at CDC – infection entered through the fingers, at a time when they didn't realize the hazard of contagion through skin contact.'

She answered flatly, 'It also means transmission can be prevented if people avoided skin contact with anybody who was infected.'

He blew out his cheeks, let the air out in a puff. He began taking a series of x-rays down from the viewers. 'How much further have you got, Susie?'

'I can tell you where we are with cultures and serology. Bacterial plates, including special stains for beta hemolytic strep, staphylococcus and clostridia, have all stayed negative. So has the serology.'

'So we are not dealing with a flesh-eating bug?'

'No way.'

'Or bubonic plague?'

'All tests have drawn a blank.'

'Viruses?'

'Viruses are problematic. You can screen for them using standard serology. But that only works with established viruses. To date serology has proved negative.'

Ric gripped his nose between forefinger and thumb, sniffed, blinked the tiredness out of his eyes. 'I can add something really bizarre. There's no antibody response at any stage in the disease. None. In fact it's the exact opposite. Every hematological parameter just nosedives into a spectacular crash.'

'This is getting scary.'

'It's like the bone marrow just went belly up.'

Susan studied Ric again, his face like chalk in the pallid light. Yes, she thought, he definitely looks more excited than petrified. It didn't seem to be getting to him as much as it was to her. She was unable to stop her hands from twitching, even when they were supposed to be at rest. 'The histology,' she added, 'is just the same. More bizarre than anything I have ever seen. I can't find anything useful from the autopsy specimens, because of the advanced state of decay. It's unbelievable that even the biopsy samples I'm looking at came from a patient when he was still alive.'

Ric shook his head.

Susan looked at him directly. 'You understand what I'm saying? Every cell in these people's bodies appears to be dying, before any failure of the heart or the brain or the lungs, or any other vital organ. It's the most disturbing thing I've encountered in all of my professional life.'

'Where does the disease process begin in the cells?'

'The mitochondria.'

'The mitochondria?'

'It slate wipes them, Ric.'

'Jesus, Susie!'

She shook her head. 'You don't get much in the way of common diseases that affect mitochondria. It's rare stuff, mainly muscle and neurological disorders.'

'Hereditary?'

'Some really bizarre syndromes. Even some links to the aging process. It seems to be down to the fact they have their own DNA, separate from the nucleus.'

He said, 'They do?'

'Hey, you won't believe this, but mitochondria even cause problems with excessive bleeding after cuts affecting astronauts in space.'

'That's interesting.'

'Sure,' she said. 'But nothing remotely resembling what we're seeing.'

'Oh, man!'

Mackenzie's gaze flattened. 'I have something to tell you, Ric. I've had it with this. I'm heading out.'

He looked at her, with his Homer Simpson slack-jaw mouth. This was the familiar Ric, the clowning colleague she recognized from years of friendship. 'Aw – c'mon! You don't really mean that?'

She shook her head. 'I just can't hack it any more. I mean, this is awful – this thing. We've been lucky so far. But we keep getting exposed –'

'Nah! You can't be heading out.'

'I'm leaving, Ric.'

'Leaving for where?'

'Halifax, Nova Scotia.'

The tone in her voice was definite enough to worry him. He was close to shouting. 'You're clearing off to go work with your brother?'

'Larry's concerned about me.'

'Shit – Susie! We need you here.'

'I have a family.'

'So do I.'

'Ric, I'm sorry.' She had hoped it would be calm and rational. But she could see now that it wasn't going to work like that. She just left her papers and hurried from the viewing room.

Ric chased her, as far as the door. She could hear him yelling after her through the thirty yards of corridor, but his voice sounded in some distant part of her mind, the kind of place where you put the memories you didn't ever want to find again.

05: 22/ 12h58

Will Grant was running late when he found himself squeezed uncomfortably close to Evelyn Maurice, head of Epidemic Intelligence Service, in the overfull elevator heading for the admin block. Maurice had just gotten back from leading the investigative team in the Southwest. They arrived together at the office of Aaron Kronstein, the CDC director. Clara, Kronstein's PA, waved them into the adjoining conference room, where they found the departmental heads already linked into a video discussion with a bald man wearing gold-rimmed eyeglasses. There were individual video monitors in the allocated places around the table. Even before he was seated, Will recognized the man on the monitor as Dr. Jez Burke, the epidemiologist from Phoenix.

Kronstein deflected from his conversation with Burke to address Will. 'It seems we could be facing a new twist to the problem.'

Will heard Burke explain how he had worked with colleagues in LA to draw up epi charts, contact tracing maps of how the epidemic was spreading locally. There was a murmur around the table as people on the periphery of the investigation became aware of the actual figures but they hardly came as a surprise to Will. In all, covering Arizona, LA and Kristina here in Atlanta, the total number of cases, all of them fatalities, amounted to 37. Kristina's death had deeply shocked Will. It had shocked everybody working at the CDC. Of the 37 fatalities, 16 were in LA and the remaining 20 in or about Thirless. The sporadic nature of the outbreaks complicated the epidemiology and so Burke suggested that they print out what he was now sending down the line. Within minutes, Will, like everybody else in the committee room, was handed copies by Clara. The bundle was 32 pages thick.

Like most doctors employed in the American Public Health Service, Burke had spent some time training in EIS at CDC. His report was thorough. Apart from Kristina's case, which had a number of unusual features about it, there had been nine separate mini-outbreaks, two in LA, one centered on UCLA, and the remaining seven in Northwest Arizona. The nine epi charts looked like branching family trees, each individual outbreak starting with a single infected individual. From here the person-to-person contacts spread out, sometimes with nobody other than the one case involved, on other occasions ramifying to a scatter of first-generation contacts. There had been no second-generation contacts to date.

Kronstein asked Burke, 'You think this means we are preventing secondary spread through the existing measures of hospital isolation?'

'Looks like it.'

'That's reassuring.'

Burke continued: 'Assuming that spread is through skin contact, the individual epi charts make perfect sense. But now I want you to look at the overall pattern.'

They turned to the final few pages, in particular the summary page at the end.

Evelyn Maurice, hazel-eyed, long-necked, more giraffe than swan, and with prematurely graying mousy hair pulled back behind generous pink ears, exclaimed, 'But this makes no sense at all!'

'No, it doesn't.'

Of the nine epi charts, only two had any known connection between them. Seven appeared to have no possible connection with each other.

'Then the outbreak must be multifocal?' Will asked.

'That's my conclusion.'

Will saw Kronstein frown. Maurice scowled, her wide thin mouth compressed. 'I'm not sure you can conclude anything like that. There may have been contacts you don't know about.'

'That was what I thought at first. But look at pages 20 through 30. Northwest Arizona is mainly desert. These are outbreaks in isolated communities. We've gone through this closely and, believe me, there is no way that there could have been any direct contact between first cases.'

'Then your index case, Reickhardt, is no longer important. He's one of many.'

'As far as we know, he's still the first. And his wife, MayEllen, is still alive and well.'

'Then we need to know why she lived when all the others died.'

'Yes, we do. But she's uncooperative. She's gone home. Refused to take part in any further investigation.'

Maurice said, 'Should she be subpoenaed?'

Burke shook his head: 'I don't want to do that unless it's absolutely necessary. I don't even know if it'd be legal. She isn't a criminal.'

Kronstein interjected: 'With all those deaths, we haven't got time to wait very long. You'd better look into it, Dr. Burke. Meanwhile, if I can turn to you, Dr. Valero, do we have any idea what might have been the external source of all of these different individual foci?'

On the video monitor Burke was replaced by Valero. 'None at all.'

Kronstein asked, 'Any therapeutic angle?'

'Nothing,' Valero grimaced. 'The only useful clinical information I can give you is the variability of progression. In some cases, involving previously fit and well individuals, they can be fine in the morning and dead by nightfall. The shortest so far is eleven hours forty-five minutes. Others, like your tech, lasted for up to three days.'

Kronstein returned to Burke. He said, 'Dr. Burke – do you have any explanation?'

'Maybe differences in individual immunity. But it's possible it might also depend on the mode of contagion. If it's through skin, for example commonly the fingers, progress can be slow. But if it's inhaled!'

'What are you implying? Are you saying you have evidence of aerosol spread?' Maurice demanded.

Burke pinked. 'No, I'm not. But there have been curious aspects. In every case, the index cases appear to be rapidly lethal. It might suggest a different mode of contagion.'

'That hardly amounts to evidence of aerosol spread.'

The director cut the argument short. 'Thank you both, Dr.s Burke and Valero. Whatever differences of opinion we might have on some aspects, the situation is more complex than we originally thought.'

Burke was still on line, as were the public health authorities in Thirless, Phoenix, Los Angeles and Dallas. They were looking to the CDC for some suggestions. The director turned to Will. 'How about Special Pathogens? Will, have you gotten any further with identifying the agent?'

Will shook his head. 'No identification. But we do have a few more facts. The agent, whatever it is, is small. It's about ten times the size of the influenza virus. For people not familiar with this, the influenza virus is 80 to 120 nanometers in diameter, and a nanometer is a billionth of a meter. The entity is 800 to 1,000 nanometers.'

'Then we should easily be able to see it on EM?'

'What we have seen to date is fuzzy. There's something very strange about its composition. It appears to be extremely compact - denser than a virus of similar dimensions. Yet it stays suspended in air like foot-and-mouth virus, which is much smaller and lighter. We're working on it. We're also working on how it might be transmitted. We know, for example, that in infected animals it's excreted in all body solutions, urine, faces, saliva, sweat and vomit. Any amount of excretion, however tiny, appears to transmit it with lethal effect.'

'To what extent, lethal?' The speaker, now on video link, was a stranger to Will. He introduced himself as Charles Davies, State Epidemiologist for California.

Will said, 'Our data confirms those of Dr. Valero. So far, it's proven one hundred per cent lethal in every mouse, rat, rabbit and guinea pig that we have tested. Upwards now of a hundred and twenty animals.'

'Lethal by what routes?'

Will glanced over at Maurice as he continued. 'Lethal by any kind of a route you choose to pass it. Whether you brush it onto skin, add it to food or water, inject it through any route from subcutaneously to intravenously.' He hesitated, his eyes confronting Maurice's directly. 'If you blow it into the airways, it's highly contagious.'

Maurice looked disparagingly skeptical.

Davies interjected: 'Then Dr. Burke could be right. It could be airborne in some cases?'

Will nodded. 'That's the big question. If we separate animal cages physically and screen imported air through HEPA filters, there is no spread. When I've connected cage to cage and allowed air to mix by simple diffusion, there is some spread, but sporadic and limited in extent. But when I blew air from cage to cage using a fan, it slate wiped the animals.'

'That's downright hair-raising.' The Californian epidemiologist shook his head. His colleagues around the table had fallen silent.

'Yet,' spoke up Maurice, 'the only person-to-person contagion we have observed is through skin contact?'

Burke's tired face reappeared on the video link. 'Other than close contact, within families, or professional carers, we have nothing so far to indicate significant spread between people. The epigraphs of the individual outbreaks are not the pattern of airborne spread.'

Valero interjected: 'So far - thank God!'

'No more,' countered Maurice, 'is there clear clinical symptomatology to suggest it. No spread through coughing or sneezing!'

Burke pressed: 'But Dr. Grant has just told us that he can infect animals by blowing it into the airways.'

'That's right,' Will added. 'In very close contact, I couldn't rule out contagion between people through inhalation of dried secretions. But human circumstances are very different from animals living in cages. Animals soil their cages with vomit, saliva, urine and feces. Forcibly blowing air about would create an aerosol containing contaminated dust particles. Given normal hygiene, people shouldn't be exposed in the same way.'

Still Burke pressed him: 'How then, without airborne spread, do you explain the multifocal origin?'

'I don't know.' Will shook his head slowly, knowing how important such information was for the Public Health authorities. He felt the weight of Burke's frustrations add to his own. 'The multifocal origins worry me too. They obviously imply some critical unknown factor. Maybe some additional tier of contagion? Until we know more about the lethal agent, we just can't be sure what that could be.'

After another half-hour or so of tense discussion, the meeting closed. The mystery epidemic was now top priority for the CDC. Maurice made arrangements to travel to the Southwest to work with Davies in California. She was assigned three subordinate EIS officers to help her. Her first priority was to study the LA epi stats to see if she could glean any information additional to what Burke had found. Knowing Maurice, she would do everything in her power to give the Phoenix epidemiologist a scientific slap in the face. Kronstein motioned to Will to stay back for a private word after the others had left.

'You getting much sleep, Will?'

'Not a lot.'

'Me neither.' The director walked to the window to look down onto Clifton Road. 'What do you think?'

'I'm baffled.'

'Me too! I have Ruth Galbraith on my back. I'm going to have to call her. Problem is, I don't know what to tell her.' Galbraith was the Secretary of Health and Human Services.

Will was silent.

Kronstein's gaze froze on the Stars and Stripes, which hung limply from its flagpole in the humid heat.

'Scary, huh?'

05: 23/ 15h07

'Monty's, Sunset – how may I help you?'

Sitting poolside in the shade, Nora Seiffert took a drag of her Sobranie, talking through the exhalation of smoke: 'This is Officer Duhane, San Bernardino PD. Can you put me through to the manager?'

A classical piano jingle played while she waited: Beethoven, *Für Elise.*

A salesman's oily voice: 'Officer Duhane – how can I help you?'

'And you are?'

'Monty Feinstein – manager and owner.'

'Mr. Feinstein – I'm investigating a hit-and-run on a teenage girl yesterday morning. I'm hoping you can help me.'

'I'll do what I can.'

Docking the cigarette under a sandaled foot, she adopted a world weary tone of voice. 'The perpetrator was driving a red Ferrari. And you came up on the statewide sweep.'

'Sure, we've got a red Ferrari.'

'A Maranello?'

'It's a Maranello – so what! No way was our car involved.'

'I haven't given you any details.'

'You said yesterday.'

'Early morning. Say 7:00 a.m.'

'I've got one red Maranello and it's on a rolling wax and shine for the studios. They call. We take it out to them. They call again. We bring it back and stow it for the next time. Like I wouldn't know if it was involved in a smash.'

'We have a witness who got part of the plate.' She read him what they had read off Ray's license plate.

'Sure – it would fit our plate all right. But like I say, there's no way our vehicle was involved. Yesterday, all day, it was in front of my office.'

'Mr. Feinstein, it's curious – wouldn't you say? I mean, a red Ferrari Maranello – would fit the plate. Can't be many of those around.'

'You ask me – it's downright screwy!'

'So convince me!'

'This vehicle has no exhaust under her skirts. Can you imagine driving a Ferrari without an exhaust? The goddamned stunt freaks pounded it on a rock. You wouldn't believe how slow those guys are to pay up.'

'So you wouldn't mind if we paid you a call?'

'You people got time to waste, be my guest.'

Nora replaced the cordless. Jamie Lee, climbing naked out of the water, stood close by, assessing her reaction.

'You want me to go down there? Check it out?'

'I haven't decided yet.' She shook her head. 'If that salesman's telling the truth, the guy suckered us!'

'That important?'

'A Ferrari same color and model. False plates that matched. That's going to a whole lot of trouble.'

Jamie Lee kissed her brow. 'You'll figure it out.'

She lit another cigarette.

'Just wrap your mind around what's important, Nora. This is the big one. We pull it off and there's nothin' but them hot Mexican beaches.'

She turned her face up so they could exchange another kiss: but she was still too distracted to take him seriously. 'You see, what I got to ask myself is what are his reasons. First the shades and the hat – and now the car. Why the mystery?'

He grinned. 'Search me.'

'Oh, Jamie Lee – sweet lover boy!' She tugged his face down so she could hard-kiss him again.

'Okay – so I go down, check it out – or what?'

She was thinking: *Ray's expecting us to go down there and check out the car. Like see if on this one occasional somebody other than the studios hired it. He's several moves ahead of us. Jamie Lee is going to come right back – nada!*

She clicked the remote to set a song starting: Foreigner – *Cold as Ice...* She hauled the boy closer with her arm curled around one thigh.

'You're right. This is the big one. But I can't help this feeling. You heard that expression – dicing with the devil. I think, maybe, that's what we're doing right now, Jamie Lee – we're dicing with the devil.'

He reached down and moved her hand to somewhere more interesting. 'So what we do is we play it smart?'

She was getting somewhat interested herself. She pulled him down, so he was lying on the towel alongside her. She brushed her fingers through his hair.

'What we got to do is figure how to play it a whole lot smarter than just plain smart – we play it smarter than the devil.'

'How're we going to do that?'

'Maybe the devil ain't as smart as he thinks.'

'Like he took the cell phone!'

'Yeah – he took the cell phone like we wanted him to. But I've got another idea – one he planted right here in my lap.'

*

MayEllen Reickhardt clutched the pot that contained all that was left of Bill after the compulsory cremation. She looked out of the pick-up window at the reporters that were waiting for her at the gates to her farm. Lucille and Paco had taken her to stay with them for the first few nights she was out of the hospital. Today, Paco was in the driving seat and Hobo, MayEllen's old and cantankerous Scottish terrier, was barking furiously in the back. 'You let them have it, Hobo!' she shrieked over her shoulder. Paco pulled in close as he could get to the barred iron gate and Lucille followed, bumper-to-bumper, in the Mazda.

The reporters must have picked up MayEllen's address from the radio interview. They must have been camped out here for days. Some of them had gone through the trash, since the black sacs were spilled open, their contents trodden into the dirt. She had no doubt that if they could they'd have gone through the mail. But Bill had welded the mailbox out of plate steel and it carried a lock, opening on the inside. MayEllen hoped that when they had put their hands into her trash, they had found some nugget from Hobo.

Paco wasn't big, like Bill, but he was as mean as a bobcat. He pushed and jostled a way through for MayEllen, so she could get the gate open and then he drove the pickup on through, with Lucille following on his tail. One of the reporters, a woman wearing a two-bit surgical mask over her nose and mouth, squeezed past both vehicles to confront MayEllen through the open window. She stuck a microphone up into MayEllen's face. A camera was rolling over the reporter's shoulder.

'Tell me, Mrs. Reickhardt, how you feel about the fact that your husband's illness has now killed twenty people in Arizona?'

MayEllen looked down at her and considered punching her smug face through the mask. As MayEllen opened the pick-up door to give her some grief, Hobo jumped down and snapped at the reporter's legs. The reporter toppled back, also throwing the cameraman off balance, and they both finished up with their butts in the dirt.

MayEllen shook her head. 'Oh, dear - I hope my rabid dog didn't bite you.'

Helped to her feet by the cameraman, the woman abandoned her fashionable veneer to swear at the jeering throng of fellow reporters.

'I'll sue you.' She screamed at MayEllen, the mask dangling below her chin.

MayEllen unlocked the mailbox and gathered up the bundle of post as Paco ushered the woman and cameraman back out of the driveway and clanged the gate shut.

'That felt wicked,' MayEllen grinned as she unlocked the door to the single-story farmhouse.

Lucille agreed with her, following on after MayEllen with a bag of groceries. 'I enjoyed it after what they made you do at the funeral. I don't think they got the right to say it's got to be a cremation and Bill is all sealed up in a ... a whadyacallit?'

'Hermetically sealed casket.' MayEllen didn't want to think about that as she led them through the door.

Paco held the door open for the two women.

They walked on through to the dining kitchen, where MayEllen put Bill's ashes down on the table. She sat down heavily on one of the oak chairs. 'That radio interview sure was the pits. I should never have let you persuade me to go up there.'

'You're right. You always are.' Lucille put her bag on the able and threw her arms around MayEllen's shoulders. Then she told Paco to pour a finger of Jack Daniels into each of two glasses and two fingers in one for MayEllen. They all clinked and downed in unison. There was an awkward pause as they put the glasses back on the table in a triangle around the pot with its cargo of ashes. Lucille started taking the groceries out of the bag. 'Now, MayEllen - I got you fresh milk and a whole pound of your favorite hazelnut coffee.'

'Bill was the one who liked hazelnut.'

'Aw, MayEllen!'

'Oh - just kiddin'.'

'You're never gonna change.' Lucille rolled her eyes. 'But I can see how it's upsetting you coming back.'

'I'll be okay. I just want to be by myself a while.'

'You got to promise me, anytime you feel a bit lonely you'll call me. Paco and me, we want you to know that anytime you want to, you just come back and stay with us. In the meantime, let me know what you need from the mall and I'll bring it out with me when I call tomorrow.'

'Thanks.' MayEllen accepted her friend's hug and a kiss.

Lucille asked her, 'What you goin' to do with - well, you know.'

MayEllen looked over at the ashes and her eyes filled with tears.

After they had gone, she poured herself a second generous glass of JD. She carried the ashes into the living room and placed them down centrally on the mantel, under the panoramic photograph over the grate: Milwaukee 88 - the eighty-fifth Harley anniversary. She drew in her lips and her breathing came noisily out of her nostrils as she gazed at them both, so happy astride the bikes that Bill had brought home as a surprise: the crimson-painted Heritage Softalk for her, with its windshield up front and huge black leather panniers on the back. Bill had thought how useful those would be for her desert collections. And he had thought about himself too in the mean machine, FXSTS, bullishly macho in black and chrome. They had posed for the picture in front of an ant's nest of other HOG members over the shores of Lake Michigan. The good times. No way was it ever going to get any better.

She made herself some coffee, took it black, and began to work her way through the messages and mail. Several calls had come from Dr. Burke, in the public health department in Phoenix, who wanted her to go back there for some more tests. Well, he could go and whistle. She wiped his messages. There were condolence cards from friends, mainly bikers. Two letters marked urgent had come from Phoenix. The dog was following her around the room. 'Well, Hobo,' she said, 'they sure seem to want me bad!' She screwed up the letters, dropped them into the stove and set light to them.

Suddenly she felt consumed by restlessness. Her skin felt so hot she opened all the windows, walking systematically from room to room. She looked out the back window at the cactus field. MayEllen felt faint and her heart was thumping, as if it had swollen to twice its size in her chest.

*

Will Grant stared at the map of the Southwest that was pinned to the wall in his windowless office. His eyes swept over northwest Arizona, where he had just stuck in a series of red pins, to plot the multifocal index cases according to the latest data on the developing epidemic. He asked himself the same questions he had asked himself a great many times since the beginning of the epidemic.

What are we really dealing with here?

He didn't think it was a new virus. But what else could it be, with something the size of a large virus? Something with that degree of compaction, that density! Nothing about the lethal agent made sense.

He stared at those red pins. What he was seeing on the map was clusters, each cluster gathered around a single human focus. What if Burke was right and they were looking at more than one manner of spread?

His gaze moved across to Los Angeles. The spread to the big city was worrying. Cities were mass amplification zones. His gaze held there for several moments before he moved on to Dallas, Texas. Two days ago they had confirmed Texas as the fourth state to be affected. The package from Thirless had been flown out of Phoenix to Dallas, where it had been handled during the exchange for Atlanta. That handling had infected a single airport employee, a freight handler, who had died and taken with him his wife, his elderly mother, and his three children.

Five more deaths! The ripples were spreading. Will felt a wave of alarm rise in him, like some malign spirit rising out of a pit of darkness.

He knew he was missing something important. He was reminded of Marje, who had been a compulsive crossword solver. Sometimes, when they were relaxing at weekends, Marje would call out some clue, when there was a word she couldn't quite figure out. Sometimes it was easy: he got it straight away, a second mind seeing the answer. But sometimes it appeared to be completely impossible for either of them to solve. It was as if the word had to be unusual, like something from a specialist dictionary. But in the end it turned out to be just another ordinary word. The problem lay in the fact they had been hoodwinked by the clue, which had led them in the wrong direction.

Was that what was wrong? Was his approach, based on emerging viruses, leading him in the wrong direction?

The telephone was ringing.

He picked it up. A woman's voice. 'My name is Kay McCann. I'm speaking from the Ivan Wallin Field Reserve, in the Mojave. Are you Dr. Grant?'

'Yes, I am. How can I help you?'

'I believe you're investigating this epidemic.' There was a note in her voice that suggested uncertainty. 'You any closer to finding the cause?'

'I can't discuss that.'

'Which means you're not. People are getting very itchy about it here in California. I've just lost my colleague to the illness.' She hesitated.

'Uh-huh?'

'I was there when the police found his body, Ake and his wife Agnietta. It was a terrible shock – well, I guess you already know what this thing does to people. But I'm not ringing just to tell you that. There was something going on that seemed really strange to me. In fact there were two things that struck me as odd.'

Will found it hard to keep the impatience out of his voice: 'What seemed odd?'

'I don't want to appear stupid. But could this thing have something to do with plants - or insects?'

He fell silent.

'I know how strange this will sound. But I feel I should go ahead and tell you anyway. My colleague, Ake Johansson, was an ecologist. He got sick while working here on the reserve and he went back home. He died in LA. Back of Ake's house there was a bed of newly planted geraniums. They were dead too. They had gone completely rotten, just like Ake and Agnietta. That struck me as a very peculiar coincidence.'

'I don't see —'

'Bear with me, please? The policewoman, the one who contracted the illness at that same visit, she touched the dead stems. I recall, afterwards, that she complained of some discomfort, pain and itching, in her fingers, where she touched the dead flowers. And then, there were the flies.'

'Flies?'

'The police officer, Brentford, commented on it. He said he's never seen a dead body surrounded by so many dead flies.'

Will stiffened. He wiped the back of his hand across his brow, to give him a moment or two to think. Epidemics attracted cranks like dead flesh attracted blow flies, but his caller didn't sound like a crank.

'What's your field?'

'I'm Professor of Evolutionary Botany at Berkeley. Ake Johansson, the guy who died, co-directed the field reserve with me. He was based in UCLA.' She hesitated and when he said nothing, she continued, 'One thing I do know about is plants, Dr. Grant. And what I saw was bizarre.'

Will thought about his dead wife and her crossword puzzles.

'Evolutionary biology? Tell me, Professor, does that mean that you know something about mitochondria?'

'I should know about mitochondria. My Ph.D. thesis was based on them, as has been a good deal of my subsequent research.'

'The pathology starts with a catastrophic destruction of mitochondria.'

She was silent a moment or two.

He cut through her silence. 'Look, maybe you and I should talk?'

'I honestly don't think I can help you. I know nothing about medical microbiology. I deal with plants, not people.'

'I'd still like to talk to you. Could you come here to Atlanta?'

'I wish I could help you, Dr. Grant. I really do. It sounds like you could do with all the help you can get. But things are a little hectic here right now.'

'Then perhaps I should go see you?'

05: 24/ 07h12

Kay's hair blew wildly as she stood on the asphalt with her arms about Sean and braced herself against the downdraft of the rotors. Mike had just set down on the parking lot. He had arrived unexpectedly. Sean, who had been sleeping in a bag on the floor of her bedroom when she had quietly slipped out for her morning coffee, at 7:00 a.m., must have woken with the sound of the chopper approaching. He had guessed who it was. She found him out here, bowled over by Mike's cavalry entrance. Now she raged at the figure in the bubble cockpit over the white paintwork with the McCann Bionano Inc. logo - the inverted M on M, looking like two trapezoids in parallel.

Mike knew just what he was doing. Sean, barefoot, wearing T-shirt and jeans, could hardly contain himself. As soon as she let him go, he ran across the parking lot and leaped into the cockpit.

'What the hell do you think you're doing?'

'Good to see you too, Kay!' Father and son sat there smugly grinning at her, Mike's arm around Sean's shoulder.

'You're not taking him.'

Mike laughed, causing a flush to invade Kay's face.

There had been a time when she had been entranced by Mike's showman extravagances. The day he proposed to her, they were enjoying a meal out in San Francisco, on the veranda of an Italian restaurant down by Fisherman's Wharf. A place by the waterside, overhung with ornamental willows and maples. Only in retrospect had she realized how much trouble he had taken to make the day special. Even the music – he had made arrangements for them to play the song, *Windmills of Your Mind*. While the music was playing, the waiter brought a gift to the table, under a silver cover. When he raised the lid, the veranda became a fairytale landscape, filled with giant butterflies. Kay didn't know the species then, but she discovered later they were *Dryas Julia Fabricius*. An absolutely gorgeous subtropical variant. The males had a wingspan of three and a half inches, golden-orange with black borders, like the sun coming through a tropical storm. Mike's betrothal gift to her was in their wings. He had done something to the wing buds of the larvae, so the wings were emblazoned with purple hearts. Even now she had no idea how he had quite managed to do that. The gift had been impossible to refuse.

She couldn't let him see the effect his arrival was having on her so she stalked back towards the doors. Father and son hopped down and followed her.

'Kay - can't we talk about it in a common-sense way?'

'You're not taking him.'

'Have you heard the latest figures out of LA?'

Kay tried to storm off through the door but he held her arm and turned her to face him. 'Hey, now, will you listen to me? It's serious. They're understating the figures, Kay. It's really spreading - getting worse by the minute.'

She shook her head. People were watching them argue. She saw Andy Yang grinning.

'How long before it arrives here? For God's sake, look around you. Where are all these people running from?'

Kay said, 'No!'

'I'm sorry to have arrived unannounced. Okay, it was stupid. Truth is, Kay, we've both been pretty good at behaving stupidly. But we love Sean.'

'Let go of my arm!'

She pushed past him but she knew it was true. Too many people had been arriving here. They had been pulling in all day yesterday. At least a dozen grad students were packed into a single dormitory where normally there would a maximum of four. They had filled the bunk beds and were sleeping on the floor. One or two of her scientific colleagues had brought out their wives, on the pretext that they were lab assistants. The atmosphere was increasingly tense.

'It could be here already and you wouldn't know it.' Mike was tailing her, speaking softly now, because Sean was getting fractious at their arguing. 'I'm not asking that he stay with me. Reno isn't much safer than LA. I've talked to your Mom and Dad and they've agreed to have him.'

Kay's parents, Tom and Marilyn Monaghan, had a farm in Wyoming. It was a very isolated place. She knew there was good sense in what he was saying. Still, she felt so humiliated she pulled herself away from him and headed for reception.

A tall man was standing by Michelle's desk, watching her run her hands through her disordered hair.

'Kay McCann?'

Oh, shit! Not now – not at this moment!

'You've got to be Dr. Grant.'

He offered his hand. 'I've just arrived.'

What was the guy doing, arriving this early! He must have flown over in the middle of the night and driven here from LA while still dark. 'I did try to warn you over the telephone. It's approaching pandemonium here.'

'Compared to where I'm coming from, it's positively restful.'

He was more youthful looking than she would have imagined, athletically built, black-haired. And those blue eyes didn't hide their look of appraisal. Struggling to adjust mentally from maternal concern to scientific duties, she murmured, 'I guess you'd better come back to my office.'

He said, on route, 'I'm grateful to you for giving me your time.'

She noticed that he was carrying a briefcase. She hardly dared to wonder what it might contain. 'You got a name for it yet, this plague that is frightening the wits out of everybody around here?'

'No name, not yet.'

She turned her head and there was a brief flash of eye contact. 'Believe me your plague has a name.'

'It has?'

They entered her office, cluttered with papers and files.

'The Zombie Plague.'

'The Zombie Plague?' He shook his head, accepting her offer to sit down.

'I was listening to a radio interview with this woman, MayEllen something...'

'MayEllen Reickhardt.'

'She claimed her husband was the first to be affected.'

'That's right.' He lifted his briefcase onto his knees and said, 'I hope you won't mind if we kick off straight away?'

'If you don't mind, I'd like to know about this Reickhardt woman. She was in close contact with her husband and she survived?'

'Yes, she did.'

'So it can't be one hundred per cent contagious as well as lethal.'

'We don't know the degree of contagiousness, or fatality, not yet. If she was infected, she had no symptoms. I'd like to talk about the death of your colleague.'

'Ake Johansson.'

'You noticed some unusual aspects. You talked about plants - dead flies.'

She was unable to suppress a shiver. 'You think they might be significant?'

'Right now, I'm prepared to consider anything that could be even remotely relevant.' Suddenly his cell phone began to bleep. He picked it out of his pocket and clicked off the connection.

'But first you want my help with mitochondria?'

'That's right.'

He took some 10" x 8" electron microscope photomicrographs from the briefcase on his knees. There hadn't been room to open it on the desk surface, which was littered with journals and papers. He passed the pictures to her, over the jumble: 'As you can see, these show the appearance in animals after we have passaged the agent and studied the development at half-hourly intervals. They move through all the stages, from normality to death.'

The pictures had been taken at various magnifications, from 10,000 through to 100,000. He waited in silence as she looked through them.

She said, 'I see what you mean about the mitochondria.'

'What would you have done that we haven't done?'

'Well, for a start, the preparations and stains are not quite as we would set them up here. We're looking with different eyes, I guess.'

'In what way different?'

'It's hard to encapsulate in a few words. But you're a virologist, right?'

'A virological pathologist.'

'You think disease. I think life.'

'You have an EM suite here?'

'A little dated, but we have one, yes.'

'I've brought some tissue specimens. Before you get alarmed, they've been Gammacelled - irradiated so they aren't infectious. You could mount them here, if you're willing. Prepare them for EM examination your way. Show me how you'd go about looking at this differently.'

'I'm not sure —.'

'Professor McCann – out there, people are dying. I'd appreciate anything you might be able to do to help.'

She looked at him again. 'I can't promise anything.'

'A different perspective?'

Kay gazed down at the small pile of EM photographs. Abruptly, she picked up the desk phone and made a call.

'Hi, Andy. The guy I mentioned - from CDC - is with me right now. He's brought a batch of EM pictures, along with some fresh specimens. Can I bring him over?' She paused to listen. 'How soon?' Another pause. 'Okay!' She got to her feet.

'Andy is already in the EM suite. He's somebody you'll want to meet.'

05: 24/ 09h19

When Harvard-based emeritus professor, Miroslav Janovic, was lonely, he spent time in what Americans called the yard. He had been lonely a good deal recently, with his daughter one year imbedded in her paleobotany degree at the Museum of National History in New York and his son lost to marijuana on the hippie trail in South-East Asia. The fact that there was just the two of them echoing around in a ten-room barn of a house had not helped the relationship between Janovic and his postmenopausal wife, Annie. She had found her own escape as a member of a group of art-appreciating women who took every excuse to go visit Europe.

All of this made Janovic angry. His anger made him more difficult to live with, which in turn made Annie even happier to stay away.

A Czechoslovakian by birth and a mathematician by inclination, Janovic had won the Nobel Prize for his solutions to the evolution of complexity in biological systems. Despite the intelligence that revealed to him exactly what was wrong with his relationship with his wife, he was so trapped in his obsessive-compulsive personality that he couldn't do a damn thing about it - other than to spend time in his yard-cum-garden, weeding, hoeing and turning over the wood-bark chippings between the flowering shrubs.

Janovic was scarecrow skinny, with large hands and strong bony fingers: he looked like he'd been designed by his farmer ancestry for the fork and the hoe. He was enjoying what he was doing when the tall stranger appeared through the gate, carrying a bunch of chrysanthemums in a presentation bouquet.

The gardening had brought on a sweat and Janovic paused in his hoeing to wipe his eyeglasses. He took his handkerchief from his pocket, breathed onto each lens in turn, then wiped them in a circular motion as he watched the man approach. A young man, as Janovic now assumed, although the stranger's face was hidden by the dark visor of a motorcycle helmet. Huge shoulders: muscled like an ox.

'Is this the Janovic residence?'

The stranger had long tawny hair that came down under the back of the helmet in a ponytail and he spoke with a kind of cowboy accent. He wore blue jeans and a sleeveless denim shirt. There was something curiously pale about his hands, half hidden among the bouquet. Janovic put his eyeglasses back on so he could take a closer look at the stranger's hands. He was wearing latex surgical gloves. Janovic had lived through the struggle for independence from communism in his native Czechoslovakia. He had encountered predators before.

Quick-thinking as to how he must appear, with his gnarled muddy hands, his old gardening corduroys, he said calmly: 'Mr. Janovic isn't in right now. But you can leave the flowers with me and I'll see he gets them.'

The stranger studied Janovic's face. His eyes roamed over the garden, to the big three story house at the top. The perusal was clinical. There was a moment during which the professor sensed how the world had grown still and quiet. A low-pitched drone invading his hearing.

'The flowers come with a message from his wife. I got to hand them to Janovic in person.'

Annie had never sent Janovic flowers in her life. He loathed chrysanthemums. Janovic regretted he had dropped the hoe in order to wipe his eyeglasses. 'Like I told you, he isn't at home.'

The stranger fired a short barrel Fabarm through the flowers, directed into Janovic's face. His body fell back into a baby palmetto, a shower of petals falling into the sticky embrace of blood and gore. The backlash had splattered the stranger's visor. Jamie Lee Weiss hinged it up so he could lean forward and inspect the mess. Then he turned his head one way and then the other to confirm that all was quiet. Nobody around. The floral garden was as still as a grave.

*

Will Grant shook the hand of Andy Yang, a Korean senior tech who was built like a Sumo wrestler. Kay McCann had abandoned him at the door. She had urgent things to attend to and would catch up with him later. Will had to go through the tedious business of explaining it all over again.

Yang took it all calmly. 'So these are tissue sections of lab animals showing sick mitochondria, huh?'

A rhetorical question. Yang was already making a spread of the photomicrographs. Without lifting his eyes from the pictures, he indicated that Will take a stool. The walls were decorated with photographs of scantily clad young women in between a proliferation of black and white microscopic images of shapes that resembled hollow pea-pods. Mitochondria!

Yang grinned: 'Impressive, huh?'

'In more ways than one.'

'I'm talking about the Prof - Kay!'

'So am I.' Will assumed he wasn't the only man to find her attractive. 'She seems a little tetchy.'

Yang cackled: 'It isn't you, Dr. Grant!'

'No?'

'It's Sean – her kid. She and Mike have been fighting over Sean ever since the breakup, and that's what - must be three years ago. And now he flies in here, looking to take Sean out to Wyoming.'

'Wyoming?'

'Kay's folks have a farm up in the mountains.'

'Right!'

Yang chuckled again, a heavy vibration that rattled his bulk. 'But hey, I can see what you mean, about the mitochondria. These are some sick looking bozos!'

'I'm hoping you can cut some fresh specimens. Maybe help decide what's going wrong with them.'

'We'll see.'

Will handed over the specimens.

'I'm not going to turn black overnight?'

'You'll be safe.'

'I believe you.' Yang had a jokey way of talking but there was tension in his body language as he moved the specimens onto the bench in front of the microtome slicer. 'I've already noticed something interesting about your pictures.'

'Yeah?'

'The mitochondria on just about every view are moribund or dead already. Only on the very earliest views – say fifteen, thirty minutes after you have injected your agent – do we see any distinguishable changes. So that's where I'm going to concentrate.'

'Makes sense.'

Yang shook out the first specimen onto his preparations board. 'I better get on with slicing and dicing. Why not cut yourself a little free time.'

'I'll stick around. Give you a hand.'

Yang grinned, his broad open mouth filled with strong wide teeth, like a steel trap. 'Thanks - but no thanks.' He reached his arm over, rapped his knuckles against the door of a fridge that stood conveniently close to his workstation. 'You look like a guy who could maybe use a beer.'

*

Dr. Jez Burke leaned forward until his visor was touching the windshield of the truck to peer out at Sheriff Horlon, who was arguing with an elderly man on the other side of his makeshift roadblock of reinforced concrete blocks laid across oil drums. They were about a third of the way up Black Mountain, one of Arizona's premier tourist attractions. A dirt road led from the other side of the road block to a trailer park on a sandy plateau. Below them, in the distance, he could make out the small town of Carefree, hemmed in by buttes and dunes. The elderly man was accompanied by a younger version of himself, wearing denims and brandishing a rifle. Horlon had hand-painted "SHERIFF" across the chest of his field suit. His deputy, Menz, dangled a pump-action shotgun at his side. The body language was scary: no need for further confrontation here but if you want it you're sure gonna get it. In the storm-laden sky overhead, reporters in choppers buzzed the scene, like vultures.

Burke was thinking: if this gets to shooting, I'm going to be too tired to run.

In the wing mirror he could see the column of four military ambulances that trailed behind.

'We've got to do something.'

The voice belonged to Jamie Sanchez, the veterinarian, who sat next to Burke in the front of the truck. Miller, the virologist, sat suited and sweating in the back, surrounded by Sanchez's traps and equipment, which included an autopsy table for animals that could be extended out there in the dirt.

'Shit!'

Burke alighted from the vehicle. From now on every movement would be made awkward by the suit. He wondered if the old guy with the rifle was one of those people who had been taking pot shots at the reporters in their choppers. There had been reports of that happening. So far, thank God, nobody had been killed. Soon there would be no need to shoot at them. The coming weather would clear the skies. He walked forward, in the direction that the thunderheads were building up.

'Don't be an asshole!' Menz was losing patience with the men at the roadblock. Now that Burke was approaching, the young man with the rifle turned it on him. Burke saw the same yawning terror in the young man's eyes. He thought: *I'm in a plague zone and there's a guy with a rifle in my face!*

The old man waved a newspaper in front of his face. The front page carried a four inch banner headline:

CAGING A VICIOUS PLAGUE

His eyes were wild, the muscles in his neck standing out like straps. He shouted: 'We're the ones caged in here!'

Burke wasn't surprised they were panicking. He had read other headlines in the last day or two:

DEADLY PLAGUE MYSTIFIES SCIENTISTS
ZOMBIE PLAGUE CREEPS ACROSS THE SOUTHWEST
ARIZONA DEATH TOLL TOPS 100

He said, 'Sheriff – can I talk to them on my own for a minute?'

Horlon and Menz took a few paces backwards and then watched.

Burke approached the two men with his glove-covered hands in the air. He spoke as softly as he could through the microphone incorporated into his suit. 'Listen to me, please. I'm Dr. Burke, from the public health offices in Phoenix. I'm coming around there to talk to you.'

He stopped walking, close enough to touch them: 'I want you both to know that I fully understand why you're angry.'

'What we are is goddamn terrified. This is a thing that eats whole families.'

It was no exaggeration. Burke had officiated at an extraordinary press conference in Phoenix two days earlier, during which he had informed about fifty newspaper, radio and television journalists that the situation was grave. They had just set up a raft of forty employees taking telephone calls in a converted school gymnasium in Phoenix. Those lines were hot, 24/7. Doctor's offices had lines around the block: people who thought they had the Zombie Plague. A small minority of them did. You didn't know who the infected people were until you examined them and by then it was too late. They'd had dozens of contacts, including family, people on buses, people in the shopping malls, the bars and 7-Elevens, nurses and the other people ahead of them in the long winding queues. Secondary call-in centers had been set up in Flagstaff and Thirless and they were equally busy. He had heard from colleagues that much the same was happening in LA and, to a lesser degree as yet, in Vegas and the rural areas around Reno.

Burke reached out and put his hand on the old man's shoulder. The muscles there were shivering and jerking. Burke could tell that the skin was hot even through his gloves. This guy already had a high fever.

'What's your name, sir?'

'Jason Bardon. This here is my grandson, Moss.'

Burke said hello to the younger man, then turned back to talk to his grandfather. 'How many people live here?'

'Upwards of sixty, normal times.'

'How many dead?'

'Five, I reckon. Two of them just kids. Three more pretty far gone. All the rest took off two days ago.'

'Show me!'

'I can't go into them places. They got contagion.'

Burke stared into the old man's frightened eyes. He just plain lied: 'It's okay. You're safe now. The last thing we want is some kind of accident. Ask Moss here to hand the rifle over to the Sheriff. We're going to take care of you – get you out of here.'

'You ain't takin' us nowhere. This is our home. We ain't leavin'.'

Maybe the old man was right to just stay. Burke had already concluded that neither he nor his grandson were salvageable. Behind his back, so only Horlon could see it, Burke made a fist with his right hand, then upended it, with his thumb pointing down.

*

Two and a half hours later, with Miller left behind to finish the epidemiology, Horlon drove Burke and Sanchez on up a winding track that led higher into the mountains. They had discovered one more case. A Vietnam vet named Vincent Ellroy lived several miles up the track, wheelchair bound and alone. One of the dead women in the trailer park had been his wife, long divorced. Until a week ago she had still cared for her ex-husband, fetching him a couple of five gallon barrels of water, food and booze once a week. Nobody had been up there to see him for a week. The old guy at the roadblock had been checking he was all right via a cell phone. For the last two days he hadn't been answering any calls.

The three men sat in silence as the four-wheel drive whined in low gear. They were high enough to look out over the desert for a good twenty miles. Far below them, and extending out into the distance, they could make out four or five separate thunderstorms, with lightning bolts arcing down out of the black underbellies of clouds. You felt it in the air: soon it was going to come down out of those thunderheads in a deluge. They were all itching to get the business over and done.

Burke had questioned the old man in some detail about Ellroy. Now he rewound those answers in his mind:

'He had no visitors during that week?'

'He never had visitors, not even in a year.'

'He came into contact with nobody at all?'

'Nobody.'

'What did he do all day?'

'Sat on the porch lookin' out at the desert.'

As soon as they left the shelter of the trailer park behind, the wind caught the truck. Every time they emerged from behind a butte, it tossed them around, like a raft in a maelstrom. The rain fell, hard as hail. There were signs they could barely decipher along the way pinned to stakes or painted onto the desert rocks:

STRICTLY PRIVATE
BEWARE OF DOGS – OFF THE LEASH
KEEP OUT
YEAH – THAT MEANS YOU

From the looks of things, Ellroy was a regular hermit. Very likely armed and not altogether sane. Sheriff Horlon had brought along the pump action. After about five miles of bone-jarring concussion, they came out into a clearing, dotted with Joshua trees and piñon pines. They stopped in front of a dilapidated trailer, extended to a porch with a covering of corrugated iron out back, all thrown together among a scattering of abandoned cars.

Sanchez muttered: 'What's with the wrecks? I thought this guy is some kind of a cripple.'

Horlon gave a snort. Maybe, like Burke, he objected to a war veteran being called some kind of a cripple: 'My guess is they predate him coming here.'

The wrecks were a mixed collection up to half a century old. The archeological relics of people abandoning their trash before moving on.

Sanchez shook his head, his eyes widening: 'No point laying out rodent traps!'

'Jesus!' Burke was staring with distaste at about half a dozen dogs. Starveling mongrels. And corpses of others, half-devoured by the pack.

Sanchez whined: 'Man – we're going to be popular with the animal patrol people when we call them in here.'

'If we bother to call them!' Horlon pulled up. Nobody was in any hurry to get out of the vehicle.

'Tell me, Dr. Burke – why are we bothering?'

'The guy's wife hasn't been out here for a week.'

'Yeah – so?'

'The incubation period is shorter than that. She's only been dead a day. That means she wasn't infected a week ago when she last visited him.'

'I still don't get it.'

'Let's just wait and see – huh?'

Burke was the first to climb out of the truck. The Sheriff came after him, toting the shotgun. One of the trailers had a makeshift wooden step. It had to be the living room. Horlon kicked in the door using the sole of his gum boot. The room was laid out for a man at wheelchair level. Garbage everywhere. Unwashed dishes on the table. More piled up in the wash basin. Family photographs decorated a dresser. Burke inspected what he took to be Ellroy in his wheelchair, his wife's arm around his shoulder. Happier times. The photographs looked decades old. They heard music coming from out back.

Spooky.

They found the body on the veranda, a round-faced balding man in his early sixties, nestled in his wheel chair, his skin turned black. The yard was littered with chicken bones and hundreds of empty Coors cans. An amputated car radio, jump-leaded to a battery, stood on the bare wood floor tuned to one of the cowboy stations. Ellroy had been dead for maybe a couple of days. A cigarette roll-up device lay upside-down on the boards beside his right foot.

Horlon whispered into his suit-mike: 'Jesus!'

Burke spent several minutes inspecting the body. There was no evidence of dog or rodent bites. Insect vectors were unlikely at this altitude. He straightened up. Stared out into the worsening storm. He shouted, 'Fuck Evelyn Maurice!'

The other two clapped their hands to their helmets at the thunder of his voice through the speakers.

Horlon asked him: 'What the hell is bugging you?'

'This poor guy! What we're looking at here has to be a fast-track. He couldn't have picked it up from the people down the track. No direct contact for a week. That means two groups. Two primaries.'

'That tell you something?'

Jez Burke gritted his teeth, staring out through his visor into the inblowing squalls of rain. 'It means that I was right and she was wrong. It's airborne. It's coming from out there. Out of the desert.'

05: 24/ 10h00

Kay McCann was not religiously inclined. But she felt blessed, in something close to the religious sense of the word, in her vocation of studying life, its diversity and beauty, and most importantly of all, in the mysteries of its evolution. She resented any interruption of her work. This plague, while terrifying, was also having a devastating effect on the normal routines and protocols at the field reserve. Ake was dead. Mike had arrived with the express purpose of taking Sean away from her. And now this pathologist from the CDC was an additional distraction, even if he seemed rather pleasant and dedicated.

She had made the mistake of arriving back in the EM room several minutes ahead of him, giving Andy the opportunity of pestering her further about his girlfriend. When Will Grant arrived, she was in a fidgety stew of resentment, worry and restlessness. He joined them on one of the wooden stools around the towering machine and they waited in silence as Yang warmed up the field.

When ready, Kay took a half step from her stool to douse the main electric light, plunging the room into darkness illuminated only by the actinic green of the screen.

'Okay, let's flick on through those early grids.'

Yang had prepared twenty-five grids from tissue specimens taken fifteen, thirty, forty-five, sixty, and seventy-five minutes after intravenous injection of the lethal agent into three mammalian species. Now he fed the 15-minute grid into the mouth-like port in the tower stack.

There was a sudden clutch of anticipation as the first views swung into view. The magnification was low power, mere tens of thousands.

Kay explained: 'We're not so used to looking at animal and especially human mitochondria. Fortunately mitochondria don't look a whole lot different between plants and animals.'

'Okay,' Yang added, 'I'm going to concentrate on the membranes.'

The viewer zoomed in as he flicked through increasing magnifications. Fifty thousand. A hundred thousand. A copper grid smaller than a shirt button expanded until the nucleus would have filled a house. He worked his way through further magnifications. A tiny portion of a nucleus became the size of a room. A single cell expanded until it became the size of a village.

Will asked him, 'You see any change?'

'Nah! I would say this is normal.'

'That would fit with the fact the animals didn't show symptoms until about half an hour after injection.'

'Okay, so let's go to the half hour specimens.'

They went through that same slow process, ratcheting up the magnification in and around another eerie landscape.

Will asked Yang, 'You see anything now?'

'Nothing definite.'

Will voiced his frustration: 'At this stage, these animals are starting to get sick.'

Yang shook his head. 'What about you – spot anything unusual, Kay?'

Kay moved closer, so the screen light reflected off her face. She saw her own reflection in the screen, her expression intense, her hair a confection of tarnished copper.

'Let's increase magnification.'

'You got it.'

Will pressed Yang: 'So, what do you think?'

'I see something, maybe. Could still be normal.'

Kay narrowed her eyes to peer more closely at the screen: 'I'm not so sure. Look at the outer surface of the membrane.'

Yang tried focusing in and out on the membrane. Will asked Kay: 'You can't see anything else happening?'

Kay turned to find him studying her face. 'Nothing I could be sure about. What about you, Andy?'

'I think there's something happening. You see that?' He moved the mouse on his pad, which synchronized with a pointer on the screen. 'There's a slight fuzziness. A loss of detail.'

'Maybe that's important,' she sighed. 'Maybe it's important to realize that that's all there is to see. I mean, nothing else looks even remotely unusual. And these mitochondria, the changes might be fine but the disruption of function could be major.'

Yang took photographs, flicked on a dim light, walked over to his developing slot and fed them in. He loaded the next grid: one of the three-quarter-hour tissue samples, flicked quickly through the magnifications.

'Now,' he muttered, 'you can't miss it.'

Will shook his head. 'What's different?'

Yang went over to extract the now developed films of the previous set so he could place the films for comparison against the images on the screen. 'Look here at the outer membrane.'

'I see it too,' Kay murmured. 'A kind of frothy appearance?'

'I'd call that lacy - and a significant change.'

Will asked the technician. 'Do you have any idea what could be causing the loss of definition?'

Kay answered for him: 'I think Andy and I may be thinking the same thing. But let's put it to one side for the moment and come back to it.'

Yang moved onto the one-hour grid. 'Okay,' he murmured. 'Now you should be able to see it for yourself.'

Will murmured, 'I do see something now.'

Kay agreed. 'I'm convinced, Andy. That membrane is positively frothy, bubbling. And there's a ground glass opacity spreading into the surrounding cytoplasm.'

'But what does it mean?' Will added.

'Okay,' she answered, 'we'll come to that. But first let's move on a little further. I want to see how it progresses through a time-frame series.'

They moved on the 75 minutes specimen.

'Jesus!'

The mitochondria were going out of shape. They were swelling up and bursting, like miniature explosions. Will turned to Kay. 'You've looked at a lot of mitochondria. Have you ever seen any progression like this?'

'Only in autolysed cells - or living cells in which the mitochondria were killed off by an antibiotic.'

Yang asked her, 'You can kill mitochondria with antibiotics?'

'Sure. With certain antibiotics, and in relatively large doses. It's another of the ways they still behave like bacteria.'

Yang nodded, 'So if an antibiotic could do it?'

'A chemical similar to an antibiotic could do it.'

Will disagreed. 'Toxins wouldn't explain contagious spread, person-to-person.'

Yang asked him, 'Could it be some kind of self-replicator that produces a toxin.'

Kay leaned close to follow it around the mitochondrial membrane with a pointer, 'You think this might be particulate?'

Will stared at what she was indicating: 'Now that would be interesting.'

'You must have the particle size for your agent.'

'Between 800 and 1,000 nanometers.'

'What do you think, Andy? Could the haze be particles that size?'

'Yeah – could be.'

Will stared at the screen, his tiredness forgotten. 'What's really going on in there?'

Kay hesitated before answering. She didn't want to make a fool of herself. She said, 'Dr. Grant – if I could hazard a guess?'

'Will – please, Kay. And go ahead.'

'Okay – Will. I believe I've seen something like it before.'

'You have?'

'Have you considered genetic engineering?'

'I've never heard of any engineered entity that remotely resembled what we're dealing with.'

'So it's new.'

'Now hold on a minute, Kay. Are you implying something deliberate?'

'If it's engineered, it's got to be deliberate.'

'I find it hard to believe –.'

'It doesn't have to mean that the plague is deliberate. Could be the thing was manufactured for some entirely different reason.'

'It's a horrifying thought.'

'There's another possibility, a good deal more horrifying. Have you considered an engineered bioweapon?'

05: 24/ 12h10

Will laid his second cold beer against his sweating brow. He was sitting back in the passenger seat of the Buick out in the parking lot. The rental car had been standing out in the open sun but he had no time to wait for the air-conditioning to cool it down. He took a sip of the beer and then called Aaron Kronstein.

Kronstein wasn't in his office. His PA, Clara, said he was attending some important meeting and should be available in an hour. 'Never mind the meeting,' Will replied. 'Get hold of him and have him call me back. It's urgent.'

'I'll do my best.'

With his cell phone on his lap, Will watched some of the biologists relaxing on their noonday break. They sat around in shorts and T-shirts in the paved area, next to two large Apache ovens. He wondered how often they got around to using those. He envied them the possibility that they might even cook their meals in them and eat them out of doors, drinking beer in the cool of evening.

Kronstein was taking his time. Will checked his cell phone, made sure he hadn't inadvertently switched it off.

When it did ring, it wasn't Kronstein. It was Martin Kennedy, Evelyn Maurice's deputy in epidemiology.

'Hello, Dr. Grant. I was told you had something urgent?'

With Maurice away and Kronstein busy, Kennedy must be holding the fort for emergency calls. But Will didn't want to talk to anybody other than Kronstein. He changed tack. 'Did we check out the neighboring states?'

'Yes we did.'

'What did we get back?'

'Nothing unusual so far. We're still making calls.'

He sighed. Kronstein had asked epidemiology to make those calls as a proactive measure. He didn't think they should wait for the other states to make up their mind before coming through to them. He knew that state public health directors tended to wait until they were reasonably certain before calling up the CDC. Maurice had found more than a hundred cases so far in LA alone, and people were getting increasingly jumpy. It didn't surprise him that people were heading out of the city.

'I need to speak to Kronstein personally.'

Sitting back in the car, taking another swig of the cold beer, Will saw a tall man come out of the building with his arm around a boy's shoulder. He recognized Mike McCann from his championing of nano-engineering. The impression he had, McCann took it to extremes. He had a reputation for being a maverick. One of Will's colleagues, a geneticist, went so far as to predict he would go down the tube, scientifically and financially, because of his over-ambitious ideas. The golden-haired boy had to be Kay's son.

His cell phone rang: Kennedy again. 'You told Clara it was urgent. I've just called Evelyn. She wants to know what's so urgent.'

'She can want all she likes. Like I told you, it's something I need to discuss with Kronstein personally.'

'He's had to go to Washington. I could try to get in touch with him, if it's so urgent.'

'Thanks, Kennedy. Do what you can. Have him call me.'

Kennedy added, 'I've just taken an interesting call from Burke. He says he's now certain the fast-tracks are aerosol spread – it's coming in off the desert.'

'On what evidence?'

'You'll have to ask him.'

Will's pulse quickened. *The possibility of airborne spread – Jesus!*

Will cut the line.

Father and son were climbing into a white Robinson R22 Beta II chopper with red accent stripes. Kay McCann hadn't appeared to wave goodbye. It was so humid in the driver's seat that sweat ran into Will's eyes. He had another swig of the beer, as the rotors began to whump the air. He was back in the darkened room, the green light back-illuminating the microscopist's features. He heard

Kay McCann's voice: *'Have you considered an engineered bioweapon?'*

*

Kay had found Mike and Sean in the cramped confines of her bedroom, sitting on the bed and playing computer games. She'd forgotten how childish Mike could be, how he'd play games with Sean for hours on end. He left Sean engrossed with the computer game to come out into the corridor to talk to her.

'Kay,' he murmured, 'I didn't want to shout it to everybody on the parking lot. But I really do know somebody in Public Health in LA. It's getting really frantic. They don't know how to control it.'

'You're not taking Sean. Go back up to Reno, Mike.'

'You think I'm exaggerating? I know you've got this guy here from CDC. Why's he here? Don't tell me you haven't been asking yourself that question. They don't have a clue what's happening.' He took hold of both her shoulders and tried to hug her but she held him off. 'I want to take you both out of here.'

'No!'

He was whispering now, that old husky whisper that would once have melted her. 'I'm very worried about Sean. But I'm worried about you too.'

'Oh, go try it on one of your bimbos!' She pulled herself out of his grasp.

He raised both his hands. 'All I ask is that you consider the situation. You're a logical person. So ask yourself this question. What happens when the first one of you here gets it? Or one of them arrives with somebody who is already sick? You haven't even got a nurse here, for chrissake! What are you going to do then? Are you going to take them out into the desert and dig a big hole?'

'Don't be ridiculous!'

She saw real emotion in his eyes. She recalled those EM pictures of the mitochondria. Maybe Mike was right? She had already asked herself that question. What if somebody here did get the infection? They had nothing more than basic first aid, stuff to manage allergies and snake bites.

'How do I know you're telling me the truth?

'I've got his number - the guy I mentioned at Public Health in LA. I'll call him up right now, let you talk to him.'

'Don't bother!'

Michelle had come barging in. 'I had to find you, Kay. Two of the grad students have gone missing.'

Kay looked at Michelle. 'Which two?'

'The two I told you about earlier. The ones who wanted you to help them with their project. They went out last night to do some black light counts and they didn't turn up this morning.'

'Where did they go?'

'Sector 5-32.'

A spasm of fright registered at the core of her. It grew into a nauseating sensation, heavy and sickening, like a cramp in the pit of her stomach. Mike seized her shoulders again as soon as Michelle had left them. 'What did I tell you. It's already happening. Let me take Sean out, immediately.'

She nodded, close to tears. She went into the bedroom and hugged Sean. She kissed him roughly on the cheek. He was so startled he tried to pull away from her. But she just wasn't able to help herself. She hugged him and then hurried out of the room.

*

Kay heard the chopper take off and she closed her eyes, held them closed for several seconds, before opening them to gaze down at the jumble that covered the surface of her office desk. Her misery was interrupted by a rapping on the office door. Will Grant came in. 'Something wrong?'

She blew her nose, told him about the missing postgrad students.

'They do that - they go out there, stay all night in the desert?'

'A lot of insects are nocturnal. One way of confirming insect densities is through black light counters, which only work at night.'

'What time would they have been expected back?'

'Soon after dawn.'

'That's seven hours!'

'I know.'

'You look worried.'

'They were working in Sector 5-32. That's where Ake was working last week. I think he must have asked them to check out whatever it was he found out there.'

'Before he got ill?'

She nodded. 'I'm kicking myself. They asked for my advice but I've been so goddamned busy since I arrived yesterday.'

Will sat down heavily in a chair. 'I've just spoken to Burke – the state epidemiologist for Arizona. He thinks the fast-track cases are airborne infections. He thinks that the infection is coming in off the desert.'

'How sure is he?'

'The evidence is still circumstantial.' Will put his cell phone onto the desk. 'This sector, 5-32 - do you have any idea what it was that Johansson found out there?'

'I don't know. But he thought it was important enough to try to call me when he got back here on Thursday.'

'There's got to be some way we can find out. He must have kept notebooks - a computer log?'

'There is one thing, something I should have thought about earlier.' She was already on her feet and heading towards Ake's office. When they entered, they had to shove boxes of equipment out of the way to get to his desk. So many people were arriving they were using any unused space for storage.

Now Kay explained, 'Ake was clever with computer programming.' She booted up the computer. As she waited for the desktop to load, she thought about Ake: how funny he could be, cigar-smoking, rangy, bony, uncaring about his appearance or fashion in clothes - his shirts holed here and there where burning tobacco had fallen through it, and his fair hair already half turned gray. 'What I'm thinking is he would occasionally leave messages for me on his desktop. For example, if we missed the crossover, like when one of us was on vacation. I didn't consider it because this time he couldn't have realized that he wouldn't be coming back after what he thought was the flu.'

One of the shortcuts caught her eye. The folder looked out of place, like Ake had intended it to be no more than temporary: it simply read 'File'. When she clicked on it, there was a request for a password, the request itself a simple code Ake sometimes used for her alone: *O-K*. She inserted the code, which was her own initials, followed by her date of birth, the year, the month, and the date, in that order. It was Ake's little joke.

The file opened.

> *We have a problem in Sector 5-32. There have been amazing fluctuations in insect populations. Some monumental crashes. But some others* - she scanned a series of Latin titles for genera and species, had the impression they were all carnivores - *running riot. You will have already noticed that the crisis is mainly affecting plant feeders. I have been observing some irregularities for several days. But then I saw the densitometer readings - and this morning, those Landsats! I don't know what the hell to make of the anomaly. The scale of devastation is alarming. I hesitate to think it but I believe we may be witnessing an extinction paradigm.*

'My God!' Kay sat back in shock.

Will came round the desk to read the message for himself. 'What could have shown up on the Landsats that got him so alarmed?'

'I just don't know.'

She knew that Ake worked very closely with the NASA-based Landsat terrestrial surveillance programs.

She found the Landset-7 gateway icon and clicked on it. The screen filled with subsidiary icons, all relating to monitoring data from the Mojave Desert. Kay struggled to comprehend the program. Ecology data at this level was more Ake's baby. Nevertheless, she clicked away through field after field, ranging through the various data downloads. The program had a large number of specialized functions but what interested her this morning was a specific program known as DARS: Disturbance Assessment by Remote Sensing and Spatial Analysis. The purpose was to pick up change, disturbance to the ecology, using a number of computational markers. She juggled the keys until she was looking at a patchwork quilt of the desert ecology, with densities of plant growth, temperature gradients and surface humidities showing up as different colors and tones.

'Can you make out anything unusual?'

'Too much data!' She shook her head. 'And there's the problem that insect densities won't show up on the Landsat maps.'

'Of course – Will, that's the answer!'

'What do you mean?'

'Plant density will show on the Landsat. But you can't tell anything about insects from these charts. For that Ake would have to rely on his resonance scanners.' She paused. 'And with what he was seeing —.'

'He'd have gone out into the desert to check?'

'Yes, he would.'

'Surely,' he urged her, 'we can call somebody. Landsat is a NASA program. Why don't we just call them up and ask them what's going on?'

Kay picked up the telephone and connected through to reception. She asked Michelle to do it and then put them through to her.

Will was looking very solemn. He asked her abruptly, 'Do you keep field protection here?'

'What kind of field protection?'

'Masks, gloves, clothing, eye protection?'

'Against what?'

'Against a lethal agent the size of a virus.'

'I... I don't know for sure. The need has never arisen. But I guess we have something left over from the Hantavirus epidemic.'

'Well, maybe we better go check things out,' he murmured.

Kay exclaimed, 'Those poor students!'

05: 24/ 14h10

Will found the field protection gear in a cardboard box, covered in dust. He unpacked it, inspecting each item carefully and laying out a suit for each of them that included a lightweight PVC coverall, a separate hood and vinyl boots. He insisted that Kay watch and listen as he checked the connections to the HEPA filters. Then he tested the pumps that would supply clean air under positive pressure for breathing and cooling. He charged up four batteries, two of which would function as spares. It couldn't be hurried and took more than two hours.

Only when he was satisfied did he ask Kay: 'If you feel ready?'

'I'm ready.'

'Okay. When we get to within a few hundred yards of the suspect area, I want you to let me know. We're going to have to put on this gear in the open. You sure you don't want to stay with the vehicle?'

'I'm coming with you.'

Will gathered the gear and they left the lab complex, almost running. Knowing the territory, Kay took the wheel of the yellow Wrangler, and Will sat alongside her, speaking tersely to someone at the CDC on his cell phone. 'The protection is ten years old. I have to hope it isn't compromised.' His eyes avoided hers, knowing she was thinking about her son while following his words. 'Get Aaron Kronstein to call me back, no matter where he is, or what he's doing.'

They had traveled no more than a few miles along the rutted track when his cell phone bleeped. He clicked the answer button: 'Grant!' Kay assumed he was through at last to his boss, Kronstein. She heard the voice say something about three more states.

'Which states?'

Kay did her best to eavesdrop as the vehicle lurched over the uneven track. Her heart began to beat very fast. *Not Wyoming, please God!*

'I don't know if you heard, Aaron, but Burke thinks the fast-tracks might be aerosol spread.'

She couldn't catch the answer.

He talked with Kronstein for several more minutes, explaining the EM conference and the genetic engineering possibility. When he switched off, Will fell silent. Kay drove for another thirty minutes through mile after mile of plains and arroyos before finally approaching the butte that over looked the flat basin of 5-32.

'We're getting quite close.'

She took a detour to her right that ascended over rocky ground, heading upland to what Ake had liked to call his observation platform. As she stopped the vehicle, Will's cell phone beeped again. In the quiet, interrupted only by the wind and the cooling ticking of the engine, she overheard the voice she assumed to be Kronstein's say, 'It's very worrying. But I can't say I understand where it's leading us.'

Will spoke tersely. 'Me neither. I've got to go. But before I do so, Aaron, I need your help. Two grad students were expected back from a nighttime field trip to the zone in question. They haven't come back. We're about to check out the area to see what's happening.'

Kay heard the tinny distant voice, 'Is that wise?'

'We'll be wearing field protection. Anyway, before we set out, I'm going to put you on to Professor McCann, who needs some advice from the Landsat people at NASA. Tell them it's important. They were working with Johansson on some ecology data and they may have picked up some unexpected changes in this area of the field reserve just before he got the disease. Johansson was the first reported case in LA. He died after he visited the affected part of the reserve.' He handed Kay the cell phone.

Kay could not suppress her anxiety. 'I overheard, Dr. Kronstein. Three more states. Please tell me one of them isn't Wyoming.'

'Not Wyoming, Professor. Utah, Colorado, New Mexico.'

The flush of relief must have been visible on her face. 'You seem less than surprised to hear that it has spread?'

'I wish I wasn't.'

'If it was so damned inevitable, why didn't we anticipate it? Why didn't we damn well prevent it?'

'Because we couldn't. Do you imagine we could have stopped all movement out of Thirless - out of LA? Even if we had grounded all the flights, it wouldn't have stopped people getting out. You can't put 20 million people into quarantine.'

'I'm sorry. It's just that I'm worried about my son.'

He said, 'We're all worried, Professor. There was something Will wanted me to do for you. Some data from the NASA Landsat people?'

She explained, then switched off the cell phone, handed it back to Will. She said, 'There's an observation point a hundred yards that way. We're going to have to walk from here.'

Wordlessly, they climbed out of either side of the vehicle. Kay blushed at the fact she had to undress to underwear even though he was gentlemanly enough to turn away. They donned the coveralls, leaving the gloves and the helmets, with their respirator backpacks until last. Kay was taping the seals over her gloves when the cell phone, lying on the passenger seat, rang again. Will picked it up, spoke a few words into it, then handed it back to Kay. 'NASA,' he said.

She took the cell phone. 'This is McCann.'

A female voice: 'You worked with Johansson, right?'

'I was his partner in administering the field reserve.'

'Well, there's something very odd showing up on the thematic mapper - and it shows up even better on the multispectral digital videos.'

'Is this Sector 5-32?'

She paused, as if examining her data: 'That's right. What we're seeing is foliage density changes.'

'What sort of density changes?'

'Circles.'

'Circles? What do you mean?'

'These appear to be naturally caused circles in desert vegetation. Not easy to see at first but you can spot them once you suspect they are there.'

'What does it mean?'

'I don't know. But I understand you're speaking from the reserve right now. I'd be intrigued to hear what you find when you go take a look.'

They completed suiting up. Then, stepping away from the vehicle, Will said, 'There are going to be lots of sharps out there. Just about every plant is carrying needles that could penetrate these suits. So we're not going to take any risks by hurrying.'

Kay was careful where she placed her feet, trudging the hundred yards of incline that brought them to the top of the butte.

The space suit felt decidedly alien to Kay as she stood and gazed over the familiar desert landscape. They were buffeted by hot gusts of wind that rattled sand against their visors as they looked down into a landscape that epitomized the wonder of evolutionary struggle. From this elevation it was easy to see how every cactus, shrub, bush and tree was circumscribed by its own little patch of scorched dirt, its battleground for survival.

Will tapped her shoulder and pointed. She followed his direction to the oblong of orange that marked the position of the grad student's Jeep. It hadn't been obvious because it was half obscured by a copse of cholla cactus. Kay scanned the area around the vehicle. For a minute or so she failed to see what she was looking for, because she was thinking too small, but then she saw it and her heart faltered. The Jeep was within a zone of discolored vegetation - a circle.

'Oh, Jesus!' she murmured.

It was gigantic, at least a mile in diameter. This must have been what Ake had seen. All of a sudden, Kay felt overcome by panic. She couldn't get enough air into her lungs. Will, who held her by the shoulders and peered through the visor at her, appeared to understand what she was feeling.

'Take it easy.' He spoke through the radio intercom, so his voice seemed to come from another room. 'Open your mouth and breathe through it rather than your nose. Breathe in deep and breathe out slow.'

She breathed as he told her and slowly the panic subsided.

Examining it more carefully, she saw that what had first appeared to be a confluent circle was actually a series of concentric circles, rather like a target, a dark thin ring at the periphery, paling to gray in the inner circle and the bulls eye itself was bleached bone white. She glimpsed what might be smaller circles extending out from the periphery of the original.

'Ake must have seen this too!'

He nodded, pointed to something else. Even from this distance you could make out that there was at least one figure lying in the middle of a clump of cacti, a short distance from the orange vehicle.

*

They retraced their steps down from the plateau and Kay drove them, still wearing full safety gear, to the boundary of Sector 5-32. It was a few hundred yards' walk in the stifling heat before they arrived at the orange four-by-four. Cholla cacti with needles that still glowed a brilliant golden, but whose arms were a tarry black, surrounded them. Inside the vehicle they found a cool bag containing some water and sandwiches. In the glove compartment was a cell phone the postgrads had also left behind.

Kay and Will walked deeper into the circle, heading for the bodies.

'I presume you recognize them?' Will asked her.

Kay nodded.

The tiny body of Sara Goldsmith - Kay recalled her as a sensitive, shy girl - sat back against the sharp needles. Her friend, the enormous Sameeha Prakesh, lay among the chollas with her head cradled on Goldsmith's lap. There were drag marks leading back out of the desert to where they found them. They had made it to within fifty yards of the Jeep.

Will followed their tracks for a distance, observing that they were irregular and wandering. He brought back a single collection bottle, containing dead insects.

'My guess,' he said, 'is that the big girl was the sicker of the two. The other one wouldn't abandon her and so they couldn't make it back to the vehicle.'

Kay didn't want to hear the details. 'I can't believe that they were alive and well only yesterday.'

'We better take a good look around.'

On the surrounding slopes they saw the skeletal remains of creosote bushes, milkweed, mesquites, burro bushes. Lower down it changed to Joshua trees, barrel cacti, whipple and Mohave yuccas. Everything was dead. Through the helmet, Kay heard no sound. She saw no movement, no ground squirrels, no quail, not even a cactus wren. There were no banded geckos clicking a warning.

She tapped Will's arm. 'See if you can spot any insects.'

'What am I looking for?'

'Flies, bees, butterflies - and arachnids too, scorpions and spiders.'

In ten minutes of further searching, they didn't find one. Kay's sharp eyes picked out a dead rattlesnake, a young male, no more than three feet in length, an angular shadow on the ground, like a fractured bough, its mouth stiffly agape with fangs extended. She had no idea how long ago it had died but its flesh was already half desiccated.

Will put a gloved hand on her shoulder. 'Kay - listen to me carefully. We have to regard our suits as heavily contaminated. Your vehicle too, once we get back to it wearing these suits. You don't have the facilities to decontaminate us back at the complex. I'm going to have to think of some alternative arrangements. In the meantime, I want you to follow my instructions to the letter. Do you understand?'

'Okay.'

Exhausted and sweating after the long trek back to their vehicle, and still wearing full biosafety gear, Will switched on the cell phone and, clumsily, through the gloves, he sent a text message to Aaron Kronstein.

LETHAL AGENT CONFIRMED. NEED HELP.

The reply, also in text, came back within minutes.

CHRIST! HELP BEING ORGANIZED. STAY AWAY FROM FIELD RESERVE. LEAVE CELL PHONE ON FOR POSITIONING.

They seemed to wait for an eternity before the cell phone beeped again. The message read:

TEST HOOD RADIO.

Will shrugged at her perplexed expression. He pointed upwards, into the sky. 'My guess is they're trying to pick up the suit radios and relay them through some army spy drone!'

Kay looked up there but she could see nothing.

'What – they can pick us up from here?'

'They've probably been watching and listening to every move we made.'

There was a sudden crackle in the hood receivers. Will tried talking: 'Aaron – you picking this up? '

'I hear you but you're muffled and very faint.'

'I'm having to shout, over the noise of the pump.'

'Okay. Hold on a while. They're working on amplifying your voice minus the background. Keep talking to me. You hearing this, Professor McCann?'

'Yes, I am.'

'That's better. I can hear you clearer now. Will, you still hearing me?'

'Loud and clear.'

'I've just had a call from Lilley, the Director of the FBI. The White House has received a spooky e-mail.'

'How spooky?'

'Detailed and challenging. Purportedly from the source of what we're dealing with.' Kronstein paused, and Kay assumed somebody was working on making the conversation even clearer. 'I told Lilley about your idea about an engineered bioweapon. It would fit with the message.'

'The idea wasn't mine, it was Kay McCann's. Anyway, the White House must be flooded with challenging e-mails.'

'Yeah, but this one hit the button. Whoever sent it, they appear to have accurate knowledge of what's going on.'

'What exactly did it say?'

'I'm waiting to hear if the FBI is activating a full CONPLAN response.'

'What's CONPLAN?' Kay said.

Will explained that in January 2001, following the 9-11 attacks, the government had set up an interagency Concept of Operations Plan that would be activated in the event of a terrorist attack involving a weapon of mass destruction.

'A weapon of mass destruction?' Her mind was reeling.

Kronstein's voice returned, to ask them to remain on hold. This time they could hear him speaking into what Kay presumed was a different telephone. Within half a minute he was back on the line. 'CONPLAN response is confirmed. Will - its orange on a potential Omega-3 situation.'

Will's head fell back against the headrest.

'What does that mean?' Kay pressed him.

'There are four Omegas, Kay. Each is a perceived WMD threat. Omega #1 is nuclear, Omegas #2 and #4 are radiation and chemical. Omega #3 is biological.'

3
The Entity

Top Secret
Operation Globalnet
Surveillance Mode: E-mail
Retrograde analysis: Index minus 06/12
DELICATE SOURCE: RESTRICTION CODE:
eyes alpha
L of E/ he→ee

Dear Lyse,

I've only been back at work here for six weeks but it seems more like six months. So much work already done and still there is so much left to do. But we're getting there. I really believe so. At the same time the pressures of what is really at stake are telling on everyone.

E.S. makes us all nervous with his jokes. He and his nanotechs are the only ones allowed to work in the new high security lab, a fact he rubs in by walking into less secure labs wearing his gear. He makes remarks, like, 'We're going to change history, Henri.' But then he refuses to explain what he means by these cryptic statements. To be frank even when he does speak to me about nanobiotics, it's beyond me. But I wish that he wouldn't bully the women, Nancy Chong in particular. I think he's just a frustrated Billy goat but she has come to me on several occasions, upset about it. I have given him a formal warning but he takes no notice. I suppose that some fractiousness is only to be expected, given our present workloads and the ever-accelerating pace of development. If only there were 48 hours in the day!

Not a word as yet to Penny and Martin. I don't want to raise false hopes. But I've made some interesting progress.

Love,

H.

05: 24/ 16h20

Ingrid Mendelson waited until they had slipped the narrow mouth of Belmont Harbor before she pulled the University of Chicago baseball cap tight over her head, wriggling the knot of blonde hair through the hole at the back. She had to wrestle with the tiller as the wind swelled both sails, shrieking with laughter at the remonstrations of her husband, Charlie, aft, whose cheeks were blown out like a glass blower's from the strain of dealing with the mainsail.

Growing up in a middle-class suburb of Minneapolis, Ingrid had not shared the teenage concerns of many of her girlfriends. When, at age sixteen or so, they had focused on cosmetics and the latest fashions, she had devoted herself to curiosity about the world. That curiosity had brought her a scholarship to Harvard Medical School where she had graduated top of her class. She had followed this with a medal-winning Ph.D. in molecular biology at MIT, two steps towards her greatest success of all: her contribution to the Human Genome Project. This had been sufficiently innovative to lead to her appointment as Professor of Molecular Genetics at the University of Chicago.

These days, Mendelson, still just 35 years old and retaining her maiden name for professional purposes, found time from a gruelingly busy work program for leisure pursuits. Four years married to Charlie Hackman, a consultant gynecologist, she was ready to consider offspring. That decision explained the sharing of glances and smiles as today, like every late Wednesday afternoon from the start of the season, they sailed the J/22 away from the harbor, and out into the slate-blue waters of Lake Michigan.

*

For Tony "Two-horn" Moldano, who had forced entry into a condominium block under construction off Lake Shore Drive about a mile south of the Irving Park exit, that Wednesday ritual was the key to his instructions.

He had scoped the territory yesterday and decided on this perch, then laid low in a motel overnight, arriving back a little after two. Now, with his hair tucked under his cap, he put on the surgical gloves. The earliest he could expect the target was some time after five. The description of the sailboat as a J/22 meant nothing to him. What he had was a photograph of a guy and a skirt on board a boat with two white sails. The guy was of no interest. The skirt was the hit. Nora's way of thinking: six hits, four guys, two bitches. J-L gets three of the guys: Nora insisting on keeping the fourth kinda special to herself. So good old Tony gets the bitches. J-L had been pulling his tassel about that, when they were sinking a pint of bourbon between them. Nora's reason, as Moldano figured it, just cracked him up. She didn't want lover boy acing other women – not while J-L still had the hots for her. So Moldano was thinking about that and laughing to himself while rigging the platform. Afraid stud-boy might develop a taste for it. Well Nora and J-L could service each other to doomsday for all he gave a shit. That love tunnel was too fuckworn for his tastes. One hundred big ones would buy him a barrel full of prime young pussy.

Okay: focus on down now!

The hit was even older, mid-thirties, medium height. But a whole lot fresher than Nora, he'd be willing to bet. Distinguishing features: natural blonde hair, below shoulder length, logo on the main sail – a blue circle, with a deeper blue surround. Within the circle the red outline of a human figure, enfolded by two parallel golden spirals. So distinctive you couldn't miss it.

Hot sunshine was angling in through the window. He twisted the baseball cap back-to-front, so the bill shaded the back of his neck. He plugged the headphones into the iPod, connected them to his ears. The Stones, *Forty Licks*. The fact was he wasn't musical. But contract hits brought on a buzz that was music-connected in some inexplicable way. That masterpiece movie, man: *Apocalypse Now*. Jesus – that scene when the boat was a bucket to hell heading on up the Mekong River – in the movie sugar-coated as the "Nung" River – and the nigger on board was jiving to *Satisfaction*. That tripped the switch for him. Just the music and the nigger dancing. That was the thing – the hell-fucking object of desire!

Oh, yeah – *Jesus!*

He recalled that scene as he lit up a Marlboro, the candy tin open to collect the butts. Okay, baby! He thought about it, not for the first time: he thought about the missed opportunities that came out of having to waste these women! Why waste it, man? They were gonna die anyway. Simple fucking logic. He fantasized about what it'd be like to engage with them first; to let it all out – go, man, with a sawn-off tickling one of them bitches' throats. *Aw, fuck – I mean, why* waste *it man...*

He began to scope the lake with his 10 x 25s.

*

In the desert, about a mile on the return journey from Sector 5-32, Kay watched as the huge shape of a Sikorsky 60G Pavehawk clattered over them, dangling a truck decorated with army camouflage. The Sikorsky dwarfed the UK-60L Black Hawk that swatted the sky in its wake. As the truck hit the desert a hundred and fifty yards away, they received instructions over their headsets. They were to abandon their vehicle and, still dressed in field biosafety gear, make their way towards the truck.

As they neared the drop zone, the clatter becoming deafening and a storm of sand rattled their visors. The Sikorsky wheeled away and the Black Hawk descended onto a spot alongside the truck. Two figures, also dressed in full biosafety suits, alighted and made their way to the truck, yanked open the back doors and climbed on board. After a minute or two, a loud rattle of radio static filled the desert air. A woman's voice bellowed out over a loudspeaker: 'IF YOU CAN HEAR THIS, RAISE YOUR RIGHT ARMS.'

Kay and Will both raised their arms.

There was a thunderous boom of laughter. 'HOW IS IT, DR. GRANT, THAT WHENEVER OUR PATHS CROSS YOU'RE IN TROUBLE!'

'Who is that?' Kay asked Will over the suit radio.

'The goddam army.'

'OKAY. NOW FOLLOW MY INSTRUCTIONS EXACTLY.'

'You know who she is?'

'Major Josie Coster - my opposite number at Fort Detrick.'

'APPROACH THE TRUCK AND STOP WHEN I TELL YOU. STAND WELL APART, WITH YOUR HANDS OUTSTRETCHED.'

'Some friend of yours?'

'You must be kidding.'

They trudged through the settling clouds of sand until they were about twenty yards from the truck. Coster instructed them to stand by. The two figures in field suits emerged from the cabin of the truck, carrying cylinders over their backs. As she got closer Kay glimpsed their faces through their visors, one male and one female. They began to spray Kay and Will down with decon fluid, walking in a systematic circle around them.

LEAN ON EACH OTHER'S SHOULDERS AND LIFT UP THE UNDERSIDE OF ONE BOOT.

Decontamination was pernickety and lasted several minutes. Then the woman lifted a hand, instructing them to wait. The two figures re-entered the back of the truck and after a much longer wait this time, perhaps ten minutes, the woman's voice sounded out once more from the loudspeakers: 'ONE AT A TIME, CLIMB IN THROUGH THE REAR DOORS AND UNDRESS THIS SIDE OF THE AIRLOCK. LEAVE YOUR SUITS IN THE BAGS AND STEP THROUGH THE SHOWER INTO THE LOCKER SPACE. YOU'LL FIND SOME FRESH CLOTHES.'

Will motioned to Kay: ladies first.

She stepped through the rear doors into a gleaming white interior. Stripping completely, she dropped all of her clothes into a green plastic bag, tied it off at the neck. Her body was dripping with sweat and her hair was plastered down onto her head. 'Take a shower,' the woman's voice called out from the front. Kay stepped though an airlock door and found herself in an ordinary shower cubicle with a soap dispenser. She set the spray as cold as it would go, filled her cupped hands with soap, closed her eyes tight shut and let the luxury of the freezing water run over her. Then she spent several minutes soaping away the sweat and smell of the suit. Shivering, she passed through the door on the other side of the cubicle, where she found underwear and army fatigues.

'I hope the clothes fit,' the same woman's voice came through from the cabin.

Major Coster was waiting for her, sitting in the front passenger seat next to a driver. Kay took one of the two seats in the second row and she leaned forward to shake the hand of a woman about forty years old, of medium height, and slim build. Coster's eyes were a twinkling hazel and her short-cropped hair was mousy, interwoven with gray. She did the introductions.

'Josie Coster - pathologist. My driver is senior tech, Sergeant Haseler.'

Kay ran her hands through her damp hair while waiting for Will to come through the shower.

'Don't worry about the Wrangler,' Coster added. 'You'll get it back after decontamination.'

They waited for Will to shower down and don military fatigues. Then the truck headed south towards the lab complex.

'You better tell me the worst,' Will muttered to Coster.

'Omega #3 is now operational. FBI and Army are headbutting as to lead Fed agency. But between you and me it's a done case. The biological nature is going to decide it. RIID will take charge.'

Kay whispered, 'RIID?'

Will answered, 'USAMRIID – our rivals in the army virology research group at Fort Detrick.' He leaned forward towards Coster and shook his head. 'What's going to happen here?'

'All the people working in the field reserve will be treated as suspect.'

Kay exploded: 'But that's ridiculous!'

Coster ignored her and kept talking to Will. 'That part of things falls to the Feebies, who are already here with the big cheese, Willson, on his way out of LA. All personnel will be evacuated. The buildings haven't yet been assessed but we can assume that they will serve as zero-rated. We're about to set up full BSL-4 facilities in the car lot.'

'And CDC?'

She shrugged. 'Not for me to say.'

Will shook his head again. 'How long have you people at been on the case?'

'Oh, I guess from about the morning after you got involved.' She cackled, a smoker's laugh: 'We been two steps ahead of you ever since.'

'My ass!'

Coster emitted a prolonged burst of laughter as the truck jerked and rolled, the army driver, Haseler, accelerating over the rutted ground closer to the field reserve.

Will said, 'We know about the President getting the e-mail.'

Coster didn't reply.

'Are you going to tell us about it?'

'I'm already telling you more than I should. Anything else you want to know, ask Jingle Jangle. He should be arriving any minute.'

'Shit!'

*

For Moldano, chain-smoking, day-dreaming, music-popping, setting up the M40A3 had taken fifteen minutes. Shit-ass half-finished building – he couldn't find any easy resting platform. The McMillan stock and 24" barrel called for four feet horizontal. He had to improvise with two carpenter's wooden horses overlaid with a door ripped off its hinges. Testing it one way and then another, he found that by turning the door to run with its long edge under the window, he could kneel on the floor and steady the cheek stock. But this brought the muzzle only two inches above the ledge of the window. He figured he'd get by on that, with a potting angle of 15 or 20 degrees. He butt-lit another Marlboro. Then, with his eyes slitted against the smoke, he accommodated using the Harris bipod.

He spent the next thirty minutes practicing on the steady flotilla of sailing boats that traveled by from the north. In one half of his mind, he was pumped up to high G in his own dream-world; in the other half he was detached, professional, observing how they swung in towards him as a matter of routine, following some kind of course. They all did exactly the same thing, like the course was laid out in the water like lines on a freeway. Closest they came – he scoped it again and again to make absolutely sure – was 380 yards on the gun sight.

*

Kay found the lab complex in a state of uproar. Soldiers were arriving by road from existing bases in the far south of the Mojave. Michelle's desk in the lobby was already taken over. Michelle had been among the first batch of people to be taken for interrogation by an FBI team, which was setting up a Joint Operation Center, or JOC, in the old rangers' station down by the highway. FBI agents, assisted by the military, were posting guard throughout the buildings. Nobody was allowed to remove anything, not even personal belongings. All paper documentation and computers had been requisitioned. The same applied to road vehicles. These were being taken away in convoy so the asphalt parking lot was completely vacant. Coster informed them that the Ivan Wallin Field Reserve was now an integral part of the same JOC, the FBI and army linking as part of the requirements for the response arm of CONPLAN.

Kay exclaimed: 'You've done all this in just a matter of hours?'

Coster shrugged. 'The FBI will want to question you too, Kay - even Will. In the meantime, if you could run me over the facility. I need to get some idea of the general layout.'

Her words startled Kay. Only now were the full implications sinking in. Her beloved Ivan Wallin was no longer a biology research station. Coster wanted to see offices, sleeping quarters and whatever technical equipment might be available for BSL-zero rated investigation. There was hardly time to ponder the implications as they rushed through corridors and from building to building. They had barely arrived back in the reception area when a new convoy of Sikorskys and Chinooks began downloading adjacent to the parking lot.

'Hey, Will,' said Coster, 'here comes your buddy already.'

Kay looked out the window to see some caterpillar-chained behemoths pull into the diminishing space available out there. Armed soldiers swarmed out of the back of more regular trucks and took up positions around the parking lot and by the doors of the building complex.

Two figures climbed out of a personnel chopper, a small man in a civilian suit and a much taller man in an army officer's uniform. The small man stopped to talk to another tall figure, who was one of four gray-suits carrying briefcases. These had to be senior FBI. She watched the small man run to catch up with the officer, who was striding through the entrance, held open for him by saluting troops. He was taken to what had formerly been Michelle's desk where he commandeered the paging system.

A booming voice, nasal and brassy, sounded out over the public speakers. 'My name is General Hauk. A state of martial law now prevails. As part of the federal response to a presumed terrorist incident, I am requisitioning this facility for military purposes. Because this attack is deemed biological, FEMA has placed the army medical division in charge of consequence management. Any remaining civilian staff will make themselves known to the FBI, who will accompany them to their JOC offices for interrogation. Anybody lacking transport should report immediately to this desk. A cordon sanitaire is already in place around this facility and unauthorized personnel will be forcibly prevented from entering or leaving. You have until...' he consulted his watch, '... 18.10 hours.'

'Will - I want to help. I want to do what I can to help.'

'You hold on here,' Will spoke to her quickly. 'I'm going to have a word with that asshole.'

He strode up to Hauk and spoke loudly enough for anyone in the reception area to hear him. 'There are one or two things I'm going to make clear. First, I don't take orders from you.'

'Is that so?'

'Moreover, I have just accompanied Professor McCann to a site out there in the desert and what we saw is likely to be significant. There are problems with this epidemic that won't fit neatly into USAMRIID's experience - or CDC's for that matter. It's important we keep Professor McCann here to help us. She knows more about what's going on out there than anybody. And we'd better hold on to some of her technical support staff.'

'You heard me declare a state of martial law.' Hauk's eyes flicked from Will to Kay and then back again to Will. 'Under the direction of the House and Senate

Appropriations Committee, I am, under statutory authority, directing a military Joint Task Force under the direct supervision of the Joint Chiefs of Staff. What I say goes. In the words of my orders, and I quote, "There is a risk that, in preventing or responding to a catastrophic terrorist attack, officials may hesitate or act improperly because they do not fully understand their legal authority or because there are gaps in that authority." I am empowered to implement extraordinary measures in the face of an extraordinary threat. I intend to act on that authority without hesitation, not only with civilians but also with any official I consider to be in the way of that authority.'

'I'll just call up Kronstein and see if that's right.' Will grabbed the telephone on the reception desk.

General Hauk slammed the button down on the telephone cradle. 'You'll call nobody without my permission.'

The small balding dark-haired man who had run after Hauk earlier now spoke into his ear. Then he addressed Will directly, in a voice that carried an unmistakable Boston twang. 'If I might presume, Dr. Grant - this conversation should not be taking place in public. Can we go somewhere private?'

Kay McCann suggested her office, where Will faced off Hauk and Moran. The three men ignored her as she flopped down in the single chair behind the desk.

'You go ahead and act like a moron, Hauk, but I doubt that even you could be that stupid. I've had almost twenty years of experience at the cutting edge of plague virology, and Professor McCann here has a great deal of experience in evolutionary botany. What we have just witnessed has implications for both fields. So we're both going to stay here and do our jobs. Now you try to stop us and you'll discover just how dirty I can play too. And don't you forget that I work for the government too.'

'We'll just see about that!'

'General!' Moran lifted a placatory hand. 'Dr. Grant, Professor McCann - allow me to introduce myself. My name is Patrick Moran. Formally, I represent the National Security Council. You can regard me as in loco for President Dickinson. Now it seems to me that the last thing we want is to have our own experts and institutions crossing swords with each other. The extraordinary measures of an Omega situation necessitate cooperation. I would suggest that we put our differences aside and employ common sense and reasonable judgment to work together.'

Moran looked up at Hauk. 'General?'

Hauk snorted. 'Seems, Grant, that at least for the moment, your boss has his thumb up the President's ass. I'll let you stay. And you can pick just two key people from the biology group here. But let me warn you, at the first excuse, it will be my pleasure to replace you with people I choose.'

His face still white with fury, Will led Kay out of the office and down the corridor in search of Andy Yang. 'If he's still here, tell him to stay. If he's already gone, find him and bring him back here. Meanwhile, maybe you could find me a cell phone so I can get in touch with Kronstein.'

After Will had left her to have a private talk with Kronstein, Kay stared out of the window, utterly bewildered. Not a single pickup or 4 x 4 was left in the lot. She listened to the loud rattle of caterpillar chains as heavy lifters shunted a honeycomb of army-camouflaged Portakabins into position, filling every square yard of black top.

*

At 17: 37 Moldano scoped target at three quarters of a mile distant.

The boat was hauling the expected course. Everything was looking A-OK. A little closer and he started to get antsy. No blonde hair. Then he made out the ponytail poking out of the back of the baseball cap. No doubt in his mind about it – the logo on the sail was unmistakable. He barked a laugh scoping the same logo on the breast of the target's white polo neck. She was working the tiller close to broadside. Candy from a baby. He sucked a final drag of smoke. Docked the cigarette through the aromatic cloud of his breath in the candy tin there on the floor.

Go routine!

He checked posture: a wriggle, relaxed. State of readiness: mag at full capacity – five rounds. He doubted he would need more than one.

A minute later, he was scoping 420 yards. He accommodated for 380. Steadied again. High readiness. A nasal whine of excitement came out of his nose, indicating the fact he was subconsciously humming: keeping track with the number *Sympathy for the Devil*. He crossed hairs on the center of the breast logo. *Apocalypse now, baby!*

He squeezed.

A hit – eleven o'clock on the outer target. Upper central on the blue circle. Blood fountain – he saw the tiny arc appear, like the dots on a cartoon drawing. The tiller swung loose, the boat was rocking. The guy was on his feet with his mouth forming a wide-open circle, trying to get back to the stern where the hit was lolling against the rail. It was his movements that were rocking the fucking boat.

Time for one more. Hold... hold on there...

Two seconds, three, four... having to adjust again. Check posture... positioning... squeeze.

Perfect hit.

Clean through the logo, through the heart of the figure within a figure.

05: 25/ 06h58

Kay was sitting down at a table in the ad-hoc breakfast room, cradling a coffee, when she physically jumped at the beeping of her cell phone. There was what sounded like static on the phone but then she realized it was the gusting of wind against the distant mouthpiece. Mike's voice sounded as if it was coming from some place out in the open, against the background of a storm.

'Hi, Kay! I thought I should call you.'

She was still so shocked by what was happening at the field reserve, her throat was dry and her voice struggled to wake out of its early morning huskiness.

He misunderstood her silence. 'Sorry to call early. But I heard that things have gotten more tense down there.'

She moistened her throat with a swig of coffee, started again: 'You're right, thing's are difficult.'

'I knew you'd be worrying so I wanted to let you know that everything is fine. I dropped Sean off with Tom and Marilyn. By now he's likely to have tired them out so they'll be having an extra hour or two of sleep.'

'Thanks for calling. I appreciate it.' Kay felt a wave of release flow through her and she actually yawned. Outside the window, a new cavalcade of military transport trucks had arrived, their engines drumming, as they maneuvered into drop-off places.

Mike's voice softened. 'I still worry about you, you know.'

She had to suppress the instinctive angry response. He was what he was and there was nothing he or she could do about it. 'Yeah - I know you do.'

'Hey, you wouldn't believe what's happening, even up there in Wyoming. They're starting to hoard stuff, food, fuel. There's a real hysteria building up.'

*

Kay was still feeling somewhat disorientated she sat around a table rigged from shoving four dining squares together in what had formerly been the rest and recreation room. It was a few minutes after 7:30 a.m. They were all so close to the giant plasma screen that their faces looked ghostly with reflected light, in perfect keeping with the current of anxiety that circulated, as if by contact contagion, among the small group of people, who included General Hauk, Patrick Moran, Fred Duhan, the Environmental Protection Agency Administrator, and two FBI representatives, gathered around the table. Will Grant was arguing the case that Kay be allowed to sit in on the meeting.

He said, 'Kay McCann has already proved her usefulness.'

One of the FBI agents, countered, 'We haven't completed their assessment of the staff here, including Professor McCann.'

'Hey,' Kay countered, 'if you don't want me here I'll go.'

But Will insisted, 'She's the only one here who can offer an expert opinion on what we saw out there in Sector 5-32.'

Moran lifted a placatory hand. 'Let me propose that Professor McCann attend a preliminary discussion. If we stick to biological analysis without discussion of security issues —?'

Hauk shrugged.

'Is that agreed?'

The FBI representatives said nothing.

General Hauk began with a thumbnail sketch of the state of readiness.

'I don't need to remind you folks of the urgency of the situation. The biosafety labs will be up and running by early afternoon. The non-secure chemical and molecular biology labs will complete the picture by the end of the day. Admin is taking up some of the pre-existing offices. Meanwhile we're setting up twenty-four-hour links with the FBI Forward Coordinating Team.

'May I also remind you people that every aspect of your work here is classified. If I might address you, in particular, Professor McCann. You are not Federally affiliated. But nevertheless this caution also applies to the preliminary discussion at this meeting. Do you accept that caution?'

'Yes, I do.' Kay forgot her personal worries and listened attentively as Hauk took over again from Moran and summarized the national situation.

Will summarized the clinical situation. 'We have close to two hundred deaths and rising. There are four states involved in a sporadic manner, all in the Southwest but extending into Texas. Given the circumstances, we must presume that America is under attack by an unknown agent. Although the numbers are still modest, its lethality appears to be 100%. We assumed to start with that we were dealing with an emerging virus. But no virus has been found by our people at CDC or by the Army medical people at USAMRIID.' He glanced towards Josie Coster, who was sitting next to him. 'Assuming that what we saw yesterday is relevant, the agent responsible also slatewipes plants, animals and maybe insects as well.'

Hauk turned to Kay. 'Professor McCann – maybe you can describe what you saw out there?'

She began with the death of Professor Johansson, his messages, the Landsat findings. She explained why she and Will had made the journey to Sector 5-32, where they had discovered the dead grad students in the huge circle of ecological destruction.

Duhan looked somewhat skeptical as he questioned her: 'Professor McCann - how many species of plants would you say there were in that circle?'

'I couldn't say for certain.'

'But we're not talking about a single species, say of prickly pear or yucca. We're not even talking of a dozen species, are we?'

'No. We're talking about fifty, sixty - maybe more.'

'All wiped out?'

'As far as we could determine in the brief time we were there.'

'But you examined the circle from a headland and estimated it to be about a mile in diameter? And every species of plant you saw was dead?'

'As far as I could judge, it was most if not all species.'

'What could cause such lethality?'

'Nothing we would ordinarily encounter other than a brushfire, spraying with Paraquat ... or, without wishing to be facetious, a nuclear bomb.'

'Nothing biological?'

'Not as far as I know.'

'You mention Paraquat. How do we know some unhinged person, or someone carrying a grudge, hasn't gone around the area spraying it with a poison?'

'This field reserve is not well known outside of biological circles. It is also reasonably secure. It would take local knowledge and expertise to break through that and spray enough toxin to cover a mile diameter. And besides, I think we are going to find other areas affected. The first case - what you call the index case - got sick after he dug up a circle of dead vegetation on a cactus farm in Arizona.'

'That doesn't rule the scenario out. We have similar crazies treading sci-fi circles in fields of crops all over the world.'

'They don't tread on cacti.'

'Surely you agree that we need to remain skeptical. Paraquat, for example, doesn't only kill plants, it also kills people - and animals too. Have you considered something entirely natural? The effects of climate, extreme drought for example, the drying up of a water table under the ground?'

'Drought is something we're familiar with in a desert reserve. The plants involved have different defenses. Mesquites and creosote bushes have very deep roots. Cacti store water in their trunks and branches. So we're looking at two very different survival strategies. If there were some groundwater calamity, the mesquite and creosote bushes would be affected first. It wouldn't immediately affect the cacti. No more would a drought form a circle, with secondary circles around the edge.'

'You never mentioned secondary circles!'

'Well,' she spoke with a rising irritation, 'I'm mentioning them now!'

Will came to Kay's defense. 'I think we can rule out a toxin such as Paraquat. We know the agent is transmissible, at the very least from human to human.'

Duhan shook his head. 'You might suspect it, Dr. Grant, but you don't have evidence to link the desert circle with human deaths.'

05: 26/ 08h55

The first real day's work began with a division of labor. Will and Kay took control of the field investigation while Coster oversaw the biosafety laboratory installation. It was Josie's first priority to get the bubble up and running. The very idea of the bubble - an environment for isolating people suspected of being infected with a BSL-4 agent - was enough to frighten everybody.

Kay set out with Will at 7:30 a.m., leading a three-vehicle expedition to gather samples from the circle of dead vegetation. Their brief was to search intensively for the slightest signs of life, as well as tabulating the full extent and diversity of death.

Just before nine, and last to leave for the sector was a detail of three soldiers led by the med-tech sergeant Haseler, who was ordered to bring back the bodies of the graduate students.

In seventeen years working at USAMRIID, Chuck Haseler had survived by being cautious. He had cut his teeth working with the most dangerous live agents in the world, including top-secret bio-engineered variants of Ebola, Marburg and America's own deadly pathogens, including the Sin Nombre hantavirus and the West Nile virus. It was one of his jokes that AIDS was a piss in virgin snow when compared to what he worked with every day. This was just another working day. He knew he had to be extra cautious. He wasn't in the clinically ordered and controlled environment of the BSL-4 suite at Fort Detrick: he was garbed up in BSL-3 field gear and walking through a war-zone in what until a week ago had been the tourist landscape of the Mojave desert. The detail he had been given by Jingle Jangle - sitting on his fat ass in the office that still had "Professor Johansson" stenciled onto the door - was to take an isolation ambulance out to Sector 5-32 and bring back the bodies to the newly set-up mortuary, where they would be autopsied by Major Coster.

They got to the target area just before 09:30. Breathing noisily through the belt-held respirator, Haseler and his two assistants recced the ground around the bodies, which were lying in a black and bloated embrace inside a tangle of chollas, with prickly pears and barrel cacti all swarming up close.

The little woman, on whose lap the great coconut head of her friend was festering, would be no problem. He could have lifted her out in his arms, like a baby. The nightmare lay with the large one, who, in his estimation, must weigh 250 pounds. Haseler was of medium height, and weasel-thin. His weight had remained at 154 pounds since he was seventeen years old. One of his assistants was a woman, Private Mary Ellen Moore, who weighed all of 98 pounds. The only beefy one among them was Mule Cavenaugh, whose massive muscles were guided by a peanut-sized brain. The way Haseler figured it, he was facing a very considerable problem. The chollas that made up the surrounding tangle of dead plants were made up of about a million sharp needles, all pointed at him.

With a glance into the distance, Haseler saw groups of people similarly dressed, mapping out square meters and then digging in the ground. None of them was near enough to call for assistance. Nowhere did he see the tool he really needed: a mechanical digger with a bucket on the front big enough to carry a whale.

He put his gloved hand to his head, as if to scratch it. 'Hellfire and damnation!'

He walked around the two figures, in their death embrace, visualizing every which way he could possibly imagine getting the job done. The problem was the prickly pears and the chollas were too goddamned rooted and awkward. There was going to be no easy way to get those bodies out. However they approached it, they were entering the equivalent of a still smoking battlefield with unexploded bombs all around them and ticking.

'Only one way we don't add to the body count here,' he spoke his thoughts aloud through the hood mike, 'is you guys get yourself spades and hack a path clear through.'

*

By ten the convoy of three investigative vehicles arrived back at the field reserve, where it was met by biosafety-suited soldiers driving a mobile refrigerated storage unit. Kay sat sweating in her suit as the truck doors opened. She watched Will oversee the transfer operation, loading a small mountain of specimens through an air-lock into the tall-sided gray vehicle. The haul amounted to several species of snakes, rattlers, corals and striped whipsnakes, a variety of rodents, including deer mice, kangaroo rats and packrats - several nests had had to be excavated in the heat - and half a dozen geckos. Every creature they had found was dead, and recently so judging from the still bloated and decaying corpses. Surface combing had turned up dead invertebrates, huge quantities of ants as well as lesser quantities of scorpions, tarantulas, cicadas and mantises.

They had dug eighteen aliquot trenches, a meter square and half a meter deep, extending in a range from the center of the circle to and beyond the periphery, including some representative areas of the satellite circles. In the superficial soil all the insects that turned up in their sieves were also dead.

Whatever was killing wildlife in Sector 5-32, it was viciously indiscriminate.

They had recovered eggs and pupae in layers deeper than eighteen inches. Only time would determine if these were alive. They also hoped that some of the great variety of buried seeds might prove viable.

The haul transferred, a new battery of troops arrived to spray down the suited scientists with decon. As Kay stood with arms uplifted to be to be hosed down, she watched the refrigerated unit reverse up against a door in the newly rigged lab complex on the parking lot, a docking maneuver so painstakingly coordinated that it resembled a lander-to-orbiter coupling in space.

A change facility was incorporated into the Portakabin assemblage and she headed in that direction. She had to line up and take her turn for the shower, emerging into the bright sunshine, her skin refreshed and her hair tied up. She was about to call up Wyoming, and talk to Sean, when a group of three men in white short-sleeved shirts and gray suit pants corralled her at the entrance to the building.

'Professor McCann?'

'Yes?'

A tall man with a horse-shaped face and close-cropped white hair showed his badge. 'Willson - FBI Special Agent in charge of the investigation of this incident. I'd like you to come with us for interrogation.'

'Don't be ridiculous!'

'I must warn you that we can arrest and detain you.'

'I am - or rather I was - the scientist in charge of this field reserve. My presence is needed for the biological research here.'

'Ma'am – we have to question everybody. Whoever triggered this attack had local knowledge as well as considerable scientific knowledge and expertise. Now - are you going to come with us voluntarily or do I have to read you your rights?'

*

'Okay,' Haseler called to the heavily perspiring Moore and Cavenaugh over the suit radiocom. 'Now we got us a way into the problem. So what we're gonna do is first drag Moby Dick off the sprat. Cavenaugh - go bring the stretcher up as close as you can. Okay, now we're gonna drag, lift-and-drop Moby Dick into it. Get that sequence fixed in your brains. Drag - stop and look - drag - stop and look - got it? All this is happening in slow motion. We're gonna keep re-orientating ourselves with regard to the sharps during the stops. Got that?'

He looked from face to face, watched each of them in turn nod their heads.

'The legs are the easiest. Cavenaugh! That's your baby. Moore and me, we gonna take one arm each.'

'Fuck, Sarge! I'm gonna be walking backwards,' moaned Cavenaugh.

'Fuck you too, Cavenaugh - you been doin' that all your life.'

All three soldiers braced their legs wide for stability. Cavenaugh, with his head screwed through ninety degrees and his eyes a good thirty degrees further, took one huge calf under each of his armpits. Haseler and Moore each hitched an arm through the interlocked crooks of their own. 'When I count to three!' Haseler ordered. They yanked and slid the huge body six inches off the little one. All three of them rested. They were already panting.

'Okay, now – we shift her towards the path a foot at a time. We find a rhythm. Take little baby steps. Stop when I tell you but don't let go. If either one of you let's go, I'm gonna fuckingwell shoot you.'

They crabbed their way out of the cholla, leaving about half the scalp, full of blue-black hair, stuck to the belly of the little one. Haseler cursed Moore, who was making snorting noises. Through her visor he saw that she was swallowing like a stork that had just eaten a small porcupine.

'Don't even think of puking in your helmet,' he hissed, through gritted teeth. 'Come on - drag - stop - drag - stop. Deep breaths! A rest break after another five yards!'

He kept a wary eye on Moore as they staggered forward. And that was his mistake. The one he should have been watching was the thick-ass mule. Cavenaugh's huge gloved hands began to slip from the legs as he was keeping his back arched to avoid a branch of a prickly pear. There was a scraping noise as a needle touched him. He panicked and started shuffling his legs sideways, swiveling the lead direction through sixty degrees. Haseler shouted. 'Stop! Hold it!' Cavenaugh was attempting to look over his shoulder at the huge cactus behind him. Haseler saw the whites of his eyes bulging out of a mask of sweat. He shouted: 'Hold it, asshole!' But there was another long scraping noise and Cavenaugh's oversize boots began to slip on some pebbly ground. He was falling backwards, twisting and turning to get his body out of the way of the prickly pears. The miracle was that Cavenaugh had managed to save his own skin. He had fallen back into the space they had cleared with the shovels, his butt landing on hard ground.

Haseler suddenly felt the weight on his arms double.

He turned to Moore. 'Don't you drop her!'

As if in slow motion, he saw Moore arch forward. She was vomiting into her visor. Meanwhile a quarter-ton whale was pulling him down. Haseler tried to stop this happening. He twisted his body in the opposite direction, still gripping the arm. But a slimy lubricant was running between the skin and his gloves. The skin was coming clean away, unraveling from the underlying flesh, like a bloodied glove that went up to the armpit. The unraveling had reached her wrist by the time he let go. His ass was already down and engulfed by the body, which seemed determined to roll right over him. He caught a glimpse of Moore and Cavenaugh just backing away. Meanwhile, his arms flailed and his right hand went down under the body and it was squashed against something spiky and vicious as a fistful of scalpels - a Spanish bayonet yucca. There was an agonizing pain in his hand. Already the flesh was throbbing as if it had taken fire.

'Get her off me, you morons!'

They were staring at him, eyes like saucers.

'Now!'

They didn't even dare to apologize. They just came over looking sheepish. Then Cavenaugh, with a huge grunt, pulled the heavy weight off him.

'Now, get me to the truck.' They looked at one another. 'What about the bodies, Sarge?'

'Fuck the bodies. Do it - running!'

By the time they got him into the back of the ambulance, Haseler was writhing with the pain in his hand. While Cavenaugh drove and Moore sat next to him, Haseler ripped off the double layer of gloves and examined where two of the spikes had penetrated into the pulp of his ring and middle finger and another had gone deep into the flesh at the root of his thumb. 'Moore - we're going to stop this thing spreading up my arm. Okay?'

'Yes, Sarge.'

'There's a towrope under the passenger seat up front. Tell shit-for-brains to pass it back to you.' With that look of panic still haunting her vomit-stained face inside her visor, she brought him the belt. He told her to loop it around his forearm to make a tourniquet. 'I want you to put your gumboot against my elbow and get it tight!' He indicated the crease of his elbow. 'Tight, like down to the bone.' Moore was clumsy because of the suit. But he had to force himself to be patient and allow her to follow his instructions. Then he shrieked at Cavenaugh in the front: 'As for you - you better drive like the devil was up your ass.'

As they tore through the desert, with tires beating up a cloud of dust, he tried to stop writhing so he could keep on talking to Moore. 'Now you see those scissors. I want you to cut the arm off this suit below the tourniquet. Do it!'

She obeyed him, trembling.

'Now, Cavenaugh - you capable of getting through on the radio? Talk to the Major and tell her what happened. Tell her I'm heading for the goddam bubble.'

Cavenaugh made the call.

Haseler's forearm was bare by the time they screeched to a halt under the decon shower. While the shower was still running over the windows, he growled at Cavenaugh. 'I want you to lift me out of the back of the truck.'

Cavenaugh did so. All three of them stood against the vehicle, drenched by the shower.

'Okay. Now you see that Apache oven over there next to the tiles.' His voice was a harsh breathy monotone. 'Help me across to that bunch of logs.'

Cavenaugh picked him up and he carried him, dropping him onto the asphalt next to the log pile.

'Moore! You go fetch Major Coster.' Haseler was forced to take deep breaths, waiting for her to disappear. 'Now you, Cavenaugh, look for the axe.'

Cavenaugh searched behind the logs. He found a machete, with a rusting blade. The big private was staring down at Haseler's arm, blinking sweat out of his dumbass mule eyes.

'Cavenaugh - you're not going to let me down again, are you?'

'Aw, fuck, Sarge!'

'I'm going to lay my arm across this log.' Haseler's vision was already clouding with sweat. 'You do it in one - or I'm gonna rip off your helmet and bite through your neck like fucking Dracula.'

It took more like half a dozen chops. Haseler stopped counting after two. He was screaming so hard he lost his voice. If he only could, he'd have sunk his teeth into that stupid fat neck. But he needed the mule to get him to the bubble in a hurry. He almost wept to see the petite figure of the Major. She was already kitted out in her biosafety suit.

'Oh, Haseler – you lunatic!'

Through his raw throat, Haseler managed a whisper: 'Don't forget to send shit-for-brains back for my arm!'

05: 27/ 04h00

Kay climbed out of her sweat-soaked bed and padded barefoot down the corridor to the common bathroom, where she cooled herself off in the shower. Heading for her office, she just flopped in the chair and waited for the dawn. She kept drifting in and out of the memory of that godawful interrogation by the FBI yesterday. They had taken her to their makeshift JOC in the rangers' station, a place that still smelled of mildew, and they had talked for two hours over black coffee in Styrofoam cups. Willson conducted most of the interrogation, playing hardhead against a quietly-spoken man named O'Keefe. They wanted to know whether she could see any possible links with what had happened and Islam or other radical groups.

'No - I can think of nothing.'

'What about you yourself. Are you a member of any pressure group?'

'No.'

'To your knowledge, do any of the staff here support Islamic fundamentalist causes.'

'We get people of every faith working here. One of the two students who died, Sameeha Prakesh, was a Muslim. But she wasn't any kind of extremist.'

'Not to your knowledge.'

'Mr. Willson – there are a billion Muslims in the world. The great majority are no more extremist than you or I.'

'You knew her that well?'

'No, I didn't know her well. But I still don't think –'

'Professor – let's keep to facts. I believe that you're environmentally active?'

'I support the Green movement, yes.'

'Support it?'

'Like many biologists I am concerned about issues like the greenhouse effect, global warming.'

'There's an active movement here? Or back at Berkeley?'

'There's nothing active in the sense you imply. Anyway, why would environmentalists set out to destroy the environment?'

'Crazy people do crazy things.'

'Well I'm not linked to anything crazy, if that's what you're implying. I've written articles, supported the need for public education.' She squeezed her eyes shut in a gritty blink. It had been a long and difficult day and she resented this dimwitted cops-and-robbers style interrogation. 'Oh, for goodness sake - this field reserve is my work. It's my whole life, other than family. You think I would do anything to jeopardize that?'

'Let's think more specifically. This place is a long way from anywhere. Nobody knows about its existence except a bunch of scientists. There's a fence around the perimeter. You can only get in through a security-coded gate. We've looked over the entire perimeter fence and there's no evidence of a break-in. So perhaps you can explain to me why it began right here in the field reserve?'

'What are you implying?'

'Professor McCann - you found a circle a mile in diameter. The only other circle we know about was in a cactus field outside Thirless, Arizona. That circle was thirty feet in diameter. Wouldn't that suggest that the circle here was the primary one? You don't have to be Einstein to figure it out. We're dealing with a WMD whose primary target wasn't Thirless. It was slam-dunk Sector 5-32.'

His words had shocked her. They had interrupted her sleep. They still shocked her now, sitting exhausted at her desk.

They had gone on questioning her, but now, in her mind, their voices receded into the distance, like echoes.

'Has to be somebody who knows his or her way around ... an inside job. Has to be one of you.'

Her exhaustion was suddenly cut through by a sense of outrage. Somebody had gone out there and deliberately planted the agent in Sector 5-32. That somebody must have known that Ake Johansson would be the first to investigate the effects of that agent. That somebody had deliberately set out to kill her best friend.

*

'Hi, Janie!'

It was still early and Will's call, made to her cell phone, had woken her. He allowed for the surprise to register through her still sleepy head.

'Hi Dad - is there something the matter?'

'I'm really sorry to wake you this early. But there won't be time later on. I'm going to have to ask you to stay with Aunt Lucy and Uncle Bret for a while longer.'

'You're not coming home today?'

'Not today.'

'When?'

'I don't know. Maybe several more days.'

'Oh, da-ad!'

Will saw Janie in his mind's eye, how her senses would already be switched to high alert. Janie had taken the death of Marje badly. He imagined her sitting up in bed, the fingers of her right hand twirling distractedly through her black hair.

*

At a little after 8:00 a.m. Kay was at her desk, compiling a list of the additional personnel and equipment they would need, when Moran called her on her pager. He said, 'Professor! We need to touch base.' She sluiced her face with cold water before heading out to find him a hundred yards down the access track, where he was monitoring the arrival of a fleet of giant trailers with corrugated aluminum walls.

'You're looking at better dormitory accommodation.'

She nodded her appreciation. 'How's Sergeant Haseler?'

'Major Coster has been up nursing him most of the night. But he's doing okay. If he keeps it up, she's planning to ship him out in a day or two.'

'Ship him out where?'

'Army hospital. General Hauk has requested a field hospital to be set up on some former military base north of here.'

'A field hospital in the desert?'

'This is a war zone, Professor.'

Kay hesitated, feeling the effects of the lack of sleep. 'You didn't bring me out here to talk about sleeping accommodation?'

'No, I didn't! The FBI has activated a full Strategic Information and Operations Center at Quantico. You'll be pleased to hear that you have been designated the "Biological Lead On Site."'

She stared back at him.

'You came highly recommended.'

'You had some say in this?'

'Maybe.'

Kay shook her head. That damned interrogation yesterday – maybe that was why they had leaned on her so hard? She said, 'I know it's an honor – a big responsibility!'

'I'm sure you're the right person for the job.' He added, 'There's something else I need to tell you. That SIOC also itemized eleven world-class scientists they might want to call on. Three days ago, two of the people on that list were killed.'

'Who?'

'Janovic, a Nobel laureate, was killed in Cambridge, Mass. That same day Ingrid Mendelson was killed in Chicago.'

'Dear God!'

'You knew them?'

'I've met Ingrid and her husband, Charlie. Janovic I only knew of by reputation.' Kay inhaled, let it out in a sigh.

'The manner of the killings suggests professional assassinations. The timing and distance between them suggests at least two different assassins.'

'It's incredible.'

'The FBI is drawing up a revised list – people to be protected. You're on that list, Professor, as well as everybody now working here.'

She thought about that for several moments. 'I have some requests.'

'Fire away.'

'An experiment I want to set up with plants. But I'll need expert assistance. I have in mind two people, one from Stanford and one from Davis.'

'You got their names?'

'I've written it all down.' She gave him the handwritten sheet of paper.

'Okay.'

'There's one more thing.' She hesitated. 'You might not approve.'

'Try me.'

'All the admin files from the field reserve have been requisitioned by the FBI. I need to recover a few.'

His eyes met hers. 'Something in particular?'

'Anyone who had business in Sector 5-32.'

'Why?'

'The FBI doesn't know these people like I do. They've got me so I'm beginning to wonder if I know them myself. I'd like to start with the two dead students.'

'This is hardly biological, Professor.'

'I agree. It's not biological. But somebody went out there and deliberately triggered this horrible business. That somebody had to have insider knowledge. I'm familiar with things the FBI might overlook. I might spot some irregularity they wouldn't notice.'

'I'll make no promises. But I'll see what I can do.'

'There's one thing in particular I'd like you to help me with.'

'Uh-huh?'

'Professor Johansson's files. His personal computer. And the mainframe from the lab. We must keep hold of them. They're bound to have useful information.'

'We talking biology now?'

'Yes – or kind of.'

'The FBI has the mainframe but I believe we still have the ecology printouts together with his personal computer.'

'We do?'

'General Hauk - he's still monitoring the Landsat data.'

'For what purpose?'

'He's watching the circles.'

*

Kay decided she had better go see how Sergeant Haseler was doing. She found him fast asleep inside the bubble. A med tech was injecting a shot of morphine through a porthole. She spoke to the tech in a whisper.

'Is he okay?'

'Okay enough to curse and swear whenever he's awake.'

'Major Coster somewhere around?'

'She's with Dr. Grant in BSL-3.'

Kay had to dress up to go find Josie Coster and Will working on opposite sides of the Perspex tunnel, operating through glove ports. They had something rigged up with tubes and pumping equipment. She was shocked to discover that it was a human hand and forearm.

'You've heard the old chestnut about the army calling for volunteers to give a hand?' Coster cackled back over her shoulder.

'You've kept Haseler's arm alive?'

'Not me!' Coster nodded across the tunnel towards Will.

He grinned fleetingly at Kay: 'I cut my teeth keeping organs alive on pumps so we could examine the impact of BSL-4 viruses. An arm is not much different.' He demonstrated how he had rigged a blood infusion pump and oxygenator to the two main arteries feeding the arm, with side-feeds of nutrients. The ad-hoc contraption was keeping the arm alive long enough to see what developed.

'What about the autopsies on the students?'

Coster said, 'Both showed fast-track patterns.'

Kay thought about that. 'And Haseler's arm?'

'If you look here, those penetrating wounds to the palm and the fingers came from a Spanish bayonet yucca in the big circle. Go ahead, use the magnifier!'

Kay inspected the wounds carefully. The flesh around them for a distance of a few millimeters was turning black. She observed whorls of that same iridescent black spreading over the fingers and the palm of the hand. They were inching up into the forearm. She could see the stitches where Will had taken biopsies.

He added: 'I've taken blood samples as well as tissue, although the blood is full of artificial substances. Now look real close along the flexor surface of the wrist.'

'Red lines!'

'Just as you'd expect in a nasty strep infection. But I just came off the telephone with Dr. Valero in Thirless and guess what? He's been seeing the same red lines in the staff who got infected through their fingers.'

'Amazing!'

'He de man!' Coster joked. 'But I can lay claim to the suggestion that we use cooling to slow down its progress so we can study it in more detail. Valero told Grant that worked with whole patients. So we kept the temperature about 40 Fahrenheit. As you can see, it's turning into a peach.'

Kay might have described it otherwise. 'I guess that congratulations are in order.'

Will stood erect and stretched his aching back. 'I've taken serum samples for you too, Kay. You need to complete the cycle, find out if we can transmit the agent back from Haseler's arm to plants. A proof of causation we medics call Koch's postulates.'

Coster tapped Will on the arm: 'Lighten up, you guys. In an uncontrolled experiment featuring one army grunt, we've just proved Duhan wrong.'

05: 27/ 09h40

At the International Conference Center, San Diego, Forman, the more senior of the two FBI agents from the local office, spoke in an exasperated tone to his companion, Stuyvesant: 'I think we better page him.'

'You want me to head back to the lobby?'

'You do that – I'll keep on looking.'

A few minutes later, he heard Dr. Mike McCann's name come out over the public address system. McCann was proving very difficult to locate in the labyrinth of lecture halls and meeting rooms that accommodated the international biotechnology meeting. Now, here, in the crowded main hall, obstructed and cluttered by dozens of company exposition stands, he could be anywhere.

The FBI agent hopped up onto one of the desks, ignoring the company's representatives who were shouting at him to get back down. He caught a glimpse of what looked like McCann in the distance. If it was McCann, he didn't look like he was responding to the pager. He looked like a guy in a hurry. He was carrying a lightweight notebook computer in his left hand and a bulging briefcase in his right. Sturveysant hopped down and hurried after him. It took him just thirty seconds to barge his way through the crowded Hall and out through the glazed doors. Facing him was a battery of elevators. One of the doors had just closed and the elevator was heading down.

'Damn! We're losing him!'

He took the staircase at a run, clattering two steps at a time, to emerge, breathless, into the lobby. Stuyvesant was standing point by one of the desks, looking for McCann to respond to the pager. The elevators were easily visible from where Stuyvesant was standing. More milling crowds filled the lobby but Foreman barged his way through.

'You didn't see him – coming out of the elevators?'

'No.'

Foreman spun round to talk to one of the women manning the desks. 'FBI, Ma'am. What's below here?'

'The garage.'

'Come on!'

They pushed and jostled their way through to the staircase. Wound through two more spirals, to emerge into the gloom of the basement. A gesture from Foreman and they split up, running from car to car, hunting the parking levels. A minute, two minutes, three... there was nothing, no McCann, no trace of movement. Then suddenly an engine started up, began screaming into high revs. Foreman was nearest. He sprinted in the direction of the sound and was almost run down by a black BMW. It headed straight at him, forcing him to leap aside. It accelerated past him. Through the driver's window, he caught a glimpse of McCann staring back at him, goggle-eyed.

He struck out with his fist, a single hammer blow against the trunk, as it pulled away from him. Drawing his Smith and Wesson, he adopted a firing position, took aim at the disappearing car with the gun outstretched in two hands. He could have loosed off two or three shots in the time he had McCann in his sights. But he didn't pull the trigger.

'For Christ's sake!' He shouted. 'All we want to do is talk to you!'

*

Patrick Moran was shaking the hand of a heavy-set and florid-faced man with thinning sandy hair. Moran said: 'Dr. van den Berg – if you need any more equipment or personnel, please let me know and I'll see that you get them.'

Kay, in her new role as on-site scientific lead, was in the process of introducing Moran to the chaos of BSL-zero labs under construction. Anton van den Berg, who had been co-opted from MIT, was preoccupied with setting up a bank of Hybaid PCR machines in one of the aluminum trailers.

'Thank you.' Van den Berg inclined his nose high in the air to look down onto the presidential adviser. 'Can I ask you if you were one of the people who picked my name out of the hat?'

'You were chosen by the SIOC at Quantico, Doctor.'

'That still doesn't explain, why me?'

'Your name was on the list drawn up by their scientific advisors.'

Moran seemed oblivious to the susurration of disquiet that moved underneath the chemist's features. Kay wondered if van den Berg knew that his name was not the first choice. That had been Ingrid Mendelson in Chicago.

A frown wrinkled van den Berg's brow. 'Do you people realize that I could have done all this back in my own lab? Very likely I could have done it better.'

Moran backed off a pace.

Many of the scientists being recruited to work at the JOC were resentful at having to move out from their home laboratories. Now, suddenly, they found themselves working under the threat of contagion.

Kay reassured the molecular chemist. 'The material you'll be working with will not require biosafety protection.'

'Well, I certainly hope not. This equipment isn't designed to work in a bio-hazardous field.'

'All samples will be rendered non-infectious before they get to you.'

'Well, thank goodness for that!' Van den Berg didn't look entirely reassured.

Moran said, 'Before we leave you to your preparations, there are one or two questions I would like to ask you?'

A look of annoyance ignited those florid features. 'Excuse me a minute, will you.' The molecular biologist forced Moran out of his way so he could move to an adjacent trailer, where a technician was connecting two ABI automated gene sequencers to a mainframe computer. Van den Berg instructed the technician to link the computer to a continuous paper roll and polychromatic printer outlet, capable of copying the base sequences of an entire gene. He watched it through before returning to Moran.

'What is it?'

'There's something I don't quite understand. This entity is capable of infecting plants and insects as well as humans, right?'

'Right.'

'But how is that possible? I mean, plants and insects and humans - genetically they're very different?'

Van den Berg blinked. 'As Professor McCann will confirm, all living organisms have a good many genes in common.'

'They do?'

'Darwin himself put forward the theory that all of life came from a common ancestor. While it might not be quite as simple as Darwin thought - he didn't even know of the existence of genes - in essence he wasn't too far off the mark. A bug in your gut, E Coli, has some of the genes that you have in your nucleus. Plants and insects have even more. And we're not even looking at nuclear genes. We're looking at mitochondrial genes.'

'Uh-huh?'

'People out there, non-scientists, assume that all the genes are contained in the nucleus. But that's an oversimplification. The mitochondria live in the cytoplasm, which is outside of the nucleus. Every cell in your body, and that of the ants, and the cacti out there in the desert, contains thousands of these tiny mitochondria. Once upon a time, maybe about two billion years ago, those mitochondria were free-living bacteria that could breathe oxygen. They infected, or they were gobbled up by, a cell that couldn't breathe oxygen. So they came to a kind of partnership arrangement. The bacteria gave the cell the ability to breathe oxygen in return for a permanent home inside the cell. Those bacteria started out with thousands of genes. But hey, if twenty or thirty years is a long time to be married, two billion years is a lot longer. Over that time, the bacteria lost a lot of their genes to become the much simpler mitochondria we recognize today.'

Moran shook his head: 'That's amazing.'

Kay was watching van den Berg's face, which showed increasing irritation.

'Isn't it!'

Moran said, 'And that union of the cell and the bacteria only happened once.'

'Very good!'

Kay signaled to Moran. 'I think it's time we left Dr. van den Berg to his arrangements.'

But Moran was persistent. 'Which means all of animal and plant life shares those same mitochondrial genes?'

'Well done! So now you know how busy I am going to be.'

Kay tugged Moran out of the lab and hurried him back to the cluster of green plastic tables and chairs laid out on what had formerly been the tiled dance area next to the Apache ovens.

He asked her, 'So where did I do wrong back there?'

'Don't worry about it.' She looked at Moran assessingly. He was no scientist. But she read a keen intelligence in those solemn brown eyes.

'Professor – you have something on your mind?'

'Yes, I do. I wanted to talk to you about the fact I've written a preliminary report on the field trawl for the NSC.'

'You look worried.'

'Every species we brought back, every mammal, every insect, every plant – the pathology was the same in every case.'

'That tell you something?'

'You and I, we're ordinary guys. But Will Grant and Josie Coster – they work with plagues every day of their lives. I'm looking at the way that they're reacting to this. It worries me that they're worried.'

Moran was looking straight into her eyes. He said, 'Professor – there's something I want you and Dr. Grant to see.'

*

They gathered together in the ad-hoc meeting room. Moran operated the screen himself. 'By now,' he said, 'you will be aware that President Dickinson has received an unusual e-mail. I'm going to share the contents of that e-mail with you. Please consider it carefully. I would remind you that this was received more than a week before you saw the circle in the desert. Unfortunately, its importance was not realized until recent events drew it to our notice. I would be obliged if you could go through the experience of receiving it, just as the President was intended to receive it, together with the sound effects. '

The e-mail appeared on the screen, accompanied by an eerie tune that sounded like a musical box in a horror movie.

E-mail: *to President J C Dickinson, The White House.*
Sender: *Yawm Ad-Din.*
Subject: *Circles.*
Priority Code: *Omega #3.*
Verification: *Molecular weight 40.27×10^6. Acid labile.*
Genome ratio: *DNA/RNA 61: 39.*
Message: *COUNTDOWN!*

The hairs on the back of Kay's neck prickled. In the silence that dragged on after the message was screened, she turned to Moran. 'The security agencies have had time to work on this. Maybe you could tell us what they've already figured about the message?'

'I can point out that the sender knows the code Omega #3. But I suppose a lot of people know that code. I wonder if Dr. Grant recognizes the verification parameters?'

Will replied, 'I can confirm that the molecular biology parameters fit those we have of the entity.'

Moran addressed them both. 'So, it would be reasonable to assume that whoever sent the e-mail has detailed knowledge of this entity, as you call it?'

Will said, 'Definitely.'

Kay asked Moran: 'The name of the sender – *Yawm Ad-Din*?'

'It's Arabic for the Day of Judgment.'

'As in the Book of Revelation?'

'As also found in the Koran.'

'Then we're dealing with Islamic fundamentalists?'

Moran said: 'Nobody's heard of *Yawm Ad-Din*. The FBI think it could be a cover name for any number of known Islamic terrorist organizations. Who knows – maybe it's some individual psychotic or a bunch of off-beam zealots.'

Kay sat back in bafflement, attempting to come to terms with what she was hearing. She pressed Moran: 'You've sourced the music?'

'No known tune.'

She looked thoughtfully at the message still filling the screen. 'Can I ask you, Mr. Moran, how the e-mail was routed?'

'NSA believes it was through a cell phone.'

'Well then - it should be easy to trace.'

'Triangulation of the cell pointed to the middle of the Atlantic Ocean.'

'You're kidding!'

'I'm not kidding.'

'I presume we looked for something out there - a boat - or a plane?'

'We looked damn hard. There wasn't any boat or plane. There was nothing out there but two miles deep of water.'

05: 28/ 06h12

Barely three-quarters awake, Kay donned scrubs, cap, boots and surgical gloves before proceeding through BSL-2 into the BSL-3 laboratory. It was the same lab where Will had worked on Haseler's arm. The room was perhaps fifty feet long and forty feet wide and the glove ports formed a broad horseshoe running along three of its four walls, essentially lab benches sealed from the room by semi-cylindrical corridors of a thick Perspex-like material. At regular intervals thick rubber gloves extended through circular ports into the vacuum-maintained corridors. The pressure of air in the room caused the gloves to poke stiffly into the working space, a grisly reminder of the origins of the serum she had worked with yesterday evening.

Inside the glove-ports, and filling four of the separate compartments on either long arm, were thirty different varieties of plants. They included species she had worked with in normal times, such as cacti, yuccas, poppies and desert primroses. Under Will's guidance, Kay had spent an exhausting four hours, with her gloved hands inside the clumsy rubber overgloves of the ports, drawing up a hundred-fold dilution of Haseler's serum into a syringe and injecting the serum into each individual plant's vascular bundle. By the time she had finished the injections her arms had ached so badly she had needed two Tylenols to help her sleep.

She had arrived early to read the results of the experiment. She came equipped with a ballpoint pen and notebook, into which she had sketched out rows and columns to tabulate the results, cross-referenced to the control injections she had made into a matching series of plants injected with sterile water.

But she entered no data into the notebook. Her hand simply fell to her side. Every test specimen of plant was dead. She should have anticipated this. But the reality shocked her. These plants were not dead in the sense the flowers you kept in a vase too long were dead. Those flowers gradually withered and died – and still they looked like faded objects of beauty. These plants were obscenely dead. They were swollen and bulbous, like poultices drawn from a gangrenous wound. She could not smell them through the glove port housing walls, but she had no doubt that if she could they'd have stank with the same nauseating charnel reek as the geraniums on the windowsill of Ake and Agnietta's home.

Suddenly Kay's mind was overwhelmed with those awful memories, the stinking black bodies in a house that had become a sepulcher of dead flies.

Sweat erupted over her entire face and neck. There was an overwhelming instinct to run from there, to discover the wholesome light and warmth of the sun. She had to force her breathing to slow down, to keep herself focused.

Inspect the controls.

She walked down the opposite glove-port corridor, observing that the controls were all healthy. There was a fleeting and wholly unscientific comfort to be taken from their healthy gloss, in a variety of subtle greens, of their hardy dehydration-resistant leaves. But the moment faded and it only seemed to amplify her fears by comparison with what she now needed to do.

She had to go back to the stinking dead and take extracts for passage into insects, to confirm the nature of the contagion. At the very thought of putting her hands into those gloves and working with that stinking vileness, panic took hold of her. She couldn't bring herself to do this. She couldn't stay a moment longer in this place. Hitting the broad square switch plate that operated the airlock door, she rushed through the second door into the change room, where she flopped down onto the bench seat in a daze.

Her reaction shocked her.

How was it that she had coped with the inoculations lasting for hours on end last night and yet, this morning hysteria had so overwhelmed her? How was she going to lead the scientific effort if she allowed her fears to interfere with her work? Kay knew she would have to confess her failure to Will. She would have to ask his assistance – hope for his indulgence. She would have to promise it would not happen in the future. But what guarantee could she give that panic would not overwhelm her again?

It was several minutes before she had calmed sufficiently to remove the scrubs and bootees and surgical gloves, to wrench off her ridiculous cap and put on ordinary working clothes.

That was where they found her.

A tall figure, gowned and masked, obstructed her exit through the open doorway. Mentally, she was so hyped up it took her a second or two to recognize him as the FBI chief, Willson. A second gowned and masked figure was hovering immediately in the actual doorway. She guessed it had to be O'Keefe. The two men came further into the tiny change room, practically filling it.

Willson said, 'We need to talk to you about your ex-husband, Mike.'

'This is not a good time.'

'We tried to get a hold of him, yesterday. It seems he ran from the building, ignoring our call over the public address system.'

Kay felt her face flush with frustration. It was almost impossible to physically climb to her feet, they were taking up so much room. She said: 'Mr. Willson! Will you please get it into your head that I can't concentrate on Mike, not now. There's a problem here that I need to deal with. I have to go talk to Dr. Grant.'

'Not before you talk to us.'

She elbowed her way to her feet, shoving Willson out of her way. 'Please? Not now! Okay?'

He grabbed hold of her arm. 'You don't seem to grasp the situation. It's very serious. Two more scientists have been killed.'

All resistance ebbed from her. 'Who?'

'An Englishman, name of William T. Freeman, and a German, Julius Eigner. They were killed in their hotel in Pasadena. Came here to address some NASA conference. You heard of them?'

'Only remotely. If I recall, their work was on genetic engineering at a very basic level. The definition of life.'

'Looks like somebody has taught them the definition of death.'

'Oh God – none of this makes sense! Why would anybody want to kill these people?'

'We were hoping you might be able to see a pattern.'

Kay shook her head.

'Yesterday, at a conference in San Diego, two of our agents caught sight of your ex. He bolted. They confronted him again in the underground garage, but he just about ran them down, crashing through the ticket barrier. There's been no sign of him since then. You have any idea what is going on?'

'Mike,' she said quietly, 'is perfectly capable of behaving stupidly. It's nothing unusual. He can take off for a week without bothering to tell people about it.'

Willson stared at her, as if he didn't altogether believe her.

'Professor – I want you to come with us. The President herself would like to speak to you.'

*

In her seat at the ad-hoc table in the meeting room, Kay looked up in astonishment at the slim and elegant African American woman whose face and upper body was the focus of the big plasma screen. She could hardly believe she was going to speak to the President in person. Jackie C. Dickinson had a natural grace that had stood her in very good stead in her rise to power. Up close she looked five years younger than her chronological age, which was 47 years. Dickinson was friendly, but businesslike. 'Professor McCann – I presume you are receiving us as clearly as we are receiving you?'

'Yes, Ma'am – thank you!' Kay was still feeling shattered after the morning's experimental results. She had had a very brief opportunity of talking to Will about it before the tele conference. Will had been great. He had persuaded her that she had merely failed to prepare herself mentally for what she was likely to find in the BSL-3 lab. She hoped he was right.

'Professor - we're grateful to you for your dedicated work and for sparing us your time for this conference. Can I cut to the chase and ask you if you have formed any opinion on what we're dealing with?'

'Dr. Grant would perhaps be better able to answer that question, Ma'am. He's the viral expert.'

'But I understand we're not dealing with a virus?'

'No. It's unlike anything we have ever encountered.'

'What more can you tell us about this – this entity?'

'It appears to have been designed to move not only between individuals but also between different species.'

'By move about, you mean infect them?'

'Yes.'

'You know about the e-mail from some individual or group hinting at responsibility for this entity. Are you putting together any clearer picture of what we might be dealing with here?'

'All three of us - myself, Major Coster and Dr. Grant - are agreed. We're convinced it is the result of genetic engineering.'

'But who would want to construct such a thing?'

'I can't understand why any reputable biotechnology company would do it, that's for sure.'

'Please explain.'

'What would they gain? There would be no rational purpose.'

'Not even as a weapon?'

'There's a big negative against.'

'What's that?'

'A weapon would be directed against a specific target, presumably people. The lethality of the entity has no biological direction. It appears to be universal.'

President Dickinson was silent for a moment or two. 'Professor – isn't a nuclear weapon just as universally lethal.'

'Yes, Ma'am – it is!'

'And the universality of this – this entity – is made possible because all of life shares the same mitochondria?'

'Yes.'

'Then it would be fair to conclude that this agent has been designed to attack mitochondria.'

'Yes – it would.'

'Professor McCann – do you think that what you're investigating could be the construct of a single individual as opposed to a group?'

Kay answered: 'I doubt it.'

'Why?'

'Maybe in Batman movies, you come across some egghead scientist who mixes chemicals on his kitchen table and comes up with some spectacular creation. In reality, the construction of something as complex as this would require the coordinated efforts of a host of technical experts, not to mention capital underpinning in terms of buildings, plant, salaries and access to high-tech equipment.'

Dickinson pressed her: 'This is an important realization, Professor. So let's be absolutely clear about it. In your opinion, we're dealing with a bioengineered weapon, made by some group with considerable technical know-how?'

'I can't say it was engineered as a weapon.'

'Meaning?'

'It might have been engineered for another purpose.'

Dickinson's face was frowning on screen: 'Such as what?'

Kay was too cautious to answer that. Everybody knew that governments, in particular the military, were as interested in genetic engineering as any major biotech company. 'I couldn't say.'

'Okay, so let's look at funding. What level are we talking about?'

'Millions of dollars, certainly.'

'Which narrows the field considerably. It would have to implicate big business, or wealthy supporters?'

'That would be my conclusion, yes.'

Dickinson nodded: 'Professor -- Mr. Duhan, the EPA Administrator, has suggested a solution to the circles.'

Kay sat back in surprise.

'This agent, entity or whatever you call it – he informs me that it would be destroyed by fire.'

'I don't know of any biological agent that wouldn't.'

'His suggestion is that we burn it. Incinerate every circle.' Dickinson turned her attentions to General Hauk, who was also sitting at the ad-hoc table. 'General, is that practical?'

'We could hose the circles down with gas and torch them. But this is a hot dry season. The big area, coming out of Sector 5-32, would need to be ringed by a fire-break, or the whole southern Mojave could go up in flames.'

'Is it your advice that we do it?'

'It's Duhan's advice that we do it. My advice is that it is practicable, Ma'am.'

'Anybody object?'

Nobody did so.

'Consider it your baby, General'

05: 29/ 11h45

'Hi, Janie!'

'Hi, Dad. Don't tell me. You're calling to say you're not coming home?'

Will hesitated, glancing over at Kay. They were taking advantage of a fifteen minutes break before the second heavy schedule of the day, sitting out in the fresh air.

He said: 'I'm sorry. Not just yet.'

'Why can't I come and stay with you?'

In the distance, medical orderlies wheeled Haseler, in a portable isolation chamber, out to the makeshift helipad. So far it was good news. In two days of observation the tough little soldier had shown no signs of infection.

Will said, 'I'd really love to have you here with me. But it'd be too dangerous. I want to know you're safe.'

'Oh, safe is boring! Even during the season, Uncle Bret watches women wrestling when the Hawks are on another channel.'

'He does?'

'You know he does.'

Janie loved basketball. At their home in Monarch Village, he had rigged a hoop and backboard in the yard. Nancy and Brett lived in a condominium in Fairlie, next to the downtown facilities of Macy's, the Rialto Center and Georgia State University, where Brett worked in admin. There was no yard. Not so much as a convenient garage wall. Will gazed skywards as the Medivac chopper took off with Haseler on board.

'Phillippa's dad is taking her for a summer special autograph session.'

'Maybe he could take you too.'

'It's competitive, Dad. Phillippa is aiming to get to summer camp.'

He knew that Janie was desperate to spend five days at the Atlanta Hawks' summer camp, where the kids had expert coaching from professionals. He had promised her she would go there when she was 12 years old. Janie wasn't winning the battle to control her voice: he could tell she was close to tears. 'Last year Dominique Wilkins was there.' Dominique Wilkins was the Hawks' all-time leading scorer, with a grand tally of 23,292.

'When's it happening?'

'June 19 through 24.'

'Maybe Aunt Nancy –?'

'Nancy doesn't like any kind of sport.'

'Well, let me see what I can do about it!'

A sob broke through: 'I never get to go anywhere.'

'When's the signing?'

'Sunday.'

'I'll see if I can get Sunday off.'

Kay's face swiveled around to look at him. She didn't need to speak. He could read the empathy in her eyes.

Janie said, 'Yeah – sure!'

*

At two minutes before noon, a mix of excitement and anticipation infected the reporters demanding information at the edge of General Hauk's cordon sanitaire at the bottom of the dirt road leading to the Ivan Wallin Field Reserve. A sprinkling of national television trucks was now part of the scene. Even from a distance they couldn't miss the armada of earthmovers and back hoes chugging and clanking out there in the desert. Cameramen pitched in the crow's nests of cherry pickers and vertical man hoists were zooming in on the thick clouds of dust thrown up as the hundred yard wide firebreak was being hacked out of the scrub. Suddenly, the cameras and microphones found a new focus as a convoy of Chinooks and Sikorskys, underslung with the huge tanks of kerosene, clattered overhead.

*

Moran had somehow persuaded O'Keefe to accompany Kay in confronting General Hauk in his office. 'I know that you kept Professor Johansson's computer and the ecology printouts.'

Hauk glared at O'Keefe. 'You told her that?'

Kay persisted. 'I'm not questioning your reasons. All I'm suggesting is that you allow me access. There must be something in there that will help us find out what happened here.'

O'Keefe merely shrugged.

'Ake – Professor Johansson – was obsessive with detail. You have to be that way to be a good field ecologist, and he was the best. I think that somewhere in those files I can figure out exactly when the circle began.'

O'Keefe nodded, 'Let her do it. But I want to be present.'

Hauk still glared at her, like an overly aggressive alpha male gorilla. 'Even if you look at the readouts, what's that going to tell us?'

'Somebody had to go out there and deliberately seed that circle. There's no evidence of a break-in. That somebody came in through these doors. We date when it happened, then we look to find out exactly who had business with Sector 5-32 at that time.'

'When do you want to do this?'

'Right now.'

She began by clearing the desk of everything other than Ake's former computer. With O'Keefe and Hauk watching over her shoulder, she started by working through the Landsat data on the computer. She said, 'Logic suggests that the seeding happened right at the heart of the circle. We find the smallest visible circle, with the advantage of retrospect, on the thematic mapping. That's got to be my starting point.

'Okay, so we start with the fact the circle was first detectible as a tiny discoloration on May 5.'

'So?' O'Keefe was making brief notes of her progress.

'So I know that there were two of Ake's monitors within the circle, one close to the center and one on the periphery.' She lifted a large cardboard box of IDITD readouts off the floor, rummaging through thirty or more rolls of paper recordings until she found the one she wanted, the trace for Sector 5-32 for the months of April and May.

'Now, Mr. O'Keefe, if you wouldn't mind making yourself useful,' she indicated that she would unroll at one side of the desk while he re-rolled at the other. She skipped speedily back to May 5. Then she ran through the examination of insect density count printouts, browsing a few feet at a time before rolling on backwards. For the twenty-four hours prior to May 5 the dips and fluctuation in the five-color pen lines were so bizarre, she was able to skip through an hour at a stretch. The fluctuations continued back through another twelve hours after which they began to clear somewhat erratically. The going became slow and tedious. It took Kay forty minutes of eye-aching scrutiny to be sure. By then she had gone all the way back to May 3. She stopped dead.

'You got it?'

She tapped at the blip, the first clear sign she had been able to discover. O'Keefe drew a red pen from his pocket and handed it to her, so she could circle the anomaly. 'Right! That's the first to appear on the recording. But what's the betting it took two or three days on the ground to actually show!'

'So what's your best guess?'

'May 1st.'

'You think that has some symbolic significance?'

'I don't know about that. I'm seeing a more practical implication. Ake and I directed alternate months so the first day of any month was a changeover day.'

'So somebody who knew this might have taken advantage of the temporary confusion?'

'It's possible.' She thought, *Damn! More evidence of inside knowledge.* 'I guess it's now over to you, Mr. O'Keefe. You took away all of our admin data.'

'What am I looking for?'

'Let's add in a margin of error. Say, anybody who had business with Sector 5-32 from April 28th through May 2nd. But we need to keep a special eye on May 1st.'

'You want a job with the agency, Professor?'

'All I ask is that you let me see it when you have your list of names.'

05: 29/ 12h52

Kay activated the laptop, so she could project the first of the PowerPoint projections onto the giant plasma screen. 'Welcome,' she said, 'to your first sight of the enemy.'

The small gathering of about a dozen people in the meeting room, gazed up at a full color reconstruction.

She added, 'The magnification is 40,000.'

They were looking at a blow-up that, at first glance resembled a pineapple-shaped object with a feathery frond, like a dandelion seed, on the top.

Kay said, 'It's possible these projections give it buoyancy in air.'

She waited for somebody to question that. But nobody spoke.

'The body, here, has what appears to be a roughly spherical core, like a planet with four horizontally distributed moons. We have decided to call these the equatorial nodes. Here we see two distinct discs, occupying the north and south poles. We just call them as we see them, the north and south poles. And here we have a series of intricate conduits that curl in a clockwise direction, looking from below upwards, linking up these subsidiary structures. There are other connections, like nodes and poles to core, that mesh the entire entity into an intricate whole.'

One of the scientists called out: 'It's incredibly complex.'

Kay said, 'Yes, it is!'

Moran murmured, 'Professor – it's the most terrifying thing I have seen in my life. Will you kindly explain to us exactly what it is we are looking at.'

Kay tapped new instructions into her computer and the entity began to rotate through its X and Y axes. She allowed them time to examine the moving three-dimensional geometry. Then, with a few more taps of the keys, it disintegrated into its component subunits.

She said, 'Shout if you don't understand. What we're looking at is a computer enhancement, based on what we have been able to put together from the electron microscope and molecular analysis to date.'

She projected a new image of what looked like a tangled ball made up of many different twisting ribbons, each a different color. 'What we're looking at is a blow-up of the core with the overlying membrane removed. This is where most of the genes are located. I don't want to say a lot more right now because we don't know enough. We're having to make a whole bunch of assumptions at this stage.'

O'Keefe asked: 'What are the colored ribbons?'

'Some of the ribbons are proteins and others are genes. There are far too many of them to represent each with a primary color. We've had to be inventive.' Kay turned her back to the image and faced them. 'Nothing like it has ever been seen before – nothing even remotely like it.'

Moran's lips tautened. 'Could you explain a little further – keeping it simple?'

'I'll try.'

Kay returned to the screen and made the amplification jump through two orders of magnitude, so the core became a fuzzy multicolored planet too big to fit onto the screen. Around its equatorial horizon four equally fuzzy satellites rotated, each at ninety degrees to the others in the horizontal plane. 'The actual angle and direction of orbit of the satellite nodes must be important to how this thing actually works. And these link-ups – they look almost like cables, don't they – spiraling from south pole to all four of the horizontal nodes, and then from there up to the north pole!'

Kay turned to van den Berg. 'Anton, would you mind explaining - these equatorial nodes, what's their biochemical composition?'

'They're a tightly woven composite of proteins around a matrix of RNA. Each node appears to be a little different. That would suggest they serve some different function. But the complexity would demand very precise coordination in how it works. If our preliminary findings prove to be correct, we may be looking at RNA genes in the satellites and DNA genes in the core.'

Kay thanked van den Berg and tapped some more keys to cause the image to spiral and turn, against several whistles of awe. 'As you've heard, the core appears to be based on DNA genes as opposed to the RNA genes in the nodes. At least a hundred, maybe more. Anton has been comparing their sequences to the known sequences of other genes. That's about as far as we've gotten so far.'

Moran asked her, 'So you don't know as yet how it kills the mitochondria?'

'No.'

Will spoke up. 'We do know, however, that the entity somehow takes control over the mitochondria, just like a virus takes over an infected bacterial cell. But it doesn't just kill the mitochondria. It also reproduces itself. We know it self-replicates inside the mitochondria in vast quantities.'

'Just a minute,' Moran countered. 'Are you implying that this entity is alive?'

'That's the big question.'

Moran looked back at her, stunned.

Kay explained, 'In 2002, a group of US scientists took the first step toward recreating artificial life when a guy called Wimmer reconstructed the polio virus, using mail-order DNA. A lot of other people are now following his lead. I know one syntech company, AS Biosynthetics, has been pioneering the reconstruction of plant viruses, like the tobacco mosaic virus, using little more than their genetic templates. The owner and scientific director of AS Bioinformatics is someone I know personally – Arafim Sultan. Ari was a Ph. D. student at Berkeley when I was an undergrad. He's brilliantly innovative, a protégé of my ex-husband, Mike. It's possible that his expertise might be helpful to this group.'

Kay bit her lip, aware that Anton was staring back at her with a spreading flush of resentment.

*

'Hi, Mom!'

A beat, while Kay registered it was Sean. 'Hi!'

'I just called to tell you I made a new friend.'

'You did?'

'His name's Charley Wieldstone. His father's a deputy in the Wyoming P.D..'

'Sounds impressive!'

'Charley and me, we're going river fishing for Cutthroat.'

'You be careful now!'

'It's no big deal. The river's only three feet deep.'

'Oh, I don't mean to patronize you. I'm just so relieved to hear you're making new friends.'

'How's it going with the zombie plague?'

'Things are a little crazy here right now. I'm really glad Mike got you out of harm's way when he did.'

'We had a visit from the FBI. Mom, they're looking for Dad, like he's done something really awful.'

'You father hasn't done anything.'

Sean fell silent.

She said, 'You wait and see. He'll suddenly pop up, like he always does.'

'I got a bad feeling.'

'It's a difficult time. People are getting a little bit excitable.'

'They're going crazy here.'

'What do you mean?'

'Charley's dad says Wyoming is being invaded.'

'Oh, that's being silly.'

'It's not silly. Lots of people are trying to escape from down south. They're filling up all the recreation areas with campers and RVs.'

'Well, you just keep away from them – you promise me that?'

'Charley's dad tells us to do the same. He says they're no-goods. They've been breaking into places, stealing food and stuff when people are out. Charley's dad says there's going to be trouble. It's just around the corner.'

Kay couldn't believe what she was hearing. 'There hasn't been any trouble at grandma's and grandad's, has there?'

'Couple of days ago some people came up to the gate. Guys in one of those old VW buses. They tried to make grandad give them some food.'

'They threatened your grandad?'

'I'm just telling you what he said. I didn't see them. Grandad took out his rifle and he told me to stay in the house.'

'Tell Grandad I want to talk to him.'

'He's gone out. To some kind of a meeting.'

'A meeting about what?'

'I don't know, Mom. But Charley says it's only a matter of time before people start going vigilante.'

'Sean – I don't want you to go near anything like that. I'm not even sure I want you to go fishing.'

'Mom – I gotta go. Charley's waiting.'

'Sean – Sean, you stay on this line. Get Grandad to ring me back, as soon as he comes home. Tell him I want to know what's going on.'

'Catch you later, Mom!'

*

From the top of a dune, about 200 yards from the house, FBI Special Agent Gary Maisley watched his subject exit the Pueblo style single story house and lock the door behind him. Maisley was part of a huge FBI operation underway countrywide. Anybody with the remotest connection to terrorist activities or sympathies was being brought in for interrogation. Human rights issues no longer mattered. Homes and workplaces were being searched on a massive scale. Maisley's subject, Arafim Sultan, was one of 57 scientists put under DEST - Domestic Emergency Support Team - surveillance by FBI Director Jon Lilley. DEST worked under the joint authority of the FBI, the Attorney General and the National Security Council, to provide rapidly deployable interagency teams. It was just a routine local assignment, but Maisley had done his homework on his subject.

A youthful prodigy and ex-assistant professor in the department of molecular genetics at Berkeley, Sultan had risen like a rocket through every undergraduate and postgraduate stage of his education. For several years, he had been managing director of his own incorporated bio-engineering company, based in Reno, Nevada, on the same industrial estate as Mike McCann's MM Bionano Inc. Maisley's surveillance had been given added importance now that Kay McCann had asked the FBI's permission to include him in her scientific team working on the WMD.

Now the youthful FBI agent watched as the tall, slim figure strode past the huge satellite dish installed in the yard. The FBI knew about the satellite dish. An unmarried man who lived alone, Sultan used it to control all aspects of his home from abroad, from sprinkling water onto his desert garden to looking after internal security and fire precautions. Now, through his field binoculars, Maisley watched the big dish swivel towards Sultan as he climbed aboard a burgundy-red Enstrom F28F chopper and started up the engine. The rotors, almost twice as long as the wasp-shaped body, began to turn. Suddenly, the door swung open again and Sultan leaned out, a cell phone pressed against his ear.

Maisley ran back to a truck parked below the observation dune, where the cooperation of the NSA tech - a working partnership born out of CONPLAN - would allow him to listen in to that telephone conversation. He grabbed an earpiece and was gratified to hear a woman's voice in his headphone. She sounded relieved. 'Hi, Ari, how long has it been?'

'Kay – we haven't spoken in years!'

'I wish the circumstances were a little more social.'

Sultan's voice was raised, to climb above the background noise. 'So – what can I do for you?'

There was a flare of interference. 'I can hardly hear you. There's a lot of noise in the background.'

Maisley swore under his breath.

'I've got the rotors moving. Maybe I'd better call you from the office.'

'No! Please don't hang up just yet. You know I'm heading the scientific group at the Ivan Wallin. I've been thinking about you and the wonderful work you did with the synthesis of plant viruses.'

Maisley picked up the thinking pause on Sultan's part. 'Well, thanks for saying so.'

'What's going on here - you'd be fascinated.'

'I'm hooked to every news bulletin.'

The woman hesitated. 'They're setting fire to the desert. I can see black smoke rising out of Sector 5-32.' Whatever was going on, the sight seemed to be enough to make her catch her breath. 'I've got to attend a meeting in fifteen minutes. I wanted to talk to you first. Where exactly are you?'

'Just setting out from home, heading for work.'

'Ari – I've talked to the people here. It's just an idea,' she said. 'But we're looking for people like you.'

'What? You want my help?'

'If you wouldn't mind the two of us working closely again. I guess that that's the only reason I ... well, I could have asked you earlier. But I know your brilliance would be invaluable here.'

There was more background crackle for a moment or two. 'Kay, I'd be glad to work with you. You know I'd do anything to help. But wouldn't it be better if I could assist you using my own lab facilities?'

'You wouldn't believe the security conditions. They wouldn't allow it. I'm sorry but you'd have to come here.'

There was an exhalation. 'I'll have to tie things up at the plant. I'll get back to you later. We'll talk about it in more detail.'

Maisley jerked a thumb at the NSA tech. 'We recording this?'

'Of course!'

He heard Kay McCann's voice fall to a murmur: 'I'll look forward to it.'

Sultan said, 'Take care, Kay.'

Maisley dropped the headphone and ran back to the top of the dune. He was in time to see the rotors blur as the chopper took off, with the cabin door only just closing. There was a flash of orange light, followed by a thunderous explosion.

'Jesus Christ – son of a bitch!'

Maisley automatically ducked his head down, even though he was two hundred yards away. When he looked again, the chopper was down in flames, the big blades disintegrating as they whacked into the security fence surrounding the yard.

05: 30/ 05h45

The morning dawned freezing cold. Reporter Mark Stanwyck cupped his hands around a flask-cap of hot coffee, waiting for the balloon to fill. The balloonist turned from directing the plume of flame into the expanding canopy to look over at him because Stanwyck had suddenly burst out laughing.

Stanwyck would have had difficulty explaining the joke. In fact he was recalling how the Reickhardt woman had pushed Emilia Valdez, wearing her drama-queen facemask, down onto her butt in the dirt. Mark and Emilia had been rivals for years, working their way up the ladder from independents to writing for the Phoenix media. Well, Emilia had won that pissante competition, not so much from merit - he didn't think she was any good as an investigative reporter - but because she was ruthless when it came to the deployment of her assets.

Well, now!

He shouldered the pack that contained his notebook computer, Soni digital camera and JVC camcorder, then clambered into the wickerwork basket. Stanwyck had the opportunity to get around the cordon thrown by the military and show the world how he could deploy his own investigative assets.

The balloonist, JJ Draper, was a friend from way back in high school. JJ was excited at the prospect of flouting the law. He had paid for two chase crews to follow their progress from the ground. You could call it a medium-term investment. If and when the ground crews came to a halt at the military cordon, they would film the balloon passing over the heads of those dumbasses in helmets and uniforms. That would add just the right piquancy for JJ's own kudos as a daredevil flyer. So over the previous two days Stanwyck and Draper had planned it together, getting the timing just perfect. The dawn flight had been chosen because it was the time of day when the wind was calmest and the positioning was calculated to get Stanwyck near enough to get shots of where they had been burning holes in the desert. He didn't have long to wait.

'Hey, man – holy shit!'

Mark grinned at JJ's wide-eyed stare. They had reached five thousand feet and the target zone was right below them. He was delighted to discover that they had it entirely to themselves. A single gigantic black hole, still smoking in places, stood out as clearly as if it had been punched out of the painted desert with a cosmic laser. Mark started to click-through on the digital, panning in and out so he could get an idea of its overall size, the occasional licking flame and trail of gray smoke drifting skyward. He switched to the JVC and went through a moving version of the same exercise, this time adding his voice to the tape, against the dramatic background of the breeze whistling through the wires and the muffled roar of the burner on steady. He had canned five minutes when JJ clapped his shoulder.

'Get a shot of the bandits - north-east!'

At this distance, the Apaches looked no bigger than sparrows, but they were closing very rapidly. Stanwyck whooped: magnificent!

'Okay! Burn her, JJ. Give us enough lift to find some decent wind.'

JJ turned on the heater full blast to get them skywards as Stanwyck kneeled down in the basket and rested his arms on the rim to get a firmer frame to zoom the JVC, and he froze the frame through half a dozen shots that would add dramatic digitals of the closing gunships.

*

Ari Sultan opened one eye and looked around himself at what appeared to be a hospital room. There was a disorientating sensation when he moved his head. When he coughed, pain shot through every muscle, joint and tendon. *Jesus Christ!* Even lying still, his lower back and legs were itching and smarting. A woman swam into his vision, bending over him. She was dressed in surgical scrubs, with a bonnet collecting up her hair and a cloth mask over her face. 'Thank God, he's awake,' she said. It was Kay McCann's voice. He couldn't believe it was Kay's voice. He screwed his eyes shut and attempted to think.

A different voice registered: he had to reopen his eyes to peer at a young man, wearing a green coverall and a facemask. 'Mr. Sultan – or should I call you, Doctor?'

He moaned.

'My name is Maisley. I work with the FBI out of the Reno office.'

Their eyes met.

'Please excuse me, sir, but I need a few minutes of your time and then the Professor here can have you all to herself. Is that okay with you?'

'You can... you can go –!'

'C'mon now, Ari!' Kay reached out and held his left hand, around the i.v. line that was running into it. 'This man saved your life.'

He clenched his eyes shut again.

The man's voice persisted: 'There was a C4 bomb, with an ultra-sophisticated trigger device, attached to your fuel tank.'

His eyes darted open, flitted repeatedly from one face to the other.

'I don't know how they got to you. My guess, it was attached the day before, at your factory, because we had your home under constant surveillance. I managed to reach you just in time.'

Sultan groaned aloud, clenching his teeth.

Kay McCann's voice switched to cajoling: 'Agent Maisley was quick-thinking - he drove through the security fence and put out the flames. Got burned himself in doing so.'

Sultan saw dressings on the FBI agent's hands.

'Ari! You might not think yourself lucky. You've been concussed. You have a dislocated left shoulder. You broke a few ribs. But it could have been a lot worse. Your burns are confined to your legs and lower back and they're mostly second degree. You owe it to this guy.'

Kay was shaking her head at him.

'In fact,' the FBI man said, 'it was really the Professor here who saved your life. You opened the cockpit door to take her call on your cell phone, so the door was open when the bomb went off. You got thrown clear of the worst of the explosion.'

He managed a weak grin. 'Kay —!'

'You think we could manage without your help?'

*

The balloon was drifting gently northeastward at about fifteen thousand feet. Two Apaches hovered on either side of it, rocking very slightly from side to side. The noise from their engines was deafening. Another hovered no more than fifty yards ahead of them and directly windward, with its guns and missiles aimed their way. Stanwyck's nostrils were choking on the combined exhausts. He hoped to God that his chase teams below had canned a few decent pictures of what was happening from their perspective. They were about forty miles northeast of the field reserve by now, over rough ground and deserted tracks, so close to the meeting of states that he couldn't sure if they were over California, Nevada or Arizona.

'Up ahead - I can see a road,' JJ was hoarse from shouting over the noise of the burners. He pointed into the distance, past the menacing Apache.

'Can we go around him?' Stanwyck was pretty hoarse himself.

'No chance!' JJ replied. 'The only maneuver we got is up or down.'

Even from this distance, Stanwyck could see the hand of the Apache pilot to their right jerking his thumb downward.

He shouted: 'Let's try to get above him!'

JJ shouted back: 'Okay. I just hope that raptor isn't gonna rake his claws through my beautiful balloon.'

Mark Stanwyck didn't believe that an American army chopper was going to turn its cannons on two civilians in a balloon. But still his heart was hammering as the burners roared and the balloon began to lift. The Apaches on either side moved closer. The chopper ahead of them lifted so that it still blocked their passage. JJ emptied sacks of sand, which drifted in a slow curve into their slipstream.

By now they were even closer to the Apache ahead and the current from its rotors was rocking the basket.

'What the fuck's the matter with them,' shrieked JJ. 'All this for a burnt hole in the desert!'

After five or six minutes of this cat-and-mouse, they were over the road. It was a two-lane blacktop and there was some visible traffic. Stanwyck peered down through the telescopic viewfinder on his JVC and saw that the traffic was a column of a dozen or so military vehicles. He could make out the camouflage. Then he glimpsed red crosses on the sides. Ambulances. 'Hey - see if you can steady it a little, let me get off a few shots.'

A ten-knot wind was carrying them roughly parallel with the blacktop. He used up five or six minutes of JVC tape, with a few decent freeze frames. Suddenly there was a crackling noise and JJ started roaring profanities. 'I can't believe it. Bastard is shooting at us.'

'We hit?'

'Nah! Don't think so. But hey, this is still America. What the fuck's going on in the world?'

Stanwyck stared into the distance beyond the threatening helicopter gunship. With the naked eye, he could see that further along the road was some kind of building complex. Zooming in with the JVC, he made out a cluster of low buildings. The basket was jerking and wobbling, with a wind of hot kerosene exhaust rifling through his hair. He tried kneeling, splaying wide his knees for stability, and allowing his body to roll, like a gyroscopic platform. He could just about make out a red cross and a chopper landing target on the flat roof of one of the buildings.

'What in the hell!'

Now he saw parallel rows of thick lines of green running off to either side of a central clearing. He made out ten each side, a total of twenty.

'Give them a signal, JJ. Tell them we're going down.'

'No way!'

'Do it, JJ. There's something up ahead and they don't want us to film it. Oh, man! I think I'm beginning to understand.'

It was every journalist's dream to get a scoop. But how did you recognize the big one when it was in your face? Mark Stanwyck wondered if he was looking right down on it. He said, 'You see those buildings a mile ahead? Get us as close as you can while pretending we're doing exactly what those assholes are telling us.'

JJ strained his eyes and saw the buildings. He waved an arm at the lead chopper, pointed down and made a show of letting out some air. They began to descend. The

Apaches, if anything, thundered in closer. Their guns were pointing right at them. 'You don't think they're gonna let you keep those films?'

'Hell, no!' Stanwyck thought they'd be lucky if they kept their lives. He rubbed at his brow, attempting to focus his thoughts. The thick green lines were tents. Pulling the notebook computer, he booted it, loaded Photosuite, plugged the modem into his cell phone. The basket was rocking like crazy but he ignored all distractions, kneeling with his elbows clear of the edge and focusing on the arrival of the ambulances into the building complex. One of the accompanying Apaches slanted through forty-five degrees and began to drop. Goddam! The pilot was attempting to cut off his viewing angle.

Stanwyck got a reasonable zoom on figures that had come out of the buildings and were clustering around the ambulances. He just let it run as those same figures helped people out of the back doors. He began to freeze-frame, clicking through shot after shot. Some of the sick people were being lifted onto stretchers. The figures receiving them - he presumed they were military doctors and nurses - were suited up in biosafety gear. The Apache was maneuvering below them, inching closer, attempting to block off any further views.

'Oh, shit!' JJ was looking down with an expression of rage. They were drifting further eastward, away from the field hospital complex.

A sudden swing of the basket threw Stanwyck around to the other side, where he moved from side to side, attempting to see beyond the aircraft below them. There were more figures coming out of the buildings. He caught the flash of reflection in binoculars. Stanwyck shot off a few more stills, capturing the rows of tents. How long had the field hospital been up and running? Not very long, he thought. But even if only half the tents were occupied he figured that still amounted to a lot of people.

JJ pointed. 'Over there, man! Get a load a' that!'

Stanwyck slid his elbows around the rim of the bucking basket. The Apache below was now peeling away, to take up its former position to the right hand side of them. The ground was two thousand feet away. At first Stanwyck couldn't see what JJ was pointing to. But then he realized that he was looking too near the hospital complex. Further out, about five miles into the desert, was another cluster of vehicles. He had connected up the JVC to download into the computer but there was just about room, if he put the notebook on his lap, to pan. He panned.

Gotcha baby!

He zoomed onto a big army truck, in desert camouflage ... two earthmovers ... He began filming. He stopped, involuntarily, when he noticed the pit. What it contained. His hand felt leaden as he freeze-framed a couple of shots. There was only about a minute or two of tape left and he just let it run. The ground was only two hundred feet below them when he ran out of tape.

*

A male nurse was waiting for Will Grant when he came out of the hermetic chamber of the Gammacell. He had just irradiated the most dangerous batch to date, their first harvest of highly purified and concentrated entity. The nurse told him that Major Coster wanted him to go to the bubble immediately. Stopping just for the few moments it took him to label and secure the samples in the deep freeze, he ran after the nurse.

He found Josie in the ICU, where she was manipulating the robot arms that reached into the bubble, adjusting a central intravenous line that ran into one of two new residents, one male and one female. She murmured, 'Two of them, Will – two of our scientists – they've just been admitted.'

'Definitely infected?'

'The man for definite – the women almost certainly.'

Will peered through the Plexiscreen at the two sedated figures. The man looked mid-thirties and the female late-twenties. Their faces were flushed, glairy with a sweat. Their bodies swarmed with fluid lines and recording cables. The woman was breathing for herself but the man, a stage deeper, was already plugged into a ventilator. In spite of the oxygenation, his lips were black.

Will pressed Josie: 'Fast-tracks?'

'I'm afraid so.'

'Who are they?'

'Two of Kay's botanists. The guy's an assistant professor at Irvine, brought in to work on seed counts.'

'Damn!'

The man groaned, a terrible sound, and Josie fiddled with the infusion, bumping up the poor guy's level of diamorphine. 'How in Jesus' name could this have happened, Will?'

'I don't know.'

'Maybe you better find out – fast!'

'I know what they were measuring. In normal circumstances, you find dozens of annual and perennial seeds in every handful of desert soil. Peak samples from last year showed viable seed densities of more than 7,500 per square meter. In the samples these guys have been collecting, this is down to 2%'

Josie asked him: 'This kind of work, I assume it's got to be important?'

'The 2% could be important. That's what interests us right now. We're looking at the survivors, no matter how rare.'

'And these two guys - they've been out there, digging in those circles?'

'Yes, they have. But they were suited up. I trained all of the incoming staff myself. They shouldn't have been at risk.'

'You know that Jingle Jangle will say?'

Will nodded. 'It's all I need right now.'

05: 31/ 06h10

In central Wyoming, rancher Tom Monaghan grabbed the phone in his office before it woke up the whole household. He heard the voice of his daughter, Kay. 'Hi, Dad. Sorry if I woke you.'

'Kay – you know very well you didn't wake me. Sean told me to expect you to call back last night.'

'Things got a little hectic.' Kay sighed.

'How's it going? You any nearer to cracking this thing?'

'Not yet. We're working on it.'

Tom Monaghan heard the tension in his daughter's voice. He injected a little levity into his own. 'Sean wanted to tell you himself. He caught his first trout. You mother fried it for his dinner. Today we plan to combine some horseback riding with the ranch chores.'

'Dad – you know why I'm calling.'

'What's Sean been telling you?'

'He's been telling me what's going on up there.'

'There's nothing you need to worry about. Just a bunch of hot-headed people is all.'

'Hyped up, hungry – maybe dangerous people?'

'The law will take care of it.'

'That what your meeting was about?'

'Well, I guess it was – that and some other things.'

'Like what?'

'The Sheriff is recruiting more deputies.'

'Sean said you loaded up your rifle.'

'He doesn't miss much!' Her father chuckled.

'You volunteering for deputy?'

'At my age?'

'Dad – you listen to me! I don't want Sean getting mixed up in any vigilante kind of thing. I sent him to you so he could be safe.'

'Kay – are you okay?'

'I'm fine!'

Monaghan didn't think Kay sounded fine. He thought she sounded fearful – maybe even frightened. 'Don't worry your head about Sean. Mom and me, we'll take good care of him.'

'Thanks, Dad.' She hesitated a beat. 'Sean told me you had a visit from the FBI – looking for Mike?'

'Yes we did.'

'Oh, Dad. I don't know what to think. You never know what's going on in that man's head!'

'You should forget about Mike. Take care of yourself!'

*

When Will woke up an hour later than usual, he had a headache from a mixture of overwork and lack of sleep. It wasn't improved any when Clara called him when he was still at breakfast. She told him that Kronstein was on his way to Washington and in his absence there had been a number of urgent phone messages. Kronstein had redirected the calls to him. Will groaned. He suggested she fax him the list. Then, with the two-page fax rolled up in his hand, he headed for BSL-2, where he browsed through them over his third mug of strong black coffee.

The first item to catch his eye was a request to call a public health director, Maria Lopez, in Chihuahua, Mexico. *Shit!* He couldn't concentrate with the screeching of the centrifuges, so he rolled up the list and hurried over to his office in the Portakabin sprawl.

He tried the Mexican number and got an assistant, who said Dr Lopez would call him back. He took a couple of Tylenols, washed them down with yet another mug of coffee. The high caffeine levels in his blood were stoking him into a state of hyperactive imagination. Ideas were flashing through his mind and there was every danger he would forget them when he wanted to remember them later. He took time to scribble down just one of them, the one that struck him as the most important. He wrote it in a hand afflicted with caffeine tremor on a yellow post-it note, then stuck it onto the top right corner of his monitor screen. Mitochondria had once been bacteria. Up to now he had, unconsciously, been focusing his efforts on the entity as if it were a virus. His note read: *Think about bacteria!*

He returned to the list of urgent messages.

Calls from Evelyn Maurice in LA, and from Jez Burke in Phoenix. The epidemiologists could only be communicating more bad news. Others were from people he didn't recognize at all: some guy in Mississippi, another in Arkansas. His perusal stopped at a particular name: Dr. R. Feyerbend.

The name was familiar. Will was so tired it took him a second or two to remember who Feyerbend was. He was the director of public health for the state of Texas. They had communicated - God it really seemed a year ago - about the Dallas baggage handler and his family who had gotten infected from handling the first batches of samples from Thirless. Feyerbend was a knowledgeable and sensible colleague. His message read: CALL ME. URGENT. Will dialed the number.

Feyerbend picked up the call after two rings. As Will explained Kronstein's absence, he heard background noises, suggesting that Feyerbend was not in his office but more likely out somewhere in the state, on site. The Texan colleague sounded like another professional suffering from lack of sleep. He said, 'Dr. Grant, we've got a serious situation here. A definite major outbreak. A farmer and his family, their work hands and their herd of cattle.'

'What makes you so certain?'

'The pattern fits with everything you've been putting out in the MMWRs. We have six fast-tracks, all dead in nine or ten hours. Five slow-tracks. These fit the pattern of person-to-person spread.'

'That's what - a total of eleven?'

There was a pause. 'I think we might be facing a bigger problem. Looks like a multifocal outbreak in San Angelo.'

'How likely is it?'

'We're pretty sure.'

Will's headache pounded and his throat felt dry. He asked Feyerbend: 'You taking measures to contain it?'

'We're doing our best.'

'You must have some idea of the total suspected cases?'

'We have a team out there counting. It's looking scary.'

'How many?'

'Dozens, maybe a lot more.'

'Dozens of contacts around one local index?'
'Dozens of primaries. Fast-tracks.'

*

By mid-morning, Kay was kneeling in the desert, where she had been directing a small team of assistants since daybreak. It distracted her from worrying about the two infected scientists. They were the same two she had recruited for the very work she was now engaged in, collecting plant and insect specimens on the periphery of the burn zone where the Landsats had spotted a bubble-like fenestration effect in the thematic mapping. It was vital they assessed the efficacy of the burning. But to add to her worry, she had found multiple small new circles, thousands of them, extending as far as the horizon from the burn site, coalescing and overlapping. The net effect was a lacework of annihilation, extending out in a gigantic collar, too wide to assess from the ground, yet all focused on the epicenter of black scar. The implications were alarming. From all appearances, the burning had achieved nothing. In fact, if these appearances told her anything, the burning had somehow made things worse.

She was so intensely focused on her thoughts that she overlooked the fact she had a visitor. Only when one of the nearby techs began tugging on her sleeve was she alerted to the fact that a vehicle, some quarter of a mile distant, was blaring its horn and flashing its headlights in her direction. She had turned off the suit radio com so she could concentrate on her work. Now she switched it back on:

She said, 'McCann!'

'Professor – I've gotten hold of you at last!' The voice was that of the FBI man, O'Keefe. 'You asked me to let you know about who had access here on or around May Day.'

A well of excitement rose in her throat.

'We've checked your theory. Nobody other than Professor Johansson and his students had access to Sector 5-32 in the three days you pinpointed.'

She couldn't help but shake her head within the flexible field helmet. 'I just can't believe it!'

'I'm afraid it's true. We also checked out the two students who died. Wasn't easy. You can imagine – talking with their families. The caskets had to be hermetically sealed. They weren't even allowed burial.

The little one, Sara Goldsmith, had a phobia against cremation. We had to go against her wishes and cremate her remains.'

'You came up with nothing?'

'Sameeha Prakesh was a devout Muslim. But there's no law against that. Both she, and her family, seem boringly respectable.'

'It just doesn't make sense.'

There was a silence between them during which her eyes drifted to the horror of what was now going on in the surrounding landscape. Kay urgently needed to talk to Will and Josie. She had to get back to the lab at once.

'You hear anything from your ex-husband?'

Kay thought back to this morning's conversation with her father.

She murmured, 'No.'

'Neither has anybody at his company. I think we can regard his disappearance as more than idiosyncrasy. He was expected back at work days ago. He's missed important meetings.'

'That does seem odd.'

'What about your son?'

'Sean hasn't heard a peep.'

*

Will sent a voicemail message to Kronstein, asking him to call him back urgently. It was now close to noon. Ever since his conversation with Feyerbend, his worries had mounted. The urgent calls just never stopped flooding in. He had been working on the cork-backed map on the office wall where a rash of red pins tracked the spreading statistics. He had just put a red pin in Chihuahua, Mexico, after Dr. Lopez had called him back and told him she suspected they had a case. Nationwide, the incidence of new cases had accelerated considerably. Up to yesterday, which was thirteen days since the outbreak had begun, 267 people had died from it. In the last 24 hours, given just the approximate figures to hand, that number had increased to 423. He did the math – a sixty per cent rise in a single day.

The pattern was changing and they didn't know why.

He called Evelyn Maurice and did his best to persuade her to return to Atlanta and take charge of the nationwide epidemiology. But she refused to be uprooted from the worsening situation in California. While he was still thinking about this, Burke came through from Phoenix.

'I got a message you wanted me to call you.'

'I think we should be looking harder for cases that have shown evidence of resistance.'

'Up to now, everyone who has come into close contact with a victim has died.'

'That isn't quite true. There's the wife of the index case.'

'MayEllen Reickhardt?'

'If I recall, she came into close contact with her husband?'

'Yes she did.'

'Then why isn't she dead?'

'It's a good question.'

'Maybe she's resistant?'

'Possibly. But we can't be sure.'

'Why not?'

Burke sighed: 'She's still refusing to cooperate.'

'Then go see her personally. Persuade her. Explain what we are dealing with and why we need her help.'

'And if she refuses?'

'Subpoena her.'

When Will put down the telephone, his head felt as if it were exploding with every new pulse. He stared at the post-it note stuck to the right upper corner of his monitor. *Think about bacteria!*

Forget the chaos surrounding him, he needed to cut himself time to think!

Okay, so there was an idea he should be exploring. A subject he had been thinking a lot about – one he had covered as an undergraduate and early graduate student many years ago. In the jargon it was known as prokaryotology. Prokaryotology was the study of life before it got to the stage of nucleated cells – like in animals and plants. It boiled down to the study of bacteria. Mitochondria had evolved out of bacteria. Oh, shit – if only his head would stop pounding and let him think! Bacteria could turn out to be the key. Bacterial cells had no nuclei and their DNA was arranged differently from humans. It took the form of a ring of DNA instead of 46 chromosomes. Damn, damn – *Damn! Think!* There was something hanging there in his mind, something he felt was important. Bacteria were infected with viruses, much as human cells were.

There was an idea here, if he could just pluck it out.

The viruses that infected bacteria, these were called phage viruses. Phage from *phago* – he couldn't recall if it was Greek or Latin – he didn't give a damn where the word came from, only that it meant "I eat". Phage viruses had acquired their name because they gobbled up bacteria. The bacterial body became a factory for making huge numbers of viruses and then it just went pop – it burst. It flooded the surrounding microecology with more viruses, which went on to infect more bacteria...

Wasn't that exactly what was happening to mitochondria infected with the entity? Mitochondria that once upon a time had started out as bacteria. He saw it happening in his imagination. He saw a phage virus attach with its syringe-like connection onto the cell wall of the bacterium that had once been a mitochondrion.

Gobble, gobble, gobble – pop!

Will added another post-it note to the sidewall of his computer monitor: *talk to evolutionary bacteriologists.*

Only now did he force his attentions back to the map. The outbreak was confirmed in seven states, including New Mexico and Oklahoma. If Dr. Lopez was right, it had crossed the border into Mexico.

What was causing the change in the behavior pattern of the outbreak? What the hell was really going on here?

*

On screen in meeting room Kay watched as the President made a direct appeal to the small gathering that included Will, Josie, Hauk and Moran: 'This sudden increase in deaths – do you people have any notion as to why this is happening?

Moran spoke tersely: 'Ma'am, Professor McCann has an observation that should be heard.'

'Go ahead, Professor.'

Hauk's eyes were burning into Kay's from three feet away as she replied. 'Dr. Grant and I both believe that the upturn in deaths was caused by setting fire to the desert vegetation.'

Hauk's roar cut through her final few words: 'Professor McCann is trying to shield her pal, Grant, who is trying to save his own neck. He's been careless in harvesting the entity in massive concentrations. That carelessness has cost the lives of two young and inexperienced scientists.'

Kay wasn't going to let him get away with that. She looked straight into the camera: 'May Dr. Grant be allowed to explain?'

'I think he had better do so.'

Will ignored Hauk's glare to focus on speaking simply and calmly. He needed the President to understand. 'Before I came out here, when I was working back at CDC, I did some investigations of the pattern of transmission of the entity. I tested the possibility of air-borne spread in animals. Left to simple diffusion between chambers, it spread but only slowly and erratically. When I introduced a fan to disseminate the air more efficiently between chambers, the entity spread uniformly, and rapidly. At that time I concluded that aerosol spread didn't happen between people. But now I've changed my mind. We now believe that this entity is primarily designed to infect plants. Plant cells, under observation by Professor McCann, have been found to rupture under a burden of self-replication. Plant cells are where it most efficiently multiplies.

'Then there's a second factor. The entity is small, the size of a large virus. Viruses can become suspended in air. For example foot-and-mouth virus was carried by air currents across the channel from France into England. Burning circles would result in a natural uplift of heated air. With that uplift over desert sites, it could carry the entity well above the limits of a ground-based fire. Today, Professor McCann has come back from an inspection of the desert around the burn site, where she found a massive new proliferation around the perimeter. It seems to me that there can be only one explanation. Setting fire to the desert has brought about a huge increase in uplift and subsequent distribution by means of wind currents. If we're right, that would explain both the wider geographic spread and the sudden jump in the numbers of human cases over the last day or so.'

Hauk's bull-voice roared: 'Bullshit!'

At the White House, Ruth Galbraith, the Secretary of Health and Human Services, was staring fixedly at Grant's face on the screen. She whispered, just within earshot of the President: 'My God – if this is really true!'

The psychological profiler, Rachel Minkowsky, overheard her. She was rubbing distractedly at the goose-bumped skin over her bare arms. The others began to stare at her. She murmured: 'Excuse me! My parents live in San Antonio.'

An assistant hurried to the psychologist's side with a glass of water. As she drank it, the noise of swallowing was audible in the room.

President Dickinson commanded the screen once more: 'Can this theory of yours be tested, Dr. Grant?'

'I've knocked heads with Dr. Coster. We're not going to be able to test it in any simple lab experiment. We already know that fire kills the entity. But the dynamics of a burn zone out there in nature are going to be a lot more complex. There would be major air lift at the centre of the burn, but a whole different ball game around the periphery. My guess is the rising air at the centre creates a funnel that sucks in everything, including contaminated air from outside the burn zone. It's possible it gets sucked high up into the atmosphere. Ma'am we need to know if this is true. But the only thing way we're going to test it is to reproduce those conditions in the field.'

'What would that involve?'

'It would require a very unusual experiment – plus the help of the army.'

'Then do it.'

06: 01/ 03h50

A convoy of army trucks was trundling through the valleys of the Gypsum Hills, where northwest Oklahoma bordered southern Kansas. The trucks were so big they filled the two-lane roads. Overhead, in the pre-dawn sky, an aerial cohort of Sikorsky Pavehawks, Chinook 47Ds and VH-3D Seakings shattered the quiet of the rolling farmland.

Hedda Kingsmill, aged eleven, looked out of her bedroom window and saw the vast spectacle of thunder and light approaching. She knew exactly what it was: it was the giant flying saucer she recalled from the film, *Close Encounters of the Third Kind*. And it was racing towards her. She shrieked with excitement, ran downstairs and into the yard, then stood still as a flagpole, to watch the gargantuan circus invade her father's farm. Her gaze swiveled into the sky as a Seaking descended right over her head. Then she bolted back into the house and ran upstairs and into her parents' bedroom, shrieking, 'We're being invaded!'

Mom was adjusting the bedside fan onto Pop's face. Hedda had never known Pop to be sick before in her life. She had never seen Mom look so worried. Suddenly, there was an almighty hammering on the door.

Mom's face was tearful as she patted Hedda's head: 'You look after Pop for me while I go see what they want.'

Hedda felt very grown up as she picked up the cloth from the basin, wrung it out and mopped the sweat from Pop's brow and cheeks. She was careful how she did it because of the rash. But no matter how gentle she was, Pop's skin bled and he moaned. The moaning frightened her and she began to cry. Mom was calling out to her from downstairs as heavy steps came running up the stairs. Two huge figures came into the bedroom, wearing space suits. One of them put his gloved hand around her shoulder. 'Come along, sweetheart. It's time to take you all to the field hospital.'

She began to wail, trying to get away from the gloved hand, trying to run downstairs and find her Mom.

*

In his bedroom, Mark Stanwyck was woken by the telephone ringing. It sounded as loud as a fire alarm. He grabbed at it, still clumsy with drowsiness, knocking it painfully against his ear. A strange voice asked, 'Mr. Stanwyck?'

'Ummh – huh!'

Stanwyck couldn't quite focus, however hard he blinked, on the time on the illuminated face of his digital alarm clock. He had had a few beers before hitting the sack. But he didn't think that explained it. It was pitch black outside. *Fuck!* It had to be the middle of the night. He jerked into a sitting position, murmuring. 'Who the hell –?'

'Piers Zoco.'

Even in his drowsy state it rang a bell.

'You e-mailed some artwork to us – *The New York Times*.'

'Oh, sure – *The New York Times*?'

'That's right.'

'Oh shit... I mean... Godalmighty!'

He rushed to the light switch, returned to sit naked on the side of his bed. The light was blinding. 'I thought – you know – the military again.'

'That's okay. I realize that the material you sent was gathered under conditions of duress.'

'You could say that.'

'I'm sorry to wake you in the early hours. But if we're to consider using it, we don't have much time. Convince me that the pictures are factual and representative.'

The New York Times! Piers Zoco – and he's asking me to convince him!

'You want to run with my piece?'

'There are questions I want to ask you. First, as to the material, I need to be sure about its credibility.'

'Believe me, it's real.'

'Well, we know that some very alarming things are happening. Meanwhile, the government is being economical with the details.'

'You have a nice way of putting it.'

'We like the pics. But I want to hear some more about the circumstances in which you took them.'

Stanwyck brought his inchoate thoughts under control: *Watch these guys!*

'I don't want you to just take the pictures and cut me out of the article.'

'Nobody is suggesting that. What I want is for you to explain a little more of the circumstances in which you took the pictures. You were arrested when you landed the balloon?'

'We spent the rest of the day and night under interrogation by the military police but they couldn't establish anything.'

'How come they let you keep your cameras and film?'

'Are you kidding me? They took the tapes out of the camera and the JVC. But I'd already uploaded everything into my home computer.'

'They didn't suspect you'd do just that?'

'Why should they? I stuffed my cell phone and notebook into a bag of ballast and dumped them over the side while we were descending. No way could they tell I had already posted the shots. When they let us go, I had to rush home and check the pics had arrived. I copied everything into a new notebook and deleted the shit from my home computer, so they wouldn't be able to tell it had ever been. The stuff I sent you, it was just some representatives as soon as I was able to do so.'

There was a pause. Stanwyck thought, maybe Zoco is not alone over there. Shit – maybe the Feebies are standing next to him.

'Look, Mark - I'm not committing, you understand. But if we did, we'd expect exclusivity.'

'Well, I don't think–'

'I know you must have sent the artwork elsewhere.'

Damn right I did. The Post, the LA Times.

'We have a deal – but only if we're guaranteed exclusivity.'

He was willing his heart to come down off the moon. 'And if I give you that?'

'On that basis, I'm prepared to talk terms.'

'I have plenty more to tell. I've been involved in this since day one. Lots of other pics and stories from way earlier, when the epidemic was first breaking. Folks looking frightened out of their wits. Queues outside doctor's offices. Deserted farms.' He surfaced, like a diver needing to take a breath. His teeth were chattering, but he no longer gave a damn. 'I have the full story of the index case – with pictures.'

'Can I take it that, in principle, we have you exclusively?'

'I want a guarantee you'll go with the slant I'm taking.' He was proud of himself saying that.

'What slant is that?'

'I guess you could call it doomsday arising out of corporate greed and perverted science.'

'That's quite a line.'

'You don't agree with it?'

'There's the question of terrorists. But I daresay we could find some scientists who'd be willing to talk to us. Get them to help us with background information on the entity itself. You know anything about that?'

'Not much.'

'Our sources have confirmed that it's man-made, a genetically engineered bioweapon of mass destruction.'

'Shee—it!'

'Well, before we agree a thematic slant, we really need to talk some more. I'll get back to you and we'll figure how best to cobble it together. We'll be splicing in hard data on the science with what you'll be writing. How quickly can you get your material to me?'

'How soon are you going to press?'

'Tomorrow. If you can get your material to us on time.'

'Front page?'

'Every page.'

*

From an MH-53J Pave Low at 10,000 feet, Will Grant stared down into the confusion of choppers and ground vehicles as the armada of giant balloons began to emerge into billowy existence in the dawn light. He shook his head, not quite believing the experiment that was under way. Yet it was a vital experiment. Setting fire to the holes was central to their current strategy in dealing with the entity and they simply had to know if this was, in reality, making the situation worse. The President herself had authorized the balloon experiment, thanks to the influence of Patrick Moran. In part its bizarre nature reflected the fact they had no more than twenty-four hours to plan and prepare it, a day in which they had gone without sleep. It had been his idea to pick out two affected farms, close enough for ambient atmospheric conditions to be similar yet with sufficient geographic separation from one another to make the comparison work. He returned to his bucket seat amid the group of military and air force coordinators.

Will primed Josie to be ready. She was heading the study of the control farm. Over Farm 1, red plumes of dye were rising from the ground and dispersing over the affected wheat fields, the belly-mounted cameras capturing the vectors of wind direction and dispersal velocity at time zero. Within minutes, a red haze was obscuring the circles that spread like a gigantic pox through the fields of crops. And through this battlefield haze, the first of the two armadas of balloons were already rising, with their wire baskets of experimental animals slung underneath them. The test and control Sikorskys and Chinooks were in constant touch with the coordinators as they painstakingly juggled into position, taking care not to snag the guide cables that were tethering balloons, some to the ground and others to the underbellies of the hovering choppers overhead. Within five minutes, they had written off a balloon that was in danger of snagging a rotor blade.

The coordinating scientists were now hovering two miles above the test areas, waiting for the ground-based transports to clear the two areas and their surrounding hinterlands of people. Immediately, military vehicles poured in, manned by biosafety-garbed figures, who, even when viewed with binoculars from this mile-high elevation, resembled ants. A second battery of hot air balloons began to take off the ground upwind of the second farm, within minutes assuming half a dozen different altitudes. As the uppermost balloons rose to a height of a mile, Will called Josie again, then kept the line open so they could coordinate the monitoring of Farm 2, where no fires would be blazing.

'Your group in position?'

'Primed and ready.'

'You have the wind direction at all relevant elevations?'

'We have it.'

'Your mobile group primed?'

'In position.'

'Okay, Josie. When I give the word, cut free all balloons - you getting this?'

'Loud and clear.'

Will signaled the lead pilot in the cluster of three Apaches. Within moments, the infected field of Farm 1 exploded into flame. Through the binoculars, he watched as the rivulets and streams of fire rushed and coalesced into lakes, the lakes further coalescing into an ocean of lurid orange over the kerosene-impregnated landscape. The effect on air movements over the circles was immediate, and dramatic. Black smoke was already billowing into the sky, melding with the red of the flares, and rising several hundred feet into the sky.

06: 01/ 08h40

They timed it so they hit Mike McCann's house and the Bionano Inc factory simultaneously. The FBI agent, Willson, headed the raid at the modern brick and stucco two-story house in the suburbs of Reno while O'Keefe headed the mainly techno squad at the offices and factory complex. As expected, McCann was not at home. They had already put out an APB for the still-missing black BMW. And now, poised on the front step of the large detached house, Willson gave last-minute instructions to the men and women in white overalls, and wearing white masks, caps and overshoes.

'We're looking for contacts of any kind, personal, business, academic. Mail, fax, e-mail, telex, telephone, texts – gather up everything, no matter how trivial it looks. Everything – and I mean *everything* – bagged and tagged. Quick as you can. Let's do it!'

They broke through the solid oak front door with fire axes, then fanned out through lobby, reception rooms, closet and kitchen. Willson took the stairs two at a time and located the two-room office complex on the second floor. He hauled up the tech team, instructing them to make a detailed inventory.

The office complex was a ramshackle mess. Books and journals spilled over every horizontal surface. They had to fight for space with papers, scientific, letters and scribbles. It had to be exactly as McCann had left it en route for the meeting in San Diego. Three floor-based computers, linked to big flat screens, reared like islands out of the flotsam and jetsam. Willson cursed McCann's lack of self discipline, hunting through the garbage of the scientist's untidy mind.

He said, 'Put anything that resembles designs, drawings, biochemical formulae, into a separate collection. The same applies to anything weird.'

He didn't specify what he meant by weird. He felt so out of his depth, the whole shebang looked pretty weird to him. But the very untidiness also struck him as a stroke of luck. McCann couldn't have known that he wouldn't be returning. He hadn't had time for a tidy-up. And computers could tell the right kinds of people so very much.

'I want you to take cams and stills of everything, just as it looks. Close-ups of anything interesting, which probably means everything. I want you to bag the computers, disks and anything related, as a specific unit. Get them on the first flight to Quantico. I want to hear back soon as they find anything interesting – you got this – any time of the day or night.'

He paused to look at photographs on the wall: McCann's kid, Sean, all the stages from baby to present – and guess who was coddling him! Divorce had not caused Mike McCann to throw away images of his ex-wife. There were just about as many pictures of her as there were of the kid.

*

Kay was sitting in a wood-slatted chair around a bleached garden table in the back-porch of what had been the rangers' station. The time was close to midnight. She was sipping iced tea she had just poured for herself from a jug placed in the center of the table. Even in the dark, waves of lukewarm heat washed in from the surrounding desert. The FBI agent, O'Keefe, had shepherded her out of BSL-2, past the startled faces of the scientists and technicians who, like Kay herself, had been working late. She was so tired she could hardly grasp what was happening. And now O'Keefe was leaning back against the closed door, his head down, in what appeared to be a reflective, maybe even an embarrassed, silence.

Willson, who sat directly opposite her, looked curiously elated. His hands wrestled with one another on the table surface, reminding her of a famous picture by Albrecht Durer.

'Professor McCann, I've been coming down hard on you, and I am sorry I had to do that. You know what I think? I think you're the injured party here. You're a good woman, doing your best to make sense of a nightmare.

You've been tainted by association with that arrogant son-of-a-bitch.'

He was so wound up he was unable to sit for long. He got to his feet and paced here and there, as if turning something over in his mind. He wandered to the edge of the veranda, turned his back to her, so his figure was outlined against the gloom. He spoke to her, without turning to face her. 'I need to find out as much as I can about your ex-husband, the way his mind works, how this figured in his line of work.'

Kay had to think for several moments before answering his question. She said, 'Mike can be both idiotic and arrogant. But there's no way he'd stoop to doing something that endangered people's lives.'

Willson was silent.

'You're asking me to recall ancient history?' She glanced over at O'Keefe, who had sunk his head in his chest. She said, 'Mike was a post-grad from Caltech, only just moved to Berkeley, when I started as an undergraduate. You get a whole mill of rumors in a situation like that. Already the word was out that he was brilliant. Berkeley headhunted him from even before he completed his Ph.D. I guess we were in awe of him. You ask me how his mind works? I can't pretend to answer that. Nobody ever knows what is in another person's mind. But I can tell you what interests Mike – and I think it was what interested him from the very beginning – which is genetic engineering.'

Willson's body stiffened, like a soldier who had just been ordered to attention.

Kay tried to sip at her tea, her hands trembling. *They have something on Mike.* She sensed it, her fingers finding the wedding ring. Without thinking, she began to twirl the ring around her finger.

O'Keefe cut in. 'Do you hate your ex-husband?'

'Of course I don't!'

'Do you still love him?'

'No.'

The two agents fell silent, considering her replies, no doubt wondering whether or not they believed her.

'What I'm trying to explain is that it wasn't enough for Mike merely to observe nature. He had to interfere with it. He had to *control* it.'

Willson remained silent, staring out the dark. It was O'Keefe, again, who asked the next question.

'What does that mean – to control nature?'

'He studied different disciplines. Biochemistry, molecular genetics, evolutionary development – you name it. He had to be a master of every relevant discipline. Then, when he knew enough, when he figured he understood life, he looked at how science could go about changing it.'

Willson's turned to face her. 'Isn't that a very arrogant thing to do?'

'It's what we're been doing since we first herded animals and grew crops.'

He came over, towered over her seated form. 'So what went wrong between you and him?'

'Maybe I was selfish.'

'You're not making sense.'

'He believed he loved me. But it wasn't love. It was... I guess the best description of it is some kind of intoxication.'

'Some people, like some poets maybe, use words like that to describe love.'

'I know what love is. It didn't feel the way love should feel.'

Willson returned. He slumped down noisily on the seat directly facing her. 'People confabulate when it comes to things like love. Don't lie to me, Professor. I know there was more to it than that.'

'Like the fact he saw other women?'

'Like some guys have an itch they have to scratch – and some guys have a permanent nettle rash.'

She was silent.

'Okay. So let's get back to this idea – tell me how your ex-husband likes to interfere with nature?'

'Mr. Willson! I know what you're thinking, but I doubt that you can put my ex-husband into one of your pigeon-hole categories of offenders.'

'Professor – can we come down to practicalities. What's McCann's current scientific interest within the field of genetic engineering?'

'Nanotechnology. Living machines. Machines so small you can only see them under the microscope – or even the electron microscope.'

He stared at her. 'You don't think that might be relevant?'

Kay's head fell.

'Professor – I don't think you can deny that it is absolutely and positively relevant?'

She said nothing.

'We have people – our own experts – looking into that right now. But I'm interested in something else about your ex-husband. Something you should have owned up to right from the start, but instead you were mighty careful to keep it to yourself. When you guys divorced, he ended up in hospital.'

Kay felt frozen into her chair.

Willson pressed her. 'He had a breakdown. But then you knew all about that. I mean to say, that was some flip. And it was the divorce that did it, wasn't it?'

'The divorce upset both of us very deeply.'

'Divorcees don't usually end up in a loony bin!'

'You're allowing your prejudices to show.'

'Then enlighten me.'

'You can't just pin people down to categories. I know it's what the profilers have to do. But it's never really that simple. People are individuals. They react differently to things – to stresses. Mike was impossible to live with from the beginning. Great innovative intelligence can be a curse like that. He's extremely creative. He's likely to come up with two or three new ideas in a single pot-blown or whisky-sodden night.'

'He took drugs?'

'He craved excitement of any sort, new sensations, new experiences. I was the mother of a demanding boy. Sean needed normality.'

'Mike was half crazy and then he flipped, all the way. He stayed crazy after that, didn't he? He was a guy with a whole hive of bees in his bonnet.'

'He was never crazy. He was – he still is – vulnerable.'

Willson leaned over the table staring at her. 'Mrs. McCann!'

'You know I'm divorced.'

'You still wear his ring.'

'*My* ring. I was married. I have a son. I love my son and it reassures him to see me wearing the ring.'

'You stayed in regular contact with your ex-husband.'

'We share an important piece of our lives. We share our son.'

'You met up with him here.'

'He came here for Sean – to take him to Wyoming.'

'Because he knew, better than anybody else, what was coming?'

'Because he was a worried parent.'

'We asked the psychologist, Dr. Minkowsky, to draw up a profile, assuming we might not be dealing with terrorists. Let me quote you her psychological profile: "*A scientist, male, in his 30's or 40s. Probable history of mental instability. Maybe an obvious mental breakdown? Extremely capable, a technical genius.*"' Willson compressed his lips into a taut line. 'That remind you of anybody?'

Kay shook her head. 'Mr. Willson! I know you have to ask these questions. But you've gotten Mike wrong.'

His voice was low-pitched, but keen as a knife. 'Now you listen to me. I'm going to tell you something. My daughter was a freshman student at UCLA. She was one of those who died from this goddam bug during the first week.'

'I – I'm really sorry to hear that.'

O'Keefe came forward. He took some papers out of a briefcase. He slid them over to Kay, until they touched her trembling fingers. He returned, wordless, to his vigil, leaning against the door. Willson leaned over the bare wood until his face was only inches from hers: 'Read them!'

She glanced at the papers but she was so nervous her eyes couldn't keep still enough to focus.

'Go ahead!'

'What are they?'

'Let me explain exactly what they are – where they come from. We spent all day going over your ex-husband's house for evidence. We took away three computers and passed them to our experts at Quantico. It didn't take long – these guys know what they are doing. Clever boy – your ex-husband. At least you've got give him that. We had to enlist the help of the NSA. You probably know already that NSA captures every electronic message ever sent from, or received into, this country. It becomes a lot easier when they can use those supercomputers to focus down on a single e-mail address.'

'I have no idea what you're implying.'

'An irregular series of financial payments. It started about nine months ago. But not into Mike's company account – his not-too-healthy account, according to his bank manager's reckoning. Oh, no, no, no – these payments headed off into a whole bucketful of offshore accounts. The kind of accounts that carry no names, only numbers. But every number traced right back to your ex-husband.'

'No!'

'There's absolutely no doubt about it. We're talking about huge sums of money, all unexplained, and all heading Mike's way. And from his e-mail records, we've tracked them to... well, you name it... the Cayman Islands, Belize, Liberia, Bermuda. The guy is smart. Every time we ended up losing them. NSA lost them. Imagine that! Money in – money out. Gone where? You asking me? Well you've told me all I want to know. The guy's a genius. Okay – he's a genius. A genius like that, he can make money go anywhere and nowhere – like an e-mail that leads us to the middle of the Atlantic Ocean.'

Kay's mind had gone blank. She inhabited a three-dimensional space of white chaos, white chaos running away from her in every direction.

'Smart, huh? You know what the techs tell me. A guy would have to be a mathematical genius as well as incredibly computer literate to brainstorm that. But then that's exactly what you've been describing.' He laughed without humor. 'But hey – you haven't even asked me how much he was paid?'

Her eyes closed.

'More than five million dollars. Hey, let's go for scientific accuracy – close to five million and a quarter. Enough to buy him shelter somewhere nice and cozy. Maybe somewhere in the Middle East – what do you think?'

She was a statue, unmoving.

'You know what, Professor – or shall I call you Kay? Hell – I want to call you Kay. Everybody does that, don't they – everybody you work with calls you Kay.' There was a movement of his eyes so fast and subtle, she might not have caught it, but it was definitely directed to the silent O'Keefe. 'You see, Kay, there are people who think I should resign my job as FBI Special Agent in Charge of this investigation because of what happened to my daughter. But I was given this position of responsibility by the Critical Incident Response Group at Quantico. In this capacity, I am answerable to nobody other than the Strategic Information and Operations Center, the very SIOC who appointed you lead scientist. You know what that actually means? I have a line straight through to the FBI director, Jon Lilley. I have no intention of surrendering my job. I intend to carry on until I've nailed that bastard, whose ring you've been twiddling around your finger.'

06: 02/ 00h05

Her limbs were trembling while she was knocking on Will's bedroom door:

'Who is it?'

'It's me. Kay.'

When he opened the door she almost fell through it into the room.

'Kay—?'

'I'm so relieved that you're still awake.'

He was naked except for blue boxer shorts. He'd been lying propped against the bed head, listening to Charles Mingus – *Ah Um*. She looked away while he took a few seconds to throw on a clean white T-shirt and blue jeans.

He spoke as he was dressing. 'I doubt I'll even bother to sleep... not tonight. I'm waiting for the results of the balloon experiment.'

That calm voice – that familiar look in his blue eyes! Her head was shaking. She fought to control it.

'Kay – my God! What is it?'

She shuddered. 'Oh, Will – I'm off the case.'

He put his arm around her shoulders, supported her, guided her so she was sitting on the side of the bed. 'When you're good and ready, tell me.'

She took a deep breath, shuddered. 'I'm suspended. I've got to pack my things. They're taking me to LA. First thing, tomorrow.' She laughed, in a momentary hysteria. 'First thing today!'

'They're taking you away from here?'

'FBI headquarters. More interrogation.'

'They can't seriously believe that you're involved?'

'It's Mike – he's still missing. They raided his house. They found evidence of payments of money into offshore banks. More than five million dollars.'

'Jesus!'

'Of course I don't believe it.' She just about had control now. 'I've got to go wash my face – do you mind?'

He gently let her go.

Kay threw cold water over her face in his sink. She dried herself off with his towel. She peered at her grief-ridden features in his wall-mounted mirror.

Oh shit, shit, shit!

She spoke to him, to the image of him in the mirror. 'They claim his business was going under. They think... Well, you can guess what they think.'

She watched him shake his head from side to side. She felt his hands take hold of her shoulders. She heard him exclaim: 'This is ridiculous. Don't you worry! I'm going to do something about it.' He led her back to the edge of the bed. 'I'm calling Moran – right now.'

'I don't want you to get involved.'

She just couldn't lift her face to look at him directly. When she blew her nose it made her feel faint. She leaned for support against him, with the wad of tissues still in her hand. 'With what they've found, they've no choice other than to probe it. You've got to stay well clear of this – take over as lead scientist when I'm gone.'

'I'm not just going to let them take you.'

He stood up and lifted her face to look at him. Her muscles felt stiff and waxy at the same time. He put his arms around her and embraced her. She was ashamed to think, in that comforting moment: *He's used to it. He must have gone through times like this with Marje.* He kissed her on her brow.

She said, 'I'm not going to sleep, any more than you are. Would you mind if I just stayed here with you tonight?'

He hugged her, wordlessly.

'You don't have to stop talking. I'd like it if you just talked to me.'

'What would you like me to talk about?'

'Not work. Just the ordinary things.'

'Like what?'

'The things you like. Music. I know you like music. Talk to me about the music you like.'

'I don't know what to say.'

'Please try.'

He was silent for a little while longer. She could see that he was thinking about her, what she wanted from him. He said, 'You want me to put the music back on?'

She shrugged. Leaned in against his chest.

He leaned over, still holding her in the embrace of his left arm, and got the tape to play again. 'You look like, maybe, you could do with a drink?'

She nodded.

'Something strong?'

She shook her head.

'Wine then – it's all I've got other than whisky. Chardonnay okay?'

'Please.'

He had to let her go to untwist the screw cap. He poured her a generous glass. He patted the top of the bed, so she could sit propped up in the same place he had been reclining when she had first entered the bedroom. He pulled up a chair so they could face each other while they talked. He poured himself another whisky.

Her eyes moved from the whisky in his hand to his eyes.

He said, 'I don't know where to start.'

'Why don't you tell me more about yourself. How you got interested in jazz.'

'It'll bore you half to death.'

'Maybe I want to be bored half to death.'

'Like where I come from – my family?'

She finished her glass with a gulp. She held it out to him for replenishing. 'You know, it's the first time you've ever talked to me about your family, other than Janie.'

He refilled her glass. 'What do we think we're doing here, Kay?'

'I don't know. I don't even care that I don't know.'

He laughed. 'You know I like you.'

'It's the first time I've heard you say it.'

'You know damn well I've liked you from the moment I first saw your hair color match your eyes in the light of the EM.'

Her voice was soft, liquidly jittery. 'You're kinda nice, too.'

'Really?'

'Yeah – really kinda nice!'

He grinned at her.

She said, 'So why don't you come and sit here next to me and hold me again?'

'I gotta top up my glass first.'

He topped up his glass, took a swig, came back over beside her. She said, 'Don't stop talking.'

'Because you really like my voice?'

She smiled, wanly. 'Tell me how you came to like jazz.'

'You think boredom could actually be fatal?'

'Stop teasing me.'

'Okay. It was all down to two uncles, a Harry, trumpet player, and JJ, who played tenor sax.'

She inhaled. She just loved hearing him talk about things other than their work. She hugged him around his waist.

'You feeling a little better?'

She snuggled up closer to him. 'Tell me more... your two uncles, Harry, the sax, and JJ, the trumpet.'

'It was the other way round. But —! Well, you know, the funny thing was I never knew anything about their music until I met them at my grandmother's funeral.'

She laughed without thinking about it. 'Harry and JJ, they were good?'

'Really good – as I subsequently found out. Professionals. To make a long story short, I heard them play. That was when I started to take notice. I found this record store called 23rd Precinct. I trawled the racks for albums with horns on the cover.'

'Give me an example.'

'Girl from Iponema. Stan Getz – he played sax.'

She hugged him tighter.

'The tone he found – it was kinda unbelievable. Like, maybe like your breath on my face right now, with a sigh attached.'

'That's beautiful.'

'Maybe it was the first time I thought about music like that – like realizing that music could be something that beautiful.'

'23rd Precinct educated you.'

'I couldn't get enough of what I was hearing. I just drank it all in. I still liked blues and soul. But nothing really hit me like jazz. It had the resonance for me.'

'How old were you?'

'Fourteen... maybe fifteen.'

She brushed his right bicep with the tips of her fingers. Her touch caused his arm to jerk.

'I decided I had to learn how to play for myself.'

'You learned to play?'

'I borrowed an old acoustic guitar from my cousin. A few of us ... I guess we just got it together. My brother-in-law's younger brother, Joe. Joe played electric bass. I happened to be sitting next to the amp. Wow – the first time I felt it! It felt like the music was coming up through my feet.'

She laughed aloud, clinging still tighter.

'I was probably fifteen or sixteen by then. The age when you start asking yourself, "Hey – what's pushing my buttons?" When I thought about it, the tracks I was cool with – it was always the horn sounds.'

Kay could hardly believe this was the man she knew as Will talking. Somehow, without needing to look at him, she knew he was smiling.

'If you analyze music, everything about it, the voices, sax, lead guitar, every one of them does something a little bit different to your soul. But if you think about what makes your feet want to tap. What makes you want to just get up there and dance. What gives you the real rush. The base gives you that.'

Charles Mingus was playing *Self Portrait in Three Colors*. She kissed him lightly on the shoulder: a butterfly kiss.

'You ever see Miles Davis play?'

He was holding her more loosely now, in a more relaxed way. She noticed his eyes were blinking very slowly.

'I saw him, once, on stage. He just stood absolutely still. The horn was pointed down. His head was over to one side. He was there – in that kind of special place. That's the place in all of us that lets us feel the magic of music. The passion, the rhythm, the timing – it all comes out of that place.'

She tightened her hold on him, clung to him like she never wanted to let him go.

06: 02/ 07h12

Will hesitated for several moments, staring down at the phone on his working surface. Kay was more than an hour gone. He had looked into the back seat of the black FBI Lincoln and seen her face puffy from lack of sleep looking back at him. He had remembered his promise to her and shown her that by the act of pressing the flat of his hand against the glass, her hand coming up to meet his gesture, both of them holding it there until the very moment the car took off. *Oh man!* He'd do something – he wouldn't rest until he got her back, got her reinstated – her courage and contribution recognized.

Blinking now, forcing the memory from his tired mind, he refocused all of his attention onto the fresh data that had arrived a short while earlier by fax.

He read it through again, to make sure there was no mistake. Then he picked up the telephone, dialed the number. Four beats, then he heard the answering voice:

'Moran!'

Will knew that Moran was at the White House. He had been recalled by the President as a matter of urgency. 'Patrick – this is Will Grant. You asked to be informed immediately if we had the results.'

'The balloon experiment?'

'Yes. A summary is being encrypted so I can e-mail it to you. But I thought I'd better call you with the news.' Will rubbed at his brow with the heel of his free hand. He felt so shattered, he was almost stumbling over his words. 'I'm afraid it's not good. We found 68% lethality in the test group of animals.'

'Is there any room for doubt?'

'None at all. The mortality in the control animals was 18%.'

'I'll be damned!'

In the silence, while Moran considered the full implications, Will heard a commotion behind him and turned to see Josie standing in the doorway. She was making throat-cutting signals with her hands – a serious problem, judging by her agitated state. He shook his head, lifted a finger. Moran's voice had fallen to a monotone. 'So you were right. The fires made things worse?'

'I don't think there's any doubt about that.'

'I'm going to have to inform the President. I don't mind telling you, things are already white hot here. She's making a public broadcast.'

'Because of this?'

'Because *The New York Times* is breaking with the story. We had advance warning but we had no idea how bad it was going to be.'

'I'm sorry to add to the President's worries. But there's more.'

'Go ahead.'

'Terrestrial ecosystems – I've been doing some background checking. I'm talking about deserts, Patrick. Deserts form in the subtropical high-pressure zones between the latitudes of 15 and 25 north and south. Those latitudes play an important part in the general system of atmospheric circulation.'

'Give me the punch line.'

'What it means is a desert location, given thermal rises and meteorological forces, is the perfect location for this entity to spread.'

'To spread like – how far?'

'Locally, to begin with – but given time, and add to that the effect of torching the circles, pan-continentally. Then maybe even globally.'

Moran was silent for a few moments.

'Does Professor McCann agree with your conclusions?'

'I can't say since she's been taken to LA for questioning by the FBI. We desperately need her back here. Maybe you could put in a word?'

A beat of hesitation, which told Will that Moran already knew about Kay. 'I'll see what I can do.'

Will heard the normally mild-tempered Patrick Moran swearing as he dropped the phone back onto its base. He turned to Josie. 'What the hell is it?'

'You seen the latest Landsats?'

He shook his head.

'I think you should go right now and take a look.'

He scrubbed the exhausted mask of his face with his hands. On a sudden impulse, he went to the stainless steel sink and stuck his head under the ice-cold water. He shook the water out of his hair and followed Josie as she led at a run in the direction of General Hauk's office.

*

In the Oval Office, Patrick Moran kept back in the shadows as President Dickinson waited for the cameraman to make a last-minute adjustment to his tripod distance, to ensure that the twin standards of the Stars and Stripes and the presidential seal were an artful frame in the background.

He heard the President ask: 'Are you happy with the shot?'

The question was directed not at the cameraman but at Arnie Schutz, her Chief of Staff. He replied, 'Yes, Ma'am.'

Dickinson rested her hands on the leather surface of the Resolute Desk, made out of the timbers of a British ship and presented to President Rutherford by Queen Victoria in 1880. Outside of the window, the sprinklers were already working over the grass, the water-laden air creating a miniature rainbow in the bright sunlight. Around her the room, an elegant composition of oil paintings, Chippendale chairs and eighteenth century mahogany furniture, felt strangely still, as if holding its breath. Moran raised his eyebrows, lifted an arm in a gesture to catch her attention.

She waved him to come forward. He slid the single hand-written sheet with its ten lines of summary over the leather, so it rested next to the early morning issue of the *Times*. It detailed the results of the balloon experiment the President herself had championed over army resistance, together with Dr. Grant's conclusions about potential spread from plants to people through inhalation. Her eyes fell away, one hand tapping with a 'signing pen', which, like the sugar packs that came with the coffee, was imprinted with the seal of office.

Moran caught the slight movement as the cameraman tensed: on instructions from Schutz, the woman holding a reflective silver screen adjusted her stance: the light mellowed over Dickinson's face. He saw every nuance of her startled reaction: the summary had shocked her, just as it had shocked him. Their eyes met in the instant before Moran pulled his gaze away. Through Moran's mind went visions of all the fires that had been burned in the affected desert and farms since that had become recommended policy – recommended by Dickinson's own appointee, Fred Duhan, at EPA.

She called out: 'How much time to go?'

Schutz answered: 'Five minutes.'

She whispered in Schutz's ear: 'See to it they sack Duhan – immediately!'

He whispered back, 'Consider it done, Ma'am.'

Moran watched as her attention returned to the opening article in *The New York Times*. The central picture, taking up two thirds of the front page, showed army techs, wearing field protection gear, sitting in the cabs of two bulldozers that were about to push a mountain of soil over a pit containing human bodies. The four-inch caption read:

WHAT'S REALLY GOING ON IN AMERICA?

He was familiar with the opening lines, by journalist Mark Stanwyck: *The scenes you are witnessing above don't come from a horror film - and they don't come from some refugee camp in Africa, hit by cholera or the Ebola virus. They are taking place right here and now in America.*

*

Will was sharing the monitor in Hauk's office with Josie, who had opened up the Landsat 7 gateway on Johansson's former computer. She was clicking through the Mojave section. He murmured. 'There are new circles cropping up over an ever widening radius.'

'You haven't seen anything yet. NASA called me. Hauk has had them taking closer views. Thematic mapping down to the very smallest circles. Down to 25 yards.' She flicked through grid references as she was talking. 'Now, look at this.'

Will stared at a particular circle she was highlighting with the pointer. At first he wasn't certain what he was looking at. Then he saw it and his jaw dropped open. It was just a half mile down the track from where he was sitting.

*

'Ten seconds ... nine ... eight ...'

President Dickinson took a breath, nodded, the cameras rolled.

She spoke: 'My fellow Americans. I understand and deeply sympathize with your worries about what is happening in our country. So it is my duty to inform you that in the considered opinion of this government and our expert scientific advisors, we face a serious problem. I know there has been speculation, even paranoia, in certain quarters, that this is the result of a deliberate ploy, or a mistake, on the part of military scientists. Let me assure you, absolutely and categorically, that there is no truth to these rumors. What we face is a hitherto unknown threat, a biological agent designed with specialist knowledge and wicked intelligence combined with utter disregard to loss of life.'

Moran had moved from the Oval Office to join Oliver "Rolly" Trivers, the Press Officer, as he scanned a battery of screens under five clocks showing different time zones. The President's words were being transmitted to a giant screen behind the podium in the pressroom, known as the "Gaggle Room", where more than a hundred journalists were taking notes. Trivers was concerned that global American trade was becoming affected. Half a dozen countries had halted incoming flights from southwest American airports, leaving dozens of business people stranded in the no-man's land of intermediate stops. The Secretary of State for Foreign Affairs had been dispatched on a mission of shuttle diplomacy. But it was no easy matter to calm the growing concern in foreign countries when the situation wasn't adequately controlled at home.

'You know,' Trivers whispered, 'that Duhan's just been fired?'

'Yeah – I heard.'

'Question is, is it gonna be enough to satisfy the thirst for blood out there?'

Moran shook his head. He knew that what concerned Trivers just as much as the formal address was the more intimate briefing, from leading experts, that would follow in this same room. They could anticipate some awkward questions. Another monitor panned the lawn on the north side of the White House, an area known as "Gravel Beach", where several camera teams, including CNN, were laying the pitch for a series of live broadcasts.

The CNN coverage would go out to more than 100 countries. Equally problematic was the fact that more than half the journalists came from outside America, fanning the flames of a growing international media paranoia. Something had to be done to stop America being treated as a pariah state.

Trivers turned up the volume on the President's words:

'I have been personally involved in the response to this threat since the beginning. I know enough not to underestimate it. But it would be counterproductive to exaggerate it also. This is a great nation - the greatest nation on Earth. We have faced serious threats before and we have always overcome them. We have the best military organization and the best scientists. So you may rest assured that we are going to defeat this too.'

Patrick Moran murmured under his breath: 'Jesus, Ma'am – I sincerely hope so!'

4

Exponential

Top Secret
Operation Globalnet
Surveillance Mode: E-mail
Retrograde analysis: Index minus 02/12
DELICATE SOURCE: RESTRICTION CODE:
eyes alpha
L of E/ he→ee

Dear God, Lyse,

I'm not sure this will get to you since there has been a tremendous increase in the security here. Agents from the local government are everywhere, armed to the teeth. One of our technicians is dead and two more are desperately ill. They won't allow anybody to leave the agricultural station. They're insisting on bringing in doctors and nurses to treat the sick in a makeshift facility on site. It appears that we have become a plague zone.

You can imagine the impact this is having on morale. But what worries me even more is the source of the outbreak. E.S. was conveniently off campus when all of this blew up. I have the sinking feeling we won't be seeing him again until this outbreak is contained. People are talking about a viral hemorrhagic fever, but I saw the look on the epidemiologist's face when he saw the victims. I had the distinct impression he was out of his depth.

The military have thrown a cordon sanitaire around the facility, including the little harbor. They have confiscated computers with in-built modems and cell phones. This is my only outlet - for as long as I can keep it hidden. Don't be too surprised if there are no more transmissions for a while.

I love you all,
H.

06: 04/ 08h45

'Professor – time to wake up!'

Kay heard the voice but it had no meaning. She was a child looking into the knowing face of an older woman.

'Professor!'

That irritating interruption again. Her eyes blinked open. She was sitting up, her head jammed into the angle between upholstery and hard metal in one comer of the bench seat at the back of a large car. 'You with us, now?' She was looking at the back of a man's head, a man with premature graying hair, close to white. She recognized the back view of FBI agent O'Keefe, who addressing her from the front passenger seat.

She mumbled, 'Leave me alone.'

'You were talking in your sleep.'

Her eyelids closed again, refusing to open. She was too exhausted to care. She wondered if this was some kind of hallucination. Maybe they had slipped her drugs to make her open up? They seemed to be determined to drive her mad with their interrogations.

'Stop that. Stop asking me those goddamned questions!'

The same questions, over and over. When Willson and O'Keefe had run out of options they had brought in a team of three scientific experts. One day merged with another as it started all over again, variations of the same questions, over and over and over. Her political affiliations, her work prior to the crisis, her work during the crisis, her past interests in environmental issues, her past interests in political issues, her attitude to patriotism, the names of anybody and everybody remotely connected to Mike and to herself, whether professional, social or commercial.

Throughout the nightmare she held onto a single thing, the one thing that kept her grounded, sane: the memory of loving, and being loved by, Will. She had clung to it, like somebody drowning clings to a life buoy. Will, the real Will. She felt his arm around her again. Just holding her. Accepting her. *Oh, Will!* She murmured his name again. Something had happened. At some point, in the middle of the nightmare, her interrogators had disappeared as utterly and completely as if they had evaporated. Somebody had ordered a halt. Had to be somebody very powerful. She had wondered about the President. O'Keefe came into the room where she sat disconsolately in front of a table. He said, 'I'm taking you back, Professor.'

I'm taking you back.

He said other things. He never actually apologized, but there was something in the tone of his voice.

Kay wanted desperately to sink back down into the comfort of the dream she had never fully woken out of.

Suddenly her eyes sprang open again.

'Stop the car!'

'You still dreaming, Professor?'

Through the window she saw they had just cleared the city outskirts. The driver, a man much younger than O'Keefe, had shaved his hair almost to the bone. He was battering through heavy traffic – no possibility of stopping dead.

She heard her own voice sounding too manic: 'O'Keefe, have you got some paper – anything I can scribble on?'

'You serious?'

She squeezed her eyes closed, then blinked them open repeatedly in an attempt to clear the exhaustion from her mind. 'I'm deadly serious. And I don't want you interrupting my thoughts. I've got to write it down while it's still fresh in my mind.'

O'Keefe shrugged. He shuffled around in the glove compartment, gave up. Over his right shoulder he passed her his official notebook. 'This do?'

She grabbed it out of his hand. 'A pencil or pen – anything I can write with?'

His hand was reaching back once more. 'Professor – I sure hope you're making sense.'

'I hope so too.'

She tested the ballpoint – a preliminary scribble. 'Ask Michael Schumacher to slow down so my hand isn't jerking all over the place.'

Notebook open, pen poised, she pressed her brow against the cooling glass of the window to her right. She fished for the memory in her mind: something that had come to her in her dream.

She felt such a flare of excitement, her heart misfired. It was something from a conversation she recalled between Patrick Moran and Anton van den Berg. Patrick had been irritating Anton with one of his naïve questions about the structure of DNA. There had been such a look of impatience on van den Berg's face: flushing at having to dumb down his thinking to Moran's level. He had been attempting to explain the DNA code... only four nucleotide bases ... regard them as letters. Now Kay wrote out the letters in O'Keefe's notebook: G, A, T and C. Just four letters – yet they were the key to creation. And somehow they linked to her dream. Her subconscious mind had made the link between the coding letters of DNA and composers and musical keys. The tune sent with the e-mail to the President had been in the key of G minor. Kay rearranged a two-page spread of the notebook so it made a comfortable platform under her right hand. *The key of G minor.* She ran lines across the two pages. Her fingers tapped out the notes on the paper surface: do, ray, me, fah –. Haltingly, through a mind space that was thick as molasses, she scored them onto the pages – A, B-flat, C.

A sudden thought. 'Mr. O'Keefe?'

'Professor?'

'Where's Willson?'

A pause. 'He's been recalled to Quantico.'

The thought exhilarated her: Willson gone, if only temporarily, was like a dark cloud evaporated by the light of the sun.

She said, 'Thank you!'

'I don't know what you're thanking me for, Professor.'

She smiled as the car threw her sideways, careening onto Highway 15. She held the pen poised, until the dizzy feeling in her head settled. She began, however slowly, to scribble a series of letters. It took her something close to an hour, crossing out the early attempts. Then Kay slapped the notebook with the flat of her left hand.

She muttered: 'Gotcha!'

*

Will grabbed his beeping cell phone. He had been discussing the latest news on the protein sequences with Anton and his Japanese assistant, Sami Kitisato.

He heard Kay's voice: 'Hi, Will.'

'Kay! Hey, am I glad to hear your voice.'

'I'm on my way back.'

'Everything okay? You sound beat.'

'I'm done in, Will. But a little excited too.'

'Kay, there have been developments. Some good news, some bad. The bad will keep until you get here. The good news is Sami's back from Stanford.'

Sami Kitisato had taken the entity to the physicists working the synchrotron.

Kay said, 'She get quality pics?'

'We're hoping so. They're sending us the pics today.'

'Fingers crossed.' Over the phone, Kay's voice hesitated. 'I've got news too. You can tell me I'm crazy. Just an idea I want to pass by you before I make a fool of myself.'

'Uh-huh?'

'I'm talking about it like it's a problem. But it's more of a puzzle. I want to talk to you and Anton about the possibility of a DNA-based musical code.'

'A code?'

'You remember the music that came with the e-mail to the President.'

'Yeah.'

'We know that DNA has a four-letter code. We also know that music, any musical key, is based on a code of one octave.'

'I'm not altogether sure I'm following, but go ahead.'

'Have you got a piece of paper and a pen?'

He motioned to van den Berg. 'Some paper?'

'Let's just look at the first four letters in the key of G minor. That was the key of the tune that came with the e-mail.'

'Okay.'

'The first four notes in the key of G minor are G, A, B-flat and C. Now equate those with the code letters of DNA.'

'Uh-huh.' Will scribbled the letters down horizontally. He pondered aloud, 'G, A, T, C. So what are you saying – the third letter is T not B-flat?'

'Yes.'

Van den Berg and Kitisato were staring closely at his scribbles.

Kay added, 'We know enough about the rules of codes to know that they work to basic assumptions. I've been jotting things down, working out permutations.'

'Okay!'

'I can predict your next question. Which note is the first C? What happens when you go higher – or lower – than the first C? Or when you come to G again, an octave higher?'

'What does happen?'

The line faded a moment and Will realized that Kay was speaking from a moving vehicle. Her voice returned: 'Forget about that for a moment. Codes tend to have a simple basis, from which everything else is extrapolated. The first C heard is the core C. Above the four starting notes, the next four are repeats of the code, the four after that the same. The letters of the notes only correspond for the first four rising. After that they no longer correspond with the letters of the DNA code, only the first four, which establish the basis of the code.'

'How can you say that?'

'Because as best I can figure it, it's the way codes work.'

Will started writing down the coded letters again. 'I think I see –.' He looked over at van den Berg, who was frowning and scratching so hard at his scalp it was becoming inflamed.

'I can remember tunes pretty much as I hear them,' murmured Kay. 'I've been working with the tune and I've already worked out part of a sequence. I might be getting this wrong, but the way I see it there are one or two other assumptions. You have to assume the shortest note - a semi-quaver - is one letter. There are two possible ways in which you can allow for repeats, a full quaver or multiple semi-quavers. That's the trickiest bit – I haven't quite worked it out – the code-breakers will have to earn their keep.'

'The code-breakers?'

'NSA.'

Will sat back in his chair.

He heard Kay inhale, then breathe out. 'I can't pretend to have gotten every letter right. But I'm going to read what I've worked out as a rough draft. It's the coded sequence from the first four lines of the eight-line tune. Tell me how it looks to you.'

Will wrote down the letters as Kay read them out to her. He shared his jottings with the two molecular chemists, who started jabbering among themselves.

He said, 'I can't believe we didn't think of it before.'

'Then I'm not crazy?'

'Don't push it!'

'Are you thinking what I'm thinking?'

Will looked at his colleagues. They looked excited.

He said, 'We talking about a primer.'

'Bingo!'

A primer was a probe you could use to hunt down a specific DNA sequence. It didn't need to be very long. A twenty-letter sequence from somewhere along the gene was all you needed for a primer that would hunt down and find that gene.

Will heard Kay laugh. He heard a man's voice, questioning her, in the background. He had to assume it was FBI. The man was asking her, 'But why? I can't imagine for one moment why those bastards would want to help us.'

He heard Kay's distant reply: 'I don't know why. Who gives a damn! All that matters is we've been given a clue.'

Will interrupted: 'How soon before we can get a full sequence worked out?'

'O'Keefe is passing it on to NSA. He says that if I'm right, this will be easy. The froth on his piss, if you'll excuse the vernacular.'

06: 04/ 12h50

Arafim Sultan climbed out of Agent Maisley's Dodge Durango outside the locked gates of his home. His left arm in a sling, he hobbled around the security fence to inspect the repair in the section damaged by the explosion. 'Thanks for the lift,' he nodded to Maisley. The FBI agent had also arranged for the security fence to be repaired. All of a sudden Sultan began to sweat.

He said, 'It's stupid. I've just got this prickly feeling that every moment I stand out here in the open I'm vulnerable.'

'Go ahead. I'll stick around until you're in the house.'

Behind him the Dodge blocked the drive, its engine purring.

Sultan walked over to the reinforced steel gates and inserted his key. But he didn't turn it. Instead he shoved his hand into the mailbox, reaching for mail.

'Yeeow!' he jerked his hand back, the metal so hot it burned his skin. He picked up the mail, holding it awkwardly against his body, grimacing at the agent who was still watching him. He opened the gate, walked on through into the yard, where the shadows cast by the cluster of house and garages were dark and threatening places, the sun close to vertical. He opened the front door. He heard the sound of Maisley's vehicle reversing.

Inside the marble-floored lobby, the air-conditioned air was cool and refreshing. His footsteps echoed as he moved on through into the living room, where he poured himself a generous measure of 30-year-old Glenmorangie.

He spoke into empty room. 'Voice prompt 06ZX4.'

He allowed a two-second pause as his speech patterns were assessed and recognized by the house security.

'Status?'

A female voice said: 'Status secure.'

Everything tidy. Meant to reassure him that forensic-suited NSA techs had not combed through the house during the days he had spent in the hospital.

Walking back into the hallway, he carried the whisky into his office. One wall was lined with illuminated monitors. An immense super computer took up the entire end wall. He spoke another command: the program had to reboot. He waited something like two minutes for the monitors to show close-ups from the DEST satellite surveillance behind the sand dune. Maisley's Dodge had already pulled into place alongside the NSA truck. He cleared the screen. With a one-handed scrabble over the right-sided keys, he entered Security. He initiated a time sequence replay of the surveillance cameras throughout the house over the time he had been in hospital. Of course they had wiped the first-line recording discs clean, including the monitored infra-reds from the roof-mounted cameras outside. But they hadn't found the backup. He day-scanned, then hour-scanned until he got to the start of the search. Agent Maisley looked kind of cute, wearing white coveralls, accompanied by five others, systematically sweeping the building. Sultan spent an hour sipping whisky, slow scrolling.

Of course they found nothing: there *was* nothing to find.

*

There was no escaping the excitement that greeted President Dickinson's arrival among the scientists. Today was Sunday, a day when most people could take a break from the pressures of work. But here there were no rest days. A fearful tension still permeated the gathering. Will had introduced a trial of drowning circles with decon fluid. The neighboring circles had been treated late afternoon yesterday, but it was too early to know if the technique was working. And even if it did, how long before more circles began to close in? Kay was all the more impressed when she saw the President alight from her chopper. Dickinson was dressed in a charcoal pinstripe skirt and collarless jacket.

She spent the first twenty minutes on a handshakes tour. She posed for a camera shot with a polystyrene cup of black coffee in the BSL-ZERO lab, sitting on a stool with her arm resting on the work surface. Now she sat at the table in the meeting room while Anton van den Berg talked about his trawling of the genomes of plants, animals and humans using the coded primer provided by the e-mail. The reason the President had come to visit them was because he had found the sequence in one particular mitochondrial gene.

Anton looked like he couldn't believe the President was sitting at the same table. She had listened patiently to his presentation. Now she asked him: 'But what did you learn from that?'

He said, "Ma'am – the mitochondria can only do their job if they get coded messages from the nucleus. The gene we identified helps the messages get through.'

The President turned to Kay. 'And you think this gene is going to help us stop this entity from spreading?'

'We're calling our new discovery the E gene, because the clue came in the key of E. There are a number of unanswered questions with regard to what we're really dealing with. Is the E gene the key to the entity's lethality? If it is, we're onto something major.'

Dickinson tapped a fingernail on the table surface. 'These people – they're really playing some strange kind of game with us – giving us clues?'

'Yes, they are.' Kay left the ad-hoc table to stand by the big plasma screen but she was still addressing the President. 'Please don't worry about the scientific details. What I'm going to show is some very detailed pictures we have of the entity using the Stanford synchrotron. Ma'am, you're looking at the real thing.'

'Oh, my Lord!'

Dickinson gazed at the series of glittering three-dimensional images. It was as if a complex sculptural abstract had been woven from ribbons of ectoplasm, exquisitely varied in color, twist and direction. Dickinson exclaimed her thoughts aloud:

'How can something so beautiful be so evil?'

'It isn't evil, Ma'am. No more than any bacterium or virus is capable of being evil. What it is is amoral, devoid of any sense of good or wrong. But the same can't be said for whoever constructed it.'

President Dickinson's face reflected the myriad bright colors of the projected entity. 'The people who constructed this... this thing... they had to figure the plan of it, carry it all out with such unbelievable detail. Can I ask you, Professor McCann, how long it would take to do that?'

'Years.'

Dickinson shivered, as if chilled. The screen was so close to the table that Kay overheard Dickinson whisper to Moran, who sat next to her: 'That chemist, van den Berg! Did you see how his hands were shaking?'

Moran leaned over to whisper into her ear: 'We're all concerned about van den Berg. The guy is working himself to exhaustion. They're planning to bring in somebody to take some of the strain off him – the guy who was taken out by the bomb.'

The conversation disturbed Kay, who assumed Anton also overheard it. She attempted to deflect the President's attention. 'The million dollar question, now that we have the E gene and we know what part it plays, is how we make use of that knowledge.'

Dickinson lifted her eyebrows. 'I understand you're working on a vaccine?'

Will took his cue from where he was sitting at the table: 'I've been working on how we could deliver protection at the level of the mitochondria.'

She asked him: 'Are you testing a vaccine right now?'

'We're not quite there yet. Up to now I've been looking at maybe using a bacterial type of virus – something called a phage.'

Dickinson glanced at Kay before meeting Will's eyes. 'Because mitochondria were once free-living bacteria?'

'I'm very impressed, Ma'am. But the discovery of the E gene has changed all that. I had assumed I had to change a gene, or genes, inside of the mitochondria. But the E gene is contained within the nucleus.'

'That give you a new line of thinking?'

'Ma'am – to change a nuclear gene we'd have to use a very different kind of virus – maybe one related to HIV-1.'

'Wouldn't that be dangerous?'

'Not if the dangerous genes were extracted first. We already know how to do that. What we'd do is replace the virus's own genes for contagion with whatever genes we want to put in there.'

'Dr. Grant – you make sure to keep me posted.'

'Yes, Ma'am!'

Kay glanced at Anton's perspiring face as she projected the blown-up image of a fly. It was a *Bemisia* white fly, a parasite of crops. She showed a panoramic photograph: a field of ripening crop over which the fly population was as dense as a cloud.

'We picked *Bemisia* because it multiplies very rapidly. We cut time by grinding up thousands of flies into a soup. Otherwise we might not have found it.'

President Dickinson returned her attention to the screen.

'The sequence we were looking for was there in such minute concentration, it could only be coming from a tiny minority of the flies we tested. But once we had it, we were able to amplify it using PCR.' Kay held up a tiny test tube, no more than three inches long, and waved it mere feet from the presidential eyes. 'This is it, Ma'am. This is concentrated gene "E". Dr. van den Berg has developed a test so we can screen for the gene in the blood of any species we choose to look for it.' Kay didn't even try to hide her excitement. 'Ma'am, this could be the lever we're looking for.' Kay smiled her thanks to Anton. 'Dr. Grant will explain what this means in a little more detail.'

Will's tall figure moved close to the screen: 'Just about every individual fly appears to be susceptible to the lethal agent. But when you examine what's happening more closely, not all flies are actually susceptible. There is a tiny minority, say two per cent, that shows no sign of illness.'

'Is this the same with people?'

'Yes, Ma'am – only with people it's more like 0.2 per cent. We now believe that a natural mutation of gene E is the explanation of that resistance.'

'Not just in flies?'

'No, Ma'am – maybe, hopefully, all species.'

'So you've found it in humans?'

'Not yet – but we're planning to do just that.'

06: 05/ 09h15

After President Dickinson's visit, everybody felt on a high. And there was more good news. So far the deconned circles had not spread any further. It wasn't any kind of a miracle. They were still surrounded by millions of circles and they couldn't drown them all. But at least it was another step in the right direction. Kay felt excited by it, reinvigorated. After all the hard work they were beginning to fight back even though time was more pressing than ever. But this morning, while screening yet more plant genetic sequences, Kay sat back, aware that in the excitement that had followed the discovery of the primer, she had forgotten another important line of investigation.

She was prompted by something the President had said:

'How can something so beautiful be so evil?'

Kay's answer was the same now as it had been then: the entity was not evil. The real evil lurked behind a human face. It looked out onto the world through human eyes. It concealed its intentions behind human lies.

Anger surged in her – it froze her fingers to the keyboard. It pushed the trawling of genetic sequences out of her mind.

On May Day, or no more than a day either side of it, somebody with malign intent had come into the field reserve. That person had somehow gotten through the security of the gates and driven up the dirt track to the parking lot. He, or she, had come in through the doors into the lobby and then driven out to Sector 5-32 and laid the seeds of doomsday. Kay inhaled deeply. She exhaled in a rush. She forced her tired mind to think again: *see it!*

Imagine it, from moment to moment, as it must surely have happened.

There had to be a plan – everything about this person suggested logic, mathematical precision.

Was he, or she, one of them – one of their own? Okay, so let's assume it was a man. Was he an outsider? How could an outsider have gotten past the security lock on the gates? Whoever it was, he either knew the code, or he had a good enough excuse to call through to reception, where Michelle would have operated the gate remotely.

Michelle!

Kay reached for her desk phone, but then lifted it off the phone again. This was far too important for any telephone call. She had to have this out with Michelle.

*

MayEllen Reickhardt walked around the gable to find a large white van outside of the steel gates at the top of her driveway. She had been putting out the trash in the back yard when she heard the horn blaring around the front. Now she saw the figure wearing full biosafety gear. She knew who it was, even before she set off walking:

'Dr. Burke!'

'You haven't been answering my letters or phone calls, Mrs. Reickhardt!'

She unlocked the gate, dragged it open for him, then led him back into the house. Here she slumped in a chair by her kitchen table. 'I'd offer to rustle you up some coffee, but you'd be obliged to say no.'

He was standing by the window, staring out into the yard, and beyond it at the ravaged cactus field.

'I've been stupidly slow, MayEllen - if I might call you that.'

She shrugged, knowing he was watching her reflection in the window.

He added, 'You know that landscape is still contaminated?'

'I worked it out for myself after poor old Hobo died.'

'Hobo?'

'My dog.'

'You still got your husband's ashes?'

'On that ledge, under the Milwaukee jamboree.'

Burke turned around to look at the photograph on her wall. He walked over and looked at it for several moments, like he was interested. 'I can't believe you took the chance of coming back here – staying here.'

'I had nowhere else to go.'

He approached her at the table, reached down and picked up her right hand between his gloved two. 'MayEllen - you had every right to be angry with what happened to your husband. But right now you could be the most important person in our investigation. The key to helping us to fight back against what is happening.'

She extracted her hand, went to the percolator and poured herself a coffee. She had been up for hours but hadn't bothered with breakfast.

'You got a family, Dr. Burke?'

'A wife, three daughters.'

'They safe?'

'They're with my sister - lives in Seattle.'

'That make them safe?'

'Nobody is safe.'

He stood close to her rather than perch awkwardly on a chair. The noise of his breathing machine was irritating, that and the rustling sound his suit made at every small movement. MayEllen looked up at his face through the flexible helmet visor: what she saw was tired eyes behind the gold-rimmed eyeglasses.

He said: 'Remind me about the circumstances of that morning, when you left your husband here on May 17. He was already showing signs of sickness?'

She sighed. 'Bill thought he had the flu.'

'He was coughing?'

'Yes, he was.'

'You kissed him goodbye?'

'You already know the answer to that.'

'What it is, we know now there are two ways you can get infected. From plants directly – like Bill must have gotten infected – it had to be fast-track. He had the pulmonary form.' Burke turned his head to look once more through the window, to where the entire cactus field lay dead and withered. 'My God,' he murmured, 'I should kick myself.'

'I'd like to see you do that in your suit.'

'You had to be contaminated. But you never showed any signs of infection. MayEllen - Ma'am! We believe there may be a resistance gene. So far we're only managed to find it in insects. But we suspect it also exists in people. We'd like to see if you have that resistance gene.'

'I ain't going back to that hospital.'

'It won't be necessary. All I need is a blood sample and a swab from the inside of your mouth.'

She reached her right hand down out of habit, looking for Hobo, who would lift his head up so she could scratch him. A spurt of grief brought moistness into her eyes. She dropped her face so he couldn't see it.

'Please help us. A great many people have died. You're our best hope of finding out whether or not people also have the resistance gene.'

'Will that stop you pestering me?'

'Likely it would!'

She got up off her stool, went to the back door and walked out through it. She waited for him to shuffle out and join her in staring out into a landscape in which everything was dead.

'Dr. Burke. You can take my blood.'

*

Kay knew of a dirt road a few miles down the highway that was the route Michelle had always taken into work. She was certain of it because she had once ferried Michelle home from the field reserve when she had gotten the sad news of the death of her father. As she hit the track, the Mojave sun was big and high in a cloudless sky, scorching the landscape to a hundred shades of pinks, mauves and golden yellows, challenging the insects into clicking and whirring their counter-challenge. She made it unnoticed to the new parking lot, a half mile closer to the gate. Once beyond the gate, she felt her mood lighten. There was a passing breeze that cooled her skin. She was glad of the breeze. The temperature on the dash was already spiraling towards one hundred.

Michelle lived in a place called Yucca Valley, where her late father had worked for the U.S. Marine Corps Air Ground Combat Center. Kay had told nobody about her plans to visit Michelle. If she was wrong, and Michelle knew nothing, all it would do was add insult to the injury of Michelle losing her job.

Ten miles further on, Kay wished she had brought a hat. Glancing in her rear-view mirror, she was surprised to find she had company. A medium sized truck was tearing up a dust storm behind her. Somebody was in an almighty hurry. Brick-orange, a heavy duty bull-bar sprouting from its front fender, it caught her up within a few minutes, holding its position just feet behind her. A mile or so further, with the truck still riding her tail, Kay lost patience with the inconsiderate jerk. Slowing right down, she shouted:

'C'mon, asshole! Get to the fire!'

But the truck made no attempt to pass.

It was tailgating her so close she could see the driver: a narrow face shadowed by the brim of a black baseball cap. His bare left arm was slung out of the open window, with overblown deltoids swarming with tattoos. Kay got the impression those shaded eyes were fixated on her own in the rear-view mirror. Her whole body jerked as he suddenly blared the horn. It was a customized deep-throated tiger growl.

'Son of a bitch!'

She had to slow down at an arroyo, where the track became a cliff-pass with a drop of sixty or seventy feet to her right. Her heart was racing as she heard the roar of the truck engine overlaid with another thunderous tiger growl. From the sounds of his engine, he had down-shifted gear, probably engaged the four-wheel drive. She saw in the mirror that he was swinging the truck from side to side, like a challenge. His arm was outstretched, forefinger pointing. She saw what he was indicating – that she should pull into a flat piece of ground coming up on the left.

His face in her rear-view was the feral half-snarling mask of a satyr.

'In your dreams!'

She slammed her right foot to the floor. But the truck moved faster. Her body pitched forward as the truck slammed into the back fender of the Wrangler. The jolt was so violent she'd have been thrown through the windshield if she hadn't been wearing her seatbelt.

'Oh, mother of Jesus – shit!'

Flooring the throttle again, she gained maybe ten yards but the Wrangler lost its grip on a bed of grit as she rounded an acute right-handed bend. She could still see the leering face. His hand came to his lips, like he was blowing kisses. The truck grew bigger until it filled her entire rear-view. She swore again through another almighty smash, but this time it kept on coming, bull bar to fender. It was ramming the Wrangler towards the edge. With the engine and gearbox screaming, she slammed it into low gear, crashing her right foot down with all of her strength on the brake. She could no longer see the leering face. The truck was so close all she could see was the hood. Her nostrils were filled with the smell of burning rubber and she was inhaling the storm of dust and grit. She tried jerking the wheel, one way and then the other, but it made no difference. The truck had her in its jaws. She could feel its throaty roar through the soles of her feet as the Wrangler jerked and slid to within a foot of the edge.

The front right side suddenly pitched over. The front end screeched along the rocky edge, causing the Wrangler to see-saw. Her cell phone broke free from the dash, sliding out over the cantilevered side and took off like a diver from a high board, spiraling down into the void. The steering tore out of her hands and the wheel spun full to the right.

Kay screamed.

But something was still holding. A back tire had ruptured and the wheel rim was grinding against a ridge in the rock. She wrenched back the steering, but the wheel just spun loosely, as if both front wheels were dangling in open air. Crashing the gears into reverse, she shoved the gas pedal back against the floor. But the wheels only created more dust and fumes. She heard the awful sound of heavy metal tearing apart where the front axle was grinding against the edge. The Wrangler was groaning loudly as it cantilevered further towards the void. Kay felt another sickening collision that caused the vehicle to pivot through ten degrees. The passenger door was gone, ripped off the hinges in the last collision. She was staring out into the abyss.

There wasn't much point being strapped into her seat. She unclipped the seat belt, holding onto the rim of the door to stop her body from following the trajectory of her cell phone. She hauled herself leftwards, so she was squashed against the door. The vehicle righted itself. It had to be her weight. As she felt for the lock, she heard the sudden crack of a gunshot. The windshield in front of her disintegrated. Something in the tilt of the Wrangler and its righting with her weight to the far left had brought her attacker back into view. He was brandishing a shotgun. Kay kicked the door open, slammed it outwards with her foot – but the damned thing slammed back shut, near dislocating her knee. The truck smashed into her again. Another groaning lurch – the back wheels beginning to slip and slide. She no longer dared to move. Any loss of weight on her side and the sliding would gather momentum. Her heartbeat was frenzied, sweat washing over her eyes like tears. One more smash and she was gone.

She felt the disengagement. She heard the truck reverse back twenty yards back. He was picking up enough momentum to finish the job.

She heard the screaming revs, the taunting roar of the tiger horn. But the smash she expected didn't materialize. Instead it hit her with a controlled blow, then began to shove her slowly forward. Smart satyr! Too much momentum and the truck would follow the wrangler over the edge. She yanked the emergency brake up two more notches, for all the good that did her, then cracked open the driver's door. Her head was dangling out through the opening, with her mouth and nose filling up with dust. The thunder of the truck's low gear was drowning out her ears. She screwed up every muscle, inching further and further out, anticipating that the moment she threw her body out, the Wrangler would tip over and fall. There was a high-pitched insectile whine in her ears. She thought it had to be something to do with her heartbeat or maybe the terror of impending death.

A scrambler motorcycle screeched to a halt two feet away. Its rear wheel spun, forcing it through a quarter circle. She heard two cracks. Gunshots. They sounded faint but ominous against the truck's revving engine. In her mirror she saw the satyr's face replaced by broken glass and blood. But the momentum continued, grinding both vehicles forward into the void. The scrambler jerked forward. A hand grabbed her left upper arm and yanked her bodily out of the opened door.

'Jump!'

The same powerful arm shoved her onto the seat behind the driver, her clumsy arrival causing the machine to wobble and swerve as he accelerated forward. Behind them, the two vehicles continued forward under their twin momentums, lurching and jerking over the edge and crashing, with a loud grating and tearing of metal, down the sixty foot drop.

A short distance on, he halted the bike to look back at what was happening.

'You okay?'

Kay couldn't talk. She couldn't take a proper breath because her heart was filling her chest with every beat.

'FBI – agent Wilbur!'

She stammered: 'Mr. Wilbur – oh hell... that was close!'

The young biker didn't look like FBI. He wore a white cotton T-shirt over blue designer jeans. Pulling up a hundred yards from the crash scene, he helped Kay off the bike.

Kay murmured, 'I feel faint.'

'Maybe you should just sit a while.' He helped her to do so and spoke into cell phone as she was retching into the dirt.

'How did you find me?' She gasped.

'You slipped our ground surveillance but we've got the whole area under aerial cover. I had to travel some to catch up with you.'

She clung to his arms as he helped her back onto her feet. She continued to hold onto one of his hands for several minutes.

'Who was he?'

'No idea. I guess he was one of the people who've been killing other scientists. Kinda determined, wouldn't you say?'

Their conversation was interrupted by a series of explosions: the vehicles at the bottom of the arroyo had burst into flames. She inhaled deeply, started deep breathing.

She patted his shoulder. It was as close as she could get to saying thank you.

'You want me to take you back to the field reserve?'

'No. First... Oh, I don't even know if I can face it.' Kay took a deep breath. 'But, I'm damned if I'm going to let that jerk stop me doing what I came out here to do.'

06: 05/ 13h10

Kay sat in the familiar wood-slat chair in the shade. Her left knee was hurting so badly she could hardly bear to bend it. She was staring at the hummingbirds in Michelle's back yard, a swarm consisting of several species. They were dipping and buzzing around the pottery tree and its red-dyed sugar-filled cups. She accepted the glass that was pressed into her hands by Michelle's housemate, Miranda. A triple measure of Spanish brandy. On the other side of the wall, Wilbur was talking into Michelle's telephone.

Kay guessed it was Agent O'Keefe on the end of that line. She didn't need to overhear the conversation. She could predict its tenor.

Wilbur confirmed her prediction when, several minutes later, he strode out into the yard and told her that under no circumstances was she to question Michelle on her own. Only now did she acknowledge the brandy. She gulped it down in three or four swallows. But it had little effect on the hollow feeling of panic that still yawned inside her.

That grinning satyr – he had tried to kill her. Who was he? Was he some kind of psychopath who had just come across a solitary woman in a lonely place? Or had he been waiting somewhere nearby, waiting specifically for her?

Stuff that pretending, girl – get real! You know what – you're downright crazy. You're out of your mind!

She was still sitting there when O'Keefe arrived. She heard his voice before she had the courage to look at him. He was standing in the open door frame, rightfully furious:

'Professor McCann!'

'I know.'

'Have you got some kind of a death wish?'

'I know.'

'Are we going to get any kind of explanation?'

'Give me a few more minutes. Just a few minutes– okay?'

*

They talked in the kitchen, sitting on farmhouse chairs, one on each of three sides of the square farmhouse table. Michelle's chestnut hair was highlighted with lighter streaks since they had last met. Her blue-framed eyeglasses had been replaced with contacts. She was fidgeting under the table when she asked O'Keefe, 'You mind if Miranda sits in?'

O'Keefe said, 'I'd prefer just the three of us.'

Miranda, a divorcee like Michelle herself, was also in her late thirties. She had been hanging around in the kitchen. Now she glared at O'Keefe before slowly pouring herself a glass of ice tea and strolling out into the yard.

O'Keefe slammed the back door. 'Professor – I'm just itching to hear it.'

Kay sighed. 'Michelle – for goodness sakes – I'm not implying you did something wrong.'

'Oh, Kay!' Michelle's right hand fluttered towards her mouth, the fingers crawling, crab-like over her lips.

O'Keefe lifted an index finger. *My turn!* He leaned towards Michelle, with both elbows propped on the bare wood. His eyes were staring relentlessly into hers. 'The professor here believes that somebody went out to Sector 5-32 and deliberately set this whole thing going. She thinks this happened round about May 1st. She's also convinced, Michelle, that you know who did it.'

Michelle's face was an evolving mask of horror. In a slow motion swivel, she turned that mask to look at Kay.

Kay tried to reassure her: 'I know it couldn't have been your fault. These guys – they're very clever...'

O'Keefe's raised his finger again. His voice was firm and deep. 'Michelle – you recall May first?'

'I... I guess so.' Michelle's eyes were wide and staring.

Kay said, 'Mr. O'Keefe. Let me try? Please?' She reached across and took hold of Michelle's hand. 'Michelle – we need your help. We're relying on your excellent memory. I could be wrong in this. But all my instincts point to the fact that something unusual happened that day.'

Michelle jerked her head down.

'Okay. So let's you and me try, okay? Now on the official records, it was just Ake and the two students, Goldsmith and Prakesh?'

'Far as I can remember!' Michelle muttered the words in such a rush that Kay had to repeat them mentally to grasp them.

'Michelle – I know there was someone else!'

Michelle's head was shaking repeatedly.

'Maybe it was somebody you knew? Somebody you wouldn't possibly think of being mixed up in this?'

Michelle could no longer look into Kay's eyes. She was staring down at the table. Her hand, still held in Kay's own, was cold with sweat.

Kay squeezed it tighter. 'Nothing bad is going to happen to you. I promise you, you won't get into any trouble.'

'Kay... I didn't... I don't want Mike to get into any trouble.'

'Mike?'

She nodded. Tears condensed between her fluttering eyelids.

Kay fell back in her chair.

O'Keefe took over. 'Michelle – you better explain what happened.'

'Like... like Environmental Awareness California?'

A new fright was invading Kay's heart. Her breath was catching in her throat. 'What do you mean, Michelle?'

Michelle's voice sounded flat, resigned. 'Mike called. You were busy preparing to leave for the tripleA-S.'

The second mention of Mike caused Kay to forget her knee. She jerked the leg and winced with pain.

'Mike called?'

'He said it was going to be a surprise. He wanted you to see it. But it had to be later on, when the plants got going. It was going to be a birthday surprise. I helped him because it was Mike.'

The tears were welling up out of Michelle's eyes like rain drops gathering on the edges of leaves.

'Mike still loves you. He told me that. He just wanted to find a way to tell you. We were going to make it a surprise – on your birthday.'

'To tell me what?'

'To tell you that he wasn't indifferent, like you think, to what is happening to the environment.

Kay's neck throbbed with pain when she tried to shake it in bafflement. 'You're not making any sense.'

'That was the reason Mike picked May Day. To coincide with Environmental Awareness California. Mike told me in advance to let them through. There were two of them. The woman was from the partnership program – you know, they're linked to the California Native Plant Society. I already knew about that because I'm a supporter. The guy was the biologist. He took me out in the parking lot to let me see the plants he'd brought. He pointed them out through the back window. He was impressed when I recognized Raven's manzanita. I knew it immediately because you have a picture of it on your office wall.'

A burning feeling, like a naked flame, was running over Kay's skin. She said: 'Why on earth would Mike want to plant endangered species in Sector 5-32?'

'I knew that was why you guys broke up. Mike explained it to me but I told him I already saw for myself what it did to you. What it did to both of you. He said it was because you thought he didn't share you feelings about the environment.'

'Michelle – you idiot!'

O'Keefe interrupted: 'Just tell us exactly what they did, these two people.'

Michelle began to cry openly. Miranda must have heard her from the open kitchen window because she came in through the back door. She threw her arms around Michelle and started crying too. They had to take a break. O'Keefe let Miranda comfort Michelle for ten minutes. Then he herded her back out and closed the door again.

'You ready to continue?'

Michelle nodded. Her eyes looked raw. 'They planned... at least they told me they were planning... to celebrate May Day. Kind of symbolic. Planting endangered species where they couldn't have been better protected – where Ake would take real good care of them.'

Kay blurted: 'But the whole point of the reserve is we don't interfere. We study nature.'

O'Keefe ignored her. 'They went out there and they planted these endangered species in the field reserve?'

'Yes.'

'Let me get this clear. You telling me, these two strangers went out there and put some plants they had brought in into the middle of Sector 5-32?'

Michelle was nodding. 'Kay – it was just supposed to show you Mike cared. It was supposed to give you and Mike a last chance at getting together.'

'Michelle – I can't believe Mike asked you to do that.'

'He called me several times. We talked about it. He even asked my opinion about it. He said I didn't have to help if I didn't want to. He said I was the only one who could help him.'

O'Keefe pressed her: 'He said it was to be a surprise? That mean he asked you keep it secret?'

Michelle was nodding again.

'And so you didn't tell anybody, not even the FBI, because Mike asked you to keep it as a surprise?'

'If I told anybody, there wouldn't have been any surprise.'

O'Keefe nodded. 'And you didn't link it to what was happening, because you couldn't believe that Mike McCann would do a thing like that?'

'No way!'

Kay said, 'Michelle! It couldn't have been Mike. Someone tricked you.'

O'Keefe interrupted: 'Describe them – the man and the woman.'

'The woman was pretty. She was maybe mid twenties. Tall. I guess she was pretty enough to be a model. Hispanic,

I'd day. I remember thinking she was pretty enough to have been Miss Environmental Awareness California.'

'Describe the man.'

'He was older than the woman. Tallish. Slim. He had dark hair, blue-black I'd say. I could see it coming down under his Panama hat.'

'You didn't recognize him?'

'I'd have recognized him if I knew him – regardless of the hat and the shades.'

O'Keefe exchanged glances with Kay. 'Could he – even both of them – have been Arabs?'

'I doubt it. They didn't look like Arabs. And they had no Arab kind of accents. They had California accents, like you'd expect.'

O'Keefe continued: 'The people you say organized all this?'

'Environmental Awareness California.'

O'Keefe's face turned to Kay. 'You ever heard of them?'

She shook her head: 'I know about the partnership program, linked to the California Native Plant Society. And Environmental Awareness – there's a whole host of organizations involved in conservation, one way or another. But I don't recall a group called Environmental Awareness California. I don't believe these people exist. Even if they did, I don't believe for one moment that Mike would have anything to do with them.'

'You sure about that?'

'Mr. O'Keefe, I was married to the guy. Mike doesn't give a damn about environmental awareness.'

O'Keefe studied Kay for several seconds before turning back to the snuffling Michelle. 'Mike McCann – you know him reasonably well?'

She nodded.

'How many times have you met him?'

She shrugged, 'Hundreds.'

'You'd recognize his voice?'

'Sure I'd know his voice.'

'All these conversations – they all took place by phone?'

Michelle nodded.

'You're confident you'd know McCann's voice on the phone?'

She nodded.

'You sure about that? You absolutely and positively sure about that?'

'Like I'd know my own cheating ex-husband's!'

*

At the Thirless Memorial Hospital, the six members of the NIH medical assessment team wore field suits fitted with waist-slung pumps. Exhausted nurses and orderlies, also suited, were rushing around them, looking haunted behind their visors.

Dr. Valero was complaining bitterly: 'We're constantly running out of things, like i.v. fluids, biosafety suits, linen, opiates - workers. One in three of the local doctors and nurses running the family practices are dead or gone.'

The visiting team from the DOH squirmed with unease and Valero had no intention of letting them off the hook. He continued to berate them:

'Look at the wards. We're lucky. We're well organized. The small hospitals out there have no specialist units. At least the big hospitals have ICUs they can convert. What's the upshot? Six, or maybe up to a dozen or so beds that can be intensively managed. The first two or three affected families fill the beds. Then what? They spill over onto medical wards, surgical wards, pediatric, gynecology, ear nose and throat. No intensive management facilities whatsoever. You realize that even the big hospitals in LA only have two or three nurses trained in management of infection. Within days of the thing hitting, we start to lose staff. Some of the rest take off. You can't blame them.'

'I can assure you the government is listening. We're going back there to report all of this to NIH. I guarantee you'll get all the help you need.'

'I'm proud of the ancillary staff. The little people, the orderlies, cleaners, cooks, assistant nurses, even the mortuary assistants. They know it's a death sentence and most of them still keep on coming in. What happens when these cases come into these unprepared wards and facilities? It's hard to keep up the biosafety precautions, all day, in every area, twenty-four hours a day. It's stressful. These people are working beyond exhaustion. Inevitably, sooner or later, we get nosocomial spread. The staff don't know they're infected. They go home and infect their own families.'

'We hear what you're saying.'

'I haven't even begun.'

Striding along for thirty feet, wheeling around, he started on them again: 'What we need is the whole damn country to be declared a major disaster zone.'

'Now, cut that kind of talk!'

'Don't patronize me. You're going to have to go back there and persuade them to do something new, something big, something really constructive.'

'Like what?'

Valero felt a rush of heat come into his face as he thought for the umpteenth time about his wife, Rosalyn, the look on her face when she was fleeing with the children. 'Susan was right. She cared about her family. All you care about is yourself!' Valero felt a rush of emotion right then and he didn't want these people to see that emotion in him. So he turned on the Health Department epidemiologist, a woman called Freda Long, who had been muttering about the need to keep their feet on the ground. He faced her down, their visors practically butting.

'You people – you're worrying about whether it's an arithmetic or a geometric progression?'

'Dr. Valero, we are well aware that this is a serious situation. But it doesn't help anybody to indulge in scaremongering. The figures are no worse than a good-going flu epidemic.'

'Dr. Long, are you aiming to prove beyond reasonable doubt that you are the stupidest epidemiologist in the whole of America?'

She turned away inside her flexible hood.

'Don't do that, damn you. Don't you dare turn your face away from me. And don't you go back there comparing this to the flu. We're talking about the pattern of spread –

whether what we are seeing here is an arithmetic or a geometric progression. And I'm telling you there's no contest. Because I'd be glad to be assured it was an arithmetic progression. I'd sleep better in my bed at night. But I don't believe, Dr Long, that this is an arithmetic progression. I think that what we are seeing here, Dr. Long - who-will-not-turn-her-head-back-and-look-me-in-the-eyes - is altogether more frightening.' He stabbed repeatedly with his finger in the center of her chest. 'What I believe, Dr. Long, who-doesn't-dare-to-face-the-truth, is the graph is about to go exponential.'

06: 05/ 16h47

From behind her, Will reached his hands around and embraced Kay, trapping her arms against her chest in a bear hug. It hurt but she didn't object.

She murmured, 'O'Keefe is really mad at me.'

'He's right to be mad.'

He continued to hold her. 'At least the FBI will get the chance to go over the burned-out truck.'

'Not that they'll find much left of the driver.'

'There will be some clues, in spite of the fire. They'll get useful information about who's been killing those scientists.'

She shook her head. 'But why – why would anybody want to kill me?'

'I could think of a few reasons myself!' Will's hands paused, as if contemplating wringing her throat, but instead he kneaded the tensed-up muscles in Kay's neck. 'What did you think you were doing? Tearing off to investigate things on your own?' He spun the lab stool around so she was facing him, held her face in his hands. 'Kay McCann – don't you ever...!'

She reached up to take hold of his hands.

'Just promise me you will never do anything stupid again?'

She whispered: 'Thank you!'

'You're thanking me for what? Does that constitute a promise?'

'Thank you for being here.'

'I want you to promise!'

'Hold me!' She needed him to embrace her again. She led his arms back to surround her.

He kissed her on the brow.

She said, 'I feel sorry for Michelle.'

'Michelle brought it on herself.'

Michelle had been taken away by the FBI for more detailed interrogation. O'Keefe had called the SIOC for assistance. They were looking into every possible environmental movement linked to California. But so far nobody had come up with anything that linked Mike to the California Native Plant Society.

'I still don't believe it. I can't believe that Mike had anything to do with it.'

He tightened his hug. 'Have you spoken to Sean since you got back?'

'I can't face talking to him right now. I don't want to worry him even more.' She hesitated. 'How's Janie?'

'Missing me as much as I'm missing her.'

'Oh, Will. I'm finding it increasingly difficult to stay optimistic. I'm worrying that this situation is never going to get better.'

'You know that's not true.'

'Do I really know that?'

His hold slackened, but she held onto it. She refused to let him let her go. He said, 'I just heard from Burke in Phoenix. The Reickhardt samples are on their way here.'

She felt a stab of pain in her left knee even now when she was resting. It made her limp when she walked on it. Josie had diagnosed a ligament strain.

'Kay – it means I can check if humans posses the mutant E gene.'

'I wish I was as optimistic as you.'

'If I wasn't so tired, I'd pick you up and carry you somewhere I could show you how much I admire and respect you, Professor Kay McCann.'

'For the quality of my work?'

'A little quality testing, maybe.'

She threw her hands around his neck: held on tight. 'If this ever ends... Will, if this is ever over... I want to hear you play.'

'Yeah?'

'I want to feel the bass guitar through the soles of my feet.'

He laughed, clasped his hands over hers. His fingers found the ring she still wore from her marriage.

'Don't be paranoid. I only wear it because it comforts Sean.'

'Kids, huh!'

'Kids – yeah!'

Moran shook them out of their rapture, rapping his knuckles on the door. He came into the lab with a tall and slender man whose left arm hung in a shoulder sling. Arafim Sultan grinned at Kay, then hitched his eyebrows halfway up his brow. 'I've just been hearing what happened. Hey – welcome to the survivors' club!'

Moran explained, 'Dr. Grant - at Professor McCann's suggestion – I'd like you to welcome Dr. Sultan to the team.'

Kay limped across to hug Ari, though it was a somewhat awkward performance for both of them. 'Ari, it's great to see you made it!'

Sultan beamed. 'We got so much to talk about. Later – okay?'

He walked over to the window, which looked out onto the area of the Apache ovens. 'Do you remember, Kay, how we danced Friday evenings, with a crate of Chardonnay in the cooler and those big haunches of meat cooking?'

'How could I forget!'

Will thought Sultan looked like he was still in pain. He watched him take a handkerchief from his pocket and wipe it over his brow.

Moran caught Will's look of concern. 'What do you think of this guy! Drove with that shoulder all the way from Reno.'

Sultan laughed. 'Kay called. So here I am. I can pretty well manage now with my arm out of the sling.'

'Ari always was a bit of a joker. He's have us laughing for hours.' Kay was already looking more cheerful than minutes earlier. 'He was – is – absolutely brilliant. The only molecular geneticist I ever rated even close to Mike.'

Sultan adopted a look of chagrin. 'Only close!' He raised his eyebrows at Will. He modulated his voice to a perfect imitation Mike's New Jersey brogue: 'Okay, you guys! Don't stand around expecting me to show you. Think yourselves lucky. Go explore the fucking universe.'

Kay hooted.

Ari explained: 'The only instructions anybody ever got when they came to work with Kay's terrible ex! I guess you've been hearing about Mike. I always did admire the guy – he was more like a father to me than my own. But then he went and proved he was crazy, cutting loose such a class act as Kay.'

Will extended his hand to grasp Sultan's. 'We'd really appreciate any help you can give us.'

'My pleasure!'

'Sorry folks, but time's pressing!' Moran cut in. 'I'd better shepherd Dr. Sultan on a tour of duty. We'll see about finding him someplace to sleep.'

Sultan was still chuckling as he followed Moran's departing figure: 'Wouldn't be the first time I slept on the lab floor.'

After they'd gone, Will murmured to Kay: 'He going to be okay? He looked like he's still badly hurt.'

'Who isn't!'

He looked at her thoughtfully. 'He worked here with you?'

'You got something on your mind?'

'Just trying to imagine you guys, dancing.'

'Jealous?'

'You bet I'm jealous.'

'Later, we'll talk. Right now, I'm going to see if I can find Anton. Make sure he doesn't think Ari's arrival is some kind of criticism of his work.'

*

In the early hours, the bedroom faintly illuminated by moonlight seeping through yellow curtains, Kay leaned over Will's figure lying in the bed next to her. She kissed him on his perspiring brow. 'So now you know, Dr. Will Grant, that I'm already in deep, truly, madly, deeply... with you.'

There had been no talking about jazz this time. There had been no talk at all, just body language.

Will brought her face across, so he could kiss her on the lips. In that moment, their limbs still entwined, he savored the level of intimacy that still lingered after their love-making, their muscles still jumpy from the spent excitement. Two bottles of Sauvignon Blanc lay empty on the floor.

She buried her face in his shoulder, melding perspiration with perspiration, snuggling closer, wanting to burrow right down under his skin. He brushed his fingers through the junction of her brow and the flame of her hair.

He said, 'Your knee stand up?'

'You pulling my leg?'

He laughed: she laughed with him.

She murmured, 'You don't give a damn that it hurt like hell!'

'Let me kiss it better!'

She squealed at the slide of his lips down her thigh.

'Kay! That knee is hot – like it's burning.'

'My leg isn't the only part of me that's hot.'

Moistening his fingers in the warm welcoming cleft of her mouth, he brought his moist fingers back over his own lips.

'You think Sean would mind having a sister?'

'They'd probably fight.'

Their entwined bodies rolled and jerked with laughter.

In the faint amber light, his desire devoured her. She watched it happen with her eyes wide open. He kissed them closed.

*

Anton van den Berg cracked open the door of the molecular genetics laboratory. He peered to the right and to the left. Nobody around. Sliding the cart quietly over the threshold and into the link corridor, he hurried in the direction of the secure labs.

With shock, he realized that he had wandered straight into the scrutiny of the guard on the entrance to BSL-4.

He murmured, 'Hello!', didn't wait for a reply, instead hurried past the suspicious soldier with his pulse tugging, like a claw, at his throat. He carried on down the corridor leading towards BSL-2. He never stopped moving until the guard was out of sight. Then he had to stop and gather his breath, mopping distractedly at his brow with his sleeve.

Sami Kitisato had mastered the drill for wearing those suits. Van den Berg knew he would never be able to do so. Although he had attended training sessions with Grant, he had never progressed to practical simulation. He suffered from claustrophobia. He had done so ever since a near drowning accident in childhood. The very thought of being enclosed made it difficult to breathe. But today he would have to overcome that feeling.

He would have to break into BSL-4. And the daily routine had suggested a way he could circumvent the guard. Equipment and test species were taken into the lab through an air-lock that did not involve suits or a shower, merely their enclosure in a sealed cage that was subjected to a bombardment with ionized air. The cart he was pushing was small enough and it had just enough internal space to accommodate a man. Even so there were two codes blocking entry through the door: a card, which he had appropriated through breaking open the locked drawer of Sami's desk, and a keypad on the door, with a number that was changed once a week. No difficulty with the number code: it was van den Berg himself who had suggested the simple variation to the security technician, a woman named Caley Kresh, who was equipped with excellent administrative skills but little in the way of imagination. He was still nervous, however, tapping in the triple couplets of Kresh's daughter's birthdate, 14, followed by the month, 06, and the date, now it was the early hours, of 06.

The pin light on the lock changed from red to green.

*

The shriek of the BSL-4 alarm woke everybody up. Will glanced at his bedside clock: registered 4:55, then threw a shirt and slacks over his shorts, running in unlaced loafers into the melee. Kay followed his example. She didn't have the time to worry about the fact that Ari saw her sleep-fazed body limping from the bedroom in Will's wake. The entrance to BSL-4 was obstructed. Somebody had rammed a large metal cart into the air-lock from the inside, holding the inside door ajar, so the outer door would no longer open. Soldiers, under the orders of Hauk, directed them to the communications room, where the views from monitoring cameras inside the lab were being projected onto the big screen.

Moran had arrived ahead of them, a bathrobe thrown over his shoulders and his thinning hair awry.

Will said, 'What's going on?'

Moran nodded at the screen: 'See for yourself!'

Kay exclaimed over Will's shoulder: 'My God - it's Anton! What in the world does he think he's doing?'

Van den Berg wasn't wearing a biosafety suit. He was wearing nothing other than tartan boxer shorts. He looked insane.

'You seen his skin?' Moran muttered softly.

The biochemist's chest was covered in a confluent red and scaly rash. It looked horrific but Will shook his head.

'That's not the entity. Looks more like psoriasis!'

'No.' Josie Coster contradicted him, having just arrived to join them at the monitor: 'I know what it is because I've been treating him for it. It's seborrhoeic dermatitis. It's a rash associated with stress.'

'You've been treating him for stress?'

'Even a scientist has the right to confidentiality.'

'What does he think he's doing?' Moran shook his head. 'Can't you people persuade him to come out?'

Kay, who had been studying Anton closely, said, 'I don't think it's that simple. Look at the floor around his feet.'

They saw what she was pointing out: glittering fragments.

'Glass?'

'Looks like it.'

Will muttered: 'Shit!'

Kay turned to Moran: 'Is it possible to talk to him?'

'The microphone is connected.'

'Anton - for goodness sake!'

'Kay? Is that you?'

'Yes, it's me.'

Van den Berg approached the camera set into the junction of ceiling and wall over the workbench. His face was blown up out of proportion, like a reflection in a distorting mirror. He was blinking slowly, as if trying to clear his mind. 'It's such a relief to explain to you, Kay. What it is, you see, is I've been wrestling with the secret of its metabolism.'

'What secret?'

Those eyes widened, so they seemed overlarge in the already obscenely red and camera-distorted face. 'I've been trying to figure out the entity as a whole. I've been racking my brain but I still can't figure it out. Then I realized there's got to be something we're missing – an unknown energy source.'

'Please let us help you, Anton. At least move the cart out of the air-lock so Will can get in to bring you out.'

'I can't do that, Kay. Grant – Grant, are you there?'

'Yeah, I'm here.'

'I'm sorry about the mess. You must listen to me – both of you. Don't let them break in. There's broken glass everywhere. That's why I put the cart in the door. It isn't safe. I dropped a piece of equipment.'

'You're not wearing a suit.'

'I did my best to put on a suit, but I lost it. Couldn't breathe. I got into a total panic. That's how I broke the flask.'

Will said, 'Don't worry about the glass. I'll come in and sort it out for you. I'll sweep the glass out of the way.'

'Too late, I'm afraid. It's everywhere. Even on the bench surfaces.'

'You asshole!' It was General Hauk, shouting above their voices. 'What the fuck are you doing in there?'

'We haven't been thinking right. It's the thing as a whole, you see. How it works. I couldn't get it out of my mind. As a whole – that's the key.'

Kay pleaded with him: 'Anton, you've just got to open the door.'

'I will open it up. Just give me a little more time – okay? All I want is a little more time.' Van den Berg darted away from the monitoring camera to return to the experiment he had been conducting inside the lab.

'Keep the lunatic talking,' muttered Hauk. 'Security is cutting their way into a quiet area, around the back. In the meantime, Grant, you better get suited up and ready to go in with Coster.'

Moran took the microphone from Kay's hand: 'Doctor - keep talking to me. I really do want you to explain, for an ignoramus like me, what you're trying to do right now.'

'Ah, Lieutenant Columbo!'

'I've been called worse.'

Van den Berg stopped a moment, his hands in the air, like a surgeon at scrub. 'What was that?'

'I didn't hear anything.'

'I don't believe you. You're lying to me.'

His fingers were trembling and his arms as a whole were jerking erratically. He was having trouble concentrating on his experiment. 'Explain, did you say? I've already explained. I knew I had failed. When you called him in - Sultan.'

'No, no – *no!*' Kay exclaimed over Moran's shoulder. 'I've already explained to you, Anton. Ari is just an additional mind. He was brought in to help you. To work under your direction.'

Van den Berg laughed, a self-deprecatory mocking humor. 'That was why it had to be tonight. One last opportunity - don't you see?'

He had several glass flasks over heating coils. Each had a thermocouple immersed in the liquid. He pushed a switch and there was the sound of a motor running. 'Old-fashioned inorganic chemistry. You won't be able to see it, not with the lights on. So I'm going to have to switch them all off.' Kay and Patrick howled 'no' in unison. But van den Berg took no notice. The lab was suddenly plunged into darkness. 'Now, watch!' His voice carried the same tremulousness they saw in his hands. 'Now then, what you got is an extreme laser. It just isn't visible as yet. Nothing, until... Ah-hah!'

A circle of brilliant light appeared on the monitor.

'Excellent work has been done by the guys in Colorado at Boulder. Preliminary, that's the problem. Synchrotrons take up a whole room. This, as you see, fits on a desktop. Kay, you should be able to see it by now? Relies on a much simpler system. Uses an infrared laser to generate very high-powered pulses. Last only 25 femtoseconds. For you, Columbo, 25 millionths or a billionth of a second. It rips off electrons from argon atoms. But let's not tax you with the details. Important thing, the thing even you will be able to grasp, is it enables nanoscale imaging right here on the lab surface. So! Here we go!

'Since you can't see what I'm doing, let me tell you that I'm feeding a silicon chip from a flask in the holder within the beam.

'Hey presto!'

The piercing circle of light became a pattern of dots.

Kay shouted: 'For goodness sake, Anton?'

'Saline in the flask, zero degrees Centigrade. Can't keep talking. Have to record it, so let's hope ... hmmm! You better make sure the computer is capturing these images.' He waited a minute or so, then removed the chip, replaced it with one from another flask. 'Now, let's see again!' The pattern was no longer dots. It was blurry.

'I am explaining, quickly, Kay. This business running around the specimen feed is a powerful electromagnet. I already knew the entity had strong polarity. Lines them all up, you see. Billions of the damned things.'

'You haven't got live agent in those flasks?'

'Had to be live.' Van den Berg adjusted the controls and the pattern become a little more readable, but still somewhat blurred, like a child's experiment with rotating a card on a pin. 'Critical thing is to correct for the movement. It's about sixty percent guesswork and thirty per cent luck. Ah - here we go!'

The pattern of dots reappeared.

'Shall we christen what we have just seen? I'm going to call it the "rotational coefficient".'

'The Professor here may be following this but you've sure as hell lost me, Doctor.'

'Lieutenant Columbo - let me see how you might understand it? What we see is as wonderful as it is terrifying. Those bad guys have created a miracle. But the question remains, how did they pull it off? How did they get the damn thing to work as a self-driven, self-replicating entity?'

'Search me?'

'Aha! A joke if we really take that biologically! Top score! Ten out of ten!' Van den Berg removed the test sample, replaced it with another. The blur reappeared. He fiddled with some controls. The pattern of dots reappeared.

Moran humored him. 'Like we're talking Frankenstein, huh?'

'Revisiting Prometheus! Very good! But to create a novel human being would be exceedingly unlikely. Even the humblest bacteria would be practically impossible with present knowledge. But this −!'

'Now, you're alarming me, Doctor.'

'I know what you're trying to do. Please don't waste my time.' Suddenly the lab lights came back on and they could see Van den Berg was passing his hands over his face. 'Go tell Jingle Jangle to be more patient. A little more time is all I ask. It's far too dangerous in here, even for Grant or Coster to come in. The flask I dropped was full of live concentrated agent. There are razor sharp spikes everywhere. Several are imbedded in my feet.'

Hauk was back, shouting: 'Work with us, Doctor. Let us come to you. I promise we'll get you into the bubble.'

'Nothing to gain. I might as well complete the experiment.'

'You crazy bastard!'

'General! Let's have no heroics. It will only take ten minutes to finish the job. I'm going to do it.'

The chemist wiped sweat from his face with the bunched up surgical scrubs he had put on before discarding the biosafety suit. The lights went out again and the dots reappeared. 'Please don't distract me at this stage. Got to concentrate. Got to give it all of my concentration... Kay, someone please check... make sure the computer is recording this. Plot the rotational coefficient. Rotational speed now 2.71 turns per second. See it there. What we're monitoring is a graph of increasing rotation against a temperature of 28 Celsius in the flask. Ah-hah ... we have something.'

'What is it?'

'It's moving.'

'You mean the angle of magnetization has tilted with temperature?'

There was a jerk of the light as Van den Berg appeared to grasp the equipment in what might have been a spell of giddiness. 'More interesting than that. Observe what happens when I crank up the temperature to human level. 37° C. Now, look at the graph. You must see what I'm getting at? The speed of rotation has jumped to 6.38.'

'It's... it's forming a curve?'

'Well - let's move a little higher... say, desert ambient... 40° C.'

The speed of rotation became so fast, all Kay could see was a disk of shimmering light. The speed logged at almost 40 revolutions per second.

'I can see something dramatic is happening, Anton. What does it mean?'

'We are observing an energy soak. Now watch very carefully. As I increase the temperature, the speed of movement increases. But there's more to it. Look at the ordinates. I have placed kinetic movement on this axis and heat - energy input, which can only be explained by its required uptake - here. It isn't a straight line. We're observing more than the kinetics of simple chemistry. We're seeing something of its physiology. Jesus, Kay, we're looking at life.'

Kay shivered with fright. She looked around for Ari, to see what he thought about Anton and his crazy experiment, but Ari was no longer with them. 'But how, Anton - how could they have done this with something so small?'

'I don't know. That's the remaining mystery. But I have an idea! Something in Columbo's joke. The clue lies in every living cell.'

There was an explosion in the background and the monitors were suddenly flooded with light.

Kay grabbed hold of Moran's arm: 'What are they doing?'

Will, suited in blue, appeared through a haze of smoke. He was using a broom with a large wide head to clear a way through the shards of glass. Other figures were following along the path he had cleared. Between them, they lifted up the trembling, semi unconscious figure that had fallen under the workbench area. Kay heard Will's voice, directed at Josie Coster, who was organizing the med-techs to take Anton into the bubble.

'He's showing signs of blood-borne spread.'

06.06/ 06h45

'Kay – is that you?'

'Dad, I'm really sorry I didn't get around to calling you yesterday. Yesterday was one hell of a day.'

'We had a day of it here too.'

'You did?'

Her father hesitated. 'Kay, I have something important to tell you. Those people, they came back up to the gate. I bought them off. Fact is, I gave them two sides of beef to get rid of them.'

'What's going on? Let me speak to Sean.'

'I can't do that right now.'

'Why not?'

'He's helping the ranch hands load up the transports.'

'What transports?'

'Kay, we're rounding up the herd. We've been at it since before dawn. We had to get them fed and watered for the journey.'

'What journey are you talking about?'

'Soon as I knew this outbreak was real – I had to check it out for myself.'

'What?'

'It's hit here. No more than forty miles down the road. I had to work things our fast. I asked myself what were the risks. The farm is all given over to grazing. That's a whole bunch of plants, just sitting and waiting in the breeze.'

Kay's throat muscles had clenched up tight. She was trying to speak past it but the words couldn't get through.

Her father's voice continued to play in her ear, as if coming to her from some unreal world. 'One circle in the grass, a single animal down, and we lose everything. The way I'm thinking, this thing can't infect dead meat. So I cut my losses and decided to slaughter the entire herd. Take what I can get. The men are here right now with the transports to take them away.'

'Oh pops!'

She hadn't called him that since elementary school.

The word also brought a swell of emotion into her father's voice. 'A farm can start up again. People can't. We thought we were safe. But it turns out nobody's safe, nobody at all, nobody anywhere...' His voice tailed off.

'What about Sean?

She heard her father take a breath. 'Sean's okay. We're all fine, Kay. And I intend to keep it that way.'

'You're leaving now?'

'Heading out, soon as the animals are loaded.'

'Heading where?'

'Far north and west as we can. Maybe Montana – maybe Washington. Anywhere from anywhere that hasn't got circles.'

*

The ringing of her cell phone roused Nora Seiffert. She had been half awake anyway, tossing and turning. Now her eyes jerked wide open, like a startled cat. She sat up and grabbed the cell from the bedside table. She brought the receiver to her ear.

She heard nothing.

'What in shit!'

She switched on the bedside light. Stared at the screen through sleep-blurred eyes. A text message. She fumbled the scroll key, her fingers clumsy with sleep. She read:

RAY TO SAM: READY TO COMPLETE THE DEAL

She swung her legs out so she was sitting on the edge of the bed. She dialed the number:

'I got your message.'

His voice was icy cool. 'I told you I'd call!'

'You bastard. I kept calling you and you never answered.'

'I warned you there might be problems.'

'I don't give a fuck about your problems. I want my money.'

'You messed up on one of the hits.'

'We had problems of our own.'

He didn't even hesitate. He said: 'Forget the Professor. I'll deal with her. In the meantime I've got your money.'

She couldn't read a thing from his voice. 'When and where?'

'Same place. Say, five hours from now.'

'Just make sure you bring the cash!'

*

The Committee Room at the White House had fallen ominously quiet. President Dickinson's voice cut through the silence: 'So now we are informed that the entity is in the upper atmosphere?'

'Yes, Ma'am.' It was General Monath who answered.

Dickinson was chairing the latest Emergency Management Group Meeting. She perused the ER-2 information.

'How certain is this?'

'Dr. Grant, who did the testing, is waiting on-line.'

The cam-link picture segued to Will Grant.

'Dr. Grant - we appreciate your input. May I remind you that what we are about to discuss is absolutely confidential. You should not discuss it with anybody, including your colleagues at the lab.'

'Yes, Ma'am!'

'You can confirm this? There is absolutely no doubt about it?'

'None at all.'

Dickinson's eyes flicked once more over the charts and printouts spread out like a fan on the polished mahogany surface. 'It's even in the clouds?'

'I'm afraid so.'

The President's jaws involuntarily tensed. 'This is so very important, Dr. Grant. I have to press you. I want you to convince me.'

'The ER-2's reconnaissance planes are flown by single pilots. One of the pilots on the cloud collection runs has died.'

'Died from infection with the entity?'

'Yes.'

Her voice expressed her innermost thoughts: 'When you think it can't possibly get worse, it proves you wrong, every time.'

Kronstein, who was sitting diagonally opposite her, interrupted her thoughts: 'I'm afraid we need to turn our attention to the latest mortality statistics and Landsats.'

The President sighed.

Kronstein took his place in front of the screen, so the people nearest to him had to rearrange their chairs to watch. 'We have an accumulated mortality count approaching 2,000.'

'But that's almost double the figures in a single day. With all these measures, free biosafety protection, extinguishing circles, better diagnosis!'

'The mortality graph is rising rapidly. Approximately eighty per cent of deaths are still in and around the southwest.'

Hauk added: 'But it sure as hell it ain't gonna stay that way. We have circles in 27 states, including upstate New York. We've even gotten an affected farm on Rhode Island.'

'Nothing in New York City itself - Washington?'

'Not as yet. But it's just a question of time. I would suggest that we defoliate all green areas within urban areas.'

'You're talking like Central Park?'

'I'm afraid so, Ma'am.'

'Gentlemen, we're going to have to work a lot harder at this. I want new ideas. Something more adventurous.'

*

Will returned to his computer, trawling dozens of communications from bacteriological colleagues. These were useful but not what he needed. He felt inspired by the President's words: *I want new ideas... Something more adventurous.*

He thought about Anton, the claims he had made in that crazy experiment. Was he right? Was the entity truly the first ever artificially created life form? If so, it was mind-boggling. But Anton's explanation had been half insane. Nobody was convinced by the suicidal behavior of a madman. And even if Anton had been right, his conclusions were Kay's department. They did not help Will in his search for a vaccine.

Or did they?

The entity, living or not, was a construct of genetic engineering. A vaccine, or a treatment, could only come from the same technology. Gene therapy – therapy aimed at genetically engineering its victims!

A few years ago, a French team had made a breakthrough in gene therapy of kids suffering from hereditary immune deficiency, what the newspapers called the bubble kids. They had treated 27 children with considerable success. But a few years later, several had developed leukemia. The complication had turned the whole world of gene therapy upside down, from triumph to failure. People assumed that the leukemia was caused by the virus used to carry the gene, but subsequent examination had shown that the virus wasn't the cause of the leukemia. It was the treatment gene itself. They hadn't done enough animal studies before starting the treatment.

Gene therapy was now back on the menu.

He thought: *All I need is the right gene – a resistance gene!*

*

Kay was helping Sami Kitisato set up a three-dimensional model of the entity on a small table at the front. Kay's knee had swollen to the size of a small pumpkin. Josie had strapped it so she walked – limped – with a straight leg gait. The pain in her neck, confirmed as whiplash, had also gotten ten times worse since yesterday. For the present she was insisting she could manage without a collar. And after the conversation with her father first thing this morning, she had been wandering around in a daze. Yet she agreed with her father. He was right to run. She wished at times she could run too. She had to sit down and take a sip of water before collecting her frayed nerves together for the presentation. They had rearranged the meeting room so they were sitting on an assortment of chairs in rows. The gloom that had lightened with the visit of the President had descended over them all again with Anton's death.

She started by introducing Ari to the gathering, explaining that he would be assuming Anton's role as the chemistry lead.

'Okay, so if we learned anything from the sacrifice of our colleague, it's the fact that we've got to face the big questions. How can a single entity attack all known species?'

Her question elicited a flurry of murmurings. That was good if it took their minds away from the gloom.

Ari Sultan, pale and sweating, sat in the second row.

Kay addressed him: 'The problem is none of us fully understand, even now, what Anton was trying to prove in that final experiment.'

Ari nodded: 'I guess maybe I should spend a day or two knocking heads with Sami. Review where the molecular chemistry is taking us thus far. Then I'll see if I can make any sense of what van den Berg was claiming.'

'Thanks. That would be really helpful.' She swiveled her eyes, keeping her neck as still as she could, to nod to Will, who had come in late to take his place beside her.

Kay was determined to show determination through example. 'Okay, everybody. We've got to put aside recent events and focus our minds and attentions back onto the entity. Will, could you take it from here?'

It was a relief to sit down.

Will tapped with the end of a ballpoint pen on the model of the entity they had rigged up on the table. 'Here,' he indicated top and bottom, 'we have the polar nodes. The top node is peculiar enough, with all those frond-like attachments. The bottom node is clearly duplex and the lowermost bulge links to a spike that reminds me of a viral attachment site, like the spikes that make the influenza virus resemble an old-fashioned naval mine. The virus uses the spikes to attach and then to penetrate the walls of the cells it is infecting.' He turned to their new colleague. 'We're fortunate to have Ari here to work with us. You got any opinion on this, Ari?'

'An attachment site sounds like a reasonable working hypothesis to me.'

'Okay – say we accept that the lower part of the south pole is an attachment site. But the equatorial nodes are different. Their composition suggests to me that they could be places where genes are converted into proteins.'

Ari raised his eyebrows. 'Or vice versa!'

Will paused. 'That's an interesting thought. You want to expand on it?'

'I don't know enough as yet to argue with any conviction. But you are already questioning if this thing could interact with host genes. If that is truly so, it could incorporate some means of reading host antigens and then, maybe, changing something about its own make-up.'

'Kay?'

'I don't disagree.'

'Okay. So the way I see it, we now have a testable hypothesis. We could start by comparing the gene sequences Anton had already extracted from the core with known retroviral sequences. As a matter of fact,' Will looked down at the tiny Japanese molecular biologist, 'Sami has been working the last 36 hours to do just that. Sami, would you like to take the floor?'

Will was replaced by Sami, with her heavily accented voice.

'For entity to infect new host, this involve somehow changing entity core DNA. Already we have clue to know one way this can happen. Retroviruses, like HIV, have ability to reverse the normal process. HIV use enzyme, reverse transcriptase, to turn normal process upside down, turn RNA into DNA. Maybe, from what Dr. Sultan just say, entity could reverse whole process, start with host protein sequence, and work backwards, from protein to RNA to DNA. So I send what we got to people at GenBank, also Mishima in Japan. I ask them – nicely.'

This was interrupted by laughter: nobody could imagine the fiery little Sami asking favors nicely.

'Okay! I ask them not so nicely to cross-reference one thing. Protein sequences within entity's core. I ask them, is there something that match HIV-1 enzyme reverse transcriptase. GenBank and Mishima come back with same answer. Within core of entity is sequence that is modified quite a lot but still close enough to reverse transcriptase we find in retroviruses like HIV.'

There was such a chatter of voices, Will had to stand up again and raise a hand in an appeal for quiet.

He nodded to Kay, who groaned and limped her way back to stand behind the table with the three-dimensional model. 'Last night was traumatic for everybody. But this morning we made a breakthrough. We believe it will prove to be important.'

The room fell silent.

'It began when Sami here found a variant of gene E within the core of the entity. The entity's own gene E – I should emphasize. Then it got a whole heap more interesting. We've been working through the night to bring you some really remarkable results.'

She lifted a plastic-capped tube out of a rack and waved it before their eyes. 'You're looking at entity gene E extracted from the dead bodies of the Bemisia white fly. Now remember this is gene E after the fly has been infected and the entity has had time for amplification in the fly tissues.' She put the tube back in the rack and lifted out a second tube. 'Here,' she waved this too, 'you're looking at entity gene E extracted from dead tobacco plant – a tobacco plant that was infected with entity taken after amplification in white fly.' Kay rapped a finger against the core in the model in front of her. 'It's important you follow the exact sequence of events. Entity amplifies in the fly. Then entity from the fly is injected into the plant, where it undergoes a second round of amplification. Okay? You would expect entity gene E to be the same in both cases. But the gene from the plant is not the same as gene from the fly.'

The room fell absolutely silent.

Ari asked, 'In what way are they not the same. Are you saying gene E has somehow been replaced?'

'Not replaced. But its sequences have been changed. We have two different variants of what started out as one gene.'

Suddenly there was uproar.

Kay spoke above the babble of voices. 'We're continuing the sequencing work right now. It will go on all through today and into tomorrow. We're examining entity E genes after amplification from a number of different species of animals and plants –'

'What species?' Moran interrupted her.

'Guinea pigs, kangaroo rats, deer mice, snakes, insects, two species of lizard.' She lifted the racks Sami had prepared overnight. Everybody could see the off-white powder of concentrated DNA in each tube. 'But who wants to bet that we're going to find that the E gene changes in every species?'

Moran said, 'This sounds important. But I can't pretend to understand why.'

'It gives us a significant clue as to what is happening. The entity can change its own genes. I'll go further and speculate that it probably changes its genetic makeup to make it look like "self" to any new host species.'

'Wow!' Moran was nodding. 'So you're saying that it is designed to fool its way round any natural defenses?'

'If what I'm thinking is right. And once it has gotten past the defenses, it enters the mitochondria and takes over, first multiplying in large numbers and then destroying them to flood the tissues with new entity.'

Moran was on his feet: 'This thing always operates in the same way? It does that to everything it comes across? Including people?'

'Including people, cattle, pigs - the California redwoods!'

'I've got to report this back to Washington.'

Will said, 'Before you dash off, Patrick, there's something more.'

'Tell me!'

'The key to the entity is this E gene. We've known for days that it's important for its lethality. Every life form on Earth has its own version of the same gene. That would also explain why the small percentage with a mutated version of the gene doesn't die from it. I only had time so far for a single application. I looked at gene E in MayEllen Reickhardt.'

'And?'

'She has a mutation in her E gene.' Will allowed this information to sink home before continuing. 'It could be the information I've been looking for. The Reickhardt mutation could be the gene we need for a gene therapy – or a vaccine.'

06: 06/ 13h40

In Quebec – a bungalow overlooking the fishing harbor of Sainte-Thérèse-de-Gaspé, the Gaspésie peninsula, in the St. Lawrence estuary – a petite woman with iron-gray hair, was staring at the series of articles she had spread over the dining table. She had taken them, one by one, from a spring-clip folder. Written in black marker pen in her own shaky hand on the front cover of the file was a single name... *Henri.* Her movements were slowed by rheumatoid arthritis. There were newspaper cuttings she had been gathering for two weeks, from *The Globe* and *The* Mail, from the French language newspapers, *La Presse, Le Devoir, Le Soleil.* These had led her to discover the running series in *The New York Times* and *Washington Post*...

Hommes Des Science Assassinés

The New York Times:

Two More Leading Scientists Murdered

She had read and re-read the articles many times. Passages were highlighted in red and green marker pen. Names: Professor William T Freeman ... Julius Eisner... Miroslav Janovic... Ingrid Mendelsson. With slow and careful movements, she spread them out until they covered the entire surface of the polished oak dining table, a table much too big for her downsized retirement home. Newspaper cuttings, her own notes, letters and e-mail correspondence: they were all she had left after she had sent so many of the originals in a fruitless correspondence with the authorities. Many of the letters had official logos.

L'Université du Quebec... Letters of condolence from colleagues in university centers in many countries... *de Sûreté.*

She walked out to the kitchen to pour herself another cup of coffee. She sipped at the coffee, reading slowly, a native French speaker translating from English, the latest article in *The New York Times* by the journalist, Mark Stanwyck. She had considered making contact with Stanwyck before but had been dissuaded by his crusading style and his anti-science rhetoric. The latest article – more of the same. Why didn't he realize that there were wicked people ... *malfaisant.* What was the expression in English? *Le bien et le mal!* Bad cheeses... no – bad eggs! There were bad eggs and good eggs among scientists, just as there were bad eggs and good eggs among journalists.

She folded the paper in half, dissuaded once more from attempting to make contact. Frowning, deep in thought. She left the dining room and entered a small study, lined with scientific books and journals. She switched on a computer, waited impatiently for it to boot up and Googled: *Canadian Intelligence Services*

She read through a page under the logo of an eight-pointed star against a Prussian blue ground, capped by the British crown. The page heading read: **Canadian Intelligence Resource Centre**. She scanned the opening paragraph:

> *The Canadian Security Intelligence Service (CSIS), a domestic civilian agency, investigates, analyzes and advises government departments and agencies on activities which may reasonably be suspected of constituting threats to Canada's national security. Among the activities included in the CSIS mandate are the investigation of political violence and terrorism...*

She scrolled, found what she was looking for: CSIS could assist in the collection of foreign intelligence within Canada at the request of the Minister of Foreign Affairs or the Minister of National Defense. After several more searches and clicks she found what she was looking for: an article in *Presse Canadienne* by a French-Canadian journalist. The title of the article was: *Le Canada a-t-il besoin d'un service de renseignment de style CIA?* Does Canada need a CIA-style spy service? Reading, making occasional notes: there were a number of articles on the same subject.

The Canadian government was considering changes to its intelligence role in the world, with an eye to giving it wider powers in collecting overseas information.

People in various sections of the defense forces made arguments for and against this notion.

She had written and sent e-mails before but had received no answers. Over two weeks she must have written a dozen communications and never received any form of acknowledgement.

Returning to Google, she set up a new search. She inserted the key words: Mark Stanwyck/ *New York Times.* A page appeared with quotes from his newspaper articles. Patiently she explored nine pages without discovering what she wanted. On the tenth page, she whispered:

'Oui!

A personal website. Photographs of terrible scenes. A smaller picture of the journalist himself. *'Mark Stanwyck – J'ai vous trouvé!'* An e-mail address ...

She clicked.

Stanwyck's e-mail address appeared in her mail-to window. She considered in French, then, in the message line, she typed: *Re murders of scientists...*

There was a much longer pause, during which she scribbled on foolscap paper what she wanted to say in French, then composed the English translation. Corrected here and there, the document evolved with painstaking slowness. Finally, letter by slow letter, she typed:

Hello Mr. Stanwyck.

My name is Lyse Egremont. I am the wife of Professor Henri Egremont, a distinguished Canadian scientist. I am believing that his was the first murder. I am believing also that the other murders and the terrible things that are happening in the United States may be linked with what happened to my husband last year…

*

Nora drove the Lincoln, with Jamie Lee cradling the disassembled M40A3 across his knees. The FBI had identified the remains of Tony from the burned out truck. They would be hunting down all known associates. The heat was already incredible. All the way out of LA they had tuned in to the LAPD bulletins. Arriving at the slope over Lake Mead early, she drove around the perimeter twice – no sign of another car – and then she circled back to the parking spot. A wave of restlessness made her antsy and she couldn't stay in the vehicle. As she stepped out, the heat came up through her feet like she was standing on a griddle. She wore a hat to match her tailored olive suit. J-L, who had joined her, wore a sun-bleached rebel bandanna. They kissed. The kiss went on for maybe two minutes. It was the longest kiss she had ever shared with a man in her life. But still she didn't ever want it to stop.

J-L broke the kiss reluctantly. 'I gotta pick the right spot for the hit.'

'Okay! Go for it!'

She almost wept to let go of him. She watched him pick a low dune, rocky rather than sandy. Just enough cover with a spiky bush, a ball of yellow star-shaped flowers. She saw his mane of hair disappear as he jockeyed closer to the ground. A glint of reflection, when he picked up the sight to scope the view.

We play it smarter than the devil.

J-L walked back to Lincoln with the sight in his hand. He took his time assembling the rifle, then strapped it to his back. He picked up the five rounds, the folded-down Harris stand, a slim-line walkie-talkie, a half gallon of water. These he parceled into a rug. He rolled and folded the rug he would lie on.

Nora watched him from the driver's seat, with the engine, and air-conditioning, ticking over.

Jamie Lee turned back from thirty yards and blew her a kiss. It was so close, she could taste it. *Oh baby – sweet lover boy!*

She watched him take a roundabout route back to the dune, so he wouldn't leave a line of footprints. She wound down the window, lit the first of a new pack of twenty, settled in for the wait. She glanced at her watch: 50 minutes...

*

Listening with increasing impatience to the arguments of Dr. Jerry Rizinski, director of research for Xanthos-Max, a pharmaceutical company based in Buffalo, NY, Will was sitting at the bench with the desk phone on speaker so he could bite off the cellophane wrapping of his pastrami on rye. It was as close as he would get to lunch. He carried on unpeeling the sandwich while hearing out Rizinski, who was flatly skeptical of the proposal Will had just put to him. Rizinski said: 'You just don't have any idea the time and the protocols we have to go through to get something like this up and running.'

Will abandoned the sandwich in exasperation. 'Jerry – can I take you back to basics and ask you a simple question. Is it or is it not a fact that mass production of the MRE gene will present no problem?'

'On that we agree.'

The MRE gene - christened by Will after the E gene and MayEllen Reickhardt's initials - was an exact copy of her mutated gene. Further screening of gene databases since the morning meeting had revealed that the gene was found in just 0.2 percent of people.

'Okay, so let's focus on a single purpose. We need to find a way to inject that gene into humans before or during infection.'

'You rush a thing like this and it will blow up in your face. You know about the problems with vectors. People have died from infection, or from leukemias – and that's where the damned thing even looked like working. And the greatest problem of all is going to be delivery.'

'Not with the vector I have in mind.'

Rizinski snorted. 'That's what they all said.'

'You think I haven't thought of all the angles?'

'You're working with experimental animals, not people.'

'A situation this desperate, we have to cut corners.'

Rizinski groaned: 'You ever done work with preparing a gene therapy before?'

'No, I haven't.'

'There you are, then.'

'But I've worked in a number of ways that run very close to it.'

Rizinski sighed. 'Why don't you stick to the pathology and leave the gene therapy considerations to us.'

'You guys usually spend years on development.'

'Believe me, this will go through a lot faster.'

'You mean like months rather than years? You have any idea of the number of people who will have died in that time?'

Rizinski laughed at the impossibility of Will's impatient approach. 'It's a totally new line of experiment. Nothing even remotely along these lines has ever been tested. You'd have to go through a whole routine of base level experiments before you even got around to Phase 1 human testing.'

'We don't have months, Jerry. We don't even have weeks.'

'What you're thinking is professional idiocy. You won't be doing those people any favors taking short cuts on this. We produce a therapy, it's going to have to work without major toxicity.'

Will knew that Jerry was right even as he turned off the phone. He stared at his half-unraveled sandwich. It felt very much like his entire line of work was heading the same way. He grabbed the handset and called Kronstein's PA, Clara, at CDC. Kronstein had access to just about everybody's details.

He asked her for the contact telephone number of Roxy Penhaligan, the gene therapy supremo at NIH.

*

Nora was down to her penultimate Sobranie when she caught her first glimpse of red in the distance. She checked her watch. The devil sure timed it to the minute. She watched as he rolled the Ferrari in close to the passenger side of the Lincoln. He climbed out, wearing the Panama and shades. Through the scope, J-L had to be watching him as he took a good look around, then walked around to the driver's side of the Lincoln. He signaled to Nora through the car window. He expected her to follow him back to the rear of the Ferrari, where he popped the trunk. He took a step back and waited for her to join him.

Nora took her time. She flicked away the still burning cigarette. A signal to J-L. Ray was hefting an aluminum case out of the trunk.

She climbed out of the Lincoln. She took a cautious stroll to the Ferrari. Coming up from behind Ray, she saw there was a second aluminum case in the space behind the front seats. The trunk was too small to take both. She brought the Glock automatic forward from behind her back. She held it tight against the side of his head and padded him down. He wasn't carrying a gun.

She said, 'Let's see you crack the case.'

Ray swiveled his head round to look at the gun. His eyes darted one way and then the other, screening the desert.

'Pony-tail out there with the sniper?'

Nora screamed at him: 'We got one man down. Maybe a couple of days before every Fed in the Southwest is shooting on sight.'

'I'm sorry about your guy. But those are the risks we take – right? I kept my side of the deal. I brought you the cash.'

Nora changed her mind about opening the case in the dirt. She hissed: 'Don't tell me what I need. Just haul the case over to my car.'

She kept the gun on him as he pulled out the tow handle and rolled the first of the cases over to the Lincoln.

She popped the trunk lid, growled: 'In there!'

He hefted the case into the trunk.

'Spring the damn thing!'

'I'm going to have to put my hand into my right hip pocket – okay?'

She patted the pocket with her left hand, felt something there, the size and shape of a small cell phone. She put her hand in and slipped it out. It wasn't the cell phone she had expected. It was a gray piece of electronic equipment.

'What the –?'

'A remote.'

'What kinda game you playing?'

'The case is the kind couriers use. There's an insoluble dye in the walls. You break the locks open, the dye explodes all over the bills. Makes them unusable. The remote deactivates the protection while opening the locks.'

'Do it!'

Nora adjusted her stance so she was holding the Glock outstretched with both hands, her finger cradling the trigger. 'Just try any shit!'

'Okay – let's keep cool!' He clicked the remote and the locks sprang open. 'You want me to lift back the lid?'

'Do it!'

He threw back the lid. The sudden movement made her jump. She hit him a glancing blow to the head with the barrel. He fell in the dirt, losing the Panama.

'Take off the shades!'

He did so, looking up at her.

'Hey, I know you. Your face has been on the news. You got something to do with that epidemic thing.'

He grabbed the Panama and climbed back onto his feet. He dusted himself down. Put the shades back on, the hat on his head. His voice was cool and smooth as ice cream. 'So now you know me! Now you've got that on me.'

'Just keep your distance!'

She kept half an eye on him while scoping the case. She saw it was stuffed full of hundred dollar bills.

'There's $200,000. Count it. I'm in no hurry. That plus a bonus – the kind you're likely to appreciate.'

She shifted the Glock to her right hand, her left outstretched: 'Pass me the remote! Reach out with your left hand, nice and slow.'

He came to within three feet, passed it to her.

'The black cell phone.'

'I haven't brought it.'

'You never kept it on, like I told you.'

'I warned you it was risky.'

'Where's it now?'

'It's safe. Don't worry about that!'

She hissed at him, her finger whitening on the trigger 'Don't you tell me what I should or shouldn't worry about!'

'Okay – *okay!* But I didn't need to come here. Think about that.'

It was true. But he was too confident. There had to be something else. Some kind of a catch. 'What's the bonus?'

'In the lid of the case.'

'Don't screw me around!'

He bent over the trunk. Pulled out a plastic envelope of cocaine. 'Two ounces of pure. A peace offering.'

A sweat of suspicion erupted onto her face: 'Show me!'

'I don't have a blade to cut into it.'

'Use your teeth.'

He bit into the plastic, a hole just big enough to sprinkle a mound of powder onto the back of his hand. He snorted the mound.

She studied his expression. No sign of fear: no deadly poison entering his system. 'Put it back down – on top of the money.'

He did so.

'Go haul the second case.'

He went through the same rigmarole. He hauled it out of the car and rolled it to the trunk of the Lincoln. He had to readjust the first case, rotate it through ninety degrees, to make room for the second. Then he hefted it over the lip. He was breathing heavily when he had finished.

There was something he was keeping back from her. She stared at him, trying to read him. She couldn't work it out.

'Two steps back!'

He shuffled away from her.

She took the last Sobranie from the pack in her pocket. She turned so her face was profiled to where Jamie Lee was waiting. She shook out the cigarette to accept it with her waiting lips. But she didn't light it. The moment she lit the cigarette, J-L would start shooting. She stood over the trunk of the Lincoln, clicked the remote. Nothing happened. She clicked it again. The locks stayed closed.

Her jaw muscles clenched. 'Explain!'

'You can't open the case without my help.'

'What the fuck −?'

He shrugged: 'My insurance.'

A thrill of fear passed right through her, from her head to her feet. Her hands, holding the pistol outstretched, tensed. 'I warned you about shitting with me!'

He spoke with that same maddening calm. 'The cash is there. I give you my word. Another $200,000. The case has the same inbuilt protection. The walls are loaded with dye. Only the locks don't operate through the hand-held remote. They operate through a remotely operated UHF signal. I call it up like you'd dial a cell phone.'

Reaching into her pocket, she found her cell phone. She threw it onto the dirt by his feet. 'So do it. Operate the signal.'

'I can't do it with a cell phone. It has to be the transmitter.'

She lowered her aim to his groin: 'You want me to start putting bullets into you.'

'You willing to sacrifice £200,000 for nothing? I give you my word. I'm out of here, safe and secure, and you get it all.'

She fired the pistol, a few inches below the fork of his trousers. 'You got three seconds.'

'So kill me.'

'All my instincts tell me to do that right here and now.'

'So blow away two hundred thousand!'

She spat the unlit cigarette out of her mouth. Through the crossed hairs of the M40A3, Jamie Lee had to see her do that. The guy would walk.

She kept the gun on him as he climbed back into the Ferrari. She wanted to kill him so bad, it was a craving.

Shit – *fuck!*

She was still standing there when Jamie Lee got back. She was staring in the direction of the fancy red car long after it had disappeared.

We play it smarter than the devil...

06: 06/ 16h47

A quintessentially sunny Californian afternoon. Donald Albert Cosgard, marketing director of brokers Welles and Tsuchida, was returning to his home in Santa Barbara from a brain-storming session in San Francisco. The meeting had been precipitated by a catastrophic fall of insurance investment. He had set out from home at four that morning, reluctant to abandon the safety of the club complex, which had not experienced a single casualty in the epidemic. On the return trip a major pile-up on 101 southbound had diverted him to the Big Sur Coast Highway. The experience had been worrisome to say the least, with traffic reduced to a tenth of normal by the prevailing hysteria. No tourists. This plague business sure was bad for business. He resented what he felt was an unnecessary face-to-face meeting, thanks to Jablonska's, the vice-chairman's, panic, when a video-cam would have been more than adequate.

Frowning now, reflecting on that monumental act of stupidity, he headed home on Green Oasis Club Avenue. He passed by several vehicles heading in the opposite direction. He recognized Joe Sandisford's Lexus heading towards him at top speed.

Joe was supposed to be partnering Don in an evening nine-holer. And now here he was taking off in his four wheel-drive filled up with belongings, like his entire family was heading for the hills.

Don beeped his horn.

Joe flashed his headlights. Seven or eight times. Joe even blared his horn so long Don got a Doppler effect as they passed each other by. Don put it down to personality differences between marketing and sales: Joe was Regional Sales Director for Soni.

Braking his six speed auto Porsche Cayenne at the security barrier to the Green Oasis Club Development, Don was surprised to find no guard at the gate.

What're we paying these guys for?

In the four years he had lived there he had never found the gate unmanned. In fact, now that he took a proper look at it, there *was* no gate. The barrier-arm had been snapped off and lay splintered on the blacktop surface. Blinking with surprise, Don headed on through into the Eastside village complex of 432 residents, as wholly artificial as it was exclusive to those rich enough to pay upward of two million and a half for an architect-designed five bedroom contemporary, with organic shaped pool and spa, guarded – well, now it seemed most of the time guarded – by 24-hours security, and offering access to a polo field, archery range, tennis and club golf.

It kept playing back in his mind: *no guard on the gate!*

People were standing outside of their houses talking. Some who hardly even said hello were arguing over the fences. He saw what looked like tailor's mannequins laid out on the lawns. He saw the sprinklers sweep over a slim and elegant-looking woman but she didn't appear to take any notice. She lay on her back like she was stretched on the beach.

His pulse suddenly racing, Don swung into his pebbled drive, climbed out of the car.

His neighbor, Amelia Grundman, was sitting motionless inside the open door of her Mercedes Sports Coupe. She was dressed in a semi-transparent cream-colored Gucci blouse and green arabesque print pencil skirt. He waved hello. But she didn't seem to notice him. In slow motion, her upper body began to slide out of the open door, her head performing a backwards arc onto the gleaming white pebbles of her drive way so her platinum blonde hair fanned out over the ground. He hurried over to see if he could help her. He saw, as he neared, the black rash coming out of the cleft between her cosmetically enhanced breasts to reach up, like a claw, and take hold of her throat.

Oh, Jesus!

He was thinking back: those people lying on the lawns.
Oh, Jesus, no – please – oh, God –!

Amelia was groaning and snorting. He couldn't believe
the animal noises that were coming out of her open mouth
and half flattened nose.

Don was breathing with difficulty himself, the lunchtime shrimp salad rising into the back of his throat, as he
half ran half stumbled backward, staring as Amelia's left
hand stretched right over her head to reach out towards
him, the fingers clutching and clutching, like the scoop on a
fairground grab machine.

He got to his front door, turned the door handle: found
it locked. Annie never locked the door.

He hammered maniacally with his fist, forgetting for a
moment that he had the key to open it. Then, recalling the
key, he put it into the lock. Still the door wouldn't open. He
started kicking at the door with his three-hundred dollar
brogues. Suddenly Annie was standing there, staring at
him, in a sweat-stained tracksuit. Her face was gray, her
eyes so bloodshot she didn't look like Annie at all.

He knew now why Joe Sandisford had tore out of here,
flashing his lights and tooting his horn for what seemed like
half a minute. Why there was no security guard manning
the entrance. Why those people were lying out there on the
grass.

Inside, he slammed the door shut. He took a fierce grip
of Annie's shoulders. 'The thing – it's here?' He couldn't
bring himself to say it: *the zombie plague?* A nightmare in
which you found yourself stumbling inadvertently over a
cliff and you ended up tumbling, everything uselessly
flailing into bottomless darkness.

Annie was staring back at him, saying nothing.

'When did it happen? When did you know?'

'This morning... Amelia came to the door.'

Suddenly he was shouting: 'What time did Amelia come
to the door?'

'I don't know.'

He was shaking her.

'Maybe... like nine o'clock.'

'And you let her in?'

Annie started trembling. Really jerking under his hands.

'And you didn't call me? You didn't even think to call me?'

Annie started weeping openly. 'I did try to call you. I called you a dozen times. I was told the meeting couldn't be interrupted.'

That fucking rot-in-hell jackass, Jablonska!

He softened his voice, almost weeping himself: 'Annie, sweetheart – I want you to listen very carefully. I want you to go get the kids. Please do it right now!'

'What are you saying, Don?'

The pitch of his voice was rising progressively. 'I'm saying we gotta get out of here. We gotta run.'

Her red-rimmed eyes were scanning his face, his mouth, his eyes, like goddamned searchlights. Her voice sounded like the voice of a child in his ears.

'Run where, Don?'

'Anywhere. Who gives a fuck! Out of here, that's for sure. Maybe to uncle Ronnie's in Oregon.'

'Ronnie won't want us on his doorstep.'

'We won't tell him we're coming.'

She shook her head, threw her arms around his waist. 'No, Don. We're safe here. We've got to wait. People will come. The medical authorities...'

He had to think... he had to think really fast. *What in God's name will we need?* In the distance, he heard the sounds of police sirens. 'Annie – sweetheart – we've got no time for this. You love Donny and Betsy. We've got to hit the road for them – now.'

He ran down the stairs into the basement play room, grabbed five-year-old Donald Junior and three-year-old Betsy without a word of explanation. With one struggling body over each shoulder, he took the stairs two at a time. He shoved the frightened children into the arms of his wife.

Oh, Jesus – have I ever really begged you for anything?

In his study, where the safe was, his legs turned to lead. He was fumbling with the combination. Boy, had he been wise to put money into that safe for a rainy day. Well this was it – tsunami day.

He began stuffing ten thousand bucks worth of fifties into his pants pockets. There wasn't enough room. He wasted time picking up some of what fell onto the floor and stuffing it any which way into his left breast shirt pocket, the pocket with the golf club logo in real gold stitching. He wiped his face with his hand as he turned to the desk, tugging at the locked drawer. He knew it was locked. He had locked it himself so the kids couldn't get into it. The problem was he had forgotten where he had hidden the key. He yanked the handle off the drawer before he remembered. It was just at the back of another fucking drawer. His voice was roaring witlessly in his own ears at the thirty second delay as he emptied the drawer onto the floor, going down onto his hands and knees to search for the key. He found it, unlocked the drawer, grabbed the automatic pistol and the ammo clip, stuffing the gun into his belt and jamming the ammo into a pocket already stuffed with fifty dollar bills.

Annie was watching him from the doorway. She was staring at him, the kids hanging onto her pants, screaming.

Outside, the sirens were close and loud: the cops were here. They were doing something up there at the gate.

Annie was bawling, pleading: 'Please don't frighten us. Think about the kids. Betsy hasn't been well.'

'Annie, Annie – sweetheart. Don't you understand? It's gonna be too late!'

He pushed his resisting wife ahead of him, roughly, angrily. Didn't she understand, a guy had to protect his family. He screamed at her: 'Will you just get into the car.'

She clung to him again.

Betsy hasn't been well!

He slapped Annie's face.

It was the first time Don had ever hit his wife. The shame of what he had just done penetrated his terror like a blade. Tears of remorse sprang into his eyes, running down his cheeks, as he shoved and yanked all three of them out through the front door, their stubborn feet crackling in a percussion of panic over the stones on the drive. He forced them into their seats without bothering to belt up.

Backing out the Porsche, he maneuvered the gun and ammo onto his lap, letting go of the wheel with both hands while he struggled to slot the clip into the butt. Annie began to bawl again, causing the kids to join in the chorus.

He tried to focus.

The loaded automatic was back in his belt. He went straight into high revs, picking up speed. In his rear-view, he saw four or five other vehicles following his example, tearing out of their drives, already tailgating the Porsche. He squealed to a halt in front of the security gates. He stared with jaws clenched and his eyes bulging at the two black-and-whites forming a vee in the entrance. Four police officers, dressed in biosafety suits, were setting up no-exit signs right there in front of them. A fifth cop stood point with a rifle held in pale buff-colored surgical gloves. Don wound down his window.

He hollered: 'Who do you people think you are?'

Annie's juddering voice: 'Oh, please stop this, Don!'

The cop with the rifle was staring, widening his stance.

'Hey, you guys. Can't you just cut us a little slack.'

The rifleman was moving round the hood, closing on the open window. His visored head was peering inside.

Annie's eyes were clotted with tears. Her voice reached across Don, teeth chattering, liquid sounding, like it was coming up from under water: 'Please, officer – we're just a family. You look like you have a family of your own.'

The eyes within the visor wavered: the rifle slackening, the muzzle falling. Don started praying: *Please God... just this one thing?*

Then Bettsy was sick. She made a whooping sound, before puking over the back of Don's head and shoulders. Alarm registered in that face behind the visor. Don saw it all with a perfect clarity: for Annie, Donny Junior, for baby Bettsy, the road block was now a death sentence. The rifle was lifting up again in the tight grip of those two gloved hands.

No exit! No escape!

Don brought up the handgun and emptied the clip into rifleman's face. Blood and flecks of tissue and bone blew back in through the open window. On automatic pilot, he floored the gas. He rammed through the point of the vee, leading the convoy out into the road.

*

Gary Maisley was rapping abstractedly on the surface of his desk, while sitting in his pod in the Reno office of the FBI. In front of him were his own confused jottings. He had scribbled a telephone number down in the margin of the same sheet of paper. He had gone so far as to draw a circle round the telephone number, but it hadn't helped to make his course of action any clearer. He inhaled. He picked up the piece of paper with the telephone number on it. He balled it up in his fist. He threw the goddam thing into the bin. Then, on impulse, he yanked it back out. He brushed out the creases so he could read it. He started rapping on the desk surface again, staring hard at the name, Professor K. McCann, and her telephone number on the crumpled paper.

*

At Santa Barbara Police Headquarters, 215 East Figueroa Street, a panicky call came through to the Combined Communications Hotline: officer down. Location: the Green Oasis Club Development, upper Eastside. Green Oasis: aka "Stepfordville".

Over the next few minutes calls started coming in through half a dozen different hotlines. A wave of panic was juddering through the attractive white-washed walls of the entire police headquarters, triggering the decision by Police Chief Jose Jesus Vargas to declare a "Critical Incident" response.

Officers were running from various departments to the conference room in Communications to put into operation a plan of compulsory quarantine and full emergency powers over-ride that none, in their worst nightmare, had ever really anticipated would happen. Computer, phone and fax lines were being patched through to the CDC, the Federal Government Emergency Hotline at Washington. Chief Vargas himself was talking to the Governor's Office, demanding the help of the California State National Guard. Headquartered in Sacramento, they would have to fly into the otherwise quarantined LAX airport. Seven teams of patrol officers donned biosafety suits and headed out in an assortment of vehicles, with warning lights flashing and sirens screaming, battering their way through the largely empty streets.

*

Standing in front of the ABI 3730 sequencer in the molecular biology lab, Kay heard the bench phone ring. She ignored it to concentrate on what she was doing. Opening the glazed door that covered the front of the machine, she inspected the wafer-like gel sandwiched between two glass plates about halfway down the brilliant white background. She inserted a fine-toothed comb of white plastic into the top of the gel.

The phone was persistent. Sami Kitisato, who was standing by a screaming centrifuge, picked up the telephone. She said, 'For you, Kay. Some FBI guy.'

Damn – O'Keefe!

Kay whispered, 'Tell him I'm not here.'

With great care, she lifted the fine-toothed comb back out of the gel. She had created twenty minuscule wells. The noise of the centrifuge had ceased. Sami was putting tubes into racks, one rack marked A and the other marked P. The tubes in each rack were coded by numbers. They contained different transmutations of entity gene E.

Kay paused, held still a moment so as to steady her shaky fingers. Then she began the long series of insertions into the tiny wells pressed down into the goo between the two panes of glass. She closed the sequencer door, switched on the 2,000 volts across the plates. Already those tiny samples were beginning their journey of revelation down through the gel. They had been chemically labeled, so the nucleotide compositions would show up on the chromatogram. It was a critical experiment. Done, she slumped against the working surface, feeling utterly drained.

The desk phone was ringing again, insistently. She grabbed it, barked: 'Mr. O'Keefe, I have my own work to do here!'

'I'm not O'Keefe. My name's Maisley, Professor. We met at the hospital where Dr. Sultan was admitted.'

'Mr. Maisley - I remember you – you saved Ari's life. What can I do for you?'

'I'm sorry to disturb your work with something you may think is downright silly.'

'Go ahead – shoot!'

'It's just a bunch of little things that don't make sense. When Sultan was in the hospital, I had the feeling he was scared out of his wits. Yet he never showed any curiosity about who attacked him, or why.'

Kay frowned. She had no idea where this was leading. She said, 'What are you implying? Is Dr. Sultan under some kind of investigation?'

'I know he could have been suffering from shock. But even so, it's unusual. And it isn't the only thing that's bugging me. A number of things about Sultan are bugging me. I mean, I've discovered that this guy is extremely computer literate.'

'Most scientists are.'

'Not this literate.'

'I've known Ari since I was an undergrad at Berkeley. Ari was my ex-husband's protégé.'

'Yeah! And his colleagues thought they knew the Unabomber.'

Sami was signaling to Kay: she mouthed, 'I've got to go.' Kay had to go too. There was a mountain of work that needed doing. 'Mr. Maisley, get to the point.'

'Maybe the guy's a genius. I'm asking myself – a guy that smart, maybe he could figure out a way to make an e-mail look like it came from the middle of the Atlantic Ocean.'

'This is getting ridiculous. Ari Sultan is a leader in his field. He has exactly the kind of expertise we need here. If that's all that's bugging you?'

'You ever been to his home?'

'No, I haven't.'

'He's unmarried. He lives out there in the desert, all alone. It's not what you would expect in terms of the home of a scientist. The security is incredible – to the point of paranoia.'

Kay was growing increasingly exasperated: 'Can I ask you why you're bringing this up at this time?'

'Sultan has been under surveillance. We have a load of scientists under surveillance, protective as well as investigative. In fact, I'm writing out my report on Sultan right now. I was asked to comment on the fact that he's been recruited to the scientific group working with you at the Ivan Wallin. That makes him my responsibility as well as yours.'

'But you don't have a single concrete fact against him.'

'You're right. I've got nothing other than instinct.' She heard him sigh. 'Professor McCann, maybe you're right. You know the guy. I just had to check. But I'll give you my number. Anything worries you, give me a call.'

*

At the Green Oasis Club Development, Evelyn Maurice was repeatedly swallowing to keep herself from retching. Spurts of bile were rising into her throat. Even from a distance of two hundred yards she could hear the bedlam of vehicle horns, shouts and screams from up by the barrier. People were fighting to break through the police cordon.

A veteran from the bubonic plague containment in Surat, India in 1994, and Ebola containment in several Sub-Saharan African states, she had never encountered such raw panic as she saw here. She knew now that terror was as communicable as a plague bacterium or virus. She had felt it, tasted it in her bone-dry mouth when she had been conducted, under rifle protection, through that sea of anguished faces with the help of a platoon of panicky National Guardsmen. But there was no way they could allow those folks to get out. Something terrible was going on here. Something so dangerous it could not possibly be allowed to flee. The security fence, with a single manned entrance, that had kept the club complex safe and private was now their prison. The only way these people would leave their luxury homes was in the fleet of military ambulances, guarded by armed police outriders. These were forming a long arc that went the whole two hundred yards to where her team of epidemiologists, suited up and sweating inside their visors, were moving from building to building, triaging the dead from the living, and the obviously infected living from the rest.

Overhead a fleet of Apache helicopters formed a ring of airborne protection, keeping the reporters in their buzzing hornets out of camera shot. She sure hoped they managed to keep them well clear.

An unknown number of residents had used their four-wheel drives to batter their way through the first police barricade after shooting dead one of the investigating officers. There was no knowing where they were heading, or what they were carrying out there with them. She had to hope and pray that it wasn't some fearsome new mutation.

Clearing her throat, she spoke into the com-link radio-enhanced through to Kronstein at the White House:

'Aaron, I believe we're looking at a worst-case scenario – what we've all dreaded from the beginning.'

During the conversation with Kronstein, Maurice was unable to stand still, pacing around, walking a few dozen paces along a street lined by sprinkler-damped lawns, flowering bushes and ornamental maples. She could see people lying dead in their gardens. From the searches through the homes, they were building up an extensive catalogue of dead, folks in their beds, bathrooms, on the chairs and floors of their living rooms, skins black, eyes staring.

Kronstein whistled: 'You got a handle on how it happened so fast?'

'My guess is they're all fast-tracks.'

'How could that happen?'

'Maybe something to do with the fact that the entire development was built around a golf course. I'm no biologist. But this is an entirely artificial ecology. If we assume it's grassed by just a few selected turf species. Something close to a monoculture. No natural resistance – would make it an ideal culture medium for the entity. We're laying out bodies on lawns full of circles.'

'How many dead?'

'A hundred twenty-seven – so far.'

'Jesus H. Christ!'

'Aaron – I've got to run!'

Her attention had been distracted: a colleague, dressed in a bright yellow safety suit, was gesturing to her from a rear doorway in the building labeled **HEALTH AND FITNESS CENTER.** Her leaden feet carried her over, following his figure through the tiled ambience of shower cubicles. A flutter of panic palpitated in her chest, wondering what she was going to find inside.

From inside a single locked door among the changing cubicles, she heard a child's screaming inside.

'Break it open!'

Within they found a girl with flaxen hair. She had been doubly incontinent where she sat. Her blue eyes were blank, staring. Thumb in mouth, the screams were for her mommy.

Maurice and her colleague carried her out to one of the gurneys in the massage parlor, where they stripped her naked, washed her clean, then conducted a hurried medical examination. All the while she never stopped screaming.

She had the flushed red skin of high fever. But no rash. It puzzled Maurice. She didn't need a tongue depressor to inspect the girl's throat because her mouth was all the while wide open with the screaming. At the back of the throat she saw tonsils swollen so they were almost touching, red as lava and covered in pus.

The girl didn't have the entity.

Most likely diagnosis: a beta-hemolytic streptococcal infection. A common bacterial sore throat. It should respond to penicillin. One life she could save. They rolled her out of the building under a blanket on the gurney and Maurice told the triaging crew to put her into an ambulance on her own. She instructed them to take her back to individual isolation in quarantine. If they had put her into a common infected ambulance, it would have been a death sentence.

*

In the Conference Room at the White House, a shocked silence followed Aaron Kronstein's description of what was happening in Santa Barbara. Kronstein was staring down at his papers as they listened to Sarah Lipmann, the Secretary of State for Foreign Affairs, give them a report on the European reaction to what was happening in America.

Two days ago, the French Ministry of Health and Social Affairs had been the first European institute to recommend its citizens to avoid American travel altogether. The same day the UK Health Minister had promised any help the British Public Health Laboratory Service could give them. Rumor had it that the first circles had been found on a farm in the southwest of England. Another rumor said they had found dead trees the German Black Forest. Both countries were denying it. But if it was true, the presence of entity in the upper atmosphere was beginning to threaten far beyond America. The previous day, health experts from the 27 countries that now formed the 500 million population of the EEC had met in Germany, which currently held the EU Presidency. They had imposed an embargo on all incoming flights from America. An increasingly tense committee turned to Marcus Easterhouse, the newly appointed replacement for Duhan as EPA Administrator.

Easterhouse returned their attentions to what was happening in America: 'The Landsats fit the general picture we have been hearing about in terms of human spread. Circles are spreading with increasing speed.'

'But the quenching of circles with decon works?'

'Yes, it does. In theory, provided they are caught early. In reality there are inevitable delays, even after the circles are picked up on Landsat. It's less of a problem with farms. But it's a nightmare in natural wilderness areas. We must

somehow arrest the growth of new circles before the spread
is too rapid and extensive. In one small forest area, we
picked up more than four hundred new circles overnight.
Manpower and materials are limited. Ma'am – we're
already overwhelmed.'

General Monath was nodding: 'Dr Kronstein is right.
The situation is already out of control. It's the considered
opinions of the Chiefs of Staff that this acceleration cannot
be allowed to continue. With your permission, I would like
to demonstrate.'

He took the floor, focusing their attentions back to the
latest Landsats of the Mojave Desert in a fifty mile radius of
the Ivan Wallin Field Reserve. He zeroed in from distance
to close-up. 'The pictures are horrifying. Although there has
been some debate with the meteorologists, this is the only
area where burning on a large scale is likely to have caused
a thermal swell sufficient to carry the entity up into the
higher atmosphere.' He moved closer. 'I guess you can see
what I'm getting at. This is it. This is the epicenter.'

The President's mind caught the word, a hard word, a
word of inescapable consequences: *the epicenter.*

She saw a myriad of overlapping circles, like a colossal
smallpox extending over the entire landscape.

Monath spoke tersely, crisply: 'You wanted new ideas. I
ask sanction of this committee to engage an incisive
military option.'

'Which is?'

'A mass evacuation of all those people still living in the
south Mojave, followed by a sterilizing of land and air, using
tactical nuclear weapons.'

The President stared at Monath for several seconds.

'You're serious, General?'

'I am serious, Ma'am.'

'But the psychological effect on the nation's morale!'

'We hear the scientists are making progress. We should
do what we can to buy them a little time. Even if they come
up with some kind of a solution, for circles, environment
and people, this area is beyond redemption. From the time
it was set afire, the Field Reserve has become the source of

most of the spread to all other areas. It's just about lost to us already. If we allow the contagion to continue, the implications will be worse than any effect on morale.'

The President glanced around the table, saw downfallen faces. She looked in particular at Easterhouse. No evident disagreement with Monath. 'I presume you've put together an actual plan?'

'The weapons aspect is not problematic. The biggest hurdle would be enforced removal of the residential population, given the area and the fact that a high proportion of them are likely to be infected.'

Dickinson waited for others to object. Nobody interrupted the silence.

'You'd better explain.'

Monath projected a map of the southwest. 'The Mojave occupies 15,000 square miles. If we keep it to a minimum, we could get away with zapping just a quarter of that. It's a relatively small sacrifice if this nation is to be protected. What is needed at this critical moment, Ma'am, is the courage to make a radical surgical excision.'

Easterhouse, who must have been mulling it over, exploded: 'But how does the Pentagon know that such a catastrophic remedy would work? Wouldn't it just worsen the situation and blow the entity into the stratosphere?'

'Not if we know what we're doing.'

Dickinson sighed: 'I presume you do know what you're doing?'

'Yes, Ma'am. We have experts who can exactly calibrate the effects of such a strike. I have Lieutenant Colonel Adams waiting outside in the lobby. I recommend we invite him to address this meeting.'

*

Close to midnight, Kay was sharing a table outdoors with Will, drinking black coffee. The tail end of another exhausting day. The parasol over the table was still raised, as if to shade them from the beautiful night sky. There was a light cooling breeze, which was very welcome. She touched Will's hand. 'You okay?'

'I'm fine. Just that heady mixture of exhaustion on top of more exhaustion. How about you?'

'I'm worried about Sean – my parents.'

'You heard anything more?'

She sighed. 'I know it's irrational but right now I feel like just up and running away with them.'

He reached out and held her hands.

She said, 'I got a really weird call from an FBI Agent, named Maisley. He more or less asked me to keep an eye on Ari.'

'Really?'

'Absolute paranoia!'

But the trouble with paranoia was that once Maisley had planted the seed it set her mind to mulling things over. She said, 'I can't deny that Ari looks nervous.'

'He's not alone!'

'Exactly!' She shook her head. Who wouldn't look nervous working under these pressures? For pity's sake, Ari had survived a bomb under his chopper. Why – what possible motive could link Ari to what was happening?

She just shook her head. It made no sense... none whatsoever. So why did it set some distant bell ringing, like a peal of suspicion at the back of her mind?

06: 07/ 09h47

A hammer was pounding Nora Seiffert's head. The hammering was her pulse and it was inside and not outside of her head. She struggled to open her eyes, swiveling her face towards the digital alarm clock, which, in her blurred vision, showed some time close to ten o'clock.

Ten o'clock! What was she doing? She should have taken the charter for Mexico hours ago.

She tried to jerk her body up into a sitting position but she didn't – couldn't – make it. Pain stopped her. There was a searing pain in her back whenever she attempted the slightest movement. Her gut clenched. It felt as if somebody had rammed a bayonet into her belly and it was still in there, cutting and twisting and hacking.

A new wave of shock juddered through her. She was having trouble breathing. Her nose felt blocked. Her entire face, around the focus of her nose, felt solid, hard as wood. When she brought her right hand up to touch it, her fingers were numb. The feeling was weird, a mixture of numbness, a prickling, like pins and needles, and sudden throbs of agony. It felt like her fingers were candles... like they were on fire. When she examined her right hand, she saw what looked like burnt sausages. Her fingers were swollen to twice their normal size. Her whole hand, and part of her forearm, had turned an oilescent shade of black.

This was impossible, some kind of coke-induced heebie-jeebies.

She clenched her eyes shut, opened them again. Looked. Big areas of her skin had turned completely black. When she examined it more closely, she could make out how it had started at her finger tips and crept back to her hand, her wrist, and the lower third of her forearm, like gnarly roots, branching and ramifying. The skin was tearing away from the putrid flesh underneath in rancid bubbles. What in the hell was going on? She tried to think back. She tried to remember yesterday. Ray... the money...

Ray... the money... and his little surprises!

*

Kay McCann looked around her, in the men's sleeping quarters among the closely packed trailers. She didn't want anybody, Ari especially, to see her here. Her anxiety made her want to hurry.

Damn! It must really look like it's me who's acting suspiciously!

She found the door marked 18C. It didn't have any name written on it but she knew this was Ari's sleeping quarters. At this time in the working morning there shouldn't be anybody about.

With a furtive glance to either side, she inserted the master key into the lock. Her hand trembled as she attempted to turn the key. It jammed and refused to go the whole way round. *Oh, Lord!* Panicking, she tried to retrieve the key. But the key wouldn't budge. It would neither turn nor come back out. She started rattling and shaking it, trying desperately to loosen it. At last it released the catch and the door swung open with a loud creak that cut through the prickling silence. She retrieved the key from the open door and then shoved pieces of broken up orange stick into the keyhole, rammed them further in with the key, before entering the trailer and pulling shut the door behind her.

She leaned back against the inside surface, waiting for her heart to stop racing.

She still wondered if she was paranoid in thinking that Ari was behaving oddly. But once the idea was there, it had seemed to take root. She had slept poorly the previous night, going over her suspicions in her mind. She recalled a number of things that might give substance to her paranoia.

Ari knew the field reserve. He had worked here many years ago. He knew about Sector 5-32. And then there had been rumors. She recalled Mike saying things about Ari. Worried about the arrogant behavior of his former protégé.

It was common knowledge that Ari took risks. She recalled Mike's take on Ari's business practices: 'He's forever cutting corners. Trouble with Ari, from the start, his ambition's been bigger than his common sense.'

But none of that was even remotely convincing. None of that would have persuaded Kay to break into Ari's bedroom. But then she thought of it: she had pinned down the little bell that was ringing back there, in her subconscious.

She had recalled Ari joking about Mike when he came here. Ari capturing Mike's New Jersey accent perfectly. So perfectly, you wondered if he could talk to somebody who really knew Mike, somebody like Michelle, over the phone and convince her it really was Mike she was talking to?

Heart pounding – it just wouldn't slow down – she searched the bedroom.

It was surprisingly untidy. Worse even than Sean's, and Sean's had a notice on his bedroom door, "WELCOME TO THE PIGSTY". She combed through the clothes in the drawers. She peered under the mattress. She had to go down on her knees to look under the bed. She discovered two pairs of handmade shoes. In the closet she found more evidence of expensive tastes: an Armani suit, half a dozen silk shirts. But nothing that could be construed to be in any way suspicious.

Goddam! O'Keefe was right. She wasn't any kind of detective. She wasn't even sure what it was she was looking for.

In the bottom of the closet she found a black leather briefcase. It was locked, with a numerical code. She bit down on her lip. No way was she prepared to break the locks open. She tested the clasps. The case sprung open. Ari hadn't even bothered to spin the dials on the lock. She recalled how he'd rushed back up to Reno the day before to deal with some problem at his company office – Ari, always in a hurry. The case contained much of what she would have expected: some business cards, headed notepaper, pens, a Dictaphone and a black cell phone. She had broken into the bedroom of a colleague, not knowing what she was looking for, and here was the evidence that he was in all likelihood entirely innocent.

Okay! Wasn't that what she really wanted to find?

Suddenly she heard footsteps in the asphalt outside the door. She held her breath, waited, her heart thrusting against her ribs.

The footsteps stopped outside the door. She heard the sound of a key being inserted into the lock. She was paralyzed by dread. There was a muffled curse as the lock refused the key. She heard the footsteps tapping sharply away. *Thanks, orange stick!* She waited another minute or two. Nothing. She dragged the briefcase over bedcovers and under the window so could examine the contents in a better light.

She tested the Dictaphone: a virgin tape. She examined the cell phone more closely, clicked it on. In the stored memory she found only a single outgoing call. No menu of business contacts, friends. He must have just bought it.

What now?

A noise outside the window. Ducking down under the sill, she squeezed her body back into the wall. A shadow was blocking out half of the incoming light. She heard the squeal of skin on glass: a hand shading the bright sunlight to peer more closely.

Man alive – this whole thing is getting crazier and crazier!

The scrutiny seemed to go on for half a minute. It had to be Ari himself – Ari wondering why the hell he couldn't get into his room. She couldn't bear much more of this. She winced to hear him cursing again.

The shadow receded. She waited several minutes without moving a muscle. Squatting at the window, she peered out of the corner: nobody there. She returned to the cell phone, that single outgoing text yesterday. She scrolled:

RAY TO SAM: READY TO COMPLETE THE DEAL

What could it mean?

A business proposition? Nothing unusual there – Ari was a businessman. So why then was her heart pounding so hard?

On impulse she checked the number called. Some detective, she hadn't even brought a pen or paper. She conducted a furious search for a ballpoint and a scrap of paper to note it down. Settled with the back of one of Ari's business cards. First thoughts: Andy Yang – a wizard with technical matters. Would he be able to check out the owner of a cell phone number?

She switched off the phone, put it back in the case, returned the case to the closet. With a wary look – all clear outside – she slipped out of Ari's bedroom, closed the door. Suddenly she was rushing, heading out of there as fast as propriety would allow her, terrified of how crazy she must look to anybody who might happen to see her.

*

Whenever Nora tried sitting up, she blacked out and had to come to again. She had given up trying to climb out of bed. Instead she fell back to trying to remember... Yesterday. Ray... the money... his little surprises. Like the security gadget to open the first aluminum case. Like having to wait for the radio signal for the second case.

It could have held anything, including a bomb. It cost them a day because they hadn't dared to drive of with that locked case inside the trunk. They'd been forced to stay out there in the goddamned desert. She recalled Jamie Lee putting the case on a rock he could watch from a distance, the two of them sitting in the cab, the air-conditioning running, smoking one cigarette after another. Sitting ... waiting ... watching ... She recalled J-L peering out through the gun sight every now and then, at that shining focus out there on that rock. She recalled Jamie Lee saying that something had happened. He had walked out and approached the case carefully. He had used a tire level to pull back the cover. Even from the distance, she had heard him whooping and hollering. No bomb. Just a case packed with the stuff dreams were made of.

And something else... Some goddam thing. She tried hard to remember. But she just couldn't work it out for a minute or two. She blacked out again and then, when she came round, she remembered – the little bonus in the lid of the case! The snow!

They had carried on snorting the cocaine halfway through the night. She and Jamie Lee. Some celebration. Wild. Wild for the road... tomorrow's road. Correct that – today's road. The road to dreams.

Fuck – *fuck!*

The thing... *the thing...* had to be the cocaine. But how? How had he done that, when she had seen him snort it right there in front of her?

When you dice with the devil, what do you got to do... What you got to do... you got to play it smarter... you got to outsmart him.

*

Kay was sitting in Andy's EM suite. She was surrounded by the pictures of his female conquests amid the award-winning EM photomicrographs. Her hands were restlessly tapping on the bench surface. In front of her tapping fingers were two telephone contact numbers. One was the number copied out of Ari's cell phone. The other was the contact number for Agent Maisley.

She faced a dilemma. If her suspicions were right, Ari Sultan had something to do with the deaths of all those people. He had subverted past friendship and intimate local knowledge to seed the lethal entity into Sector 5-32, killing her friend, Ake Johansson. It was possible, too, that he was linked to Mike's disappearance. On the other hand, he might be entirely innocent. If he was innocent, she had just done something unforgivable. She had not only invaded the privacy of a colleague – she had imagined him guilty. All of this because of some paranoia that could result in her dismissal from this post.

The logical thing to do – her first option – was to forget she had ever broken into Ari's office. Her second option was to wait for Andy to return. At least Andy could be induced to silence. The third option, and least logical, was to call up Agent Maisley.

She picked up the bench phone and dialed the number.

Her lips felt numb: 'Mr. Maisley?'

'Who's this?'

'It's Kay McCann.'

'Professor?'

'I guess it's my turn to be downright anal. After your call... Well, I have to confess I did something a little crazy. I should probably be arrested.'

'What did you do?'

She had to physically pause for breath.

'I took a look round Sultan's bedroom. I think – I more than think – I just about know that he knows somebody did it. He tried the door while I was in there.'

Maisley was silent.

'I shouldn't have done that. I could very well lost my job here because of it. I wouldn't have dreamed of doing anything like that in ordinary circumstances.'

'Something strike you as suspicious?'

She hesitated. 'Yes, it did.'

'Situation we got, Professor, the normal rules don't apply.'

'Thanks – thank you for that!'

Confusedly, haltingly, she told him about searching Ari's room. Even now, while she was explaining that it all came from nothing better than her gut instinct, she realized how stupid it sounded. A house built of cards. She told him about the cell phone, the text message. She gave him the number she found in the cell phone.

He said, 'Professor, it's not much. But I'll check it out.'

*

Nora's memory was slipping. Her cell phone kept ringing. In exasperation she picked it up and there was nobody there. Vaguely, somewhere on the outside of the pain, she knew there was something she had to do. Something... what was it she needed to do? With a rending noise that was half groan, half scream, she reached out with a hand that felt it did not belong to her. She saw the alien hand take hold of the cell phone and bring it right before her face. The trouble was they made them so small, the keys so tiny. The damned thing was slipping and slithering from her grip, like some wriggling reptile. Funny how her fingers were completely numb to touching the phone and yet they burned like merry hell!

Try... she thought. *You got to try dial.*

She tried to dial. Made a mess of it. Couldn't make out the goddam keys. Let it slide onto the bed. She stared at it, this reptile thing... Stared down at it where it lay next to some stinking, rotting body.

She flopped back again. She was struggling to focus. For a moment she couldn't remember who she was. She couldn't remember what it was she had to do. *The phone. Had to make a call... an important message. A desperate... vital...*

A name kept floating up into her mind. Jamie Lee... Jamie Lee was the guy.

J-L had gone back to his place to pack his stuff. Should have been here to pick her up this morning, bright and early. The plan... the plan was they'd head for Mexico by charter plane. No way you'd get through by road, not with this thing raging around them. Jamie Lee... her sweet boy, J-L. He was coming to pick her up.

Should have been here hours ago. Something was wrong. Jamie Lee would know what to do.

J-L was hot key number 1. The hot key for sweet lover boy. Just two prods. Key 1 and then the dial key, green, top left... She was struggling through a wall of agony just to reach out her hand.... Picking up the phone again... Hit 1–.

'Shit!'

Wrong key. She had hit 4. *Hit off... start again...*

I'm trying, Jamie Lee... Can't you see I'm trying...

She slid a throbbing finger over two notches that had become valleys in an impossible landscape. She pressed the key with a finger that didn't register anything. She hit the green key, top left. Heard the ringing tone... Her entire arm was shaking like she was falling to pieces. The phone felt red hot, like a burning lighter against her ear. She was panting, waiting for a bellow of retching to pass.

She heard breathing: a man's breathing. He didn't speak.

She took a juddering breath. Her throat felt as if a flame thrower had gone to work on it. Her words sounded like, 'whoomahtakinoo'.

'Who the fuck?'

'Nooo-aaa.'

'That you, Nora?'

'Eaahhh!

'You sick? I got to tell you, Nora, me too. I feel like fucking shit.'

Licking her lips with a tongue that felt dry as desert driftwood, she summoned every ounce of her remaining energy.

'Nnnn aaa nooo!'

In the snow.

Somehow... she had no idea how... Ray had cheated her.

In her mind she saw Ray's head, complete with Panama and shades, on the body of a snake... The snake was a bright red, like the devil. Suddenly she saw devil snakes, thousands of them, all wearing wraparound shades and Panama hats. They were multiplying under the floors, inside the wall cavities, sliding and slithering everywhere, their forked tongues flicking out, scenting prey, hunting, devouring, until they had taken over everything, until they filled all the rooms in the house.

*

Agent Gary Maisley took a right off the San Bernardino onto Mountain Avenue. Everywhere he encountered streets scoured clean by terror. Where there should have been a jam of traffic held back at the lights, there was just a single emergency vehicle beating through red with siren blaring. He passed by a Texaco station, closed, without even the minimal background illumination. The restaurants and shops looked haunted as old sets in a movie warehouse. Those Angelenos who hadn't taken off were skulking inside of locked and bolted houses. There was nothing that looked or felt ordinary any more. Just the spreading, festering miasma of fear.

The situation we got, the normal rules don't apply.

He meant it. This was war: a dirty, treacherous war. He had no regrets calling the professor in the first place. He did have some regrets breaking the rules in following up the flimsy lead alone. But what did he have? Nothing other than his instincts about Sultan. That and the professor's suspicions, which had maybe just been ignited by his own. It was incredibly flimsy. An amateur Sherlock Holmes breaking into a colleague's bedroom. Lifting a number out of a cell phone. A number that had given him a name – Angelina Broddick, who lived northwest of San Antonio Heights.

He'd checked the name against known criminal associations. *Nada.* Same on DNV. Same on skip warrants, rap sheets. But there was something distinctly odd about this woman, Angelina Broddick. She wasn't registered for voting. It happened. He had met lots of people like that in his work. Very likely Angelina Broddick wasn't politically interested. But it was another tiny oddity – another whisper of suspicion.

That was all he had to go on.

Whispers!

No way could he do this by the rules. If he called for support, his office chief would pull the plug.

After four or five more miles of deserted streets, he hit an increasingly rural backdrop: pulling into Mountain View Prospect, a two-lane dirt road shaded with eucalypts and the occasional cluster of bedraggled palms. A higgledy-piggledy scattering of houses lined the road, with no real common plan: wood frames, brick-builds, adobes – empty lots between them. A locality you could live in without worrying about nosy neighbors.

Maybe a place a slightly crazy kind of woman might find amenable – the kind of a woman who didn't want to be bothered with voting?

He pulled into a dust-blown dirt track that led up an incline. At the end of the track stood a single-floor adobe, hacienda-style, white-washed, half circled by a copse of digger pines. There was no name on the mailbox, just a number: 47.

He parked the Dodge beside an overgrown hedge of bottle brush. He took a good look at the house. Nothing unusual. He slid his feet onto grit. His polished shoes crunched and grated as he approached the solid oak front door. He paused again. He went over the excuse he was going to use, before knocking. The old hammy act: a report of prowlers. He had a final glance around him, taking in the dirt road, the Dodge, the mountains looking close enough to reach out and touch off to his left and behind the house. He glanced to his right, at the copse of trees. There was something under them that caught his eye. A silvery reflection, like a chrome car part. It was catching the sunlight filtering through the pine needles.

He shaded his eyes with one hand. Could be the shape of an automobile – one with black paintwork. What kind of an idiot would park a vehicle under sap-dripping pine trees?

He decided to go take a look.

It was a black BMW. It took him maybe two seconds to make the connection. The missing scientist, Mike McCann, owned a black BMW. He had to crouch on his haunches, yank branches out of his way, to see the front plate. He found a broken light and other minor damage consistent with crashing through an underground car park barrier. There was even a splinter of wood caught up in the plate. His heart was doing somersaults when he called the office on his cell phone.

*

A new wave of trembling ran through Nora Seiffert. *Ray!* She could recall his name but not his face. She hated that... she hated the fact she couldn't recall Ray's face. She heard the doorbell ring, insistently, stridently.

Jamie Lee? *No, no – no!*

Go away!

Another wave shuddered through her, shaking her limbs and rattling her teeth.

She heard loud noises coming from the door. Blinking her sole functioning eye, she listened to the noises, trying to figure out what was going on. A splintering crack: the door frame had just broke open. Footsteps were padding through the hallway. A shadow was entering the bedroom... A tall shadow, wearing a space suit.

The shadow squawked at her: 'FBI.'

Her eyes swiveled towards the six-foot circular mirror in the ceiling. A hideous face was looking back at her. The whole centre of the face, including the nose and mouth, was a butterfly, painted black. Blood was running down in a thick stream from the left nostril, taking a detour around the swollen lips, and rising over the chin. It carried on down, like a pestilential river, watering the valley between two small hills that were her breasts.

Another shadow joined the first: two shadows, squawking out questions.

She tried to spit at them. Her eyes rolled in the furnace of their orbits. A gurgling obscenity rose out of her gut. She began to vomit. Black vileness jetted out of her mouth and something even worse came out of her bowels.

Even with her eyes closed, she heard the clattering of their spacemen feet and hands as they began to tear the house apart: searching.

A new wave of trembling was shaking her limbs and rattling her teeth. It exhausted her. Her arm fell by her side and her eyes came to rest on the obscenity overhead, the vision of hell captured in that cold silver eye.

*

O'Keefe was red in the face from shouting at Maisley: 'I can't make up my mind which of you is crazier, you or the Professor!'

Maisley was standing to formal attention, 'All I had was instinct and Professor McCann trawling through her colleague's briefcase.'

'You could have blown it. What do you think would have happened if that woman in there wasn't already sick?'

Maisley said nothing.

Six cars were gathered around the house. Two were emergency med vehicles. A search squad dressed in full biosafety gear were still combing through the rooms.

They had established that the woman's name was Nora Seiffert, not Angelina Broddick. Seiffert was a known associate of Moldano, the guy who had tried to kill Professor McCann and ended up dying in the truck. They also had hard evidence: a USMC M40A3 sniper rifle, which had been taken away for ballistic match up with the Chicago hit.

Maisley said: 'Seiffert's phone records should confirm the call from Sultan.'

O'Keefe stared back at him: 'All we got to link anything to Sultan is a phone call.'

'Sir − it's got to be him. It all fits. He's got the know-how to construct the entity. His own biotech plant to design and construct it.'

'But why would he do it? Where's the cash?'

'I don't know. I don't know whether he connects to terrorists. We do know he's got lots of foreign connections.'

'It's very speculative.'

'I know how we might be able to confirm Sultan.'

'Spit it out!'

'My guess is the receptionist, Michelle, never met Sultan. He hasn't worked there in something like twelve years. We get somebody to take Sultan's picture to her and ask her if this is the guy who took the plants out to Sector 5-32.'

O'Keefe was staring at him.

'We could add a panama hat − and shades.'

'It's another long shot.'

'What's to lose?'

O'Keefe barked instructions into his cell phone.

Maisley started to shiver and shake: 'I just gotta sit down.' He flopped onto the hood of a car. The mixture of relief, pride, anger − he didn't know what.

O'Keefe still pressed him: 'What about the bomb?'

'He had to have put the bomb under himself. To throw us off the scent.'

'That's taking some risk!'

Maisley shrugged. He had no better explanation. He blinked his eyes, as if making a sudden realization. 'Sir – she could be in danger. Professor McCann! She thinks Sultan knows that somebody was in his room.'

'Shit!'

O'Keefe got onto the cell phone again, calling the JOC. Professor McCann was also to be taken into protective custody.

A shout from the house switched both of their attentions to a biosafety-suited figure that had popped out onto the doorstep. One of the forensic guys was waving his arms. O'Keefe hurried over and Maisley followed.

The forensic technician was shaking his head. 'You wouldn't believe what we found in the cellar. There's a guy chained to the floor. He says his name is Mike McCann.'

06: 07/ 19h55

Will worked on in a mixture of exhaustion and exhilaration. He ignored the fact that the lab complex was in uproar around him. FBI agents were storming through offices looking for Ari Sultan. Nobody offered any explanations. By now he was becoming used to this type of thing: first Kay and now Ari had become the focus of their paranoia. He told them he hadn't seen Ari since mid-morning. It was bizarre. But right now it wasn't enough to distract him from putting all of his efforts into the confrontation with Jerry Rizinski, and Xanthos-Max, which was looking like it was growing into a crisis.

It had been evident from their conversation yesterday that Rizinski was reluctant to play ball with Will's gene therapy. It was no good reminding him that people were dying – and the figures were doubling day by day. Neither would Rizinski provide Will with vector to try out here in the labs. He insisted that all manufacture and trials were the exclusive prerogative of Xanthos-Max.

So, increasingly, Will had taken over the responsibility of developing the gene therapy by himself.

Roxy Penhaligan was now in the loop, ostensibly as a neutral, but between them they had decided on their vector, a monkey immunodeficiency virus, dressed up in a Trojan coat, known as VSV-G. Will was working with it already. He had inserted MRE gene into the viral shell yesterday. He, and Josie Coster, had been up halfway through the night, constructing the vector and adding the requisite additional components designed to blinker and chain the virus.

The gene therapy plasmid had been injected intravenously into a dozen animals, three species groups, and a dozen control animals. That experiment was now up and running. But he and Josie had done this without formal consultation with FEMA, or the NSC. When Xanthos-Max discovered what they had done, they would blow a fuse. Nevertheless Will was gambling on the fact that their small scale trials, if successful, would give Rizinski, and Xanthos, the kick up the ass that they needed to forget normal time lines and the worry of potential litigation that was the real explanation behind their stonewalling.

Will wasn't looking forward to a new head-butting cam-link session. But he wasn't going to shirk his responsibilities. He waited until he had both Rizinski and Penhaligan on the line and then he told them what he had done.

Rizinski exploded. 'You're crazy. You're worse than crazy! Your puerile impatience could jeopardize any chance we have of beating this thing.'

Roxy said nothing, though Will could imagine she was listening with interest.

'Jerry, if this blows up in my face, you can point the finger at me. But what if it doesn't? Do I go talk to CONPLAN and say, "Hey – look! We did this with nothing more than our diagnostic lab. Xanthos-Max refused to help us." Maybe its time FEMA, or NSC, took a good hard look at your contract. There must be other big corporations out there who'd step in.'

'This is blackmail.'

'Jerry – it's desperation.'

'You think you're playing this cute when in fact you're completely out of your depth.'

'I'm not sure that he is,' Roxy stepped in. 'I could give you two examples where government agencies tore up contracts.'

Rizinski said, 'Well, I'm not buying it.'

Will pressed him: 'You should talk it over with your legal advisors.'

'You telling us how to run our business?'

'You telling me, Jerry, you refused to work with us, an integral arm of CONPLAN, and you haven't consulted your legal guys?'

'I'm telling you to get off our case.'

'Roxy!' Will ignored Rizinski to play a variation of his own game plan. 'You get those interim reports I sent over?'

How likely was it that Rizinski was recording the cam-session? Will guessed that every word they exchanged went in front of a board of legal advisers. Even if Rizinski hadn't recorded the sessions before, he'd sure as hell be recording this one. He wouldn't dare not to, now that the implications had been mentioned. Jerry was a hard-nosed corporate shit. You could put your shirt on the fact he had enemies within his own organization.

Roxy said sweetly: 'I'm looking at them right now.'

'What interim reports?' Rizinski barked.

Will ignored him. 'Roxy – you see any glitches with our methodology?'

'Nothing I can see.'

Rizinski burst in: 'I don't know what the hell game you're playing, Grant.'

'Let me remind you, Jerry – we're the scientific arm of CONPLAN. We're in a plague situation. By implication, we're empowered with all of the emergency powers we need. You should think about that.'

'You talk to me like I'm being obstructive when all I'm being is sensible – pragmatic. No Mickey Mouse therapeutics is going to work.'

'We'll know, pretty soon!'

'Jesus! You goddam amateurs!'

'Are you telling me you're turning it down flat?'

'This is your private little indulgence!'

'There's nothing private about it. I have the support of the lab organization. And that of my boss at CDC and, through Patrick Moran, a line straight through to NSC and the President.'

Rizinski laughed. 'My ass!'

Will bit his lip. Did Rizinski know he hadn't, in fact, taken the time to speak to Patrick Moran? He'd have to see to it urgently.

'Roxy, I'm going to have to hang up. I'll let you have the preliminary toxicity results – by early evening at the latest.'

'I'll be very interested to see them.'

Rizinski cut the connection.

'Hey, Will,' Roxy's voice was more hesitant now, 'I sure hope you know what you're doing!'

*

The FBI agent was dissatisfied with the little that Mike was able to tell him. O'Keefe had begun his interrogation as soon as they cut him out of the chains. He had continued while a doctor was examining Mike's broken collar bone.

'How'd that happen?'

'She did it – the bitch from hell. When those guys were chasing the car in the underground garage in the Conference Center in San Diego. She smashed it with the butt of her gun – just so I'd be sure to get the message.'

'But our agents reported that you were driving the car?'

'Tell me about it.'

'No – it's you got to tell me about it!'

Mike sighed. 'I was at the San Diego meeting. I heard my name being paged. I was going to answer it but first I had to get something I'd left behind in my car. I didn't notice there was anything wrong until I heard her knuckles rapping on the driver's window. I look up and there's this impossibly slim blonde-haired bimbo peering in at me through the glass.'

'Seiffert?'

'She didn't introduce herself. By the time I thought about locking the door, it was too late. She was shoving a Glock automatic into the back of my head.'

'Why'd she break your collar-bone?'

'Your two guys turned up. She didn't like it. So she smashed my collar bone and told me to drive.'

O'Keefe smiled, faintly. 'You drove the car all the way here from San Diego with that smashed up collar bone?'

'I drove it.'

'Okay – so explain to me – why'd she keep you alive?'

'You want me to go over the conversation verbatim?'

'Whatever you can recall of it – yes.'

'She says to me, "Let me explain something that might help focus your thinking. I got a contract with your name on it. But there's something about the contract that tickles my curiosity. There are six names on the list. Five of these it's a simple hit, no frills. You know what I mean?" Let me tell you, I got her meaning.

'Then she says, "Not you, sweetheart. You get the special treatment."' Mike paused to cough. 'You people even thinking of letting me have a drink – some tasty little morsel of food to eat?'

O'Keefe called for somebody to bring him some water. He said, 'We'll stop and get you some food en route.'

They hurried him out of the door and into a large dark car. Mike was helped into the back seat, where he sat nursing his injury, while O'Keefe slid in alongside him. Maisley sat up front with the driver. O'Keefe said, 'Keep talking – Seiffert made you drive the car.' The interrogation continued some more while they headed out in convoy, with LAPD patrols fore and aft, strip lights flashing, sirens shrieking.

'She said, "Hey, let's not get over excited. It's still the same contract. But in your case I got to conceal the fact you're dead. So the question I'm asking myself is – Why?"'

Mike suddenly started breathing hard. His face broke into a cold sweat.

O'Keefe looked away from him, out of the window. 'You're okay. It's over. But I need to ask these questions.'

'I wasn't listening too hard after that. I knew I was meat. She was only talking to herself anyway. She says something like, "That kinda gives me an idea. If you're that important to the contract, you become interesting to me."'

'You became some kind of pawn?'

'I mean, she's going on like this... "The guy wears a Panama and wraparound shades. He goes to all that trouble. What do you think of a contract who goes to all that trouble just to hide his fucking face?" What the hell does she expect me to say – does she want me to disagree with her? "Me," I say, "I wouldn't trust that fuck."'

O'Keefe smiled again.

'"Way I see it," she goes on, "I keep you alive but I pretend you're dead – you become useful to me."'

'So she saw you as insurance. She thought, maybe, if the contract went bad on her, she could squeeze you for information?'

'Yeah – that was my take!'

O'Keefe nodded. 'Logical!'

'So, okay, she was a logical kind of murderess!' Mike groaned. 'Aw come on, guys! Do you mind laying off me until I can feed my wiped-out neurons. I'm starving!'

They stopped at a hamburger joint and Maisley brought Mike back two quarter-pounder cheeseburgers and a jumbo-sized coffee. Mike insisted Maisley go back for a double portion of fries.

The convoy coursed eastwards in the dark: the cruisers front and back butted aside what little there was of traffic and ignored junction lights. From time to time, O'Keefe stopped asking questions to take calls on his cell phone. Mike closed his eyes so he could focus all of his attention on eavesdropping.

From the conversations Mike came to several conclusions. The FBI knew Seiffert had made a call not long before her death. The call destination was another cell, at a location within LA. That call appeared to be important and its investigation had racked the FBI investigation into high gear. Sultan, meanwhile, had disappeared from the Ivan Wallin. The window to his bedroom was broken, his briefcase gone. Teams were hitting his home, his biotech plant. Their techs were trawling records, phone, fax, e-mail, whatever. Every few minutes, another message would arrive for O'Keefe, from agents everywhere. He closed his cell for the umpteenth time.

'So what you're implying is that Sultan went out of his way to set you up as a bankrupt mentally-flaky priority one subversive.'

'And you suckers sure fell for it.'

'I'm still not altogether convinced you weren't somehow involved.'

'My involvement was down in a pit with a Glock at my head.'

'There could have been some kind of falling out. Maybe you were the contract wearing the Panama and shades. And she found you.'

'Ari played you guys like puppets.'

'If what you're telling me is the truth, you're the guy he played like a puppet. He knew you've been arguing in public with your colleagues for years. You were a grudge looking for mischief.'

'When you lay your hands on that shit – I want to be in on the interrogation.'

O'Keefe laughed.

Mike insisted, 'I mean it. You're gonna need me.'

O'Keefe ignored him. 'Okay, so let's just say I buy it for the sake of argument. He figured a way of shifting the blame onto you. But I still can't get an angle on motive – I just can't figure him out. I mean, why construct this monstrous thing?'

Mike shook his head: he had no idea.

'Sultan – you see him as some kind of fundamentalist?'

Mike roared with laughter: 'Like me – Ari's a founding member of WHOGAS.'

'WHOGAS?'

'WHOGAS - who gives a shit.'

'That a real organization?'

'An unofficial one, over a few beers with some of the guys.'

O'Keefe was frowning. 'It still doesn't make much sense.' The FBI man was distracted by another call on his cell. A brief conversation. O'Keefe called to agent Maisley up front. 'We got to the desk clerk – Michelle.'

'She good for it?'

'She confirmed Sultan.'

*

Will decided he had better talk to Kay urgently. One of the techs informed him that she had been taken to the JOC offices by the FBI.

'What's going on?'

The tech shrugged. 'They tell us nothing.'

All of a sudden, he felt ravenously hungry. He grabbed a tuna and salad sandwich from the canteen and headed for BSL-3.

Josie was in BSL-4 – taking a peek at the animals. He'd have to test the tissue cultures on his own. He chewed at the sandwich as he sketched out a plan for 64 test plates in a cross-patterned grid. It would be tedious and time-consuming.

He poured himself another mug of coffee from the pot, ignoring the fact that it would heighten his jitteriness, then called up Josie in BSL-4.

'Anything showing?'

Her voice came back, raised above the noise of the air pump. 'Nothing definite. Just too early.'

He said, 'I've got urgent things I need to do. I could do with a couple of your techs to take over the cell cultures.'

'You got it.'

He put down the phone.

Such was his distraction that he ignored the phone ringing for several seconds. Then, assuming it was Josie with some additional wrinkle, he shoved the receiver against his ear, locking it in place with a lift of his shoulder, as he continued to set out the big grid of human tissue culture plates.

Janie's voice took him completely by surprise:

'Dad!'

She sounded upset.

'Oh, Janie, I'm forever apologizing to you!'

'I... I, uh ... oh, daddy!' Her voice juddered to a stop. He heard panic there, in her voice. He could still hear that same panic in her breathing down the line.

'What is it?'

'I'm going to die!'

Will was staring at the plates but seeing nothing.

'Please don't be cross with me?'

'Cross with you, Janie?' His voice was hoarse. 'I don't understand.'

He heard the snuffling sound of his daughter crying.

His own breathing had become erratic. 'Janie?'

'Phillippa... Dad, she's got it. H-her whole family.' Her voice rose to a wail. 'They've taken the whole family to the hospital.'

'Phillippa's got what?'

'She's got *it*!'

A fist of ice was constricting his heart. 'Are you saying that you were in contact with Phillippa?'

Janie was weeping openly now. 'Yesterday - Saturday - was her birthday. Last night, I decided I had to... She's my best friend. I didn't even stay for her party. Aunt Lucy drove me there, just so I could give her her present.'

'You came into contact with her last night?'

'I... I hugged her.'

'Did you kiss Phillippa, Janie?'

Another wail: 'Yeah!'

'Phillippa has been diagnosed?'

'The whole family - they've gone into the university hospital.'

'Oh, Jesus!'

He was talking to himself: *you're jumping to conclusions*. He tried to think. There were logical questions he should be asking Janie. How was she feeling? Did she feel hot? Did she feel like she was coming down with the flu? But he couldn't bring himself to ask those questions. Skin-to-skin communication was extremely infectious. Mucous membrane contact - kissing - it was just about one hundred per cent. The ice was spreading, invading his entire chest. He couldn't take an adequate breath.

His conversation a short while ago with Rizinski and Penhaligan started running through his mind, like an action replay in a horror film. The vectored treatment was untested, unproven. Even if it showed a modicum of promise, development had not even begun.

Too late for Janie!

Janie was shrieking: 'Come home for me, Daddy – please!'

06: 08/ 02h50

Kay didn't even attempt to sleep. She was under protective custody, sitting at the bleached wood table on the porch of the former rangers' station. Ari was loose. Her former friend, who had taken out a contract to have her murdered, and there was no saying he wouldn't try again. Nobody could think of a motive for Ari's behavior. People were assuming that he was crazy. Kay didn't think Ari was crazy. Then the message had come through from Will about Janie: from that moment onward here was no question of sleep.

The FBI had offered her a cot but she had abandoned it for the porch, finding it more peaceful now, the desert air cooling down.

She heard the patter first, then witnessed a sudden squall of rain.

Would rain damp down spread of the entity? She had no idea. It had never rained from day one so it hadn't been tested.

Strange to think how, with the rain, the desert around the field station would bloom. It was desperately ironic, given the proximity of millions of proliferating circles. Like a false promise of hope.

Sitting there, mulling things over, she responded little to the FBI agents coming to talk to her, asking this and that, going away, often actually running. Phones in the background were ringing constantly. Willson himself arrived some time in the early hours. The Special Agent in Charge was moving in and out of the various buildings, bossing the show. Sometimes he talked to her, sometimes he sat in silence. Sometimes he studied her with a curious expression: like maybe he was trying to figure where she was coming from, or maybe, just maybe, he was feeling a little guilty about previous encounters.

'This guy, Sultan! You reckon he's capable of constructing this thing?'

'Maybe – maybe with help. With help – probably.'

He was off again, to answer a ringing phone.

She moved her position, to sit further back in the porch, looking for the coldest spot, the deepest shade. Kay McCann: biological lead on site. But she was no longer confident she could exercise that responsibility. She was losing confidence in herself. Mike was heading for here. That much she held onto. For what ... what did they call it? Debriefing. They had told her all about finding him. He was basically fine other than ravenously hungry and needing treatment for a broken collarbone. Willson was back again, looking at her across the table.

'You said two things: maybe and probably?'

It was good, helped to keep her rooted, this demand for logic. Willson was coatless now, but she saw none of the suspenders you saw in the old Fed films. His pants were held up by the conventional black leather belt.

She was blinking through the miasma: thinking about Ari Sultan ... perhaps the most brilliant mind she had ever met. She thought about the old adage: genius and madness. Was Ari deranged?

'He couldn't possibly have done it on his own.'

'But he could have masterminded its construction?'

'Possibly.'

'Yes or no?'

Blinking slowly, aware of the shape of her eyelids, like small leaden arcs pivoting about their ends, moving through treacle: 'Yes.'

'Plus the money to front it?'

'Very likely.'

'The motive?'

'That's the thing I just can't get my mind around. I can't even begin to imagine what motive could have driven him to do this.'

*

'Sir – we have something.'

It was half an hour later. Willson turned his upper body half way in his chair so he could see who was speaking. 'What is it?'

'We've taken a call from an editor at *The New York Times*. The journalist, Mark Stanwyck, the guy who's been writing the articles – he's been contacted by a woman in Canada. Claims her husband was the first scientist to be assassinated. They want exclusivity in return for cooperation.'

'Fuck what they want! When did this happen?'

'March this year.'

'Name of the woman?'

'Lyse Egremont.'

'Her husband?'

'Henri Egremont.'

Willson turned back to Kay: 'The name Henri Egremont mean something to you, Professor?'

'Yes. University of Quebec. A Nobel Prize winner. He died a few months ago in some kind of lab accident.'

'What kind of accident?'

'I'm not sure.' She was fighting against the miasma. 'Somewhere abroad – an agricultural station in some Middle East country. I recall something about an explosion ... a fire involving gas bottles.'

The agent interrupted: 'The woman, Egremont's wife – she claims it wasn't an accident.'

'And she waits three months to tell us this?'

'She's been telling people for months. They've been ignoring her.'

'They?'

'The Canadian Defense authorities.'

Willson reflected on this for a moment: 'Three months ago – hard to see the relevance.' His interest was visibly flagging.

'His wife says he was employed by Sultan.'

'Shit!'

'Sir, you're not going to believe this. She has all these e-mails. Stuff about bioengineering. He was the head of some research project. She's been telling them about this stuff but nobody's been listening.'

Willson was puffing breath in and out of his nostrils like a train pulling out of a station.

The unseen agent fell silent, waiting.

'I want everything she's got.'

'Canadian jurisdiction?'

'Okay, talk to them first. A guy called Bernie Potter. Make it clear we want this stuff yesterday'

'Yes, Sir.'

Willson's bony hand shocked Kay when it fell on her shoulder. 'Professor, I may need your advice on this.'

It was raining again, drizzling out of a pallid grey sky. A couple of beats from the cicada under the floor. Like it was clearing its throat. Kay heard the engine first, then saw the vehicle pulling in, an FBI unmarked. Mike stepped gingerly out of the door. His left arm was bent into his chest, supported by a sling.

Kay was climbing onto tired feet. Willson was also just returning. His arm clamped down on her shoulder again: 'He isn't your husband any more.'

'I still want to welcome him back.'

'This takes priority.' He slammed three sheets of paper down in front of her. Two e-mails and a copy of a letter, faxed over from *The New York Times*. 'Look at these, Professor – this is urgent.'

Out of the corner of her eye, she saw Mike being herded into one of the buildings.

'Professor –!'

She read an e-mail:

Dear Lyse,
Such excitement!
I have enjoyed this week in London. We spent the evening in a small hotel by the Thames. My new employers had booked the entire place for the inaugural celebration – although relatively unknown in the international league, the

> *company certainly knows how to spend money...*
> *Of course El Supremo had a hand in planning this ...*

She read a fax from Lyse Egremont to the Canadian Defense authorities, telling them she didn't believe her husband had died in an accident. It was dated May 26. A day after the Mendelsons were killed in Chicago.

'Mr. Willson! Could you get me a pitcher of strong coffee?'

Willson barked the order, a pensive expression on his gray lined face.

Kay turned back to the communications, her mind struggling for a clearer focus as she moved on to the second e-mail.

> *I'm sorry we couldn't get together for Thanksgiving. And now it's the New Year and I haven't seen my little granddaughter in ages... Things are looking so much better... Dr. Ahmed's work on maize is very promising – also Chan's work on rice. ... Even E.S., after that spiteful episode with Nancy Chong, when she refused to hop into bed with him, is showing signs of knuckling down ... The fellow is undoubtedly a wayward genius.*

She clenched her eyes tight shut. Reopened them. She forced herself to a still better clarity of thought: E.S. – El Supremo – alias Ari Sultan! She read on...

> *I'm not one to get overly excited, but we have made a breakthrough - without doubt the creation of a new biological paradigm. I'd love to say more but I'm not allowed to talk about it. E.S. has pioneered new organic vectors in the eight months we have been here. We have abandoned microprojectiles. Spectacular nano*

> *linkups with bioinformatics. There are radically new structure-class charts sprouting along the entire lengths of the corridor walls!*

A few beats to consider: was she wrong? No!

Her voice stuttering with fatigue, then clearing, she said, 'Mr. Willson... *Mr. Willson!* I believe this is important. I think – I believe – it's describing the construction of the entity.'

Willson's face was a mask of triumph. He was shouting through an open door to his assistant. 'Go get a hold of NSA on the hot line.'

The assistant called back: 'Yes, Sir!'

'They intercept every e-mail,' Willson explained to Kay. 'They'll have everything. All we need to do is pin down the time span and the addresses and servers.' Then he shouted at the agent, who was standing there, listening. 'Get onto it. I want times. Locations. And copies of every exchange that ever took place between Egremont and his wife.'

Mike was coming out onto the porch. He was holding out his hand to take hold of hers. She couldn't stand up: her legs had gone.

'Oh, Mike – you goddam lunatic!'

'Good to see you too!'

Her relief was tempered by thoughts of Janie. Horror, grief, a swell of suppressed emotions were battling for space inside her.

She'd somehow missed the moment of sunrise and now the sun was clear above the horizon on a blossoming desert. The chaos around her was worsening. Agents were running to and fro, adding the e-mails and faxes as fast as they were coming through. Mike planted himself down into the adjacent chair. Willson had already disappeared, hauled away again to deal with something new.

Mike whispered: 'You think they've caught him – Ari?'

'I don't know.'

Willson reappeared. He stormed up to the table. He leaned over them both, ignoring the paperwork, his voice a rasping whisper:

'The President has received a second e-mail.'

Kay shook her head: 'Why now — I don't get it.'

'Professor!' He passed a weary hand over his face. 'Your name is mentioned in the e-mail.'

06: 08/ 06h03

A biosafety-suited Will Grant was standing in the corridor of the Intensive Care Unit in the University Hospital in Atlanta. He had to hold still to collect himself outside the isolation room, then take a breath before walking in:

'Janie, sweetheart —'

She was sitting in the chair by the side of the bed, dressed in a disposable hospital-issue pajama suit. Sweat stuck the thin material to her body in places. Her eyes were red and her eyelids were swollen from crying. She whispered: 'You're too late, daddy. I kept asking you to come home for me.'

Will went down onto one knee to be level with her. 'I haven't got much time to explain, Janie. I know that what's happening must be really frightening. I'm taking you back with me.' He waited a moment or two for his words to sink in. 'Now, forget I'm wearing this moon suit and give me a hug.'

Janie lifted her arms up and she hugged her father. Her body was frail, vulnerable. Terrible memories... déjà vu! He swallowed. He spoke as gently as the suit would allow: 'I want you to trust me. I'll be with you all the time. You believe that?'

Janie was staring into his face, her lower lip trembling.

Will gazed back at her through the moistness of his own tears: 'Some people are going to come in here, dressed like me. They'll be carrying a plastic balloon on a gurney. I'm going to have to put you into it. It won't hurt. You'll be able to breathe and to talk normally. It's a mobile isolator, so we can put you on a plane and get you out of here.'

Janie shrank down into herself, her hands buried between her thighs. 'Where are you taking me?'

'To the hospital in Thirless. You know where that is?'

She nodded.

'Then you know that it's not far from where I've been working. There's a doctor there, Ric Valero. He knows more about treating this thing than anybody else. He'll be looking after you.'

*

President Dickinson stormed into the Committee Room, assuming charge of the ad-hoc assembly of the Emergency Management Group. She didn't care if the other members of the committee noticed the loss of her normal elegance, which had been replaced by a brittle jerkiness of anger.

'Go ahead - let's see the damn thing!'

> E-mail: *to President J C Dickinson, The White House.*
> Sender: *Yawm Ad-din.*
> Subject: Circles
> Priority Code: *Omega #3: red.*
> Message: *ENDGAME!*
> This one is for you Kay...

In silence they listened to another computer-generated tune, in those same tinkling musical-box cadences.

Dickinson spoke abruptly: 'This one even I recognize.'

The psychological profiler, Minkowsky, nodded: 'It's a pop tune, *Windmills of Your Mind,* from the soundtrack of the movie, *The Thomas Crown Affair.*'

'What's it mean?'

Lilley murmured, 'Means we're dealing with a sick bastard!'

'Minkowsky?'

'I have no idea, Ma'am.'

'Are we convinced this e-mail is another genuine communication?'

Randall, the NSA director, nodded.

Dickinson, with a look of fury, rounded on the FBI director: 'Mr. Lilley?'

Lilley said, 'I've got no explanation – not as yet. With what we now have from Lyse Egremont, we can be certain that Sultan is our perpetrator. This has to be some kind of personal communication.'

'What do we know about him?'

'He's a naturalized American. Born in Indonesia, of Muslim origins but, far as we know, non-practicing. We made a big mistake, letting him go join the others working at the JOC lab. Even if it was at the insistence of Professor Kay McCann.'

'Surely she isn't involved?'

'She's being questioned right now at the JOC. But we don't think she's involved. He fooled everybody, including her. Apparently he worked there as a grad student, maybe twelve years or so ago. He was a protégé of her ex-husband at that time.'

'Any leads to his whereabouts?'

'He's taken off, we don't know where. Car gone from the parking lot. We're turning every stone looking for him right now.'

'And the terrorists, *Yawm ad-Din*?'

'We have to conclude that they never existed. They were a distraction. Like setting up Mike McCann as the fall guy.'

Dickinson's gaze swept over the committee, making fleeting contact with each member in turn. 'It's progress, I guess. But time is fast closing down our options.' Her gaze stopped at Galbraith, the Secretory of Health. 'Ruth – no sign of a slow-down?'

Galbraith, who looked like she'd been up most of the night, shook her head. 'It's doubling every twenty four hours.'

'What about the circles?'

Monath hurried to the screen, impatient for the computer link to kick in: 'Ma'am, we have Landsat pictures for the entire country. We're dousing circles in the wheat-fields of Kansas. What you now see just about everywhere is the spread of circles. We're dousing them fast as we can. But we're not dealing with the source. My opinion – it's the prelude to a goddam explosion.'

All eyes were on her: every one of them willing her to make up her mind about the nuclear solution. The President paused for perhaps thirty seconds. She said, 'We wait a little longer.'

*

Kay was still sitting on the verandah, swigging strong coffee like water. Mike had been taken away again for further debriefing. She had just read the latest e-mail to the President. It fell from her hand onto the table surface, next to the growing collection of communications from the Canadian wife of a dead Nobel laureate. The lone cicada percussed the floor, like a disjointed rhythm section to the computer generated jingle: the same eerie musical-box cadences.

Willson pressed her again: 'Did Sultan intend this for you?'

'I don't know what to think anymore.'

'There must be some kind of a clue in this tune. This tune means something personal to you, doesn't it, Professor?'

'It was our favorite. Mike requested it in the restaurant – when he proposed to me.' The memory seemed to belong to another world.

'So what does it mean to Sultan?'

'I don't know.'

Willson exhaled. 'None of this is making sense to me.'

She thought: of course it isn't making sense. The nightmare isn't over. It's going to continue.'

'Professor?'

How could she possibly make sense of the fact that she was linked in some personal way to the horror of what was happening? She wanted to get back to the lab: to join Josie Coster in pushing Will's ideas with the gene therapy – to feel she was doing something.

She looked up at Willson. 'This woman who kidnapped Mike – she was definitely linked to the killings of the scientists?'

'Nora Seiffert was the leader. Sultan hired her. We found an aluminum case full of cash in her house. We're working on tracing it.'

'But she died from infection with the entity?'

'We figure Sultan double-crossed her. Clearing his tracks.'

'So he must have hired them to kill those scientists – to kill me?'

'Certainly looks like it.'

O'Keefe had joined them: 'Professor, if you had been killed, who'd have been most likely to take over as scientific chief here?'

'Provided we didn't know it was him, likely Ari Sultan.'

O'Keefe grunted. 'Then we've got at least part of his motive.'

Willson held Kay's attention, eye-to-eye. 'Professor, we believe there's one more killer out there. Whoever it was that Seiffert called on her cell phone when she was dying. We think we know who he is. A vicious thug named Jamie Lee Weiss. You should still consider yourself at risk.'

Kay felt physically nauseous.

'You listening to me, Professor?'

'I'm very tired, Mr. Willson. I'm trying hard to think. Going through the words of the tune.'

'You got an idea?'

'Ari was academically brilliant at Berkeley. Math in particular. He liked to play mental games.'

'So it would be reasonable to assume he's still playing games with us? Challenging us with riddles?'

'Challenging me personally with this one.'

'The tune?'

'Yeah – the tune.'

'Meaning what?'

Kay began to hum it to herself, went through the words again. The chorus. She pulled out a blank sheet, wrote it down as she recalled it:

> *Like a circle in a spiral,*
> *Like a wheel within a wheel*

Never ending or beginning
On an ever-spinning reel...

She recoiled.

'Professor?'

'Mr. Willson, ask yourself the question – what possible circle could turn within a spiral? What wheel could turn within another wheel?'

Willson's face contorted with impatience.

'The spiral is DNA, the molecule of life. The circle is a metaphor for a machine.'

'A machine within the DNA of life?'

'A very special kind of machine, Mr. Willson. A nanomachine!'

He shook his head, struggling to understand.

'Oh, Ari's been so clever. I see now why he chose Mike for his fall guy. Mike pioneered the construction of nanomachines. That was what Anton was exploring in his final experiment. Poor Anton!'

Kay was already on her feet: 'Mr. Willson – we've got to set up a conflab. Bring together all of the scientists.'

06: 08/ 06h00

Will was sitting by the bubble in the plane. His mouth was dry, his heartbeat hollow, erratic. He was consumed by a feeling of helplessness. What more could he do? What would he do if Janie died? *What...?* The overnight hours had dragged by with a horrible illogic of their own. Waiting ages for the portable isolator to arrive, then for the chopper pick-up: these were the toughest hours he had ever had to endure.

Work – *Jesus!* He would work himself to death. A black tunnel – nothing at the end of it. But at the back of his mind he refused to give in. It was no good just relying on hope. What he had to rely on was logic.

Last night Josie had read the latest animal experiment. One in three of the test group was still alive. They were sick-looking. But maybe they'd survive. The treatment had worked. He wasn't sure it would convince Rizinski. It was a long way from a hundred per cent success. Will also knew that Mike McCann was safe and helping them. Kay had called Will fifteen minutes earlier to keep him posted. She had explained the shocking truth about Sultan: that a man everybody had trusted as a valuable colleague was in reality the murderous hypocrite. It was perhaps just as well that Sultan had disappeared. Will was feeling more than a little murderous himself.

His thoughts reeled, from Janie to work: from work back to Janie. He was devoid of appetite. He didn't even feel a thirst, even though his mouth was permanently dry. He was unable to prevent the same questions from coming back to torment him:

It was nine in the morning by the time they were settled in the ITU at Thirless. He lifted Janie out of the bubble, carried her over to the bed wrapped in the embrace of his rubber-suited arms.

Will hugged his daughter more fiercely.

He had to let her go so they could change her clothes. Janie still wore the pajama suit she'd had on since Atlanta. He hadn't even thought about it – about how uncomfortable it must make her feel. Sweat was soaking through it over her chest and back, the thin cotton curling up her long skinny legs to the knees. He waited until they had washed her down in the bed and dressed her in fresh clothes. They brought in a fan to help reduce her temperature, which was rising rapidly. He saw the jerks, the shiverings: the onset of the rigors that would cause her temperature to soar. He came back to sit on the edge of the bed so he could be level with her.

'I can't even kiss you through this suit.'

'It was a kiss that got me in trouble.'

A shudder registered at the very core of him as they locked eyes. Janie had cried herself out on the journey. What he now saw now in her puffy red-rimmed eyes was a haunted look that brought the moistness back to his own.

Clearing his throat he spoke to her softly: 'This is Dr. Valero, Janie. He'll take real good care of you.'

'Then it's for sure - I've got the Zombie Plague!'

He brushed his hand through her black hair, separated from real contact by two overlapping layers of gloves. The nursing staff moved back, to allow the tall biosafety-suited figure of Valero to sit on the edge of the bed, next to Janie.

Valero touched the back of her hand: 'Hi, Janie! I guess that you and I are going to get to know each other pretty well. Are you in any pain?'

It was out of Will's hands now: he could only watch Janie nod to the man in whose hands he had place her life.

'I got a major headache building up.'

'Right! You feel anything else?'

'I've got a shivery feeling like the flu, inside of me.'

'Well, we can take care of that. The nurses will get you feeling more comfortable. Get you something more attractive for a young lady to wear.'

A voice inside Will was screaming: *Do it: make her more comfortable.*

Valero's face was looking out at Janie through his visor. It made empathic communication harder: 'Janie - I can see how intelligent you are. So I'm not going to kid you about anything. I promise you that. What it is, there's something I want to try, to see if it will help you. It might seem a little scary. Okay?'

A violent spurt of anxiety. Will was doing his best to conceal his own panic from Janie, who kept glancing his way for reassurance.

'Janie – you ever heard of therapeutic hypothermia?'

She was shaking her head.

Why the hell isn't he asking me this?

'What you've got is a very early stage of the disease. Some people progress quickly, some slowly. I think you are going to be one of the slow ones. That's good. It gives us a little more time to do something about it. To take maximal advantage of that, I'm going to have to put you to sleep.'

No!

Janie whispered: 'What's the point?'

'The point is that we're working on something new. Your father has played an important part in it. But we're not ready just yet.'

'You want to put me to sleep and then freeze me, is that it?'

No way!

Valero was smiling, lightly taking hold of Janie's right hand: 'Cool you down a little, but not like in the sci-fi movies.'

'Daddy?'

Will hauled Valero to one side, whispering to him through the microphone intercom. 'What the hell game are you playing? We talked about superficial hypothermia.'

'I've thought about it since then. Superficial hypothermia isn't going to give us enough time. I want to try deep hypothermia.'

'Why?'

'You know why.'

'How deep?'

'Take her core temperature to 68 degrees Fahrenheit.'

Will shook his head, too emotional to have any chance of concealing it from Janie, unable to hide his terror that this might be the last time he ever spoke to Janie.

'I know it's relatively unknown territory. But young previously fit people have survived accidental deep hypothermia. There was a report of 46 cases.'

'Sure, but how many survived?'

'Fifteen.'

His arms were flailing. He was shaking his head: 'Jesus Christ!'

Valero said, 'We've got to try.'

'These fifteen - they looked at the long term side-effects?'

'No hypothermia-related side-effects that impaired the quality of life.'

Will muttered, 'I don't believe it.'

'There were early cognitive deficits, as you'd expect. But years later, they were leading normal lives.'

Will crossed to the bed and hugged Janie again. Their tears met on either side of the visor of his helmet. 'I think we should go ahead, sweetheart.'

'Oh, Daddy, I'm frightened.'

'Of course you are.'

Janie clung to him, fiercely, longingly: he felt the fine frail bones, and the heat of her body, even through his suit. He felt an overwhelming wave of mixed love and terror: he had to stop himself squeezing so hard, or he'd break her ribs.

'I feel like if I go to sleep like that, I'll never wake up.'

'Do you think I'd allow that to happen?'

'Don't leave me.'

'I'll never leave you, sweetheart.'

*

Kay watched intently as Mike, his right arm supported by a more substantial orthopedic sling, stood in front of the plasma screen and gazed at the synchrotron images of the entity. The only key person missing was Josie Coster. Josie was keeping in constant touch with Will, while working her butt off in BSL-4, fighting for Janie.

Mike's head was shaking, his eyes wide. 'Man – this is awesome!'

Rumbles of disapproval erupted from the dozen or so people gathered in the meeting room. The FBI agents, O'Keefe and his boss, Willson, were foremost among them.

Kay spoke from where she was sitting at the ad-hoc table. 'You're not uninfluenced by the fact that, maybe, you are partly responsible for its invention?'

'What it is, Kay, is that out of blue you see your own ideas – ideas that everyone has thrown in the trash – come to fruition. Ari did a bucket-load of borrowing. Look at the compaction. The organization. That's one hell of a clue.'

'What organization?'

'You need organization to drive this thing. No way otherwise are you going to coordinate anything as complex as this.'

Kay recalled the words of the dying van den Berg: *It absorbs kinetic energy... A new paradigm!*

'Can you explain the link to nanotechnology?'

'Kay – you're really asking me to explain nanotechnology? You've spent most of your professional life studying nanotechs. Where you see mitochondria, I see motors. Nature was always a billion years ahead of us.'

Mike left the monitor and moved to the computer open on the table behind it. His awkward gait was a reminder that this was a guy who had been chained in a pit. 'I haven't had time to familiarize myself with all you've been able to gather about its construction. But let's see if I can drive it from there.' He started hitting individual keys. The entity exploded into its component parts: the engineer's three-dimensional schematic. Then, with painstaking thoroughness, Mike analyzed the subsidiary structures, one by one.

'From what I can see, your overall thinking makes sense. The core is where gene reconstruction takes place. The horizontal nodes are where host antigen sequences are reworked to RNA. All right! But there's something else going on here – at this south pole. Something really odd.'

'What is it?'

'Did van den Berg ever talk about a programmable memory?'

'I don't recall him doing so.'

'Look here,' Mike zoomed in on the south pole. 'Watch as I flick in and out of mag. In low mag, you see there is a second bulge. And now in high mag. Jesus!'

The screen filled with a blow up of the south pole. Then the structure expanded further like an exploration into a fantastic labyrinth of starry constellations, interwoven by bright colored ribbons.

Kay muttered: 'You know what it is?'

'It's definitely nanobiotic. Let's see if we can trace its connections. This guy – looks like an influenza virus spike. This makes contact with new host membrane – new antigen. So let's follow the action from there. It enters the first bulge. My guess this reads the sequence. Passes the sequence to here, the second bulge. Hey, look at that! Suddenly there's an awful lot of cabling. Some goes straight up into the core. But most comes out and spirals right and upwards to each of the four horizontal nodes – what you call the moons.'

Kay pressed him, 'Can you hazard an educated guess?'

'Yes, I think I can. But first tell me – did van den Berg keep a record of what he was thinking?'

'Anton didn't make much sense at the end.'

'What did he say exactly?'

Patrick Moran cut in: 'I'll tell you exactly what he said, Dr. McCann.' Moran took out his notebook and he read directly from it. 'I quote, "The bad guys have created a miracle."'

Mike laughed. 'That's what he said?'

'Yes.'

'He was exaggerating, is my guess.'

Kay said, 'Anton wasn't given to dramatizing.'

'Okay, Kay. Then get me van den Berg's records.'

Kay asked Sami to get the disk from the molecular biology lab. She was back in less than a minute, carrying Anton's laptop computer.

'Folks, I apologize, but we're going to have to take a break. I need to take a good look at this. Meanwhile, I'll lay my hands on some constructional algorithms that may help us understand what's really going on.'

*

Patrick Moran followed Kay back to her office. He said, 'I've been watching your face back there. I'd like to know what's making you look so worried?'

'I'm worried because Mike is worried.'

'What's really going on?'

'You remember a conversation we had – it was very early on – about Crick and Watson and the discovery of DNA?

'I remember.'

'Do you recall we talked about the fact that Crick claimed they had discovered the secret of life?'

'And you said Crick's boast was premature.'

'Maybe it was, back then.'

'You telling me we've got to that stage?'

'I don't know for sure.'

'But you suspect it? You believe science is now playing at God?'

'Oh, I think, Patrick, you'll find there's a race on right now. A whole bucketful of scientists and institutes are competing to do just that. With a Nobel Prize for the first to breathe the spark of life into inanimate nothing.'

'Like Frankenstein's monster?'

'Some people might see it that way. But there are many who wouldn't agree with you. And these are well-intentioned people, famous institutes.'

'You think Sultan won that race?'

'That's what we're trying to find out.'

*

When Kay arrived back at the meeting room, Mike was already shuffling the two computers on the table so he could link the hard drives through the USB ports. As he reloaded the blow-up of the south pole, he spoke softly into Kay's ear. 'Van den Berg had style. Did you know he arranged for the people at NSA to run the entire E gene off as music, based on Ari's code?'

Kay gave Mike a warning look.

He grinned. The screen was illuminating both their faces, with a harsh white glare. Mike spoke up, so the entire audience could hear him. 'I figure this baby works through a kind of intelligence.'

Kay countered, 'Don't be ridiculous!'

'I'm not talking about the self-aware kind. But it gives us part of the answer to what was puzzling me earlier. If I'm right, this structure, the second bulge in the south pole, is a nanocomputer.'

'Perhaps,' Moran cut in, 'you could explain to everybody how something like that works?'

'I'll try, but it's going to be part guesswork. You have to start with the presumption that this entity turns the normal processes backwards. It picks up a new protein sequence, converts that to RNA and the RNA is then converted to DNA, which alters its genetic make-up to fit the new host. The RNA to DNA step is easy. The HIV-1 virus does it every time it hits a new victim. But the step back from protein to RNA is the ballcruncher. Up to now, nobody has figured that. My guess is Ari did. And he did so through this guy here. The nanocomputer was designed to program the switch between protein sequence and RNA sequence.'

Moran interrupted again. 'Hold on a moment. Let me try to get this clear in my mind. You're saying that this nanocomputer is the key to how it infects all those different animals and plants?'

'Yes.'

'But if we logically extend that idea, Sultan must have designed it to wipe out all of life on the planet.'

Mike shook his head. 'Only a lunatic would do that. Ari isn't a lunatic. So something must have gone wrong.'

'Like what?'

'To answer that we need to know the original master plan. And we don't know that. Maybe the question we need to ask ourselves is, what if something went wrong with the computer programming?'

Kay was staring up at the screen. 'Maybe we can work out the original plan. Can we take a step backward and return to the whole entity? See if you can take us through the entire infection cycle?'

'Okay! We're talking about an entity whose genome is designed to be plastic – flexible – through being programmed by a nanocomputer. The computer is like a primitive controlling brain. Plants are primarily where it multiplies. That suggests it was designed with plants in mind. My guess is we're looking at an agricultural project. South pole reads some designated antigens of a new host plant. The computer translates protein sequences to the corresponding RNA. This information passes to the four horizontal nodes. Van den Berg found RNA genes here, so we can assume it remodels RNA genes here. The fact there are four nodes suggests some degree of specialization. Maybe insects versus plants – maybe, and this is a frightening maybe – one of these nodes is specialized for mammals. Dare I suggest humans! From here the reprogramming is carried further up the spiral to the north pole, from where it is relayed to the core'

Mike waited for comment, but his audience was stunned into silence.

'I've got the algorithms. So let's see if we can get this baby up and running.'

Mike's audience gazed in wonder as an abstraction, like a skein of ticker tapes of many different colors, appeared to float in air. They watched as the eerie mix of seemingly random writhing and mathematical precision condensed like a self-assembling puzzle. As Mike zoomed out, the growing abstraction became the tiny south pole with its protruding spike.'

'All we've got to do now is mimic first contact with new host antigen!'

With a few more seconds of computer manipulation, the whole of the entity appeared to come alive before their eyes. 'I've set the algorithm so we get moving patterns of light for actual chemical signaling. Looking up from below, we see the programming move in a clockwise rotation around the vertical axis.' Mike waved his hand to Sami: 'Go for it – let's hear the music!'

'You mean, whole E gene?'

'Sami – let's rock'n'roll!'

Kay objected: 'Mike – you're being melodramatic.'

'Sure I am. But you still don't get it. I want you to experience it the way Ari hinted you should when he put the primer to music. I want you to hear it sing.'

Above the south pole a dark shape, at this scale as gigantic as a night-capped planet, began to turn slowly anti-clockwise as a dense skein of cabling spiraled out of the south pole and moved clockwise around the plant towards the equator. Here it made contact with a horizontal node , which began to glow.'

Kay shivered as the eerie musical box music, coding for the entire gene in the key of E, sounded. Meanwhile the entity exploded into its various components and, as the whole rotated from one equatorial node to another, each exploded into light in turn.'

Mike whistled: 'Kinda Bach-like, don't you think, only more jangly and disjointed.'

'The entity reassembled around the gigantic core and it began to rotate anti-clockwise again. A new skein spiraled from the equatorial node to the north pole, which became a matrix of moving patterns of light. As the entire north pole glowed, a cataract of rainbow-colored light spilled downwards, expanding to a myriad eddies and flows of tertiary activation, until the entire core became incandescent, like a furnace.

'Wow! Didn't I tell you this baby is awesome!'

Kay was unable to drag her eyes away from the metamorphosing nano-biotic life-form: realizing that millions – billions – of these things were inside of Janie.

'So what can we do to stop it?'

'No gene therapy is going to stop this – not out there in nature.'

'You're saying we can't do a thing?'

'I'm saying carry on with what you're thinking in terms of vaccinating people. That's fine for people. But it won't help you with nature in general – not in the time frame you've got. You only have to think how many different species of plants there are out there. Plants, insect carriers – whatever. This thing changes with every one of them. Maybe there is a universal strategy, like in a hundred years it will become symbiotic. But in the time frame we've got, there's no easy natural answer. To beat it we need to think very differently.'

'Think how?'

'Our best shot would be to think like Ari Sultan. Learn from his experience.'

'Like what?'

'Like we make a rival entity, based on the same technology.'

Kay took a deep breath. 'We construct a rival strain that would inject the MRE gene into all of nature?'

'Hey – let's be realistic. No way we're going to vaccinate all of nature. What do we do to fight a plague? We ring-vaccinate all of the contacts of an infected person. In this case we ring-vaccinate plants wherever you find circles.'

Hauk said, 'I get you – like foresters cut a wind break around a fire?'

'Exactly.'

Hauk pressed him: 'How long would it take to construct this new version of the entity, knowing what we know already?'

'From scratch it would take years. But we're not starting from scratch. Given what we already know, let's say maybe six months.'

'We don't have six months.'

'There is a way we could give this a major shot in the arm. How we could get the construction time right down.'

'What?'

'We get a hold of the original construction blueprints.'

'Where are we going to find those?'

'Go find Ari Sultan.'

06: 08/ 18h45

Kay sat in her office and stared at the dossier of e-mails and faxes that had been culled by NSA from their surveillance archives. They lay scattered around her like confetti. The key communications she just about knew word for word. These were critical to any effort at understanding what had happened. The technical mentions left her in no doubt that here was the story of the construction of the entity. Ari, as brilliant as he was egregiously impulsive, had put it together. He must have been working obsessively on the nano-biotic linkup for years. When at last he was ready to go all out for construction, he had recruited Henri Egremont as site lead. Egremont offered great organizational know-how. Indeed he offered more. Egremont was UN sacred. A pillar of the green movement, a champion of "Feed the World". His probity would have cut through official red tape with a foreign government.

Slumped against the desk, deep in thought, she read through a selected few e-mails for the umpteenth time:

> *... Tell Penny and Martin that I've been asking about Simone. Her photograph takes pride of place on my desk, among the mosquitoes and the ants ...*

She ran her gaze over another...

> *Lyse – there's a possibility – I hardly dare to mention it – but I have begun to hope we might be able to help people like Simone.*

What did it really mean? Did it mean that Henri Egremont's granddaughter, Simone, was sick?

> *... So much work already done and still there is so much left to do. But we're getting there. I really believe so. At the same time the pressures of what is really at stake are telling on everyone.*
>
> *E.S. makes us all nervous with his jokes. He and his nanotechs are the only ones allowed to work in the new high security lab, a fact he rubs in by walking into less secure labs wearing his gear... Not a word as yet to Penny and Martin. I don't want to raise false hopes. But I've made some interesting progress.*

Okay – there were things that didn't quite add up here. A granddaughter who was definitely sick. An agricultural station doing gene transfer experiments on monkeys. And there was more.

Ari had known from the very beginning the construction couldn't be done in America, not at his plant in Reno. Not in America because Ari didn't want people to know what he was doing. Because he knew he was pushing things. Taking risks, perhaps, that he wouldn't have been allowed to take here in America.

She had a clear impression from the e-mail sequences that something had gone spectacularly wrong. Her fingers scuttled back through the confetti like crab's feet. Searching... probing.

And then —!

> *... One of our technicians is dead and two more are desperately ill ... It appears that we have become a plague zone...*

Utter disaster.

She could pinpoint the timing of the catastrophe from a change of tone in Professor Egremont's communications. A change in tone accompanied by a change in Ari's behavior. The whole shebang coming off the wire, big time! There was her problem – her dilemma. What was she to do?

Mike's pithy remark... *Go find Sultan!*

That persuaded her.

She locked the door, then opened the safe, removed the blue and silver automatic pistol she had confiscated from Pocock on a day that now seemed part of another lifetime. She stared at the lettering on the barrel: *Browning BDM*. She had no idea what BDM stood for. There was a small slotted nut, silver against the blue metal of the slide, marked P and R. She left it where it was, on R, whatever that meant. She slid the 15 round clip into the butt. She put the gun down on the desk. She cursed herself as stupid. But still she began to put on the biosafety suit she had carried over from BSL-3. They had put her in charge. She was responsible.

She pushed the automatic into the belt that held the pump for the HEPA filter, where it felt as heavy as the burden of her deceit. She put on the boots, left the lab complex, hardly aware of striding the four hundred yards to the remodeled parking lot, with its giant vehicle decon showers, like old-fashioned car washes, arching over the entrance. Her entire being was a confusion of rage and uncertainty. She knew exactly where Sultan was. She knew, because he had called her within half an hour of the end of Mike's presentation. He had begged her to meet him. She'd have given her right arm to talk over her dilemma with Will. But Will wasn't here for her to talk to. Will was with Janie. And she had had no option but to lie to Willson, just as she had no option now but to go out into the dead zone in the desert. She had no option because the questions that needed answering were so big, they overrode all others.

*

Will reached out to brush as gently as the gloves would allow the pallid cheeks under the lambent blue eyes Janie had inherited from his side of the family. Her core temperature was a steady 68× F – horribly reminiscent of the fate he feared for her.

He whispered: 'Don't leave me, sweetheart. I couldn't bear it. Not after we both lost Mom!'

Two nurses had entered the room. One was checking the tubing that led to the cut-down into the femoral artery and vein. She called out the readings through her radio mike, while the other took notes: the pulse, a mere 28 beats per minute; the low blood pressure of 90/50, so low it had to be artificially maintained. Will closed his eyes but he could still hear the throb of the ECMO machine, which had taken over the blood oxygenation: the beep of the pulse on the eight-line monitor.

Opening his eyes again, he stared at the parallel scribbles of the graphs that plotted out Janie's vital signs: if this failed, those scribbles would become flat.

The nurse in charge, Delahay, was standing nearby, watching him. She said: 'You should get some rest now. Go back to the labs where you can do her more good. We'll call you if there's any change.'

He knew she was right. He should go back to work and stop ruminating, worrying, before it drove him crazy. But he just couldn't do it, any more than he could stop himself thinking: *I'll never leave you, sweetheart!*

*

Kay found Ari exactly where he said she would find him. In Sector 5-32. He was sitting in the red Ferrari, which he had camouflaged from aerial reconnaissance with piles of dead plants, and dirt – a vehicle-sized mound of charcoal and ash he must have shoveled out of the desert with his bare hands and dumped over the hood, body and trunk. He waited until she was within ten yards of him before climbing out, stretching his back and his limbs. He startled her when he extended his right arm – as if he wanted to shake her hand.

Ari not wearing any kind of protection.

He was dressed casually: designer jeans and an open-necked shirt of midnight blue. She ignored his offer of a handshake, confronting him with the extended gun.

'Please tell me, Ari, that we've gotten it all wrong.'

He was unbelievably calm. 'Let's put aside the histrionics, shall we, Kay. We go back too far for that.'

Her last shred of disbelief was replaced by rage. 'You ... *you —!*' Her voice stuck in her throat.

'Welcome to the new Eden, Kay.'

'You did it! You killed all those people!' She tried to beat him over the head with the gun. But he easily overpowered her, yanking the gun from her right hand, pulling off her double layer of gloves with it.

He threw the gloves back to her. He was smiling again, just like the Ari she remembered – that baby-faced smile. 'Put the gloves back on, Kay.'

'In God's name – why?' She attacked him again, with flailing arms. He used his elbow to block her, knocking her backwards onto the cinder-strewn dirt. He waited for her to get to her elbows and knees, so she was kneeling in front of him.

'You better cover up. This place is still hot.'

She went down onto her knees, picked up the gloves and fumbled them back on.

'Why aren't you wearing protection?'

'I think you can guess the answer to that.'

'You're immune? You have the MRE gene?'

'I discovered my personal little anomaly years ago – right back when I was working on my PhD. I told no-one, not even Mike. Little did I realize then how beneficial that knowledge would prove, one day.'

Kay swallowed saliva that tasted like acid in her throat. She couldn't believe the fact he was standing there, in this landscape from hell, talking to her in a normal tone of voice.

'Why did you do it?'

'The same reason Oppenheimer created the bomb. Because I could. Because I'm a scientist. It's how I earn my living.'

She tried to rush him, with her flailing arms. He pistol-whipped her through the helmet. Knocked her down once more. 'Don't be silly. We're rational people, you and I.'

'You sent those e-mails to the President. What did it do for you? Make you feel important, looking down on all us ordinary people. You think you're above the likes of us. Some kind of megalomaniac playing at God.'

'As James Watson remarked in answer to that same question: "If we, the genetic engineers, don't play God, who will!"'

'Right now Will Grant is at the bedside of his dying daughter. You're responsible for all that grief – that pain!'

He pistol-whipped her harder this time. She fell back into the dirt, bleeding. He came over and hauled her back to a kneeling position. He squatted down opposite her in the dirt so he could speak to her through the suit: 'What do you want me to tell you? That I didn't set out to kill anybody? That I'm really some sanctimonious idealist?'

'You seeded the whole thing in Ake's favorite patch, acting the goat on some environmental nonsense. Who was the Hispanic girl? Some dumb model you got rid of after you'd planted the seeds out here? You killed her, didn't you? You killed her, like you killed Ake and all those other scientists.'

A shrug: the girl a formality. 'Your precious partner spurned me when he took you on. I was smarter than you. Years more qualified.'

It was true. She had wondered at the time. Ari was smarter than her. Ari: Mike – she'd have been hard pressed to judge which was the more technologically brilliant.

'Just for that? My God – you wanted to hit back at the world because he didn't give you a job.'

'Oh, don't kid yourself. Getting back at Johansson was merely opportunistic.'

'For God's sake, Ari! You're arrogant, opinionated. But you were never vicious or hateful.'

He looked thoughtful, wistful even: 'It really was an accident, Kay – fate.'

'Explain to me!'

'Oh, it was obvious way back – five or six years ago – I had taken my company as far as it was going. I wasn't short of money. I no longer needed banks, outside investors. Yet still my mind was full of these amazing ideas. It was the challenge, if you want to know the truth. I got to thinking about Mike, his creativity with nanos. We both know he's a hell of a bright guy.'

'Why pick on Mike? You once idolized him.'

'I did – you're right. A shame nobody else would listen to him. Well, I was listening. You know I'm hot with computers. I hacked into his main frame, extracted every piece of information I could. I couldn't believe the ideas that were rolling around in the guy's mind. Mike "Wacko" McCann. I never thought he was wacko. I thought he was inspired. His concepts of nano and bio combined – they should have given him the Nobel Prize.'

'You set him up as the fall guy.'

'That came later, Kay. I didn't set out planning to hurt Mike.'

'He encouraged you, took care of you at Berkeley.'

'Sure he did. He's a nice guy playing by the rules in a world where nobody else does. All I did was to couple his ideas with my own. Man, once I really began to think about it, it was like an explorer discovering a virgin continent. I had to put this to work.'

'So you used Mike's ideas to create a monster?'

'We didn't set out to hurt people. What you see is pest control mode gone wrong. We were getting close to the point where we could program it to do whatever we wanted. We could select for a single species of weed – or insect pest. Think about that. We could eradicate the anopheles mosquito that carries malaria, or the tsetse fly that carries sleeping sickness. Or we could loosen up the parameters, so it was lethal to an entire class of pests. For me, that was enough to uncork the champagne. But Henri had other ideas. He was the one persuaded me we had to extend it to gene therapy. That was a whole different ball game.'

'You're just blame-shifting.'

'No. Henri convinced me that we could program it not to kill but to manipulate genomes. That was a good deal more finicky than weeding and knocking out insect pests. All I did was to give him his head.'

'I don't believe you.'

'The irony was Henri was right. We were getting there. It was like there was nothing this baby couldn't do. Every challenge we put it to, it came up with the goods. We could insert endurance genes into food plants to make them resistant to drought, high salinity – you name it. But old Henri – he wasn't satisfied. All the time he was talking about his granddaughter. Did you know his granddaughter, Simone, has cystic fibrosis? He persuaded me to start up this new line, looking for medical applications.'

'You should have said no.'

'You think I don't realize that? You think I don't go back over it in my mind, a thousand times? Easy to say now. But you should have been there, Kay. Seen for yourself what the entity was capable of! Those were heady days – days when it looked like there were no limitations. A little tweaking of the nano programming and it could have put right all those kids born with genetic abnormalities. Think about that. Think about the fact that maybe ten times, maybe a hundred times, more people are born every year with those kinds of problems than have died so far from my creation. Think about all those kids – all that grief!'

Kay's head fell. This was the Ari she remembered, the light of inspiration in his eyes with the wonder of some new vision.

'You really believe I could have set out to develop something as ugly as a weapon? You've seen it. You know it's too beautiful.'

Hearing him talk, watching him laugh: that small boy laugh with the dimples in his cheeks, it was hard to think him capable of evil.

'Jesus, Kay! Can't you see it from my point of view? It was going to be my gift to the world – my wonder child!'

06: 08/ 20h13

Jamie Lee Weiss slid the pump action and backpack under the wire. He paused for breath. Knelt down. Crabbed sideways to get his fucked-up body through. It took him maybe half a minute just to angle through the hole he had cut. He stopped right there, moaning, on his knees for a while. The pain was like a flare going off inside him. It left him panting like a dog that had caught the action from a twelve gauge to the guts. He took minutes to gather his thoughts again. *Feebies!* Watch out for the Feebies. Place was crawling with them. The Feebies had taken out Tony. Scope it, figure it out... play it smart.

Tony Moldano – the two-horned fuck – was stupid. He did crazy stupid things. He had gotten himself iced because he was crazy stupid.

Weiss was panting still, but he was also back on his feet. The Feebies were in the sky with satellites. They were monitoring the area with infra-red drones. Rumor had they could pick up a cigarette tip glowing from a mile high. He didn't have the breath in his fucked-up lungs to smoke. And not a great deal of time.

Wiping sweat out of his eyes, he looked at the map coordinates. He had drawn the cell phone triangulate onto the map with a shaky hand. Stupid jerkoff – Ray – that slimeball had even given him the time and the meet: 20:00 – Sector 5-32. He grimaced with pain, just to lift out the compass... check direction.

All he needed was to get a final fix on coordinates. Pay attention to the little things. Like lightening up his load. He should maybe dump the backpack. No unnecessary baggage. Keep a hold of the compass and pump action. Limping on, pain-ravaged, unsteady, he forced his legs to stagger over the rim of the first dune. Time for a breather. He knelt down again, out of sight of the perimeter. Removed the bandana. Used it to wipe down his entire face. Panting... panting like a dog with its guts hanging out.

Think ... get it clear in your mind.

Gotta hope... count on the fact the vermin would be there.

Mighty peculiar meet – this place at sundown. But the telephone had been specific. A call to some woman – Kay. The mistake J-L had been waiting for.

Stop, scope it out... think.

Ray had made the mistake of taking the cell phone by the lake. Smart vermin, most of the time. But stupid vermin when it came to the cell phone. Like he hadn't cottoned to the fact they'd have it tracked. Nora's thinking – ya can't trust the fuck. He heard Nora's voice: 'Oh, Jamie Lee – this is the big one ... the big chance for you and me... the one we been waiting for.

Sobbing... panting...

Clever vermin, clever like a weasel. So ya gotta ask why. All that stuff with the security locks on the cases ... and then he doesn't cotton on to the cell phone?

And then the penny dropped. The answer crept into his mind, like the vermin had gone and crawled in there and pissed in his skull. *Ah, Jesus.* Ray had scoped it all the way. Had figured every goddam move ahead. Didn't care the cell was traceable. Didn't give a fuck, because he already had it figured... because Ray knew all along he was dealing with dead people.

Aw – fuck! Aw fuck! Aw fuck...

*

Kay swallowed another mouthful of acid. The sun was being swallowed whole by the horizon. Their bodies cast enormously lengthened shadows over the ash-strewn ground. She inched a fraction nearer, all the while engaging Ari in conversation, keeping her voice reasonable, distracting his attention. 'What you've actually done, Ari, is to abuse the gift of your own genius. Genetic technology, in more cautious hands, will cure those children with their hereditary diseases. It will enable people to live longer, healthier lives, to enjoy their grandchildren and even great-grandchildren.'

He waited, with that half smile, until she was only inches from the pistol. Then he lifted it calmly and pressed it against her hood. 'Don't make me shoot you, Kay. I want you to live. You're going to be my gopher with the government. If things work out, we could find ourselves working together again.' He widened his smile until the dimples reappeared, like small round holes, in the shadows of sunset. 'How about that – you and me! Just like the old days.'

Her heart did a somersault. 'The e-mails – you were setting up to deal?'

'You don't disappoint me.'

'You're deluded if you think they'll deal with you.'

'Kay, let me tell you a little story about myself. Something I've never told anyone. I was one of twelve children of a family from the small village of Mjarjo Dirajo on the northern tip of the island of Sumatra. I grew up in poverty the likes of which you couldn't begin to understand. My father was a fisherman who died at sea. At that time, a lot of men and boats were going missing. My mother believed he was the victim of one of the big fishing boats, trying to hide the fact they were using banned trawling methods in the Malaccan Straits. But even as a child I knew otherwise. It was poverty that killed my father. When you're poor as a Malaccan fisherman, sooner or later you take one risk too many.'

'Are you offering this as some kind of explanation?'

'My mother did her best for her bedraggled brood, wearing out her heart as much as the joints of her fingers gutting fish on the *jermals*. She did that so that her favorite son, Ari, could go to school. She chose me, because she knew that I had a gift – a mathematical brain. That was how come I was the only one of my family to escape. I guess I never stopped running.'

'But you made it!'

'Oh, once I got there I found a new ideal. I had a vision, Kay. When I began to construct the entity, vision was what drove me. Arrogant, you called me! If I was arrogant it was to think I could get there and still play the idealist, feeding the hungry millions. What I planned wasn't a WMD. It was a biological revolution.'

'Talk to me about the construction, Ari – how you did it.'

'Killing is what pesticides and weed killers are all about. So I just sat down and I designed your twenty-first century garden variety all-purpose horizontal-gene-transfer pesticide machine.'

'Why did you focus on the mitochondria?'

'Because I needed something with universal application.'

'You couldn't see the danger in that?'

'All I wanted at first was ecologically aware pest management. But once the basic aim was achieved, the additional potentials just kept growing. From a commercial point of view, the sales potential was enormous. On the other hand, old Henri could feed the starving of the world so they could breed even more starving millions. I wouldn't have begrudged him becoming the hero. Meanwhile I could patent the general principle. I could ask my own price.'

'It was overweeningly ambitious.'

'Easy to say now that you've got the advantage of hindsight. But at the time it looked like the realization of all my dreams. Sure I failed. But it wasn't for the reasons you're suggesting. I don't think anybody could have foreseen what actually went wrong.'

Kay looked at Ari and suddenly felt so tense, she was aware of each beat of her heart.

'Hey – I look back on it now and I think I wasn't sufficiently imaginative. I hadn't widened my horizons nearly enough to realize –!'

'To realize what, Ari?'

The sun was already half devoured. He was staring out into the closing dark, with the glitter of what looked like starlight in his eyes. 'To realize it was alive!'

Ari's voice was full of amazement. 'How do you explain something like that? Something you never intended to happen? The first true nanobiotic life-form! That's what you guys are dealing with.'

'But how did it happen?'

'It escaped our programming. It took life all by itself.'

'How in the name of God did that happen?'

He shrugged. 'There was an accident. Things had grown hectic. We were all working too hard, following too many lines at once. My guess is that somebody got careless. That's what Henri thought too. He figured that two very different strains came into contact with one another in the same insect host. I was working with mosquitoes infecting monkeys with the yellow fever virus. We assumed there was some kind of hybrid union in one of the insect lines. Two different strains of entity fused. That botched the computer programming. It happened so fast we didn't have time to investigate it.

'Suddenly – like completely out of the blue – people started dying. The first to die was Henri's senior tech, Nancy Chong. You can imagine how I felt. It took me a while to grasp what was happening. At first all I could see was the project was out of control. I was devastated. I couldn't sleep at night. I couldn't function by day. There was a noise, like a jet engine, roaring through my mind.'

Ari halted in mid-explanation, his eyes staring.

'Well, you can imagine. You know the pattern of the illness. Nancy and Henri were close. Her death, the way she died, just about blew his mind. He was the one who called up the authorities. He didn't figure the way they'd take care of it. I... Well, I admit that I cut and ran. But even when I got back here, I couldn't get my head back into any kind of order. Then it came to me. I realized what I had actually achieved. My genie was evolving – my creation was alive. Where I was born, people believe in fate, like Christians believe in Jesus. I saw that it was the hand of fate, come knocking on my door.'

'How did they take care of it, the authorities?'

'How do you think?' He barked a laugh. 'Kay, it just about frightened them out of their wits.'

'They killed them all?'

'It was a close-knit community. They had all been exposed by that time. A military solution was the only logical outcome.'

'Dear God!'

'All that was left was ashes in the desert.'

Kay pressed him, 'There was no airborne spread?'

'This place is not the Mohave. This place is sand for a hundred miles. What the French call *la desert total!*'

Kay paused, shocked. Needing to think this through further. 'So how did it get to America?'

'I had already been testing the entity on a small scale, in the Nevada desert.'

'You conducted field tests in America?'

'The test zone was about thirty miles north of the first place the entity broke out, the cactus field in Arizona. I got some sweatbacks to dig up the ground. They buried the dead plants, sprayed the area with poisons. But even then I knew it was just buying me time. I'd seen what had happened in the agriculture station. The test zone belonged to my company. People would trace it back to me.'

'Sector 5:32 – that was your distraction?'

'I was desperate by that stage.'

'You tried to murder Mike.'

'Mike's alive?'

'The Seiffert woman – she kept him alive.'

He nodded. 'I'm glad to hear it. I really am – though I don't expect you to believe that.'

'You even tried to murder me, so you could cover up what you had done.'

'Survival is a strong instinct, Kay. It wasn't personal. There was never any real animosity toward you or to Mike.'

'Stop it! Stop this lying! Just answer a single question. Why did you give us the MRE primer sequence?'

'Call it a gift. I wanted to help you. I wanted to show you guys I'd show you how to develop it, when the time and the circumstances were right.'

He had it all off pat. In his eyes, she could see that he was unrepentant. He was proud of the monster he had created. Blood was seeping down inside the faceplate of her helmet from her nose. Kay was struggling hard to keep her voice from shaking: 'You're still hoping to profit from it?'

His eyes narrowed. 'My offer is there. People can take it or leave it.'

'You're insane if you think the government will deal with you!'

'You're naïve, Kay. They didn't hang the Nazi rocket scientists at the end of World War II. Governments fought over them. America will soon be dealing with me, for precisely the same reason. You want what nobody but I can give you.'

'Right now the FBI is swarming over your company – your home.'

'They'll find nothing.'

'They'll talk to people – those who helped you.'

'The people who helped me to construct it are dead.'

'They'll find the manufacturing blueprint.'

'Every record of the construction has been destroyed. There's only one blueprint left, Kay. And that's right here!' He tapped his own head. 'Now tell me they won't want to deal with me!'

*

His head was swiveling half around, J-L looking at where the sun had gone down. The light was rapidly fading. The air cooling.

Panting ...

Stop.

Scoping it clear...

Stop.

Sweating: thick blood-stained oily, pouring off him into the dirt.

Stop.

He was close enough to see them at last. One of them was wearing a space suit with a helmet. Kneeling in the dirt. Then he heard the voice he recognized. Ray was the one not wearing a suit. Ray was on his feet, pacing around. Ray the one doing the talking. The space suit doing the listening. J-L's mind going in and out of darkness... Fighting to keep his focus on the guy without the suit... on the guy pacing around in the desert, as night crept in... All of his focus was on vermin Ray. Getting closer to the familiar voice...

Stop.

Panting ...

Scope it clear. Focus: the pump action. Shuffling closer... Hit the fuck from behind. Focus...

Stop.

Gasping for breath... Catching a snatch of words... Down on his knees... Shuffle closer. Close enough to make out every weasel word.

'The government will have to deal with me because I'm the only game in town. You could broker that. You must do it, Kay.'

A different voice, a woman's voice, coming from the suit. 'You can go to hell!'

Another sound... A distraction, in the distance... Turning with agonizing slowness in the direction of the sound, he saw the lights of vehicles in the distance. Goddam Feebies! Having to pump the gun one-handed... The ratcheting noise in his ears... He did it! That was the shell going into the chamber. But the world was going in and out of focus. He got one foot up, wavering... Steady the fucking knee. Scope... Aim steady. Don't get distracted by the approaching lights... The white hair... The voice...

Shit! The bitch had seen him. A gloved arm was rising, fingers splayed. The tinny voice coming at him from the space suit... 'No, you mustn't – stop!'

Yeah! Sure!

First hit!

Fuckin' nectar! Nectar... for you... Nora, baby!

Automatic pilot. Trigger – pump – trigger – pump – trigger...

Three more blasts from close range ... Fast as his one hand could manage to pump the chamber. Fuckass's body pitching forward over the woman, sliding sidesaddle.

Almost cut in half... blood, bone and intestines spilling out...

For you, Nora!

Groaning aloud, his one functioning hand gone maddeningly slow. No way he was gonna get to his feet again. End of the road. Dragging himself forward, his left leg now catching and tumbling him over onto the dirt... pointing the pump action into the face of the skirt from a distance of three feet.

*

Kay had been temporarily blinded by the shower of blood and gore over the faceplate. She wiped it off with the backs of her gloves. The killer was just feet away from her, coughing and retching. His face, what she could make out of it in the near dark, was already half destroyed by the spreading black gangrene, over which his tawny hair had broken out of a silver ponytail clasp, falling over his face and shoulders, bedraggled and wild. Only the right side of his face was moving, his right eye a red-injected beacon of hatred. A rivulet of bloodstained mucus trickled out of the left nostril and ran down to drip from his chin. He was flailing an uncoordinated hand, attempting to pump the shotgun, his fingers slipping over the bloody stock every time he attempted to slide it back.

In what seemed an eternity of slow motion, Kay reached out for the pistol in Ari's dead hand.

Her wrist felt weighed down with its ugly bulk, her eyes swiveling down at it through her gore-grimed vision. She hefted the automatic between her outstretched hands, her gloved finger almost too thick to get through the guard and onto the trigger.

She said, 'Put the gun down.'

He roared like a wild beast, ripping open what had once been a sleeveless denim shirt. Kay saw the creeping black whorls over the skin of his chest. Kay felt dizzy with revulsion.

She said, 'I'm going to give you one last chance.'

She heard the ratcheting mechanism click. He laughed, a desperate low-pitched tarry sound, past a mouth now drooling with a thick mucousy blood.

The gun jerked as she fired, tearing through his left shoulder and propelling him down into the blackened dirt.

He jerked around, moaning. But then he dragged himself back so he was facing her again. For a moment she glimpsed a challenging sparkle in his good eye.

She shot him again, in the other shoulder.

This time he only managed to curl onto his side. His two arms were useless, the shotgun had fallen into the dirt by his right side. He was whispering to himself, through gritted teeth. Maybe a name...

A siren was sounding out not more than a hundred yards away. They both ignored it. The killer's face was a gibbous mask, his hand still clutching for the shotgun.

She said, 'I've never killed anybody in my life. But I'm warning you for the very last time.'

His huge body was shaking, his breath panting, as he attempted to raise the shotgun into the crook of his arm.

With her hands jerking wildly, Kay pointed the pistol at that juddering skull: she kept pulling the trigger until she had emptied the clip.

06: 09/ 06h30

'Kay! How are you feeling?'

In her dream, a voice spoke to her, sounding heavily muffled. She knew something was wrong. Opening her eyes, the confusion deepened. She was lying on her back in some kind of cloud. A disembodied hand was approaching her. The hand wiped her face with something moist. She looked again, saw a tissue. The hand was gloved, protruding into a cave of bright light, holding the tissue.

She recognized the voice now: it was Josie Coster. Josie said, 'You're in the bubble. We had to sedate you. I'm injecting flumazenil, which will reverse that. You'll be fully awake very soon – though you might notice some nausea.'

Kay turned her head to her right. She saw Josie Coster looking in at her. Suddenly she remembered... Ari in the desert.

Coster's face was replaced by Will's. He explained: 'We had to take precautions. You were upset. You told us about losing the glove.'

Her mind was confused for several more seconds. Then she felt the rush of clarity returning to her senses.

'How's Janie?'

'She's in hypothermia. The hypothermia is holding things steady. But I don't know how long Dr. Valero can keep it going.'

She tried to rub her eyes, but both her arms were tied to cannulae, drips and electrodes of various sorts.

'Shouldn't you be with her?'

'Josie and me – we're working on the gene therapy.'

The gene therapy! Oh, my God – I forgot!

'How's it going?'

'We're having problems.'

Her teeth clenched up and she began to shake.

'It's okay,' Josie comforted her. It's just the antidote taking. You're just going to have to ride it out.'

Josie's voice was replaced with another. Though muffled by the bubble, it also sounded familiar. 'We sympathize with how you feel right now, Professor McCann, but we must speak to you about Sultan.'

She recognized the voice: it was the Special Agent in Charge, Lawton Willson. O'Keefe must be there too, squashed up next to him in the narrow confines of the intensive therapy cubicle.

'You in a fit state to talk?'

She nodded: but inside her anxiety expanded.

'I realize you're just coming round from sedation. But time is pressing. We need to discuss what happened out there. I have to be sure you're lucid enough to answer to my questions. I'm going to test you, Professor.'

Her teeth clenched again but her head was nodding.

'What day is today?'

'Friday... Friday, I think June 9th.'

'Subtract serial thirteens from a hundred.'

'Eighty-seven. Seventy four. Sixty one...' She took it to nine.

'That's good!'

Suddenly she panicked, attempting to sit upright. The movement tugged on the intravenous line running into her subclavian vein, above her left collarbone. She began to explore her skin, running eyes and fingers over her hands and arms, her abdomen, her face. She scratched at the skin of her face, drawing blood.

Josie's voice reassured her: 'You're okay. You've shown no signs of the disease.'

Relief flooded her senses.

Willson's voice returned: 'I understand Sultan wasn't wearing protection?'

'He threatened everybody else but he took no risks himself.'

'He was immune?'

She nodded.

Willson pressed her: 'He told you that?'

'Yes.'

She could make out Willson's face now, pressed close to the plexiscreen surface, his eyes studying her closely. What had she said to him when babbling under sedation last night? 'Okay,' he continued. 'So let's start over. You absolutely sure Sultan was the sole perpetrator of the outbreak?'

'He convinced me of that.'

'There was no *Shawm Ad-din*?'

'No.'

The FBI boss was silent a moment, assessing her closely through the plastic: Kay heard the pulse of the monitor, the whirring of the motor on the machine that drove the intravenous line.

'The bomb under his chopper?'

'I didn't ask him about that. I assume he must have planted it himself.'

'But he nearly died?'

'Ari's trademark – over-confidence. He opened his door. I presume he intended to jump clear.'

O'Keefe butted in. She could see the blur of his face now behind Willson's left shoulder. 'But it was your phone call that made him open his door. He couldn't have anticipated you'd call.'

'He called me.'

'But agent Maisley said –'

'Maisley must have missed the start of our conversation.'

O'Keefe's face withdrew. Then Willson moved so close they were holding eye contact through the blurring transparency.

'How did you know Sultan was out there in Sector 5-32?'

'He called me on my cell phone.'

His voice was suddenly cold with fury: 'And you didn't think to inform us?'

'I had to meet him. He was the only one left who knew how the entity was made.'

O'Keefe was every bit as furious as Willson: 'So you just ignored everything we told you and took it upon yourself to tell nobody. To just go out there and confront him?'

'Of course I wanted to. I desperately wanted to tell you. But he said it had to me on my own. He threatened to kill himself if I didn't come alone. I believed him. And I had to persuade him to help us stop it.'

She felt ravaged by a new mix of emotions, of rage, resentment and bitter disappointment. A mess of aches and pains were beginning register. There was a throbbing pain in her neck when she turned it.

'Oh, Will. I failed you. I failed Janie.'

'You didn't fail anybody.'

'You don't understand. Mike needs the blueprint. But Ari told me he'd destroyed every copy. The only one left was in his head. That was the ace up his sleeve. He thought it would make him so vital to us that we'd have to deal with him.'

'That may not be entirely true, Professor.'

Kay stared at Willson. 'What do you mean?'

'You've behaved stupidly. But there's a possibility you could redeem yourself. Under normal circumstances we would look to Dr. Grant. But he's tied up with the gene therapy project. Do you feel up to a trip to D.C.?'

'Washington?'

'NSA has come up with something interesting. You have a meeting scheduled in a little over seven hours.'

06: 09/ 13h40

'What's going on?' Kay addressed the question to Josie Coster, who was sitting next to her in the black limo.

'Search me. I think these guys figure you have a taste for adventure.'

Josie was wearing her formal Major's uniform. They turned a corner to be confronted by a gigantic multivector display of white radio dishes. Moments later they were hustled up the wide steps of a skyscraper building.

Kay said, 'This is it – the famous NSA?'

Josie said, 'You see that iridescent sheen over the entire building?'

'Uh-huh.'

Josie cackled her smoker's laugh. 'It's encased in copper mesh so as to screen the most efficient and complex espionage establishment in the world from itself becoming the subject of eavesdropping.'

A woman in a gray uniform met them in the lobby. Her name badge read "Madeleine Conlon". She escorted them through a card-coded door, with the warning:

CRITIC in progress: authorized personnel only

The woman explained things while still on the move: they were entering the Crisis Situation Management Zone of the National Security Operations Center. They passed by rooms in which dozens of people sat in front of flickering screens to an inner lobby, where Conlon instructed them to take a seat. She said,

'Lieutenant General Randall will meet you in person.'

When she had gone, Kay turned to Josie. 'Is Randall who I think he is?'

Josie lifted her eyebrows and nodded.

*

Roxy Penhaligan's lean face, with short-cropped gray-brown hair, was gazing back at Will from the computer screen: 'What's happening?'

'We achieved entity elimination up to 80 per cent in the test group of animals. But then they got high temperatures and died on me.'

'Damn! The ten-fold dilutions have no effect?'

'Nothing I could see.' He massaged his face. He couldn't remember the last time he had a proper sleep.

'What about the tissue cultures.'

'That's the baffling thing. We have a gene therapy that prevents entity replication in human tissue culture. But when I inject it into animals, it first seems to cure them and then something bizarre goes wrong. Honest to God, they look like they're getting better. And then all hell breaks loose. I don't have a clue what's going on – no idea. Other than whatever kills them – the pattern of the disease – looks different. I just don't get it.'

Roxy commiserated: 'Me neither!'

Will felt like an island of stagnation in an ocean of hurry, movement. There was never enough time to really think – maybe that was not a bad thing. Kay must be in Washington by now. The FBI had refused to give him any explanation of why they were taking her there.

He asked Roxy, 'You talk to Jerry?'

'I tried. He's not taking my calls.'

'Shit!'

'Will, there are plenty others who agree with Rizinski. I've got people breathing down my neck here too.'

'All that concerns me right now is Janie.'

'They're saying you're too involved. Who wouldn't be, in your situation! We have to keep on trying. Those people – wait until we get something to work and they'll change their tune!'

Will sighed. 'I'm so goddamned exhausted I find myself dozing right here at the lab bench.'

'In spite of the difficulties, we're looking at something very interesting here, Will.'

'Do you have any suggestions?'

'The Trojan coat can be immunogenic, which might be problematic But I don't think your test animals have time enough to develop any major immune sensitivity to it. Maybe we should separate out the various steps in the plasmid construction. Test each component of the cocktail separately and see if it's down to a specific item?'

'I'm running out of time.'

'I hate to remind you, Will. But it isn't just Janie!'

'That's not what I mean. The Ivan Wallin is closing down. The labs are being moved to a new base in New Mexico. Roxy – we just heard this morning, they're going to nuke this place.'

*

Their guide returned and escorted Kay and Josie to an elevator. They emerged into a gray-carpeted corridor, where a man waited for them dressed in a navy blue US air force uniform. His hair was close-cropped white. On his right breast was a patch decorated with a five-pointed star. He introduced himself as Kerry Randall, Lieutenant General USAF, Director of the NSA.

'My apologies for keeping you waiting.'

He indicated that they should precede him into a small meeting chamber equipped with state of the art teleconference facilities. Twenty or so men and women were sitting around an anodized aluminum table with a smoked glass top. Although there were no formal introductions, Kay saw the uniforms of senior ranks from what she assumed to be all of the armed services. She had no doubt that the FBI and CIA were also represented. Randall barely gave them time to sit before starting proceedings:

'First I want to thank our visitors for coming here at short notice. Major Coster – Professor McCann – I must ask you to undertake that anything you see or hear within these walls will be treated as absolutely confidential. I assume your acceptance of these conditions.'

Kay nodded, as did Josie.

'Okay - to business! We should express our gratitude to the Canadian Security Intelligence Service, who permitted the FBI to conduct a video interview with Mrs. Egremont, the wife of the late Professor Henri Egremont. I would like you to listen in to that interview.'

Randall nodded and a film of the interview appeared on screen.

Kay saw a pale elderly woman sitting across a polished wood table, her hands folded on each other on the table surface. She recognized O'Keefe's voice. 'Mrs. Egremont, perhaps you would tell us the nature of your late husband's work for Sultan?'

When she spoke, it was hesitatingly, and with a strong French accent: 'I want you to understand that my husband was, how you say, a man of honor. Henri agreed to do this work because he think this project will help humanity.'

A Canadian-accented voice in the background asked Mrs. Egremont if she would like some water.

She shook her head: 'No, thank you. I will carry on.'

'And the nature of that project, as your husband understood it?'

'It was to make a... a biological machine that will assist agricultural production. What Henri liked to say, green the deserts. Feed the hungry.'

Randal spoke, 'We shall return to the Egremont interview a little later.' In the meantime I would like to address you in particular, Professor McCann.'

The screen now showed a series of e-mails from Henri Egremont to his wife, Lyse. 'Our interest in these,' Randall explained, 'is confined to their scientific content. I think you will agree that there is an initial sense of optimism, then a rising tenor of worry.'

Kay said, 'I agree.'

The screen now featured a high altitude view of a desert landscape taken from a reconnaissance satellite or aircraft. Kay made out a peninsula jutting out from a coastline of sand dunes. There was a dark green circle against the desert, about the size of a postage stamp.

'I can confirm that what you are looking at is in the Middle East. I'm not at liberty to name the country, which assumed the research was bona fide.'

The views jumped into a closer focus. Kay saw a pie chart of radiating fields. At the center was a rectangular cluster of buildings. At the very heart of the complex was a huge glass dome.

'What you're looking at is the agricultural station, set up by Sultan under the direction of Professor Egremont. This is where the final construction of the lethal agent was made. If we are to believe Sultan's confession to you, Professor McCann, the agent evolved by assuming its own potential for life – with the terrible consequences we now face.' Randall interrupted the screening. 'Professor, what you are about to see will be unpleasant.'

'I want to see it.'

Randall nodded, then signaled for the screening to continue.

'What you are now witnessing is a military attack on the agricultural station. You can clearly see the attack unfold. Here - if we zoom in – we can make out the radiating nature of the station, with a cluster of buildings, including the dome at the core.' He pursed his lips. 'The government involved is cooperating to the extent they have provided us with imagery from the attacking aircraft.'

Kay watched the ensuing scenes in a shocked and disgusted silence. She murmured: 'Ari told me about it. But it's still horrible to witness!'

'Yes, Ma'am, it is. The official line was that there had been a gas explosion followed by a fire. Now, I want you to observe certain frames very closely.'

Kay watched the spectacular destruction of the dome.

'Let me explain the additional implications. We now return to the interview of Mrs. Egremont.'

The elderly figure reappeared on screen. Kay heard O'Keefe ask her, 'Would you confirm for me, Ma'am, that it was your husband's custom - a lifetime's good working practice - to keep detailed records of all of his research?'

'Yes, he did.'

'What form did these records take?'

'Henri was… how you say – *très méticuleux.*'

'He was methodical?'

'He write it up in the lab book – the notebook as you call it. Then, in the evening, he copy those notes into his computer.'

'How expert was he in computer technology?'

'He write his own programs.'

'So he could have designed some of the algorithms that went into construction of the entity?'

'Mais oui!'

Randall cut the Egremont interview and addressed the assembled group. 'It is of paramount importance that we find his notebook computer.'

Kay spoke her mind. 'Surely no such records could have survived that carnage.'

'Professor, you can see from the e-mails that Henri Egremont did not altogether trust his employer. And, since you've read the e-mails, you may guessed where he would have kept his note-book computer in such circumstances?'

'In his e-mails he talked about a safe.'

'Indeed, he did. Now I want you to watch one particular part of the surveillance data. This is further montage from the same attack aircraft. We'll be watching a time-lapse extract, slowed down for our benefit. Okay – let's see it!'

They watched a clicking frame, like an ancient newsreel on a hand wound camera. Oblong buildings came slowly into view, as clearly as if they had been filmed from the roofs. They could make out the elongated shadows in the bright morning sun. A movement beginning in the left upper field revealed itself as a man with shirt tail flapping over the back of his boxer shorts.

Randall added, 'I can confirm that Mrs. Egremont identified this as her husband, Henri. We can make out that he had no time to put on trousers and the fact his feet are bare. Now, in the subsequent frames, we see him moving towards the dome. Here, he rushes in through the entrance. There's a very significant delay - we make it a good seven or eight minutes - between his entry into the dome and its ultimate destruction.'

Kay watched those seven or eight minutes of panning film made by the cameras on board the attack aircraft: the fields surrounding the dome: radial slices, containing a wide variety of crops. Maize, rice in paddy fields, a bewildering variety of cereals, fruit trees – all growing in a bountiful profusion in what was otherwise a null desert. And circles, the now familiar pock marks of death, everywhere.

Randall brought their focus back onto to the figure, with shirt tail flapping, running to the dome.

'Note the fact that it's strange behavior when you consider that the dome is a structure of glass held together with aluminum struts. It was the last place anybody would head for protection.'

Josie Coster cut in: 'You think Professor Egremont is securing his records?'

'We know his office was in the dome, which suggests his safe was too. Major Coster, what would you have done?'

'I'd have done the same.'

Kay asked, thoughtfully: 'And that has something to do with bringing us here? You want to go look for it?'

'We have to assume that the entire area around the dome, and the field lab, is still heavily contaminated.'

'Nevertheless, you're asking us to go in there and look?'

'If this mission brings back any intact notes, or computer records, it would massively speed up the Phoenix Program.'

'The Phoenix Program?'

'From the bird and not the city. It's the name we've given to the reconstruction of a new version of the entity, aimed at spreading the protective MRE gene into nature.'

Josie spoke up: 'Kay is not military. And this is a military operation.'

'You're correct, Major. We don't propose that Professor McCann enters the hot zone. But we need her nearby.'

'So I'm the patsy?'

'I would have chosen Dr. Grant, but you know the circumstances. But from what I hear, Major, you also have a reputation for such adventures.'

'You guys sure know how to make your pitch!'

06: 10/ 07h55

'Hello! I'm Will Grant, speaking from the Ivan Wallin. I'd like to speak personally with Dr. Valero.'

There was a delay of several seconds. When he heard Valero's exasperated voice, he was reminded of how this had all begun: with Valero waking him from sleep.

'Yes?'

'How's Janie?'

'She's much as you left her.' The unsaid words hanging in the line between them. *We're running out of time. In truth, we're just about out of it.*

'I have something for you to try.'

A beat of hesitation: 'What is it?'

'It's along the lines we've been talking about.'

'We talking about a specific therapy?'

'Yes.'

'You approved to conduct the first human testing?'

'Not exactly.'

Valero demanded: 'What's going on?'

'It's the MRE gene, carried in a viral vector.'

Valero was silent for another beat or two. 'So what are you implying? It isn't official?'

'If it works, it will be.'

'Shit!'

'What do we have to lose?'

'Shit!'

'This place is closing down around me. I don't have time to do anything more but try it.'

'You've tested it in animals?'

'To a limited extent.'

'And?'

'It stops the entity in eight per cent.'

'But?'

'Some bizarre complication sets in.'

'Shit and shit!'

'Maybe in humans it'll be different!'

There was a very long silence. Valero exhaled a deep sigh. 'You're asking me to put my neck on the line for some unproven therapy?'

'We wait for formal trials, we'll be waiting for months. You can claim I lied to you. I told you it had approval.'

'You know I'm not going to do that!'

'You recall the story about Jenner – how he found the vaccine for smallpox? He just went out there and damnwell tried it.'

Valero was silent.

'We're both worried about the duration of Janie's hypothermia. You know there are signs of change around her lips, even through the hypothermia. If we wait another day, she isn't going to make it. What do we have to lose? I'm prepared to put my neck on the line. How about you, Doctor?'

'How's it administered?'

'By slow intravenous infusion.'

'God help us!'

*

The two AAVP7A1s hauled themselves out of the sea, like monstrous crabs, deluging water over the bone-dry sandy shore. Designed as amphibian assault vehicles for beach landings in war, the helmets of each three-man crew protruded from the two circular hatches at the steering ends. Inside the cargo holds of the forward vehicle, the bio-suited figures of Josie Coster and the two med-tech sergeants, Holly and Armstrong, rattled like peas in a pod designed to accommodate 25 marines. The caterpillar tracks gouged deep ruts in the sand until they clattered onto the hard standing by the derelict buildings of the former desalination plant. As the lead AAV crashed through the rusting iron gates set into a two-meter concrete wall,, Josie radioed back to the nuclear powered aircraft carrier, USS Eisenhower, a gray-blue silhouette on the horizon:

'Kay, you hearing me clearly?'

'Following your every move like you were right here next to me.'

'Okay – we're on the radial.'

A combined weight of 52 tons moved inland at a cautious ten miles per hour through a desolate wasteland that bore no resemblance to the giant fields of ripening crops that had once illuminated this patch of desert. A hot offshore breeze rattled sand and carbonized organic residues against the camouflaged metal, a reminder if ever they needed reminding, that the atmosphere here was lethal. On route they stopped so that Holly, the designated cameraman on board, could film some bleached white bones that lay scattered on a parallel embankment.

The dead jogger had been identified as a Russian entomologist: Andrei Famintsyn. A shred of Bermuda shorts was still clinging to a wing of pelvis.

Josie went through her final check-list: the batteries driving the HEPA-filtered pumps attached to their belts, the inbuilt radio communication, the integrity of the junctional zones of hood onto PVC coverall. They donned the heavy chain mail style overboots that came up to mid thighs. The latter had been Josie's own ad-hoc improvisation after the Maryland meeting, and hastily constructed for them by naval engineers on board the carrier.

*

Patrick Moran was walking in bright morning sunshine beside the President. The sky was a beautiful golden orange. He said: 'My wife, Elizabeth, foreclosed on the deal more than five years ago. She said it was because I was boring.'

'My dear Patrick, I can't imagine.'

'I didn't contest her grounds. I knew she was right. I am boring, and I don't mind admitting it. I'm about as exciting as one of those fossilized turds the archaeologists find so interesting over there in Montana.'

President Dickinson squeezed the arm of her trusted advisor as they walked along the bridle path that ran around the outer perimeter. She had the latest mortality and landscape figures: the epidemic was still spreading, doubling its human tally daily. She knew about the hopes for a vaccine that would save human life: she also knew about the Phoenix Program. *Hopes!* Up ahead, the secret service guards started to wave, drawing Dickinson's attentions to the sound of the helicopter ferrying in her husband Bryson and their two children. They would be waiting for her when she arrived back at Aspen.

'Why no kids?'

'Imagine putting little clones of me into the world. You think I'm that misanthropic?'

Smiling, another squeeze of his arm: 'I think perhaps we should turn back now.'

'Yes, Ma'am.'

Moran signaled their intentions to the cordon of security men.

'Will you pray with me, Patrick?'

'I'd be honored.'

*

It took ten minutes for the lead AAV to reach the central compound. The gate on the vehicle was controlled by two immense chains, their links nine inches thick. Josie waited it out until the forward lip clanged on the ground, then led the awkward shuffle of three down onto the rubble. Once clear of the vehicle, she recalled what she could of the basic layout. The buildings were no more than shells, poking out of mounds of heat-scorched rubble. Behind them, the second vehicle was pulling up at a secure distance: backup in case they encountered something unexpected.

Suddenly her voice rang out over the radio-com: 'Son of a bitch - you guys see what I'm looking at?'

Holly, who was capturing the images in his camcorder, replied: 'Yeah, we see it.'

Armstrong swore.

The dome had metamorphosed to a harrowing ruin of twisted aluminum struts and jagged shards of glass. Sprung steel hawsers tottered, like barbed wire. The ground underneath was a minefield of shrapnel and splinters.

'Okay,' Josie added, 'we know the score. We take our time. Do what we can to watch out for each other. But if the worst comes to the worst and somebody takes a hit, we carry on.'

She led them forward. From the second AAV, additional cameras panned them as they trundled around the obstacles, mailed boots crunching human bones.

*

'Hi, Janie! I bet you don't remember me?'

Will saw Janie's eyes swivel slowly around to look at Valero. Her lids were so swollen and heavy they closed again under their own weight.

'I'm Dr. Valero. Do you recall – I was explaining how we were going to cool your body down?'

She coughed, a reaction from the removal of the endotracheal tube. She started whooping. Suddenly her muscles began to jerk and shiver and her teeth rattled. Janie opened her eyes again in a panicky search.

'I'm here!' Will spoke softly, beside her. Their eyes met.

Janie started to cry.

Valero talked to her in a gentle voice: 'The shivery feelings are just the consequences of warming up. They'll ease off in a little while.'

Valero picked up Janie's right hand and held it between his gloved two, rubbing gently at the blue-marbled skin. Will recognized the look of a man who couldn't remember the last time he had had a decent sleep. They had begun by rewarming the blood flowing through the extracorporeal loop of the ECMO machine and had completed it with blankets and water bottles. All that had been stopped, half an hour ago, because Janie's temperature was going up like a rocket – much higher than the normal 98.4. With the end of the hypothermia, the rash was spreading around her mouth.

'I want you to listen to me carefully, Janie. Your Dad is here. He's following every move we make. You know he did a wonderful thing. And because of what he has done, you're kinda special. He's given us a brand new treatment. And you're the first to try it.'

The intravenous infusion was already running. A saline line, coupled to a side branch. He adjusted the drip, watching the counter. A central venous line that went right down into the right atrium of Janie's heart. It would take another half-hour to finish running through. But already, the MRE gene was entering the living cells in Janie's body.

Her lips were reddening with astonishing rapidity. Her voice, through her inflamed mouth and throat, was distorted but intelligible:

'Will it make me better?'

Will brushed her face with his gloved hand. 'That's what we're all hoping for, sweetheart.'

*

Patrick Moran watched as, under the cedar beams of the sun porch at Aspen, Jackie C. Dickinson kissed her husband, Bryson, on the lips. Bryson put his arms around his entire family.

Moran heard the President whisper into Bryson's ear: 'Things to do. Catch up with you guys in the chapel.'

She strode the short distance from Aspen to Laurel, where she joined her defense advisors in the Conference Room, taking her place across the oblong table. On the opposite side they had removed several chairs so they would have an unobstructed view of the large screen split into quarters.

'Mr. Farnsworth!'

Her NRC adviser informed her: 'We're through to the Pentagon, Ma'am.'

The President's face popped into view on the monitor, segueing to the top left hand corner of the screen. Monath's took the bottom left. The faces of senior defense force officers appeared, gathered round a table in the top right, and a panoramic view of the Mojave Desert in the bottom right.

Dickinson went through the motions. 'All are still agreed on the necessity of this course of action.'

There was no dissenting voice.

'Then I guess we'd better go ahead.'

Monath spoke: 'Ma'am - we're beginning the countdown.'

It had been Dickinson's decision that the nuclear containment operation be explained, factually and honestly, to the American public. CNN, Sky Live, and all the major television channels had abandoned all other coverage throughout the day to concentrate on was happening. On the fourth corner of the screen, a digital clock face began at one hour, counting backwards.

*

Inside the perimeter of the dome, Josie Coster could make out what must have been a central corridor. Just about discernible in the ruins, she saw a honeycomb of what had once been labs running off to the left and right. Raising her hand, she called for a temporary halt. She spoke to Kay through the suit mike: 'We have a problem. If you look at the pics being relayed by Holly you'll see that the internal structure must have comprised two floors. We don't know if the Professor's lab was on the ground or the upper floor. Far as I can see, there's nothing left of the upper floor except for that twisted mess.'

Kay muttered back: 'It's a nightmare.'

Josie began to move forwards again: 'Okay, everybody, keep a close watch on those cables.'

A few minutes later, as they made slow progress close to the heart of the structure, they heard a grinding noise. Josie glanced up to see a disturbed a pile of twisted metal begin to slide. A screech of tearing metal was followed by a momentary silence: a single cable was still holding it tense. They stopped walking. Nobody dared to set up the slightest vibration.

Josie said, 'Abort. Let's try a slow retrace of our steps, one at a time!'

*

Back in the communications room of the aircraft carrier, Kay attempted to follow the confused pictures still being relayed by med-tech Holly. Her eyes, like the cameraman's, were fixed on the tensed strut of cable.

Suddenly, a tiny sliver of movement –

Kay saw the cable began to tear apart, a few strands at a time. There was another jerk of movement in the tottering superstructure of the upper floor.

Kay heard a grunt from Josie. There was a confused glimpse as Holly turned away from the strut and back towards his companions. Armstrong's hand appeared to be grabbing hold of Josie's shoulder. Kay couldn't tell if he was panicking or trying to protect her. Both figures stiffened as Kay heard a new creak from the background. Holly rounded the camera onto a vertical pylon, studded with shards of metal and splinters of glass. The pylon appeard to be tearing away, swinging down through a slow remorseless arc.

Armstrong's shout rang out: 'Hazard overhead!'

Kay screamed: 'Josie – watch out!'

Kay felt like she wanted to throw herself forwards, to grab Josie around her shoulders, and pull her down to safety.

She heard an agonized scream.

A man's voice began shouting: 'Man down! Man down!'

*

Will saw that Dr. Valero was sweating profusely inside his visor. The infusion had completely run through and the intravenous line was now carrying saline. But Janie's temperature was still rising. It was about to pass 105×F. Her breathing had speeded up so she was panting forty times a minute. Her limbs were writhing, her eyes wheeling.

'Oh, Jesus!' He muttered to Valero. 'What we're seeing – it's exactly what happened to the animals.'

Nurse Delahay, standing behind Will's seated figure, said, 'It's no good, Doctor. We're losing her.'

'Hush, woman! I need to clear my mind.'

Delahay stared at Valero, shaking her head.

Valero put his hand on Janie's brow. 'Let's do an urgent blood screen.'

Delahay aspirated blood, ran to the nursing console, called hematology. The test would take ten minutes. In that time, Will watched Janie grow increasingly restless. She started to jerk and shake. Valero added diazepam to the intravenous infusion.

The console beeped. The nurse was running back with the printout.

Valero gasped: 'Will you look at that!'

'What is it?'

'She's showing a massive leukocytosis.' He held the printout in a shaking hand. 'Her white cells have gone through the roof.'

Will glanced over at the doctor. 'What the hell's going on?'

'Her white count is 27,000.'

'I know what a leukocytosis is. What's it tell you?'

'The entity slate wipes the bone marrow. Everything drops through the floor, white cells included. But that's not happening.'

'What is happening then?' Will sensed Valero's excitement.

Valero wasn't listening to Will. 'Okay! Let's try adding steroids to the infusion.'

'But wouldn't that suppress her immunity.'

Valero laughed abruptly: 'I sure hope so.'

'Will you tell me what you're thinking.'

'As I see it, the infusion has to be impure. Its manufacture was rushed through. Even the gene itself was only recently engineered. My guess is it was cloned in coliform bacteria. It's contaminated by gram negative endotoxins. What we're seeing is not the progression of her disease. It's an allergic reaction – endotoxic shock.'

'You can do something?'

'I don't know for sure. But I sure as hell am encouraged by what's happening. Now, Nurse Delahay, will you go draw up that syringe.'

*

Around the perimeter of the Mojave Desert the land-based strike force, a vast encirclement of tactical missile launchers, was cocked, their crews checking times against the master sequence. The launches were computer-controlled: accuracy down to milliseconds. At 50,000 feet above their heads, B-52H Stratofortress BUFFS - Big Ugly Fat Fellows - were getting ready to air-launch their AGM-86 smarts, cruise missiles powered by turbofan jet engines, each individual missile directed to precise vectors and timed to detonate at 15,000 feet over precise geo-positional targets. Like the ground-based strike force, the air-borne force was also locked into the same master plan. They had rehearsed this attack strategy daily, three days running. After Maneuver #1- when a turbulent opposing wind had caused a cap delay of 0.5 seconds - errors had been progressively cut to a currently acceptable 0.005 seconds. All missiles would launch by the time the digital clock swept past 12:18:11.

President Dickinson stood up from the conference table in Laurel and announced that she was leaving for Evergreen Chapel. 'Anybody who likes can join me there.'

She walked alone past Walnut on her left until she reached a modest building, with a rough plank wall and a roof of green shingles. Inside, she walked the central aisle of a chapel to join her family in the front right side pew. In passing, she spotted Patrick Moran, among the service men, gardeners and camp staff hanging around near the doors.

She was already kneeling when the Reverend Joshua Cameron, who had performed their wedding ceremony and baptized the children back home in Cookeville, invited the congregation to pray with him.

*

Television screens through the nation made ready to project the message she had recorded at 7.00 a.m. before leaving the White House. For security reasons, it would be presented at 12:18:11 on the dot, as if going out live.

> *'My fellow Americans, I have to inform you that, after the fullest possible discussion with my security advisors, I have been obliged to implement this harrowing solution. The Mojave Desert is a precious domain, full of natural beauty and vulnerable wildlife. It comprises less than one half of a per cent of the*

total land area of this proud and courageous nation. But there are times when, in looking to cure a patient, the surgeon must excise the source of his illness. What we now put into effect, with heavy hearts, is equally necessary in order to protect the health of America. It will give our defense organizations and scientists the time they need to implement avenues of response that are already in progress, all aimed at bringing the present crisis under control. In the coming weeks, my government will keep you constantly informed of the progress we anticipate from these measures.

May God bless you all and keep you safe through these difficult times.'

06.10/ 11h40

Aboard the USS Eisenhower, Yellow-shirts, their traditional uniforms covered by full biosafety gear, were streaming over the four acres of deck. Every man carried a portable decon cylinder on his back. A second unit was busy in the hanger bay, where they were hosing down the giant elevator platform. With a maximum capacity of 130,000 pounds, this was capable of lifting both AAVs at the same time but the Commanding Officer, Captain Fred Osterhause, had ordered they bring them up one at a time.

The alarm caterwauled, followed by the high-pitched monotone of the lift engine. First to arrive was the support vehicle, which contained the body of the dead scientist in the cargo hatch. Although this vehicle was equipped with mobile decon sprays, and it had been hosed down on the beach before re-entering the water, Captain Osterhause was taking no chances. He ordered that it was to be sprayed all over its camouflaged surface even as it appeared on deck.

The entire ship was now stinking of decon fluid.

The body was brought out and the medics lifted it into the portable isolator. Observing the operation from the observation deck, right beside the Captain, Osterhause, Kay saw, even through the green med sheet, how the signs of head injury were apparent.

Kay had shaken hands with the shore party before they set out. Now her eyes moistened as the first AAV trundled onto the designated area and meanwhile the second was on its way up.

She watched the Yellow-shirts go through the same routine. These armored vehicles were full of pockets and crevices, where a lethal agent could escape detection. If it ever escaped into the confined spaces below decks, it would spread like wildfire. Kay's greatest worry was the underside, and right now the Yellow-shirts were down on the deck and sluicing everything, so decon was leaching out, dripping over the edges of the flight deck.

The rear hatch of the AAV cracked open, the ramp rattling down on its chains. She could hear the Chief Petty Officer from the hanger deck passing out orders over the radio com. Kay was amazed by the restraint of the watching crew. But now they could see the surviving shore party gather on deck. Here and there crew members began applauding or shouting words of encouragement. A party of engineers, fully suited, stood by. Another order from the Petty Officer and a flattop tow-engine appeared. Chains were attached that ran into the hold of the AAV. The tow began pulling. A screech of metal on metal signaled the small oblong of safe being tipped onto the ramp. The screech continued as it was pulled all the way down and clear onto the decon-drenched deck.

The quiet shattered as hundreds of crew began high-fiving and cheering. But for Kay, the anxiety, tinged with grief, was still mounting.

A communications officer came hurrying down from the bridge with a phone message. He held it up before the Captain's eyes so he could see it came from some presidential assistant.

Osterhause took the phone.

*

Outside the doors to Evergreen Chapel, Patrick Moran heard the clipped naval voice came on the line.

'Sir, this is Captain Osterhause, speaking from the USS Eisenhower. What you want to know – I can tell you that we've recovered the safe.'

'In what sort of condition?'

'Battered and charred. The door's still intact but it's buckled tight shut.'

'And the contents?'

'We've got it up on deck and right now we're drilling into it . We're going to take a look inside with fiberoptic probes. We'll know within a very shot time.'

'Thank you. The President would like you to keep her informed to the second on the safe's contents.'

'Yes, Sir!'

*

Kay donned her biosafety suit and joined O'Brien, the Chief Engineer, who had drilled the two exploration holes in the safe. She watched as he inserted a fiberoptic probe through one of them and a set of surgical forceps through the other.

'Okay, Professor, it's all yours!'

The fiberoptic views were being relayed to screens and the entire ship was watching what Kay was doing on one of them.

'What the heck we looking at here, Professor?'

'I believe we're looking at carbonized notebooks.'

'Carbonized? That mean it's been a wasted exercise?'

'I can't be sure, but I hope not. It's possible the notebooks slow cooked, like meat left too long in the oven. They couldn't really burn, or not for very long, because the oxygen was limited in the hermetically sealed interior of the safe. I'm going to try to lift them – see what's below.'

'Be careful. Even carbonized, they could be partially readable to forensics.'

'Right.'

Kay rooted carefully with the forceps in the tiny cave of the safe interior, her hand tremor exaggerated by the magnification of the fiberoptic scope. With extreme delicacy she lifted the carbonized junk from one corner.

The engineer said, 'What's that?'

'I can't see clearly so I'm going on feel. It feel's firm. I'm going to try to brush away the junk from just one edge.'

By now Kay could see it. The oblong of a notebook computer was there, lying under all of the carbonized remains. The thick plastic looked charred and disfigured. But the shape was intact.

She said, 'It looks a little cooked but not incinerated. The burning of the surrounding paper used up the little oxygen present. My guess is there wasn't all that much flammable material in the dome. After the heat of the explosion, the fire probably didn't last very long.'

'The hard drive?'

'I can't be sure – we'd better crack the save without doing any further damage to the computer.'

*

Just inside the doors of Evergreen Chapel, Moran's cell phone was beeping once more. He walked out into the garden to take the call.

'This is Captain Osterhause, of the USS Eisenhower. Let the President know we have the computer.'

'In what sort of condition?'

'Looks good, all considering. The notebooks are incinerated but Professor McCann has a hold of the hard drive. She wants to speak to you herself.'

'Patrick?'

'Kay – is it intact?'

'Well, from what I've seen so far, it's looking kind of spectacular.'

'We have the blueprint?'

'If blueprint is anywhere near the right word for it. I've never seen anything remotely like it.'

'But it's what Mike needs – right?'

'I'm about to transfer the entire contents of the hard drive to him right now.'

Moran's face flushed. He exhaled with relief.

'Thanks, Kay!'

Patrick feet were already pounding the central aisle. His voice was shouting: 'Ma'am - we've got it. Thank, God, we have the computer. The hard drive is readable. We've got the blueprint.'

President Dickenson emerged from the pews and hurried out through the doors of the church. 'How close are we to critical?'

Moran looked at his watch: 'I make it roughly seven minutes.'

The President closed her eyes, exhaled a short sigh. 'Seven minutes – it's as good as a lifetime. Let's go tell them, Patrick – stop the countdown!'

'Yes, Ma'am!'

*

The phone was ringing at the nursing console. Will saw the nurse, Delahay, go back to answer it. She waved to him and he walked over to take the call.

'Hello?'

'Will, is that you?'

'Kay!'

'Janie – how is she?'

'She's improving. The MRE gene appears to be taking. Dr. Valero thinks she's going to make it.'

Her breath caught at the other end of the line. 'Will – we found Egremont's computer. We have the blue print. But it was at a heavy price. One of the shore party was killed.'

'Oh, Christ – not Josie?'

'No – the med-tech photographer. A guy called Holly.'

'How'd it happen?'

He was silent for the minute or two it took Kay to explain. Josie had been only a whisker away from injury. Holly had been distracted by filming and had failed to duck.

He said, 'You okay?'

'I'm okay. I'm heading back.'

'See you then. We'll have the opportunity to talk a lot more. Right now I've got to get back to see Janie. She could wake up any minute. I want to be there when she does.'

'She isn't conscious?'

'It's temporary, the sedation. Ric – Doctor Valero – has it all in hand. He should be given a medal for what's he's done.'

'Give her a hug for me, will you do that?'

'I'll do that.'

Will heard the nurse call out, 'She's coming round.'

He was by the bedside in time to tell his waking daughter, with her red-rimmed angel eyes, that he loved her.

Janie's voice was croaky and slurred but he understood her perfectly well:

'I... I'm really going to get better?'

'You bet, sweetheart.'

She was silent for many seconds. 'And you... Dad?'

He wrapped his arm around her shoulders and hugged her close to him. 'Sweetheart – I'm taking you home.'

Fifty years after the discovery of the structure of DNA, a computing machine composed solely of DNA molecules and enzymes has been recognized by Guinness World Records as the smallest biological computing device... Around 60 trillion of these devices could fit in a teardrop.

Daily Telegraph, London:
February 25 2003

Printed in the United Kingdom
by Lightning Source UK Ltd.
126537UK00002B/37-498/A

9 781874 082422